PROLOGUE

AS THE RIVER surged through the forest, snake-like, into the heart of the wilderness, it carried a mystery—a lone figure splayed across a drifting log, suspended between life and death. His battered body clung to the rough timber as if it were his last tenuous link to this world. Blood seeped from a jagged wound on his forehead, snaking down his face and through his beard in slow, crimson rivulets before vanishing into the river's cold embrace. What was the story this nameless man brought to these shadowed waters? What fate had marked him so brutally?

One arm hung lifelessly over the edge of the log, swaying to the river's rhythm. Inked deep into the flesh of his forearm was a haunting tattoo—a dagger crowned with a death's head, a symbol both ominous and cryptic, that whispered about violence, secrets, and perhaps a death foretold. But why was he here, abandoned to the mercy of the river? Was he a sinner seeking redemption or a hunted soul fleeing a debt only death could settle?

The forest loomed around him, silent, as though it knew his story but dared not speak it aloud. Only the river disturbed the quiet, roaring with the relentless flow of time, pulling him deeper into the forest and beyond. In this forgotten stretch of wilderness, far from the reach of human eyes, he was a phantom adrift, a nameless figure caught between worlds; his story untold, his purpose unknown.

Onward, the river bore him deeper into the unknown, where the line between life and death grew thin. Was he the harbinger of horrors yet to come or the final chapter of terrors that had already unfolded? In the darkened forest, there were no answers—only questions, waiting, submerged, in the black waters.

ONE
LINCOLN HIGH

LINCOLN MEMORIAL HIGH SCHOOL SPRINGFIELD, Illinois, Spring 1992

It was Friday, and Jack Brooks was looking forward to the weekend. It started like any other working day, but had he known the terror awaiting him at the end of that day, he would have stayed in bed.

Jack was the head caretaker and groundsman for Lincoln Memorial High School and the adjoining college. Lincoln High was a decent school, well-funded and well-maintained. However, like many schools, it had its fair share of troublemakers, but anyone who put in the effort and stayed the course could expect a decent education and hopefully move on to the college.

Lincoln Memorial High was built in 1818, initially serving as a courthouse, with a stately mid-colonial design. Twenty-one sweeping limestone steps led to the entrance; each symbolizing one of the twenty-one states that had been ratified by the time of the building's completion. Bronze plaques decorated each of the stone slabs, commemorating the acceptance of every state into the Union. The first plaque read 'Delaware, December 7, 1787,' marking the first state to ratify the Constitution. The final plaque read, 'Illinois, 1818 – "Free Soil,"' along with the signature of President James Monroe.

At the top of the steps was a wide veranda supported by four marble fluted columns, crowned by a gabled roof and a domed bell tower. The façade featured eight sash windows framing two large oak-paneled doors. The grand building stood with quiet dignity, atop a hill, overlooking manicured lawns and stone pathways bordered by perfectly pruned rose beds. Each path led to an ancient oak tree planted by German settlers in 1810.

Jack loved his role at the school—a place he himself had once attended. Though his time there had its challenges, he left with respectable grades, thanks mainly to the support of his sister, Rose, who also had attended, and the steady, guiding hand of the school's principal. Upon finishing school, Jack took up the post of groundsman and had been there ever since, gradually rising to head groundsman and caretaker.

As head groundsman, one of Jack's regular tasks was to cut the grass, and he often started at the base of the grand oak tree. Today, as he set to work, the steady hum of the mower lulled him into a daydream. He found himself thinking about the ancient oak, wondering what stories it might tell if it could speak. Through his father's German ancestry, Jack felt a connection to the tree; his family had been among the first settlers in Springfield, and it was they who had planted this very oak.

He often mused about whether a distant relative might have once tended to the tree with the same dedication he felt. To Jack, he was the oak's guardian, responsible for its upkeep and protection—a duty he liked to think had been passed down through generations. The oak had become a favorite gathering spot for students, offering welcome shade on warm summer days, and standing as a silent witness to their carefree moments, just as it had to those who came before them.

He was also aware of the oak's darker history; it was ominously known among locals as the 'Hanging Tree.' Back when the school was a courthouse, legend held that convicted criminals met their end dangling from its sturdy branches. Though no photographic evidence supported this claim, the stories persisted, leaving an unsettling shadow over the trees past.

There were other reasons the tree had got its dark name. He

remembered an incident at the tree in the early seventies—he had been only eight at the time, so he had paid little mind to the adults' hushed conversations and uneasy glances. What he did know was that his older sister, Rose, was attending the college adjacent to the school during that period. She had also been a student at Lincoln High around the time of some rather gruesome murders that had rattled the city. Rose never spoke of it, refusing to share her memories or connection to those unsettling days. Jack later discovered the Lincoln Mauler had been her best friend, Micky—a man Jack had trusted and grown fond of during his frequent visits to their home. The revelation had shattered him, leaving him haunted by the fact that he had failed to see the monster behind the friend.

Now, as the mowing was coming to an end, Jack looked up at the branches and wondered what other secrets the oak held, watching over the grounds as silent witness to both the beauty and the buried darkness of the place.

Jack flicked off the switch of his mower signaling the end of the day's first task. He stood for a moment, taking a deep breath, and glancing up at the school building perched majestically atop the hill. Pausing, he let its history wash over him, a history he had learned in class, gaining top grades. He thought about those fifty years that it had served as a courthouse, a place of judgment and justice, until 1865, the year of President Lincoln's assassination.

During his legal career, Lincoln had walked those corridors, representing countless clients within its walls. In his honor, after Lincoln's assassination, the building was transformed into a school and officially reopened in 1866, carrying forth a legacy of knowledge rather than verdicts.

Over the years, Lincoln Memorial High had its fair share of troublemakers and dropouts. Jack, thankfully, wasn't one of them, and although he didn't excel, others did, and he knew of them all. Among its former students were seven senators, two Supreme Court justices, star athletes, and even a few astronauts. Jack once dreamed of becoming an astronaut but knew his psychological issues would have prevented him from being one; he was happy just to know he had gone to a school with such great Americans. Their achievements were immortalized in the school's high achievers' glass cabinet, proudly showcasing their photographs, trophies, medals, and even a gram of moon dust.

Jack also knew the school had its share of dark history, but nothing could have prepared him for that day he learned about Michael Beaumont. *The Lincoln Mauler.* Back then, he seemed cool. Jack remembered that he would bring his Kodak Super 8 camera around, and he and Rose's friends would make short films at the cabin, capturing the laughter and antics of youth on grainy film.

Jack remembered those afternoons, watching them act out their little stories, laughing and playing around. He felt lucky to be around them, to feel like a part of the group, even as the younger tag-along. And for a long time, those memories held nothing but warmth—until the truth about Micky came out.

To Jack, those moments now felt tainted. It's strange, he thought, to remember someone you thought you knew, only to realize they were carrying a darkness inside deeper than you could ever imagine. Those films he made—innocent little scenes—now felt like shadows of something far more sinister.

As he raked the grass cuttings into a pile for removal, Jack thought back to a time when he must have been twelve or thirteen; he remembered sneaking onto the church grounds one Halloween night with the few friends he had; they dared each other to visit Micky's grave—the infamous resting place of Michael Beaumont, the *Lincoln Mauler.* The thrill was undeniable, but as they drew closer, the group fell silent, captivated by the sight of the cold stone marker. The inscription read, *God forgives all sinners.* To them, it seemed a mockery, given the horrors Beaumont had committed, especially against their friend's older brother.

He remembered Max pulling out a can of spray paint to leave his own mark on the stone: *Cocksucker,* followed by THE LINCOLN MAULER. At the time, Jack found it fitting, a crude form of justice for the fear and loss Beaumont had inflicted on their community.

Years later, Jack occasionally passed by the gravestone, often while visiting his father's grave with Rose, and he couldn't help but notice the curious care given to Beaumont's plot. The ground was always tidy, free of weeds, and there was often a single rose placed in a pot at its base. It struck Jack as odd that someone, perhaps silently, still cared enough to tend the grave of a man so feared and despised. The mystery lingered each time he walked past.

The Lincoln Mauler left a dark stain on the school; his attendance at the school had been erased from the annals and written history. Though no official school records of him remained, the mere mention of his name was enough to bring conversations to a hushed, uneasy silence. He remained a part of the fabric, not only of the school but also of the community. The latest crop of students had no recollection of the gruesome murders and the fear that hung over the town in the seventies; for them, it made for good storytelling at sleepovers and campouts. Over the years the story became an urban legend. Like all urban legends it had a basis of truth. The Lincoln Mauler became one of America's top five serial killers, alongside Bundy, Gacy, and Nielson. It took three years to catch him, during which he notched up fifteen kills, mainly students. There were whispers that he didn't act alone, a mystery that remained unsolved.

All the murders he committed took place while he was a student at the school and later at the college campus. He lived to kill, and strangulation was his modus operandi. If that wasn't enough, the sexual violation he subjected his victims to before and after their brutal deaths was enough to earn him his moniker. There was no gender preference —male or female, they all suffered the same fate. The killings came to a grisly end after he was found hanging by the throat from the school oak tree, the 'Hanging Tree.' A fresh, strangled corpse lay beneath him: Jenny Malkovic, his final victim. Beaumont had taunted the police with a cryptic invitation, leading them straight to his location. They expected the worst when they arrived, and he didn't disappoint. Clutched in Jenny's cold, lifeless hands was a film reel titled 'A Portrait of a Serial Killer,' an expertly edited masterpiece of horror. Although there was no footage of him committing the murders, his voiceover to the piece and his explanation of why he chose his victims and what he did to them was enough to convict him and close the case. It made for pretty gruesome viewing. *60 Minutes* managed to get a copy and did an exposé of the man, which turned him into a cult figure, and many rap groups and DJs would wax lyrical about his exploits. In many respects, he had the last laugh, the final word. Criminal psychologists often commented that fame was his motive.

After several studies, papers, books, and a low-budget horror flick, he became an icon and a demigod to aspiring serial killers. However, his fame began to fade shortly before the movie's release. The film received poor reviews and failed, causing the horror of the Mauler to become a dark footnote in the city's history, one that should be forgotten. Many unanswered questions remained. Did he act alone? What happened to the missing student, Bartholomew Harris, who might have been the Mauler's last victim? Where was he? At the time, Captain Jackson had serious concerns about the case. "Serial killers don't tend to kill themselves," he was quoted as saying. He went on to point out that all the evidence was circumstantial; there was nothing directly linking Beaumont to the murders, aside from the videotape and his confession. Yet, despite these doubts, his concerns were brushed aside, and the case was closed. To this day, the lingering questions—much like the mystery of the Lincoln Mauler—remain unanswered.

But spring had begun, and the school welcomed a fresh start to the year. It was Friday, and Jack had many more tasks to complete before the weekend.

TWO
GREEN FINGERS

IT WAS A BRIGHT, brisk spring morning and now that Jack had completed the mowing it was time to get on with the rest of the day's tasks. A glistening blanket of dew spread across the well-tended school grounds. The sun was rising but had not yet warmed the keen air. Jack had gathered the tools for the work ahead and made his way over to the flowerbeds.

Jack was young and fit, his tall, six-foot-two frame both lean and sinewy, a physique forged by the grueling demands of his work. Dark hair swept across his brow, and his skin bore the sun-kissed tone of his Native American heritage on his mother's side. In contrast, his piercing blue eyes—bright, almost glacial—betrayed his German lineage, their icy depths hinting at secrets locked tightly within. Behind that inscrutable gaze and his calm, brooding demeanor, Jack harbored a mind brimming with unspoken thoughts and a solitude that gnawed at him, relentless and unyielding. Though friends surrounded him, none could claim to truly know him. He was a man who concealed himself behind layers of silence and shadow, his past and secrets buried deeper than any pirate's chest—not filled with treasure, but with agony and despair; a festering box of misery.

With a sharp thrust, Jack plunged his fork into the frost-bitten earth, feeling the resistance as he broke through the hardened crust, loosening the soil for sowing. There was plenty more work to ready the grounds for summer, but Jack welcomed the task. It kept his hands occupied and, for a while, quieted the shadows lurking just beneath his stoic surface.

Looking skyward, Jack wiped his brow, squinting as the sun slowly rose. It seemed brighter that morning, and as it climbed higher into the cloudless blue sky, it warmed the dew-laden grass of the school grounds. The mist began to rise, and to Jack, it was as though there were a sea of angels dancing and swirling majestically on the breeze.

If Jack had the time, he would sit transfixed, enchanted by the mist's quiet dance over the school grounds. "If you look hard enough," he would often say, "animals emerge, rising from the misty depths." Now, as he stared into the thickening fog, shapes began to materialize, their forms shifting as if conjured from some otherworldly place. An elephant appeared first; its mighty trunk raised high before a gentle breeze swept it away. A giraffe followed in its place, tall and elegant, only to dissolve seconds later, making way for a parade of other wild and wondrous creatures, each sculpted by the mist's languid, ghostly hand.

Two antelopes took form next, heads lowered as they seemed to graze the grass, their ghostly figures merging before locking horns in an ethereal clash that sent soft ripples through the mist. And then, like all the others, they too vanished into the swirling depths. But Jack lingered too long in his reverie, and soon the mist began to churn with a darker intent, molding itself into shapes far less natural.

Out of the murky veil emerged a towering, skeletal figure, its impossibly long limbs stretching in unnatural proportions. It was cloaked in tattered shadows that bled seamlessly into the mist, merging with the surrounding darkness. As a cloud drifted in front of the sun, a cold chill wrapped around Jack. He gazed upon its face—an empty, mask-like void, hollow and ominous, with sunken eyes that faintly glowed, as if lit by the despair it sensed lingering nearby.

A twisted, macabre grin stretched across its face—a grin that hinted at agonies untold, promising suffering in silent whispers. The creature loomed over Jack, its gaze fixed, feeding on his solitude like a predator drawn to the shadows surrounding a silent soul.

Honk! Honk!

The sharp blast of a truck's horn jolted Jack from his trance, the annoyed driver passing by with a flash of frustration. Blinking, Jack glanced back at the lawn, but the animals had vanished, as had the specter he'd conjured, frightened away by the noise or perhaps by the sun's slow but steady ascent, warming the air. *They'll be back*, he thought, a shiver tracing his spine. With a steadying breath, he gripped his fork once more and drove it into the earth, each thrust of metal against soil grounding him—if only for a little while.

The sun had climbed higher, and after an hour of steady digging, the work began to weigh on Jack's muscles, each swing of the fork a little heavier than the last. He paused, took a deep breath, and reached for his knapsack, pulling out a bottle of juice and a small cup. Pouring a generous measure, he gulped it down, savoring the sharp zest of lime and lemon that his sister had thoughtfully packed for him—his favorite. "Digging is thirsty work," he murmured to himself, chuckling, before setting the cup aside and drinking directly from the bottle, draining it with a satisfied sigh.

The air was heady and sweet, infused with the unique scent of honey pine—a local tree prized for its golden, resinous sap, irresistible to the bears stirring from hibernation. The fragrance mingled with the soft, floral notes of wild fuchsias and daisies that dotted the grounds, weaving an intoxicating tapestry of scent that no perfumer's hand could ever hope to capture. Jack took in another deep breath, letting the aroma settle in his chest, grounding him in the moment—a fleeting respite, a breath of calm before he returned to the relentless earth.

Nearby, in perfect contrast to the wildflower beds he was tending, a patch of roses stood proud, their crimson blooms carefully pruned by Jack's expert hands. He had always had a knack for gardening, something everyone who knew him could attest to. Snipping a few roses for his sister, he was momentarily distracted by a bird's song.

Jack turned to glance back at the ancient oak, ignoring its sinister history, as he listened to the cheerful, melodic trills of a pair of migrating fox sparrows. A faint smile crossed his lips as his thoughts drifted back to his childhood. Memories flickered in his mind, one after another, like an old slideshow. He recalled the time he'd bunked off school to swim in the lake by the family cabin—[click]—a younger version of himself, perhaps eight, fishing by the lake with his sister Rose and her boyfriend Bart. An uncomfortable memory surfaced, of Rose, furious with Bart, landing a slap across his face, the shock leaving Jack frozen, a hollow fear curling within him.

Then, the projector jammed [click, click, click]. Jack's brow furrowed, his eyelids tightening as the pleasant memories dissolved, giving way to one he'd fought hard to forget.

The last image of his father.

It struck him with brutal clarity, as though no time had passed—his father hanging by the neck in the cellar doorway, swaying slightly, his head tilting unnaturally to the side. His pale face twisted in agonized distortion, his eyes bulging, his cheeks a hideous shade of blue. Jack remembered the slick, unnatural sensation beneath his foot—the thick lump of tissue that had slipped beneath him: his father's tongue, torn off in his final, desperate struggle for air. The stench had been unbearable: the bitter tang of alcohol, stale cigarettes, and the suffocating odor of feces. Jack had stood there, paralyzed, as the grotesque image seared itself into his mind, forever etched in unbearable detail.

But then, mercifully, the memory stopped. Jack's mind had developed a defense, a fail-safe born of teenage therapy sessions, where he'd learned to control the darkness that clawed at him, to keep himself from spiraling into the depths where misery and shadows resided. Slowly, the song of the sparrows coaxed him back to the present. Jack opened his eyes, his gaze settling on the pair of fox sparrows, now in full song, their gentle melody anchoring him, pulling him from the precipice.

He smiled and nodded in gratitude, as if thanking the birds for rescuing him from his nightmare. He wet his lips and attempted to whistle back at the thrush, but they took flight, unimpressed by Jack's flat attempt at communication.

Chuckling softly, Jack retrieved a red handkerchief from his pocket, embroidered delicately with a gold cross. He smiled; the handkerchief always brought him a sense of comfort. He took a brief moment to inhale its sweet scent before neatly folding it and tucking it back into his pocket.

Rummaging through his other pockets, he fished out the old, dirty rag he'd been hunting for and used it to wipe the lingering dirt from his face. The freshly cut roses were now bound together, ready for his sister, and Jack attempted to mimic the thrush's tune once more—without much success. A talented gardener he might be, but Dr. Doolittle he certainly was not. Glancing down at his watch, he realized that his daydreaming had taken up more time than he'd intended. The morning was slipping away, and there was still a long list of chores awaiting him back at the school. It was Friday, and Jack knew he'd need to work swiftly if he hoped to finish his tasks before the weekend beckoned.

THREE
SCHOOL'S OUT

LATER THAT AFTERNOON, the weekend break began for Lincoln Memorial High School students. The school bell rang, piercing and relentless, announcing the beginning of the weekend. Like water from a breached dam, students surged out of the classroom doors.

The corridors became ravines and gullies, the thunder of rolling feet pushing and racing along them. They jostled, barged, and collided like rolling boulders forced forward by the power of rushing water.

The oak exit doors loomed in the distance, solid and steadfast, but they would not block the surge of young flesh and bone intent on breaking out. Centimeter-thick iron hinges strained under the onslaught as the school discharged its contents. Still, the clattering oak doors hung on until the last student raced out to join the unstoppable tsunami of youth that surged across the courtyard. A weekend of fun, mayhem, and youthful exploration had begun: forty-eight hours to push the boundaries, break the rules, and reinvent youth like every other generation past. As the corridors filtered, there was a commotion.

"Brad, you asshole, you've ruined my dress!"

Monica's voice echoed down the corridor, sharp with frustration. Brad, the school's notorious prankster, had struck again, targeting her with a balloon filled with red dye—no reason necessary. Brad never needed one; he lived for the thrill of other people's humiliation, savoring their pain like some twisted delicacy.

"I'm going to get you for this, you creep," Monica spat, furiously trying to scrub the dye from her dress.

"Ooh, I'm quaking," Brad mocked, clutching his chest theatrically. Turning to his lackeys, Fat Boy and Ginger, he begged with feigned desperation, "Please, guys, save me from her wrath." He fell to his knees, grabbing one of his friend's legs, pretending to sob. "I'll do anything," he pleaded with a theatrical whimper, burying his face in his hands.

"Eat this, you jerk!" Monica snapped, giving him the finger with a contemptuous glare before spinning on her heel and storming off. Brad watched her go, unfazed, a low, sinister laugh bubbling from his throat —the kind of laugh you'd expect from a cartoon villain. As the sound echoed down the corridor, his smirk grew, satisfied and predatory. His friends joined in nervously, chuckling along as Brad basked in his victory.

Brad was the only child of a broken home. He lived with his mother, a worn woman who had lost control of him years ago, left to raise him alone after his father walked out when he was eight. His father, an alcoholic, occasionally reappeared—often drunk or halfway there—taking Brad to the racetrack or some seedy boxing match. His mother's protests that this wasn't the place for a boy fell on deaf ears, her warnings unheeded, echoing now only as bitter memories.

Monica's distress was just another notch in Brad's reign of terror. He couldn't leave the school without one last fix; the weekend loomed, and he'd be starved of victims until Monday. With that in mind, he set off down the corridor, scouting for his next target.

Jack rounded the corner on his rounds and nearly collided with Brad. Pausing, he met Brad's smug gaze and then looked over at his sneering cohorts.

"Watch yourself, Jacky boy—sorry, er, *Mr. Brooks*," Brad mocked, his voice dripping with sarcasm as his friends snickered.

Jack held Brad's stare, unimpressed, offering him nothing in return. He had far more pressing matters than humoring Brad's petty games.

As he turned to leave, Brad's mocking laughter echoed down the corridor, chilling in its malice.

"Did you see the look on that cow's face?" Brad sneered. "I'd pay to see that again."

"Looked like she was on the rag," Ginger chimed in, lighting a joint as their laughter rang out in the empty hall.

"Serves her right. She thinks she's something she's not," Fat Boy added, his grin wide and mean.

As Jack rounded the corner, his eyes caught sight of a small crowd up ahead—a cluster of girls whispering in hushed, urgent tones. Sensing trouble, he quickened his pace.

"What's going on here, girls?" he asked, his voice calm but with a quiet authority. After a brief, tense explanation, his gaze settled on Monica, her face blotched with tears, the red dye staining her dress in lurid splashes. The anger rose in Jack, cold and resolute. He knew he had to act swiftly before Brad could slink away.

Turning sharply, Jack strode back in the direction he'd come, his eyes scanning for Brad. He was done allowing Brad's cruelty to go unchecked; the boy's reign of terror was ending today, and Jack would make sure of it.

FOUR
SHABONEE

JACK QUICKENED his pace and as he noticed the door to the boys' toilets swinging shut. *Perfect*, he thought, his pulse quickening with the thrill of finally cornering them. He strode to the door and pushed it open, hoping to catch them in the middle of whatever mischief they were plotting.

But as he stepped inside, the scene that greeted him was worse than expected. The boys had already vanished, leaving nothing behind but a chaotic, deliberate mess. The sinks were overflowing, the faucets left on full blast, water spilling over the edges and pooling across the tiled floor. The walls were sprayed with lurid graffiti and crude images scrawled in red spray paint.

Quickly, Jack turned off the faucets, watching the last of the water trickle down to a halt. *Not today*, he thought, a promise of justice settling in his mind. As he turned, his eyes landed on a school bag abandoned in one of the stalls. Just as he stepped forward, the door swung open, and in walked Brad, back to collect the bag he'd carelessly left behind.

Brad froze, his smirk vanishing as he locked eyes with Jack, realizing he'd walked straight into a trap. In a split second, he turned, ready to bolt, but Jack was faster this time, lunging toward the door.

"Oh no, you don't!" he shouted, setting off after them with fierce determination.

"Shit!" Brad cursed, casting a panicked glance over his shoulder to see Jack bearing down on them, his expression grim and unyielding. "Leg it!" he hissed to Fat Boy, who needed no further prodding. They tore down the corridor, frantic and clumsy, scrambling like wild animals fleeing a burning forest.

Their footsteps thundered down the hall, the echoes bouncing off the walls in a frantic rhythm, and the shrill clatter of their shoes betraying their desperation. Each corner they rounded only seemed to bring Jack closer, his own steps steady and unrelenting, a shadow that refused to let them slip away.

Jack surged forward, relentless, a hound on the trail. Though he wasn't as quick as they were, and he sometimes lost sight of them around the sharp turns, his knowledge of the school was his advantage. He knew every shortcut, every narrow passage hidden behind familiar doors. He could anticipate their every turn and stumble, and he wasn't about to let them wriggle free this time.

Through echoing corridors and past startled students, Jack pursued them, their footsteps hammering in sync like a frantic, unending drumbeat.

The boys split up, hoping to confuse Jack and force him to give up the chase. But Jack had no intention of giving up. His eyes were fixed on one target: Brad. His friends were small fry.

Jack paused to catch his breath. Even though his work kept him fit, Brad had youth on his side, and he was much lighter. As Jack gulped down much-needed air, he cocked his head, listening carefully.

The school was silent, save for the rhythmic creaking of swinging doors, the squeal of rubber soles scraping the polished floors, and the hurried sound of feet scurrying down a distant corridor. Jack could almost map Brad's movements from the sound of each worn, unoiled hinge; he was getting closer. The final clue was the unmistakable sound of the gym door—several clatters followed by a solid click, ending with a distinctive rattle as the floor lock slid into place. Silence fell. There was only one explanation for that silence: Brad had nowhere left to run. He would be hiding.

Now trapped, Brad's options were limited. Jack knew all the fire doors were locked and would remain so for the weekend. He'd personally secured the windows after last year's break-ins. The prey had no escape. Gathering himself, Jack took a deep breath and smirked. He proceeded calmly down the corridor towards the gym.

Meanwhile, Brad, sweating profusely, was desperately seeking a hiding place, unaware that his capture was inevitable. His black Nike trainers squealed and scuffed the recently buffed floor as he darted across the gym. Time was running out. He had to act fast. Spotting a large basketball bag crammed with balls, his heart raced with hope. He quickly discarded several balls and climbed inside, pulling the zip closed, leaving a small gap to breathe. He lay still, waiting.

For a moment, there was eerie silence, but then the gym door swung open and slammed against the wall. Brad froze as the door banged and began to swing slowly shut. The groan of the unoiled hinges sent a chill through him. Seconds later, the room fell silent again.

Brad's heart pounded in his chest, and he struggled to control his breathing. A bead of sweat trickled into his eye, stinging him. The salty discomfort became unbearable, but he knew any movement would give him away. He blinked, trying to soothe the irritation, but it only worsened. His face contorted as he fought the urge to wipe it away, but there was no relief.

Jack stood in the doorway, his posture alert, scanning the room like a seasoned tracker. His gaze swept left and right, sharp and focused. His nose wrinkled slightly as he sniffed the air, searching for any clue. Then his eyes locked onto a set of black scuff marks marring the freshly polished floor—a clear trail.

Crouching, Jack examined the marks closely, tracing them lightly with his fingers. His instincts sharpened, and a quiet surge of pride rose within him. His mixed heritage—modern experience combined with ancestral wisdom—felt like an advantage. He remembered a story his mother told him about his Potawatomi ancestors and a great chief called Shabonee, tracking deer, buffalo, or lost cavalry patrols across the plains. Today, it was Nike trainers leaving a trail instead of hoofprints.

Rising to his feet, Jack continued along the trail with careful, deliberate steps. His mind briefly wandered to those ancient hunts, but his focus snapped back as the marks led him to what seemed to be a moving sack.

Jack paused, a flicker of satisfaction crossing his face as he realized he was closing in. He allowed himself a moment to savor the impending capture before swiftly moving in. In one fluid motion, he unzipped the bag and, with a firm grip, apprehended his target.

"Up to your old tricks again, I see. Some things never change," Jack remarked, pulling Brad from the sack.

"Go to hell, creep!" Brad spat, struggling in vain as Jack easily overpowered him, grabbing his collar and dragging him towards the head-teacher's office.

"My arm! You're hurting me!" Brad cried, thrashing against Jack's hold.

Jack seized the moment, slamming Brad against the lockers with a firm grip, his voice low and fierce. "Looks like you've been caught red-handed."

But then, as he caught his own reflection in the polished metal of the lockers, Jack felt a jolt of recognition. This wasn't him—he'd let his emotions get the best of him. Taking a steadying breath, he eased his grip, letting his tension subside. He remembered what it was to be a troubled teenager himself, lost and furious with the world. He knew Brad's background too well—the deadbeat father, the broken home. In a flash of empathy, he decided on another approach, one that might reach Brad more than any show of strength.

"Listen, I get it," Jack said, his tone softer but resolute. "You're angry, and it feels like the world's against you. But your father's choices don't have to be yours. Don't let him drag you down."

"Fuck you," Brad spat back, his face twisted with defiance, rejecting Jack's olive branch with venom. Jack shook his head, letting the boy's defiance roll off him. There was nothing left to do but walk Brad down the corridor, his grip firm on the back of Brad's collar.

As they passed through the hallway, scattered cheers and jeers erupted from the few students still lingering around, their faces alight with satisfaction at seeing the school terror finally caught. Monica stood among them; her face flushed as she watched Jack stride past. He offered her a small, reassuring smile, catching her gaze for a brief moment. Her cheeks colored deeper; her admiration clear in her brightened eyes.

Jack returned his focus to Brad, resolute. Whatever punishment lay ahead, he hoped that maybe—just maybe—it would be the wake-up call the boy needed.

FIVE
MUNGO

EVENTUALLY, they reached the principal's office. Brad, a little roughed up but silent, stood beside Jack as he began explaining the incident to June, the principal's stern-faced secretary. Jack kept his tone steady, detailing the vandalism and harassment with a quiet authority that conveyed both his frustration and his resolve.

As he spoke, he noticed a thin trickle of blood beginning to drip from Brad's nose. Jack reached into his pocket, pulling out a rag and offering it to the boy. But Brad merely smirked, wiping the back of his hand across his face, smearing the blood across his cheeks in a crimson stain. The gesture was unsettling—defiant, almost taunting. Jack hesitated for a moment, thrown by Brad's odd expression, but quickly regained his composure and continued his account.

June pressed the intercom, her expression unreadable as she summoned the principal.

"Mr Henderson, there's been an incident. Jack's here with Brad Marshall."

A sigh came over the intercom. "Why do 'incident' and 'Brad Marshall' always seem to go together?" After a brief silence, the principal's voice came back. "Send Jack in."

June smiled warmly at Jack as he walked into the office. Her expression changed the moment she looked at Brad—a cold scowl replaced the smile. She pointed to the chair. "Sit," she said firmly.

Brad grinned defiantly, refusing to move.

"I said sit," she repeated, her voice steely.

This time, Brad sat, still smirking but saying nothing.

The room fell into an uneasy silence, broken only by the occasional ring of the phone and the rhythmic clicking of June's typewriter. Brad stared coldly at June, wiping the blood still trickling from his nose.

"He's gonna pay for this," Brad muttered, licking the blood from his hand and smiling maliciously. "He's gonna pay big time."

June, visibly disgusted, shook her head but chose not to respond. She despised him, and any further interaction would only give him more satisfaction. A few more minutes passed before the principal's voice barked over the intercom.

"June?"

"Yes, Mr. Henderson."

"Send Brad in."

"Yes, sir." June's eyes snapped back to Brad. "You heard him, off you go."

Brad slowly got to his feet, taking his time, as if savoring every second. As he reached the principal's office door, he paused, turning to June. "Did you have a ginger cat?"

June's face betrayed her emotions. The question struck a nerve, filling her with remorse as she remembered her beloved cat, Mungo, who had been found mutilated on her front lawn the previous summer.

"So it was you, you little bastard," she whispered angrily, her voice shaking.

Brad smiled darkly and turned away. June's eyes filled with tears as he swaggered into the principal's office, followed by Jack. The door closed behind them, and soon after, muffled voices began seeping through the thick office walls. The principal's disappointment was evident. Brad had been given chance after chance, but he had squandered them all.

The punishment was swift and severe—suspension, pending an

investigation set for Monday morning at 1:30 p.m. Brad's actions had finally caught up with him, and there was no saving him this time.

When the door opened, Jack escorted Brad out and handed him over to school security. Brad turned his head, glaring back at Jack, his face contorted with rage. The hatred in his eyes was unmistakable.

"I'll get you for this. I'm gonna make you pay," Brad spat venomously.

Jack shrugged, unfazed. He simply turned and re-entered the principal's office, closing the door behind him. Brad was gone, leaving the room in heavy silence. The principal leaned back in his chair, rocking slightly as he pondered the situation. After a moment, he broke the quiet.

"Jack, I want a full report by nine-thirty on Monday morning."

"Yes, Mr. Henderson," Jack replied. He respected the principal, a man who was fair, honest, and kind. He had known Jack since his school days and had helped him through difficult times as a teenager. The principal had been a father figure to Jack and had played a key role in getting him his current job as the school's caretaker. The trust between them was deep.

"What's the damage to the toilets, Jack?" the principal asked.

"Not much, just needs a lick of paint. The blockages will take me about an hour to fix," Jack explained.

"Alright, let me know the full cost—paint, overtime, everything—so we can bill Brad's family for the damage."

"Will do, Mr. Henderson. I'll get started right away," Jack said as he left the office. As he closed the door behind him, he noticed June had been crying.

"What's wrong, June?" Jack asked gently, noting the tears brimming in her eyes.

Amidst quiet sobs, she recounted Brad's cruel words about her beloved cat, Mungo, . Jack, fumbling through his pockets, eventually pulled out a crumpled, dirty rag and offered it to her. June glanced at the grimy cloth and shook her head, politely declining. Realizing how absurd the gesture seemed, Jack gave her a sheepish smile.

"Are you going to be all right?" he asked softly, concern creasing his brow.

"I'll be fine, Jack," she replied, retrieving a clean handkerchief from her handbag, pressing it to her eyes. Jack promised her that Brad wouldn't hurt anyone like this again, and they shared a brief, reassuring smile. Yet her hands trembled as they clasped a small tag hanging from a delicate gold necklace—a tag inscribed with Mungo's name.

As he watched her hold that pendant, a new resolve settled in Jack's heart. Brad had crossed a line, shattering the unspoken boundaries of cruelty. Today, Jack would make sure Brad felt the full weight of his actions. Whatever it took, he was done letting Brad terrorize the school unchecked; it was time for him to face the consequences he had long evaded.

SIX
GOOSEY, GOOSEY GANDER

JACK MADE his way to the toilets, bracing himself for the mess he'd have to tackle. It was going to be a late night, but he didn't mind. With his sister away on business and only his cat waiting for him at home, there was no reason to hurry.

As he began the clean-up, scrubbing away the graffiti and sopping up water pooled on the floor, Jack's thoughts wandered. He'd never actively sought out female company—his own tangled past had left him wary, uncertain of how he might come across. There was always a faint fear that they'd see through him, glimpse the shadows he kept tightly guarded and dismiss him as strange, unreachable. And even if he did manage to connect with someone, he mused, Rose would likely scare them off anyway. She had always been fiercely protective of him, seeing through his silences to the secrets he buried. A wry smile crossed his face as he pictured her stern expression, ready to ward off anyone she deemed unworthy of his trust.

For now, though, it was just him, the empty halls, and the slow rhythm of his cleaning. The solitude didn't bother him; it was, in many ways, a comfort.

The clean-up didn't take long, and after stowing away the mop and bucket, Jack made his final rounds, checking the locked doors of each classroom. He rattled each one, ensuring they were secure. As he moved through the hallways and corridors, switching off the fluorescent lights, the once-bright corridors dimmed into soft shadows.

Suddenly, he heard footsteps. Hard, neatly spaced steps echoed down one of the corridors, Jack turned to see a shadow at the end of the half-lit corridor. It didn't take long for him to recognize the figure—it was the principal, always the last to leave. Jack stepped into the light.

"Good night, Mr. Henderson," Jack said, politely.

"Good night, Jack. Don't forget, nine-thirty on Monday. The sooner we deal with Brad Marshall, the better."

"It won't be much of a loss to the school, that's for sure," Jack replied.

The principal nodded, his expression caught between a smile and a grimace. Beneath that thin grin lay a deep sense of failure—Brad's failure weighed heavily on him. Unlike Jack, the principal couldn't do any more for Brad. He was about to become another statistic, a student lost to the system. With a sagging posture, he bid Jack farewell.

"See you Monday, Jack."

"Good night, Mr. Henderson."

After locking up behind the principal, Jack checked his watch and resumed his final rounds. All that was left now was to set the alarm system. As he approached the control panel, he noticed a single red light blinking persistently. Every indicator should have been green by now. Frowning, Jack tapped at the stubborn red light, but it remained unchanged, signaling an issue with one specific room—the old storeroom tucked away in the lower level, a space filled with dusty books and long-forgotten equipment. Jack felt a shiver creep up his spine. He despised that part of the school.

The storeroom was once part of the old courthouse's cells, built to hold prisoners awaiting execution. History lessons had often glossed over that particular cell, whispering tales of 'dead men walking' held within its oppressive stone walls before their final march to the hanging tree outside. That old cell had witnessed more deaths than anyone cared to remember, and Jack had never been able to shake its haunted air, the quiet chill that lingered in its depths.

He glanced at the flickering red light once more, confirming his suspicion. It was indeed the cell storeroom setting off the alarm. Jack's pulse quickened, and a heavy unease settled over him. He hesitated, then resolved to sidestep the issue. There was no way he was going down there tonight. Reaching into the panel, he found the fuse for that connection and carefully pulled it. He'd get Will, the school's maintenance man, to sort it out on Monday.

With one final look at the panel, he took a deep breath, reassured by the silence that settled around him. As he closed the alarm panel and turned the key to lock it, a chill crept down his spine, and an instinctive notion overwhelmed him. He turned swiftly, a movement out of the corner of his eye catching his attention—a shadow slipping around the corner, silent as mist. He heard no footsteps, no rustling of clothing or scuff of shoes, but an undeniable presence lingered, clinging to the air like the cold breath of something unseen.

For a moment, he stood frozen, his heartbeat loud in his ears. He strained to hear any sound, any telltale sign of life, but there was only the low hum of the building settling, and the flicker of the security lights overhead casting long shadows down the hallway. Jack's grip tightened on his keys, his instinct to turn and leave battling with a strange compulsion to follow, to confirm that he'd truly seen someone—or something.

But Jack couldn't just leave; it was his responsibility to ensure the building was clear before locking up. He steeled himself, shaking off the prickling sense of dread that clung to his skin. He made his way to the corner where he'd seen the shadow disappear. As he approached, he called out, "Hello, anyone there?" Silence met him, thick and unyielding. He took another step, his voice firmer this time. "You need to leave—I'm locking up. Mr. Henderson, is that you?"

Still nothing.

He continued, his movements slow yet deliberate, following the corridor's bends, the walls narrowing around him. With each step, he turned lights back on, flooding the dark spaces ahead with a flickering, sterile glow. His footsteps echoed down the long, stretching corridors, a hollow, rhythmic sound that magnified his unease. It wasn't the darkness or the silence that disturbed him most—it was what might be hiding within them.

Jack realized, too late, that he was being led deeper into the oldest part of the school, to a place he'd hoped he would never have to venture. The air grew thick and stale, the faint hiss of steam created a sinister symphony. Overhead, ancient pipes rattled and rumbled like some dormant beast shifting in its sleep. He couldn't help but remember his snake-hunting days as a boy, a memory punctuated by the two small scars on his arm, relics of a lucky escape. Absentmindedly, he rubbed the marks, feeling his pulse race beneath his fingers.

Then came the unmistakable sound of a door creaking open somewhere ahead. Jack whipped around in its direction just as a shadow flickered past the corner, vanishing as quickly as it had appeared. He glanced around, his heart sinking as he realized where he'd ended up —the old prison cells corridor. The school's unsettling history crept back into his mind: tales of condemned prisoners, 'dead men walking,' waiting for their final march to the gallows. One story surfaced now, vivid and chilling—a rumor he'd heard at a Halloween sleepover about Bartholomew Harris, the last victim of the Lincoln Mauler. Bart had been a friend, his sudden disappearance shrouded in rumors that he'd been buried somewhere in these cells. Jack had always dismissed it as mere legend, a ghost story, but now, faced with the echoing corridors, the thought unsettled him deeply.

A second creak broke through his thoughts, and he realized it was coming from the very door that had triggered the red light on the alarm panel. The door stood open, a cold invitation in the shadows. He swallowed, resolved. *Well, I'm here now. Might as well close it*, he told himself, stepping closer.

As he reached the door, Jack hesitated, then gave it a push, swinging it open fully. He reached for the light switch inside, flicking it up—nothing. The bulb was long dead. With a sigh, he pulled out his torch, its thin beam cutting through the darkness, illuminating dust motes suspended in the stale air. Bracing himself, he stepped inside.

The room was cramped, filled with shelves of forgotten equipment and crumbling stacks of old books. The air was thick with a damp, earthy smell, and something else—a faint, coppery scent that made his skin crawl. The beam of his torch traced over the shelves, lingering on old, rusted tools and cracked bindings, relics of an era left behind.

Darkness always made him uneasy, and it reminded him of an old childhood memory, or perhaps a recurring nightmare—it was hard to tell which.

As Jack hesitated in the doorway, a sudden presence made the hairs on the back of his neck stand up. He spun around, but not quickly enough. A shadowy figure loomed behind him, and before Jack could react, he felt a sharp push. He lost his balance and tumbled down the hard concrete steps. The impact left him winded, and as he lay on the floor rubbing his shoulder, he looked up at the shadow standing in the doorway.

There was no time to assess his injuries. The light spilling in from the hallway began to fade—the door was closing. Jack scrambled to his feet, his heart racing. He reached for his keys, but they were gone—lost in the fall. Panicked, he limped up the stairs, pain shooting through his knee as he slipped and banged it hard on the step. He heard the keys jingling—whoever had pushed him was trying to lock him in.

He lunged at the door, wedging his foot between the door and the frame just as it slammed shut. The metal door crashed into his ankle, and Jack screamed in pain. He retracted his foot, hopping on one leg, cursing under his breath. By the time he tried the handle, it was too late—the door was locked.

Jack slumped against the door, his breaths coming in ragged gasps as laughter ricocheted through the narrow, dimly lit corridor. It wasn't just any laugh—it was calculated and cruel, as though whoever had locked him in here knew exactly how much power the room held over him. His swelling ankle throbbed in rhythm with his pounding heart, the pain sharper with every pulse.

"I told you I'd get you, Jacky boy," came the voice.

Jack froze. There was no mistaking the voice—it was Brad.

"You little fucker!" Jack shouted through the door. "Wait till I get out of here!"

Brad's laughter faded into the distance, but not before reciting a mocking nursery rhyme:

"Goosey, goosey gander, where shall I wander? Upstairs, downstairs in my lady's chamber. There, I met an old man who wouldn't say his prayers, so I took him by the left leg and threw him down the stairs."

Brad's voice trailed off into silence. Jack pounded on the door once more but knew it was futile. Brad was gone.

SEVEN
A FAMILIAR PLACE

GATHERING HIMSELF, Jack hobbled back down the stairs, knelt, and began searching for his torch, the floor cold and damp to his touch. He found it, smashed to pieces. Anger bubbled up inside him. He grabbed the broken pieces and tried to reassemble them in the dim light that leaked under the door, but it was no use. Defeated, he searched the room in the dark, running his hands along the walls, hoping to find a working light switch. Nothing.

"This isn't happening," Jack muttered, sliding down the wall and rubbing his hands through his hair. He closed his eyes, wishing it was all a bad dream. But when he opened his eyes, he was still trapped.

His breathing quickened as the reality of his situation hit him. Panic started to set in, but he fought to stay calm. He had to think. There had to be a way out.

He fumbled his way around the room, hands brushing against dusty shelves and forgotten equipment. In the darkness, the faint sliver of light beneath the door barely pierced the gloom, offering no guidance. His fingers brushed against something cold and metallic—a long, rounded handle. His pulse quickened as he traced its contours, recognition dawning in an instant: it was a toolbox. A fragile yet determined hope flickered within him as he pried it open, the hinges groaning softly, the sound cutting through the oppressive silence. Inside, he found tools. They felt rusty—a hammer, screwdrivers, a wrench. They didn't feel in great condition, but they were better than nothing.

Grabbing the hammer and screwdriver, Jack limped back to the door. His ankle throbbed with every step, but he had no choice but to move. He raised the hammer and struck the door handle. The sound echoed in the empty corridor, but the handle barely budged. Again and again, he hammered, but the door was solid. When he tried to pry it open with the screwdriver, he broke the door handle clean off, leaving him worse off than before.

Exhausted, and in pain, Jack slumped to the floor, his breath ragged. His thoughts turned to his cat waiting for him at home. Who would feed it if he didn't get out?

Panic clawed at Jack's mind, and he screamed, the sound ricocheting off the unforgiving walls, swallowed by the darkness that pressed in around him. The silence that followed was brutal—no footsteps rushing to his aid, no familiar voice to reassure him. He was utterly alone.

"Think, Jack. Think," he muttered, his voice barely more than a whisper, tinged with desperation. "Rose!" he yelled into the darkness, clinging to the faint hope that his sister would come for him—she always had before, somehow sensing when he needed her. But the thought evaporated as quickly as it had arrived. This time, it was useless. She was away for the entire weekend, and no one else would think to search for him here until Monday morning.

A cold, hollow chill gripped him, seeping into his bones as the realization sank in. He'd laughed off the ghost stories before, dismissed the unsettling history of the old cells as mere rumor. But here, in the bowels of the school, trapped with the memories and shadows of forgotten souls, his calm was beginning to crack. The darkness seemed to press closer, thick and tangible, creeping in as his hope drained away.

His breaths came quickly, clouding in the cold air. He could feel his heart pounding, a frantic beat that echoed in the oppressive silence. Monday felt like a lifetime away.

His eyes darted around the darkened room, seeking any hint of a way out. There had to be something—a vent, a weakness in the walls, anything. He remembered the pipes that lined the corridors above, hissing and groaning with the building's age. *Maybe*, he thought, *one of them leads outside*. If he could just find an opening, a passage large enough to crawl through, he might be able to escape.

Jack pushed himself up, wincing as he bore weight on his injured ankle, and limped to where the pipes were half-embedded in the wall. He traced their rough, cold metal with his hands, following them as far as he could, only to discover they disappeared into the brick, offering no potential route to freedom.

"Dammit!" he cursed, the word cutting through the stillness. Defeated, he slumped down against the wall. There was no way out.

For now, he was trapped with nothing but his own thoughts—the creeping memories of things he'd tried hard to bury. As the silence pressed in, he couldn't shake the disturbing feeling that something was watching him from the shadows, waiting, patient and silent. The dark had a presence of its own, and Jack found himself facing a primal fear he'd spent years ignoring. All the strength he gained over the years controlling his inner demons was now slowly ebbing away.

He took a deep breath, steadying himself. He couldn't afford to give in to terror. He had to survive the night somehow. Maybe Rose would come home early from her trip.

EIGHT
ROSE

"SO YOU SEE, ladies and gentlemen, what I've outlined in the portfolio would be an excellent feature for the next issue. It seems red is the color of the summer."

Rose finished her presentation, both hands firmly planted on the table, emphasizing her point. Like the sharp red pinstripe suit she wore, she was stylish and composed, exuding confidence that filled the room. There was no doubt—her authority was absolute.

The room, sleek and minimalist, with frosted glass walls and a single Warhol original on display, acted as an extension of Rose's poise. The Charles Eames table and chairs complemented the space; they were symbols of success. Rose sat at the head of the table, commanding attention. Around her were senior executives, editors, and designers, mostly men, along with a few secretaries, quietly taking notes. Rose's presence eclipsed them all.

As she closed her folder and straightened her jacket, she placed the lid back on her Montblanc pen with deliberate precision, a final gesture of confidence. The room responded on cue, bursting into murmurs of agreement and congratulations orchestrated by her mere presence.

Among the sea of approving nods, a voice cut through, challenging and direct. It was Charles, the new cover designer, eager to prove himself.

"How can you be sure, Rose?"

He leaned forward, elbows resting on the table, hands gesturing towards her presentation, attempting to gain the room's attention. His timing was off, and he'd underestimated his opponent. Silence filled the room as everyone turned to watch the exchange.

Rose uncrossed her legs, clasped her hands, and leaned forward slightly, fixing her gaze on Charles. Her eyes were sharp, unwavering. "Charles, in this industry, certainty comes from experience and results. This season, red has dominated the runways, the latest collections, and consumer preferences. Our readers rely on us to guide them, and I trust my research and instincts. Do you have a better suggestion?"

Her words sliced through Charles's confidence like a knife. His bravado crumbled, and he blushed, flustered, like a schoolboy caught in an embarrassing mistake. He forced a grin, shuffling the papers in front of him in a futile attempt to recover. It was clear he'd lost the battle. Rose had barely broken a sweat.

Rising from her seat, Rose placed the Montblanc pen into her jacket pocket and addressed the room with her signature authority. "Gentlemen—and ladies," she added, her tone cool, "I trust I've made everything clear. I expect the rest of the features to be finalized by the end of the week. No exceptions."

Everyone nodded in agreement, and as they gathered their things to leave, Rose's voice cut through the idle chatter, directing itself to Charles.

"Oh, and Charles… your Versace shirt is fake. The buttons are all wrong."

The young designer's face flushed again as Rose turned her attention back to the others, dismissing him with ease.

After the meeting, Rose made her way to an empty office to make a call. The phone rang unanswered. Annoyed, she tried again, muttering under her breath, "Pick up the phone, Jack… pick up."

Still nothing. The phone rang unanswered in the empty apartment. This time, Rose let it ring, waiting for the answering machine to pick up. The familiar click sounded, followed by her own recorded voice.

There was something strange about hearing herself in the silence of his absence.

"Hey, Jack," she began, trying to keep her tone light. "Hope you had a great day at work. Just checking that everything is okay... and that you've taken your medicine. I'll call you later. Love you."

She hung up, frustration simmering beneath her worry. Leaning back in her chair, she stared at the phone, her mind racing.

Where is he? Jack should've been home by now. She checked her watch: 6:30 p.m. Of course, she realized, he'd likely still be at work. *Stop it, you're being ridiculous*, she told herself, but the nagging sense that something wasn't quite right lingered, refusing to be brushed aside. There was something else tugging at her memory, something important that Jack had asked her to do.

She frowned, straining to remember. *What was it?*

Then it struck her—*the auction.* Jack had specifically asked her to check out the model train memorabilia auction. "Trains!" she exclaimed aloud, cursing under her breath. She'd completely forgotten.

She remembered he asked her to bid on a rare locomotive—the 746 Long Stripe J, no less. Rose knew nothing about model trains, but she intended to win it for her brother, whatever the cost.

She grabbed her coat and keys, determined to make it in time. Jack's obsession with vintage trains bordered on reverent, and she'd promised she wouldn't let him down.

She promised herself she'd call him again later. Gathering her things, she headed towards the lift, only to bump into Charles in the hallway.

"Hey Charles, where's the Pinkerton Auction House?" she asked casually.

Charles, eager to redeem himself, said quickly, "It's on 72nd Street and York Avenue." He glanced at his watch. "But it's closed now... I could take you there tomorrow if you'd like?" His tone was hopeful as he looked at her, clearly hoping for another chance to make a good impression.

She offered a polite smile and declined, but he continued, giving her detailed directions, his enthusiasm barely contained. As she turned and walked towards the lift, she couldn't help but notice he'd changed his shirt. Without turning around, Rose spoke over her shoulder, "Charles, I was only kidding about the shirt."

He smiled, relieved. But as the lift doors opened, Rose stepped inside, turned on her heel, and delivered one final blow.

"As for the yellow tie…" She let the words hang in the air, shook her head in mock disappointment, and allowed the lift doors to close, leaving Charles standing there, staring after her.

With that parting shot, Rose had cemented her authority. Charles—and anyone else who had witnessed the exchange—would certainly think twice before questioning her judgment again.

NINE
ALONE IN THE DARK

JACK, still trapped, clung to his sanity by the thinnest of threads. He could not know what time it was or how long he had been locked away; he guessed it was late as tiredness began to creep in. He knew that staying calm was his only hope. He inhaled deeply through his nose and exhaled slowly through his mouth, and the sound echoed like a train gaining momentum. As he settled in for the long haul, sitting on a dusty box, his mind drifted back to the beginning of the day, before everything had unraveled. His mind wandered to the start of his day. It had been so beautiful—the fragrant scent of roses, the endless blue sky, and the cheerful chirping of the fox sparrows. Closing his eyes, he tried to summon these happy thoughts. It worked for a moment; his breathing slowed, and a sense of calm washed over him.

But the peace was fleeting. The mental slideshow that entered his daydream that morning had started to play once more, this time picking up where it had left off. The horrifying image of his father hanging by the throat flashed vividly in his mind. Jack couldn't shake the gruesome picture, and there was no chirpy birdsong in the dank dungeon to rescue him from his dark reverie. This time, the slideshow continued to its horrific conclusion.

He recalled every ghastly detail: the thick pool of blood dripping from his father's mouth, the grotesque lump of his severed tongue that he had slipped on, and the unmistakable stench of death as the body released its contents. The smell, that awful just-dead smell, lingered in his nostrils. Jack's eyes snapped open, his heart racing. That was all he could remember, thankfully. He was relieved to escape the daydream but disheartened to return to his grim reality. He leaned against the cold, damp wall, feeling dread coil around him like a serpent. His breath hissed out, steam emerging from his mouth and nose in the cold air.

Struggling to his feet, Jack knew he needed a distraction. His eyes, now accustomed to the dim light, traced the thin sliver seeping through the gap at the base of the door, casting eerie, elongated shadows that loomed around the room like silent sentries, watching. The stillness of the shadows unnerved him, their presence almost palpable.

He began to pace, clicking his fingers rhythmically in an attempt to anchor his thoughts and stave off the rising panic that threatened to take hold. Leaning back against the cold, damp wall, he closed his eyes, allowing himself a brief moment of relaxation. The sharp pain in his ankle had settled into a dull, persistent throb, a reminder of his limited mobility.

Focus, Jack, he told himself, inhaling deeply, forcing his mind to sharpen, to find any possible way out of this tomb-like cell.

Jack fumbled through the darkness, desperate to keep his mind occupied, and he found an old, broken school chair. Though it wobbled, he hoped it would hold his weight. He needed relief from his aching ankle, so he took a chance and sat down. The chair held firm for now, and he rested his head in his hands. Before long, his mind drifted into another daydream. This time, he was a child, about seven or eight years old, recalling visits to the old log cabin with Rose. They would meet Bart, Rose's boyfriend, who reminded Jack of Grizzly Adams, a show he loved as a kid. Though Bart was young, about the same age as Rose, he had a full, bushy beard.

Jack looked back on that long summer at the cabin with a bittersweet fondness. The cabin sat near the old house where they once lived; he had just turned eight. Visiting the summer house felt like a grand adventure, it had been a place of freedom and wonder. He remembered fishing in the cool, babbling stream nearby, losing himself in the endless days under the sun. But one memory of that summer stood out sharply, like a thorn.

It was the day Rose and Bart had an explosive argument. Even after all these years, he could still recall the shouting, the tension in the air thick and suffocating. Jack had never seen Bart so angry, his face contorted with rage. The sight had terrified him. Rose looked equally shaken; her eyes wide with fear.

He watched as Rose left with Bart, leaving him behind in the quiet cabin. He remembered standing at the door, watching them disappear into the woods, a shadow of dread settling over him. Rose returned alone a short time later, and they walked back to the house in silence.

For a long time, that memory had been eclipsed by another—it had also been the day Jack discovered his father's lifeless body. The memory of Rose's tears stayed with him—he found it strange, as she had never seemed to care for their father. But she wept for a long time, and it was the last time he ever saw her cry. It was also the last time he saw Bart.

Only much later did Jack learn what might have happened. Rumors hinted that Bart had fallen victim to the *Mauler*, a grim fate that could explain his sudden disappearance, never to be seen again.

ROSE RETURNED to her hotel room with the thought of calling Jack still lingering at the back of her mind. As she entered, she kicked off her shoes, feeling the ache of the long day finally catch up with her. With a sigh, she ran a hot bath, promising herself she'd call him as soon as she'd had a chance to unwind.

But the warmth of the bath melted away her remaining energy, and by the time she slipped into bed, the weight of exhaustion pulled her under almost instantly. Her eyes barely had time to close before she drifted into a deep sleep.

"ROSE," Jack muttered, the name slipping from his lips as he jolted out of his daydream, disoriented. The thought of his sister had surfaced suddenly, breaking into his waking moments like a beacon. In the dim light of the cell, her face came to him—warm, reassuring but distant.

He did not know how long his daydream had lasted. It could have been ten minutes, a few hours, or the whole night; he had no way of knowing, locked in a box void of time. His mind began to spin, sanity fraying with each passing moment. The stench of rotten, damp books assaulted his senses, and the darkness—God, the darkness—was becoming all too familiar. Through the night his mind drifted into a daydreams and half-sleeps, returning to a childhood nightmare that had haunted him since he was a boy. Over the years, he often wondered if the terrifying dream was rooted in a forgotten reality. The thought sent a chill through him. If it were indeed a fragment of his past, it would be a secret so dark that it had to stay buried. Terror now spread across his face. Panic set in, and his heart began to race. Once again, he tried to think of the chirpy song his feathered friend had sung earlier in the day. Jack pursed his lips in an attempt to whistle a tune, but his lips were too dry. Frantically licking his lips, he tried again to raise a tune, but to no avail. He became more frustrated.

Desperation fueled his movements as he quickly got up, stumbled to the bottom of the staircase, and slowly climbed the stairs. He continued to knock on the door, hoping that Brad had had a change of heart and would return, but deep down, he knew it was unlikely.

What seemed like hours passed by. Jack began pacing the small cell, his steps uneven as he muttered under his breath, half-formed prayers and desperate wishes spilling out in a whispered litany. His mind was fraying, slipping into a dark place he couldn't control. The silence pressed in around him, thick and suffocating, amplifying the gnawing ache in his stomach and the dry, burning thirst that had started to claw at his throat.

He leaned back against the door and began talking to himself, childlike. In the background, a leaking pipe dripped, each drop smacking the floor, rhythmically clicking. For a moment he thought of drinking the water that dripped from the pipe, but he wasn't there yet.

As each second passed, the soft clicking sounds became louder and more annoying, each drip echoing around the room. Jack began to mumble.

"They're going to get me. Please, let me go. I'll be good," he pleaded, his voice trembling. Tears streamed down his face as he mumbled uncontrollably.

"I'll be good now, Daddy. Look, I'm smiling. Daddy, please don't let them hurt me," he repeated, his words growing more frantic. Jack was losing his grip on reality.

Suddenly, he froze mid-step and raised his head, alert, like a prairie dog.

"Who's there?" he whispered, his heart racing. He had heard a faint sound. Unsure if it was real or his mind unraveling, he shook his head. But then the sound came again—someone or something was sharing the room with him. Jack's eyes darted to the shadows at the edge of his vision. Had they moved? His pulse quickened. Were they here to hurt him? The human-like shadow had multiplied. Now, there were four.

"I know you're there! Please don't hurt me," Jack pleaded. Except for the dripping pipe, only silence was the reply. He slumped back on the chair and rocked like a child, crying and whimpering. It wasn't long before he was asleep. While there, Jack's past and those images of his childhood, which he thought were hidden in the darkest depths of his mind, returned to haunt him.

"Stop that crying, I tell ya!" Jack's father loomed menacingly over him; his hand raised high. CRACK. The hand came down hard, striking Jack across the face. Jack had cut his leg while playing, the deep wound bleeding through the cloth he had hastily wrapped around it. His sobbing had irritated his father, who was trying to watch TV. Jack cowered under the table, desperate to escape the blows.

"Sorry, Daddy, please, I'll be good," Jack begged for deliverance as tears streamed down his face. His father grabbed him by the scruff of his neck, pulling him from beneath the table, pinching his skin, and leaving a bright red welt that stung, making him cry even more.

"I'll show you, you little crybaby." His father again raised his hand to deliver another punishing blow. SMACK. His father had been drinking again, and when he drank, Jack knew there was hell to pay.

His father was tall, and you could see he had once been handsome underneath his tired face and sullen eyes. His unkempt hair was gray; unusual for a man his age, but the pain of his wife leaving and all the drinking and worry of raising two children had taken their toll.

He dragged Jack to the cellar doorway. Jack desperately clawed at the floor and kicked furiously, but his father was too strong. His T-shirt rose and exposed the bare flesh of his back that screeched against the hard-tiled floor of the kitchen. Almost through the cellar door, Jack grabbed the air and managed to catch the doorframe. Tears now flowed freely from Jack's swollen and tearful face. A trickle of blood ran from the corner of Jack's mouth, tiny bubbles forming around his nostrils. His pitiful screams and cries had no effect on his father, who gave one final yank, dragging Jack into the darkness of the cellar. Jack's fingers clawed desperately at the walls as he was pulled down the creaking wooden stairs, leaving faint scratch marks in the brittle plaster and flaking, bubbled paint. Now missing the top layer of skin, his fingers began to bleed. He thought his father must be able to see the pain, clearly visible, on his battered face. As they reached the bottom of the stairs, his father let go of his grip and returned up the stairs. Once at the top, he slowly turned, looked down at the terrified boy, and promised him, "If you don't stop crying, The Miseries'll get ya."

Jack, eyes filled with tears, face grimaced with fear, held out his arms, begging his father not to leave him. He cried again, "Daddy, please, Daddy, NO!"

"Daddy, no, please no." Jack awoke suddenly, arms searching, grasping the air. He was now back from his nightmare. Some time had passed; Jack was unaware that the night had come and gone. He tried to close his eyes, hoping to fall asleep again, then opened them quickly. The thought of falling asleep and finding himself back in his nightmare was far more frightening than his present predicament—but the line between reality and his nightmare was beginning to blur.

Jack once again realized the seriousness of the situation and began to cry deeply. He was lost, and time had moved on without him. Was it day, or was it night? Jack knew neither; time was the jailer that locked him away with only his nightmares for company.

Now fully awake, he resumed his banging and shouting. He tried again with the screwdriver, tapping on the water pipes, but no one was out there to hear his crude attempt at Morse code, his SOS, or his pitiful cries for help. He climbed the stairs and rammed the chisel against the lock, hoping to bust it and pry open the door—no luck. The doors were the original cell doors and made of steel reinforcement, doors that were made to hold in evil murderers and rapists—and now him.

Jack slumped to the floor and buried his head in his hands. As the sound of the dripping pipe returned, he screamed and banged his head back into the door, cursing everything and everybody; he even cursed his sister for not being there. Jack began to regress further into his childhood. The flashbacks were getting stronger, starting to cross over into his reality. He was becoming more childlike with each passing second and minute.

The rhythmic *drip... drip... drip* echoed off the stone walls, each drop smacking against the cobbled floor with maddening consistency. The sound gnawed at Jack's sanity, chipping away at his resolve. Driven to desperation, he crawled over to the dripping pipe, ignoring the gritty floor beneath his hands and knees. Thirst had overtaken him, dulling his instincts for survival, and he pressed his lips to the spot where the cold water trickled down, drinking greedily.

For a brief moment, there was silence, a reprieve from the relentless dripping that had filled his mind, taunting him like a ticking metronome. But as soon as he pulled back, the water resumed its relentless beat, each drop slicing through the stillness, mocking him. He tried to drown out the sound by counting each drip, letting the rhythm lull him into focus. For a while, it worked. But as the count stretched on, the numbers blurred, merging with his exhaustion, pulling him down into sleep.

In the darkness of his dreams, he was back in the cellar of the old house—but it was different, twisted. Shadows writhed along the walls, creeping closer with every drop of water that hit the floor. Faces he couldn't quite make out whispered his name, and the sound of the dripping grew louder, each drop a thunderous beat in his mind. Jack tried to wake, to pull himself back, but the nightmare held him in its grasp, trapping him in a place where reality and dread had melded into one.

"Daddy, is that you?" The creaking of a door opening cut through the pause. Strangely, no light entered the room. Jack knew this was the side door, the side door that let in his tormentors, and they were here; sheer terror filled Jack's face. "Please don't hurt me." Tears started to flow from his deep blue, watery eyes. His busted lip and bruised cheek were the least of his pain; the thought of what was to come was far more terrifying. He tried to scamper to safety, cowering in the corner.

The cellar was dark, a darkness that dulled all the senses. Even so, it couldn't conceal him in the tiny room. There were no hiding places, no windows to crawl out of, no cupboards—just a dark, damp dungeon. The air was thick with the stench of piss and feces. In the center, an old, wet, moldy mattress lay flat on the floor; a mottled, flea-bitten blanket lay crumpled beside it.

The groaning door closed gently. Jack faintly heard the scrape of a key turning, then the lock clicking, signaling his fate. He sensed a presence; there was no light to cast a shadow, but he had been here before and knew his fate—there was no escape. They were here, the shadows, the dark ones—The Miseries. A dark figure lunged at Jack and grabbed him tight. A hood was placed over his head, and his hands were tied. Through the hood came a vile, pungent stench. It hung in the air, soaking into the very pores of his skin. The hood gave no protection as it seeped through the cloth and polluted what little air he had. The foul stench of stale cigarettes and whiskey left an acrid taste in his mouth.

He couldn't tell how many tormentors there were—definitely two, possibly three. Other times, there had been more, but most of the time, there had been only one, usually the one that stank the most. They never spoke, just tortured and tormented him. What had he done so wrong that made his father abandon him like this, to be subjected to this vile act? Jack could only pray for it to be quick, but today, there were three.

Jack jolted awake, the remnants of his nightmare slipping away like shadows at dawn, only to be replaced by an ominous, rhythmic *thud… thud…* echoing through the room.

He held his breath, his heart pounding as the sound grew louder, each beat reverberating through his bones, sinking into the pit of his stomach. His skin prickled, goosebumps rising in sharp waves as cold fear flooded him, making him tremble uncontrollably.

"Who's there?" he called, his voice barely more than a whisper, choked with dread. Silence answered him, thick and oppressive, as the noise continued, each thud rattling his resolve. Was his mind playing tricks on him? Was this the echo of his own fear, or had something more sinister entered the room?

Images from his nightmare flared up, memories of stories he'd dismissed—The Miseries, the specters of sorrow said to haunt these old cells, feeding on despair, luring the lost and lonely deeper into madness. He couldn't shake the feeling that something was watching, lurking just beyond the edges of his reality, waiting.

"Rose!" he cried out desperately.

TEN
SOLD

ROSE AWOKE WITH A JOLT, feeling as though a distant voice had called her name.

"Jack!" she cried out, startled.

Blurry-eyed, she glanced at her watch and cursed under her breath—8:55 a.m. She groaned and stretched, but before she could fully shake the fog of sleep, the alarm on her bedside table blared to life, its digits flashing insistently. That's when the thought struck her—she hadn't called Jack last night as she'd intended, and now it was already the next day. Just as she thought of him, the phone in her hotel room rang. Her heart leapt—could it be Jack? She snatched up the receiver, but it was only her office calling to inform her that her meeting had been moved up an hour. She glanced at her watch. It was 9:15 a.m. The 12.15 a.m. meeting was now scheduled for 11.15 a.m. She cursed and sprang into action, hoping traffic would be light.

Turning on the shower, she went to her suitcase and noticed the glossy auction catalog Jack had given her, the page carefully marked. Flipping to it, she found the exact train model he wanted circled in thick ink. She glanced at the high reserve price and hoped she'd be the only one bidding.

After a rushed shower and a quick breakfast, Rose headed across town; her prayers were answered, and traffic was light, and moments later, she headed into her meeting, which was, fortunately, uneventful. They discussed final edits of a feature article with her as the subject, titled 'Power Play,' with the subtitle she'd insisted on: 'Rose to the Top.' Charles kept uncharacteristically quiet, falling in line after his previous misstep. She felt pleased, even powerful, knowing her vision was finally being realized.

A quick coffee later, she was in the front row of the auction. To her relief, only a couple of others placed bids on Jack's train, and she won it with room to spare. The rest of the afternoon was spent shopping and having dinner, her way of unwinding, and a way to soothe the guilt of leaving Jack alone for the weekend.

As soon as she returned to her hotel room, she rushed to the phone, eager to call him. But the line rang out into an empty apartment once more. Eventually, the answering machine picked up, and Rose sighed, leaving a cheerful message. "Hey, you, just checking in. Hope you had a great day! You said you'd be seeing Max—hope he's well. Oh, and just to let you know, I got the train you wanted! You owe me big time. I'll call you at the airport before I leave. Later, alligator!"

She hung up and sighed, disappointed at missing him again. But she shook off the nagging worry. *He's 28; he can take care of himself.* Yet, as his big sister, she knew it was her right to worry.

ELEVEN
GATHERING SHADOWS

JACK GRABBED the screwdriver as a weapon against whatever was in the room with him. He retreated to the corner of the dark, damp storeroom, which now felt more like a dungeon. His back against the wall, he waited, the dim light from his shattered torch casting long, eerie shadows around him.

Suddenly, a movement in the shadows caught his attention. Jack swung wildly, nearly losing his balance. "Get away from me. Leave me alone!" he shouted. "I know you're there."

Panic surged in his voice. "Please, help me. Daddy, don't let them hurt me!" His words echoed back at him in the small, confined space, amplifying his fear.

A high-pitched squeal pierced the room, bouncing off the stone walls like a ricocheting bullet. Jack's head snapped from side to side, his eyes frantically searching the darkness for the source of the sound. Then he heard it—a faint scraping noise, growing closer. Was it a demon sharpening its claws?

Jack shook his head, trying to clear the terrifying image. Desperation took over as he swung the screwdriver in front of him, kicking and lunging blindly into the shadows. His fear consumed him, and soon, the room's rancid smell of rotting books and damp walls, along with the ache of an empty stomach, overwhelmed him. Doubling over, Jack vomited violently, the acidic mix of bile and lemon-lime juice burning his throat.

The scraping noise stopped, replaced by an eerie silence. Jack hoped his tormentors were gone. But then, a deep, guttural moan echoed ominously from the far corner of the room. It was followed by a roar that seemed to shake the very walls. Jack's heart pounded so violently that he could hear it in his ears.

From the shadows, a headless figure emerged, towering over Jack, its form shrouded in a dark, unnatural stillness. Jack's breath caught, his chest tight with terror, but he couldn't look away. The figure reached out, its hand extending toward him, fingers long and shadowed, as if to draw him into the depths of the darkness it carried.

Panic surged through Jack's veins, his legs giving way beneath him. He fumbled, the screwdriver slipping from his grasp, clattering to the ground and rolling until it lodged upright into a grate, its sharp end jutting like a sinister, makeshift punji stake. In a moment of brutal irony, Jack's body crashed down onto it, a searing pain exploding through his back. He screamed as the jagged metal drove deep, piercing just below his ribs, the agony blurring his vision.

Desperate, he reached out toward the headless figure, his fingers grasping at the shifting shadows, unable to tell if it was real or a twisted hallucination born from his horror. The shadows wavered before him, teasingly close but forever out of reach. The figure's existence was uncertain, a phantom of his mind—or perhaps a ghost, echoing from the walls of this forgotten place. But the wound was real, the sharp, brutal pain grounding him in grim reality, each breath a fresh agony that reminded him just how vulnerable he was.

Gasping in agony, Jack felt the warmth of his own blood soaking through his clothes, the iron tang filling the air. He writhed on the floor, desperately trying to free himself, but the pain was unbearable. Blood trickled down the grate, draining away like the last grains of sand in an hourglass.

Above him, more headless figures gathered. They hovered, waiting. The Miseries were back, ready to feast on him. Jack weakly kicked out, but the movement only amplified his suffering. He was losing too much blood, and his body could no longer take it.

"What are you waiting for, you motherfuckers? Come and get it!" Jack screamed, his voice breaking.

The shadows didn't move. Jack grabbed the leg of the chair and, using his last bit of strength, hurled it at the gathering figures. That was all the invitation they needed. The Miseries descended upon him in a feeding frenzy. Jack writhed beneath their weight, but every movement sent waves of pain through him. His vision blurred. Darkness crept in, and just before he lost consciousness, Jack gave in to the inevitable.

The Miseries fed, and Jack slipped away, alone in the darkness.

TWELVE
TWIN PEAKS

IT WAS NOW SUNDAY AFTERNOON, and Rose, standing by the payphones at the airport, dialed home one last time. Her fingers gripped the receiver tightly, each unanswered ring amplifying the hollow ache of worry that had been building in her chest. When the answering machine finally clicked in, she let the phone drop back into its cradle, unable to leave yet another message. She'd already left so many; surely he'd have heard one by now. *Wouldn't he?*

A prickling unease crept along her spine, that unmistakable instinct telling her that something was off. She took a slow, steadying breath, trying to shake off the feeling. *Maybe he'd called the hotel and missed her*, she reasoned, but that only led to more uncertain maybes that offered little comfort.

As she waited for her boarding call, her mind drifted, the need to get home now urgent and pressing. She could almost feel the miles stretching between them, like an invisible cord tugging her back. *Stay calm*, she told herself. She would be home soon enough, and they'd laugh about this—he'd say he tried to call, she'd say she tried to reach him, and they'd both joke about missing each other like ships in the night.

But even as she tried to reassure herself, that lingering sense of dread wouldn't quite let go.

The flight felt endless, each minute stretching unbearably as Rose gazed out the window, the endless expanse of clouds beneath her offering no solace. She tried to lose herself in music, slipping on her Walkman headphones and pressing play on a mix tape Jack had made for her. But the familiar songs brought only brief distraction; every few moments, her mind drifted back to him, the worry like an itch she couldn't scratch.

Switching off the music, she glanced up at the in-flight screen. *Twin Peaks* flickered to life, a murder mystery unfolding in surreal scenes that only seemed to stoke her unease. She'd thought a bit of distraction might help, but as the program wove its twisted tale of disappearances and dark secrets, Rose's mind kept spinning back to Jack. *What if something really had happened?* The question gnawed at her, and each scene on the screen seemed to mirror her growing worry.

She tried to push the thoughts away, but that lingering sense of dread clung to her, stubborn and unyielding, whispering fears she couldn't silence.

Finally, the captain's voice crackled over the intercom. "Ladies and gentlemen, this is your captain speaking. We are about to descend to 20,000 feet as we approach our destination. Please fasten your seat belts and extinguish your cigarettes. Thank you for flying Griffin Airlines, and I hope you have a pleasant day."

"Excuse me, madam," a stewardess said, pointing to the no-smoking sign. "The sign is now flashing. Please extinguish your cigarette."

Rose smiled, apologized, and stubbed out her cigarette.

She fumbled for the seatbelt buckle, snapped it shut, and finished the whiskey on the rocks she had been nursing throughout the flight. Handing the empty glass to the attendant, Rose adjusted herself, her thoughts drifting to Jack. Glancing down at the box peeking from the auction house bag beside her, a warm smile crept across her face—until a voice interrupted her.

"A present for your son?" a man asked from the aisle beside her.

Rose turned, puzzled. The man, well-dressed but lacking real style, was beaming at her.

"Excuse me?"

"The train in the bag," he said, pointing to the box. "Is it for your son?"

Rose glanced at the box again, noticing the word 'locomotive' printed on its side. She forced a smile. "Oh, no. It's for my brother, Jack."

The man smiled wider. "Phil." He introduced himself confidently.

"Sorry?" Rose replied, turning her head slightly in his direction but keeping her interest restrained.

"My name's Phil. And yours?"

"Rose," she answered, her enthusiasm barely detectable as she returned her gaze forward.

"Nice to meet you, Rose," Phil said, thrusting his hand across the aisle. He held it there for an awkward moment, grinning. When Rose didn't reciprocate, he slowly retracted his hand, his grin faltering.

Rose placed her headphones on, turned up the volume, and leaned back in her seat, tuning him out. Without moving her head, she noticed Phil's book: *Killer Instinct: The Art of Making the Sale*. The irony made her smile slightly.

THIRTEEN
NO ONE HOME

THE SIX-HOUR FLIGHT from New York to Bloomington felt like an eternity for Rose. It was 11 p.m. when she left the airport and made her way outside to wait for a cab. The evening chill made her shiver, but fortunately her cab arrived quickly.

The almost-yellow cab pulled over to where she patiently stood. City grime clung to its battered body, which sported many gladiatorial scars. She wasn't expecting much from her ride. With her eyebrows raised, she gingerly opened the door and glanced inside. Much to her surprise and delight, the interior was neat and clean. *Never judge a book by its cover*, she thought. The drive home would be over an hour, and she believed that the inside of the car was far more important than the outside, just like with humans—an axiom she had stuck by throughout her life.

The driver appeared beside her, taking her small case. She slid gracefully into her seat as he held the door open. The driver held out his other hand to take the gift. She hesitated, not wanting to let go or let it out of her sight, but it was bulky, and the boot was the best place for it. Reluctantly, she let go of her grip. He gently removed it from her hand, instinctively knowing it was special and needed extra care. She leaned back and secured the seatbelt. The door closed with a thud; seconds later, he placed the case and Jack's gift in the boot and slammed it shut. Moments later, the driver was seated in the driver's seat, waiting for instructions.

"Where to, ma'am?" he asked, politely.

She leaned over and was once again impressed as she noticed the clean and tidy driver. Then, the smell of the car freshener hit her nostrils, a fragrance she recognized and loved. A rose-shaped freshener hung from the front seat backrest, and for a moment, she was lost in thought.

"Ma'am?" he asked.

"Brandon Apartments, Springfield, please," she instructed and relaxed back in the seat. The taxi moved away without a screech or jerk; her initial apprehension left her, and she hoped it wouldn't be long before she was home.

Rose noticed the driver's eyes looking back at her from the rearview mirror. She hoped he wasn't one of those drivers who initiated small talk; she wasn't in the mood. She just wanted to get home. Thankfully, his eyes returned to the road ahead, as he sensed her wish for quiet.

Rose turned her head, gazing out the window at the busy, neon-lit, bustling city with its bright, sparkling backdrop. She could hear faint laughter over the beeping of horns. The traffic was heavy, and the cab came to a standstill, but she didn't mind because they had stopped outside her favorite jazz club.

She looked at the neon sign: letters poured out from a brightly lit saxophone. Each letter danced into position, eventually spelling out the club's name, 'Catz Club.' Her gaze drifted to the advertising board on the right. The individually flashing light bulbs mesmerized her as they blinked on and off in sequence. The lights flashed slowly at first, then gained speed until they all blinked furiously together. In the background, she could hear the cool jazz music that bled out onto the boardwalk, sometimes dull and distant, then bright and alive as the doors opened and closed with the comings and goings of the nighttime crowd.

It reminded her of the fairground she visited as a young girl with her mother for her twelfth birthday. That was the day she met Bart and that was the day her life changed forever. She quickly put the thought to the back of her mind not wanting to progress that particular lifeline beyond the memory of the day she met her first love. Opting instead for a memory of the sights and sounds of the fairground. She could hear the distant voices of the carnies drawing them to 'The Wheel of Fortune.' *Round and round she goes, where it stops nobody knows.*

Her daydream began to blur as the music changed to soft jazz that mingled with boisterous reveling. *Don't tell nobody when you're having fun… Easy, walk, don't run. Careful who you're talking to. Big Brother Is Watching You…* Rose snapped out of her daydream as a familiar tune burst out of the club when the doors opened wide, spilling out unwanted clientele, drunk and unappreciative. It was Mose Allison, one of her favorites. The doors closed, and the music was pulled back into the club, but the tune carried on in her head. Her eyes focused again on the advertising board: 'Jo Good Live! Friday 18th.' She made a mental note to get tickets. She and Jack loved jazz; it would be a treat for them both.

The taxi continued, and she gazed at the city she loved. It was a city with a small-town feel but a vibrant nightlife with nightclubs, theaters, and late-night coffee bars. However, there was an underside, a darkness to the city that only the enlightened, the initiated, or those who operated outside the law could sense. Rose fit all three. Her polished exterior masked a complexity and darkness known to few. She hadn't simply become the woman she was; her journey had been forged in hardship, survival, and secrets. Her ties to Springfield ran deep, not just as a woman who had fought her way to success while raising her younger brother alone but as someone with connections to the city's shadowed corners.

She had been there in the seventies during the terrifying spree of the Lincoln Mauler. Not only had she been there, but she'd known him —once, they'd even been friends. He haunted the city like a ghost, leaving fear and blood in his wake, and Rose had seen it all firsthand, a silent witness to his madness. Those memories lay deeply buried, an unspoken chapter of her past that had shaped her in ways she rarely acknowledged, even to herself.

Her trauma had begun long before that. Her mother's sudden abandonment had left her and her younger brother, Jack, in the care of a father whose violent rage branded them with scars, both physical and emotional. She could still recall the final traumatic moment of that chapter—the day she witnessed her father's suicide. The images were burned into her memory, too raw to fade fully, wounds that even medication could only dull.

At twenty-one, she left college to care for Jack full-time, casting aside her own dreams to give him some stability. Yet fierce determination pushed her to return to school later, earning her marketing degree with distinction—a remarkable feat considering she balanced her studies, a job, and the role of guardian to her brother.

Today, as a successful fashion editor at an elite New York magazine, Rose had carved out a life that felt whole. Financial stability was no longer a concern, and she held the reins of her destiny, finally free from the shadows of her past. The flexibility of her work-from-home arrangement allowed her to maintain her career while still watching over Jack. And yet, beneath her composed, accomplished exterior, Rose knew those scars lingered, woven into her very fabric. Hidden from the world, yes—but never entirely gone.

Over the years, Rose's bond with Jack had shifted from an older sibling's duties to a mother's fierce protectiveness. She doted on him, standing as his unwavering shield against any threat, be it emotional or physical. In the local park, she fought his battles, and during the long, dark hours of the night, she sat beside him as he wrestled with the demons that haunted his dreams. Each time Jack awoke in a panic, she was there, ready to hold him and chase away the waking terrors. She knew these demons intimately—they had visited her in her youth as well. Rose had vowed long ago that they would never claim Jack. She would give everything, even her life, to protect him from the darkness.

After Jack was born, life became tough, and their mother struggled. Though they weren't poor, the family was strained, weighed down by secrets—secrets that were carefully kept within the family. Jack's arrival had been unplanned and unexpected, and while their mother did her best, the hidden tension and the growing weight of their father's abuse became harder to bear.

Over the years, the strain of their father's escalating violence took its inevitable toll. Then, one day, without warning, their mother disappeared. She left no trace behind, abandoning everything—her clothes, her cherished sewing kit, her favorite church hat, and even the gold cross Rose had given her for Mother's Day, which Rose later found broken under the kitchen table. Rose never forgave her mother for leaving, though deep down she understood. She knew the reasons, the same reasons that fueled her hatred for their father.

He was a brutal man, violent and unrelenting. He would beat them all—often. She never told her mother that he raped her but wished she had, as maybe they could have both escaped.

Left behind, Rose and Jack both were forced to endure her father's drunken rages. The beatings intensified, and Jack, innocent and fragile, became the primary target of his wrath. Rose instinctively took on the role of protector, shielding Jack as best she could from the escalating violence. She often thought that if only her mother hadn't left, perhaps they could have sought help—perhaps their lives would have taken a different turn.

For eight long years, Rose bore the brunt of her father's abuse, but when he was finally found dead, hanging by the throat in their home, she felt nothing but relief. The overwhelming sense of freedom liberated her. At last, it was just the two of them—Rose and Jack. She swore in that moment that no one would ever harm them again. She would protect Jack at any cost.

But Jack was never the same after finding their father's body. The trauma twisted deep inside him, and he became a troubled child, haunted by the horrors of his past. His teenage years were particularly difficult, requiring constant attention and care. Rose devoted herself to him completely, determined to make up for the lost years of his childhood, to somehow mend the wounds that their father had left behind.

They shared the pain, the scars of their past, but there was one secret Rose kept buried—a secret Jack, for now, did not need to know.

This wasn't the first time she had left Jack to fend for himself, but it was the longest—three days. She had made sure that there was plenty of food in, and he wasn't totally incapable. Rose knew she sometimes mothered him too much, but he was all she had. She was a little apprehensive about leaving him for this long, but she had needed to attend this particular meeting, and she had needed a break.

She snapped out of her daydream as the taxi slowed; they had arrived at her apartment. She instinctively checked her watch—they had made good time with no detours to increase the fare, no idle chitchat. She felt happy and relaxed. Rose lived in the upscale part of town that had been revitalized in the mid-seventies when affluent residents moved in. The tall nineteen-twenties art deco building stood as a relic of a bygone yet modern era, piercing the night sky with arrogance. Rent in this area was expensive; only doctors, dentists, and business professionals could afford to live here. Rose fitted in well as, like everyone else, she kept to herself, making the price worth paying.

She leaned over and gave the driver $30. The fare was $20.

"Keep the change," she instructed.

The grateful driver leapt out of the car and opened the door for Rose. After removing her bag from the trunk, he passed her the bag containing Jack's locomotive.

"Your boy is going to love his train," he said.

Rose just smiled back. She couldn't be bothered to explain. He carried the case to the front of the building, and after tipping his cap and wishing her good night, he left.

Rose was glad to be home. She didn't hesitate, picking up her briefcase and tucking the package she'd won at auction securely under her left arm before pushing through the revolving, oak-framed glass doors of her apartment block. The brightly lit lobby welcomed her, the familiar click of her heels echoing along the polished parquet floor as she passed the reception desk, staffed around the clock.

Scott, the night security guard, was at his usual post, and he greeted her with a casual cowboy-style salute. Their eyes met, a shared moment of silent acknowledgement lingering between them. They'd shared drinks a few times at a nearby jazz bar, their conversations easy and unforced. Although their connection had never crossed any boundaries, there was a mutual understanding—Scott, patient and quietly confident, seemed to believe it was only a matter of time.

As Rose entered, she offered him a brief glance, conveying just enough warmth to let him know the door wasn't entirely closed. But tonight, her thoughts were elsewhere, tugged back to Jack and the unsettling worry she couldn't quite shake.

"Evening, Miss Brooks." Scott greeted her with his usual warmth.

"Evening, Scott," Rose replied, pausing briefly.

"How was your weekend?"

"Fine, Scott, just fine. Is there any mail?"

Scott quickly rifled through her mailbox, handing Rose a few letters and a magazine—Jack's model train magazine, *Rolling Stock*. She knew it had arrived on Saturday, so why hadn't Jack picked it up?

"Have you seen Jack over the weekend?" Rose asked, her tone edged with concern.

"No, I wasn't on duty, so I'm not sure," Scott replied casually. "Maybe he just forgot."

But Jack never forgot. He had an uncanny memory, Rose thought. Her repeated, unanswered calls over the weekend had only fueled her growing worry that something was off.

"Thanks, Scott," she said with a tense smile before hurrying towards the lift.

Turning the corner, Rose nearly collided with Judge Harry, a sprightly eighty-four-year-old who, despite his frailty, had enough strength to steady her.

"You alright, Rose? You seem in a bit of a rush," he remarked, his eyes filled with concern.

"Sorry, Harry," Rose replied, brushing off her fluster. "It's just been a long weekend. Are you well?"

"I'm fine, sweetheart," he answered warmly.

Rose wasn't one for pet names, but she let it pass. She noticed the leash in his hand—Harry was about to take Precious, his pampered poodle, for her nightly stroll. Normally, Rose would pause for a chat, but today she needed to get upstairs. Yet, before he could turn the corner, she asked, "Harry, was everything alright while I was away?"

"No, not really," he replied slowly. Precious yapped loudly, almost joining the conversation.

"Quiet, Precious," Harry muttered, tugging the lead gently.

Something in his voice made her probe further. "Come on, Harry. Is there something you're not telling me? Jack hasn't been blasting his music again, has he?" she asked with an apologetic smile. Harry was the building's unofficial eyes and ears—if anything was wrong, he'd know.

"No, actually—" he started, only to be interrupted by more yapping.

"Quiet, Precious," he demanded firmly. He continued, "I haven't heard a peep from him all weekend."

"Yap, yap, yap," the dog seemed determined to have her say. Harry pulled on the lead again, trying to quieten her.

Oh, you little nuisance, Rose thought, keeping a polite smile. "Strange," she said, puzzled. "Thanks anyway, Harry."

"No worries." Harry turned and headed towards the exit.

As the lift doors finally opened, she stepped in, pressing the button repeatedly, hoping it would close faster. Her mind raced—she thought of her unanswered calls, the pile of untouched mail, his unopened magazine, and the silence that had settled over his flat. What was going on? She knew he'd been planning to finish his model landscape. Once lost in his trains, Jack often tuned out the world, which could explain his unresponsiveness. But still...

When the lift doors opened on her floor, she took a breath and climbed the remaining stairs. The steps seemed steeper today, likely the result of a hectic weekend. She looked forward to a soak in her hot tub, but first, she'd have words with Jack for not returning her calls.

As she neared his door, a faint whimpering caught her ear, like the cry of a child. She unlocked the door, and as she entered, a cat darted out, only to pause and wind itself around her legs, nearly tripping her. Spot—Jack's beloved cat—was usually this clingy only when hungry.

How odd, Rose thought, knowing Jack wouldn't forget to feed Spot. This was her final clue—something was indeed wrong, very wrong. Spot meowed more insistently as she moved into the kitchen. "Alright, alright, Spot," she muttered, dropping her bags and calling out for Jack. She tried first calmly, then with a trace of impatience, "Jack!"

Frantically, she checked every room, including his bedroom, where the bed looked untouched. Her disappointment quickly turned to dread. The flat was empty. This wasn't like Jack at all. Everything was exactly as it had been on Friday morning—the faint scent of disinfectant from her last clean lingered in the air.

Rose's mind spun as she began contacting Jack's friends, her worry intensifying with each unanswered call.

FOURTEEN
BREAKING POINT

SHE HAD one more call to make. It was late, and after the lack of success of her previous attempts, she wasn't hopeful. Still, she willed this call to be answered. To her relief, it was.

"Hi Max, it's Rose. Is Jack with you?"

Max was Jack's only close friend; someone he'd known since school. They occasionally played basketball together at the local park or grabbed a drink.

A tired voice came through the line. "No, I haven't heard from him all week. Is something wrong?"

"I hope not. Jack's bed doesn't seem to have been slept in since Thursday. He didn't feed the cat, and it doesn't look like he's been home all weekend. It's just not like him." Rose's voice, though stern, wavered slightly as she took deep breaths between sentences, trying desperately to hold back her feelings. Her eyes were now glazed, but her strength held up. She was in complete control of her emotions and refused to cry, but the pressure was building. A single tear trickled down Rose's cheek, a precursor to the emotional flood that eventually burst forth as the situation overwhelmed her, causing her to panic and gently start sobbing.

Max tried to calm her. "Don't worry. There's bound to be some logical explanation. Sit tight. I'll come over and pass by the school to see if he is there."

Rose called a few more of Jack's friends, but he only had a few, so this took little time. She also called all the hospitals within a fifty-mile radius, but still nothing. Constantly looking at the clock as the seconds turned into minutes and the minutes turned into hours, time ticked mercilessly away. She poured herself a whiskey and began to pace around the apartment, looking for any sign, anything that would suggest there was a perfectly plausible explanation, but it was in vain. The realization that something was drastically wrong hit her hard, and she now had no choice but to contact the police.

"Are you saying there's nothing you can do?" Rose was beginning to lose her temper now.

"I'm sorry, ma'am, but he has to be missing for forty-eight hours," the officer replied.

"I'm telling you there's something wrong. It's not like Jack. Please, you've got to do something," Rose pleaded.

"I'm sorry, ma'am, but we have some real crimes to attend to. Call back tomorrow if he is still missing," the officer said, becoming repetitive. She had obviously lost her patience with Rose.

Rose took the phone from her ear and looked at it with frustration. The phone was an easy target as she vented her frustrations. "Call back tomorrow? Yeah right! Tomorrow, he could be dead. Maybe then it would be a real crime, but then it would be too late!" she yelled angrily. She slammed the phone down hard and looked at it contemptibly, then lifted and slammed it down again and again until she heard the doorbell ring. Rose's eyes lit up as she jumped to her feet; a smile spread across her face as she rushed to the door.

"Jack, is that you? Where have you been?" she called out. She opened the door, and her face dropped. It wasn't Jack—it was Max.

"Any luck?" Max asked, his concern evident as she turned away; he followed her into the hallway. "I went by the school, but I couldn't see anything."

"No," Rose replied sadly.

"Did you call the cops?" Max inquired.

"The cops," Rose angrily snapped. "They're a waste of time. They can't do anything for forty-eight hours." Rose slumped into the chair in despair, burying her head in her hands.

"Wherever he is, I hope he's okay. I wouldn't forgive myself if anything happened to him," she cried.

"Look, there's a logical explanation for all this. Relax, and I'll make you a coffee."

"I don't want coffee. I want Jack," Rose replied sharply, frustration lacing her voice as she clutched a worn photograph she'd pulled from her shoulder bag. The picture showed only herself and Jack, with one side torn away, as if someone had literally been cut out of their lives. All that remained of the missing person was a man's arm, casually draped over Rose's shoulder.

MAX'S EYES caught on an unusual tattoo on that mystery arm—a dagger with a black handle in a golden sheath, its hilt crowned by a sinister death's head skull.

The tattoo stirred something in Max's memory. He'd seen the design before but couldn't quite place it. Questions flooded his mind: who did this arm belong to? An ex, maybe? The thought unsettled him, the tattoo's familiarity prickling his unease. But as he looked at Rose, he saw the distress in her face, and he knew it wasn't the time for questions. Instead, he stayed quiet, standing by her side.

ROSE COULDN'T HELP but weep as she looked at the picture. Each tear brought back memories of how she had always been there for Jack. She remembered the times when he would cry, too afraid to sleep because of his nightmares. She would hold him and rock him to sleep. She also recalled how he insisted on always having the light on, believing it would protect him from the monsters in the shadows, the monsters he called *The Miseries*. Even now, she had to open the door so he could see the hall light. It seemed like Rose had taken on more of a motherly role for him rather than just being his sister after their father died.

"I shouldn't have left him for this long," she whimpered.

"Look, he'll be fine. He's a grown man. He's probably—" Max paused.

"He's probably what?" Rose snapped.

"You know, went for a drink, met a girl, usual men stuff." Max attempted to reassure her, although he knew it wasn't likely.

"You have got no idea," she replied, wiping her eyes and trying to gather herself. "He needs me to protect him," she explained.

"Protect him from what? Who? What are you talking about?" Max asked, curiously.

"You don't know him as well as you think," she answered, mysteriously.

"Okay. Maybe I don't, but we can do nothing right now. Just sit and wait," Max replied with a sincere, calming tone.

ROSE RECLINED, resting her head on the plumped-up pillows that Max had arranged. Max went to make coffee, and upon his return, he found Rose had drifted off to sleep. Not even the worry of her missing brother could keep her awake after the long day of travel, particularly following the generous amount of whiskey she had consumed. Max covered her with a blanket and stayed with her throughout the night.

FIFTEEN
ACCUSED

THE ALARM JOLTED to life at precisely 7:30 a.m., its harsh buzz echoing through the dim room and shaking Max from a restless sleep. Disoriented, he rubbed his eyes and glanced toward the couch. There was Rose, awake, clutching a photograph and sobbing quietly, her face pale in the morning light. She held a picture of herself, Jack, and the tattooed arm of the mystery man.

Max moved closer, his heart tightening at the sight of her distress. He sat down, tentatively placing an arm around her shoulders, hoping the simple gesture might ease her pain.

"Get off me, you creep," she snapped, shoving him away with a ferocity that startled him.

"Rose, what—" he began, stunned.

"I know your type," she hissed, her eyes blazing with sudden distrust. "Get out, or I'll call the police."

"Rose, listen to me," Max said, keeping his voice calm. "I know you're upset, but you're safe here with me."

"Safe?" Her laugh was hollow, cold. "Just get out. You're just like the rest of them," she spat, pointing fiercely at the door, her gaze dark and unwavering.

"Rose, you've got me all wrong. I wouldn't—" But before he could finish, she picked up the phone and started dialing.

"Alright, alright, I'm going." Max rose and moved to the door. He hesitated, turning back to her one last time, his voice softening.

"Look, I know you're shaken. Just... call me if you need anything, alright? And let me know when Jack gets back."

Rose said nothing, her silence dense with an unspoken grief. She set the phone down, her fingers trembling ever so slightly, and dabbed at her eyes with a crumpled tissue, her gaze fixed on the photograph in her hands. Max lingered for a moment, his eyes on her as an intense worry crept into his mind—not just for Rose but for Jack, his friend, whose absence now loomed even larger.

With a heavy heart, Max turned and stepped out, shutting the door gently behind him. Outside, he paused, drawing a deep breath that did nothing to ease the knot tightening in his chest. A shadow of unease settled over him. Something was terribly, unmistakably wrong.

AT PRECISELY 9:30 A.M., Principal Henderson sat in his office, glancing at his watch with mounting impatience. Jack's absence was strange, almost unsettling. Pressing the intercom, he called his secretary, an edge of urgency in his voice.

"June, could you step in for a moment?"

A moment later, she appeared.

"Yes, Mr. Henderson?"

"Has Jack reported in yet?"

"No, Mr. Henderson."

"Who opened up this morning, then?"

"Will did, sir. Jack always comes in a bit later on Mondays," she explained, though her expression had begun to reflect the principal's concern.

"Yes, but Jack was scheduled to meet with me at nine-thirty sharp. It's not like him to be late," Henderson muttered, casting another look at the clock—now reading 9:48 a.m. "June, could you send Will up to my office? And please arrange an appointment for Mrs. Marshall as well."

Moments later, Will knocked on the door.

"Come in," called the principal. Will entered, wringing his cap in his hands, his shoulders hunched and face uneasy.

"Will, Jack had an appointment with me this morning," the principal began. "Any idea where he is?"

A glimmer of relief crossed Will's face as he realized he wasn't in trouble. Placing his cap back on, he replied, "No, Mr. Henderson. I usually open early on Mondays, and Jack always gets here around ten a.m."

"So... nothing out of the ordinary when you came in this morning?" Henderson asked, eyeing him carefully.

"No, sir. Everything was as usual," Will replied.

Just then, a soft knock interrupted.

"Come in," Henderson said, glancing at June, who entered with a concerned look.

"Mr. Henderson, Jack's sister is here—she's asking for him. He hasn't been home all weekend."

The principal's gaze sharpened, exchanging a worried look with Will. "Send her in."

Rose entered, her face pale and her eyes swollen from what must have been hours of crying.

"Hello, Rose," the principal said softly. "We were just wondering about Jack—he had a meeting with me this morning. Is... is everything alright?"

Rose's face crumpled, her voice breaking as she managed, "He hasn't been home all weekend, and I'm really worried. This just isn't like him."

A tense silence fell over the room, each of them caught in the weight of her words. The clock ticked on, its faint rhythm punctuating their growing unease, as a creeping sense of dread settled over them all. Where was Jack—and why hadn't he come home?

"I have to agree with you. It isn't like Jack at all," the principal replied, worriedly, offering Rose a chair.

Will spoke. "I will thoroughly search the school. He might be stuck somewhere since locking up on Friday. If he's still here, I'll find him."

"Okay, Will, I'll call the police, just in case." The principal began to dial.

"I've already tried the police," Rose huffed. "They said they couldn't help. He had to be missing for forty-eight hours."

"We'll see about that," the principal retorted. Undeterred by Rose's statement, he made the call.

"Hi, this is the principal of Lincoln Memorial. Put me through to JB." There was no time for pleasantries.

ROSE LISTENED CLOSELY, a flicker of intrigue stirring. She knew that in this town, connections ran deep—whether through family bonds or club loyalties. If you wanted things done quickly, cutting out the middlemen was key.

True to his word, the principal's call had immediate impact. Within the hour, police arrived at the school, and they began taking statements from anyone who might have seen or spoken to Jack. They scoured the building, moving from classrooms to storage rooms, their footsteps echoing through the halls. Yet, after combing through every possible space, they came to the conclusion that Jack had left the building after locking up on Friday. There wasn't much more they could do on-site.

"We'll follow up on a few leads," one of the officers had assured, but the words rang hollow for Rose, whose worry was deepening into dread as the officers left. It felt as though the school was shrouded in tense silence.

WHISPERS and wild rumors quickly began to spread among the students. In one of the quieter corridors, Monica happened to overhear a hushed conversation between two of Brad's friends—his only close friends, in fact. She strained to catch their words.

"You're kidding! Locked Jack the Rat up in the old storeroom."

"Yeah, he's been there all weekend. It's his own fault. He deserves it. If it weren't for him, Brad would still be here."

Monica's heart pounded as she caught the name 'Jack.' Though she hadn't heard every word, her instincts told her that Brad was involved. She didn't wait another second and bolted down the hallway, heading straight to the principal's office to share what she'd overheard.

MEANWHILE, Will, having found nothing out of the ordinary during his search of the school, decided to check Jack's locker with the master key. Nothing seemed unusual—though he noted that even the roses Jack had brought in earlier were gone. Relieved yet puzzled, he headed back to the principal's office to confirm the police's conclusion: Jack had likely locked up and left the building on Friday.

WHILE WILL WAS EXPLAINING his findings, a commotion sounded outside the principal's office. The principal opened the door to see Monica in an intense conversation with June.

"Monica, what's going on? What's all this about?" he asked, eyeing her curiously.

"Sir, I think Brad has something to do with Mr. Brooks's disappearance. I overheard his friends talking in the corridor."

The principal's brow furrowed. "What exactly did you hear?"

"Not much," Monica admitted, "I was too far away to catch every word, but they mentioned Jack—err, Mr. Brooks—and they were laughing, making jokes. Please, sir, you have to do something."

The principal sighed, torn between his duty to investigate and his caution over student gossip. "Monica, I know you're trying to help, and I understand you've had your own issues with Brad, but we can't go accusing people based on vague conversations."

"Please, sir," Monica pleaded, her determination evident.

The principal hesitated, then finally relented. "Alright, alright." He glanced at his watch, recalling that he had an appointment scheduled for 1:30 p.m. with Brad Marshall and his mother. It was now 11:15 a.m.

"Look," he said, "I've got a meeting with Bradley and his mother later today. I'll take the opportunity to ask him if he knows anything, and with his mother there, perhaps she can encourage him to tell the truth. How's that sound?"

Though slightly disappointed, Monica nodded—it was something, at least. But she knew it wasn't enough to quiet the suspicions swirling in her mind. Her expression betrayed her resolve: she wasn't going to let it go that easily. If there was evidence of Brad's involvement, she'd uncover it, and she already knew where to start.

BACK IN CLASS, Monica feigned illness, rubbing her forehead now and then. The teacher soon took notice and, with a concerned look, excused her to go home, assuming she was unwell.

But home was the last place Monica intended to go. She gathered her things and slipped out of the building, her destination firmly in mind: Brad's house. If Brad was truly behind Jack's disappearance, she was going to find out.

But Monica knew she couldn't do this alone if she was going to get real answers. She needed help and she knew just where to get it.

SIXTEEN
STIR OF ECHOES

IT WAS MIDDAY, and the police had done all they could. They'd taken statements from everyone involved, followed their standard procedures, and advised Rose to go home in case Jack called. The principal shook the officer's hand, escorting them out of the office with a respectful nod. As they left, he turned his attention back to Rose, who sat motionless, her gaze distant and hollow.

"Look, Rose," he said gently, "let me drive you home…"

But Rose offered no response, her bleak stare fixed on some point beyond him, as though lost in a world of worry.

"You look exhausted. You could do with a bit of rest," he pressed.

"I don't want rest. I want Jack," Rose replied flatly, her voice devoid of emotion.

The principal paused, then tried again, softening his tone. "You heard the police, Rose. There's nothing more we can do right now. If Jack calls, he'll call home first. That's the best place for you to be."

He spoke with a calm reassurance, his optimism almost tangible, but Rose was too distraught to hear it. The words felt empty, like an echo fading into the silence between them.

"Rose? Rose…" he called softly, but she didn't respond. Seeing her so lost in thought, he decided to step back, giving her a moment to gather herself in the quiet.

ROSE, lost in a daydream, reminisced. She was now in her garden, swaying happily on a rusty old swing that creaked as it swayed. The garden was scattered with wildflowers, and the wild roses she had been named for, bloomed. The garden was her mother's favorite place, and, when pregnant with Rose, she would sit for hours watching the sun rise and fall, often not moving from her spot from morning till dusk. When Rose was born, they would both sit and daydream—innocent times—happier times.

In her daydream, it was the day she turned twelve. She didn't have a care in the world. It was a lovely summer's day, with birds singing. Beyond the garden, she saw a group of rabbits playing peacefully in a field. She ran over, trying to catch them, laughing and giggling like any sweet, innocent child. Her laughter was a symphony of joy, a stark contrast to the struggles she had faced in the past.

The sun bathed the landscape with a golden glow, casting long shadows and making the grass shimmer. Rose's dress billowed as she ran, her hair catching the light in a cascade of deep black waves. She was beginning to blossom into a fine young woman, her movements graceful and full of life.

Rose's eyes sparkled with the innocent wonder of childhood. As she sat, she plucked a daisy from the ground, twirling it between her fingers, lost in thought. Though marked by moments of darkness, her life was punctuated by days like these—days filled with sunlight, laughter, and a sense of freedom that seemed endless.

As she lay there, Rose dreamed of a future where every day could be as peaceful as this one. The memories of her father's rage were distant, like a bad dream that couldn't touch her in this moment of pure happiness. She closed her eyes, the sun's warmth on her face; she imagined a life full of love and kindness.

The delicate breeze rustled the leaves of the trees, and Rose felt a sense of belonging, a feeling that she was part of something beautiful and enduring. She wished that she could hold onto this moment forever, that the simplicity and joy of this day could carry her through whatever challenges lay ahead.

Rose opened her eyes and sat up, frozen, as she heard a car screech up the driveway. She turned to see but couldn't quite make out who had arrived. She stood to get a better look, hoping that it would be her mother returning from town. She stood on an upturned pail to gain enough height. She peered over the fence and recognized the car, but it wasn't her mother's. It was her father's. She struggled to stand.

She watched as he slammed the car door and walked—no, fell—into the house. He had been drinking. Her face changed instantly. Fear now replaced her rosy smile. She rushed around the back of the house and hid in an abandoned playhouse she had as a child.

Unsure of her hideout's safety, she tried to find a more secure location. Cautiously, she sneaked into the kitchen and peeked from behind the door to the room where her father stood. He staggered through the house, in one door and out another. Rose looked for a new hideout; she couldn't risk being found now that he was drunk, and her mother wasn't home to protect her.

"Mary!" her father yelled out for her mother. "Where the hell are you?" When he realized Mary was not home, his attention turned to Rose, who had now found refuge under the stairs.

Rose's heart pounded as she pressed herself deeper into the shadows, hoping he wouldn't find her. She could hear his heavy footsteps moving closer and his voice growing louder and more agitated.

"Rose!" he bellowed, his voice slurring. "Come out, come out, wherever you are!"

She squeezed her eyes shut, praying he wouldn't discover her hiding spot. She could hear him rummaging through the rooms, opening and slamming doors, his frustration mounting. The air was thick with tension, each second stretching into an eternity.

Her father's footsteps approached the kitchen. Rose held her breath, her tiny body trembling with fear. She knew that if he found her, no one could protect her. His regular violent outbursts were fresh in her mind, and she braced herself for the worst.

The kitchen door creaked open, and she could see his shadow cast on the floor. He stood there for a moment, swaying unsteadily. Then, to her horror, he began moving towards the stairs.

Rose's mind raced, thinking of a way to stay hidden. She knew that her hiding spot under the stairs would only provide cover for a moment longer. As his shadow loomed larger, she bit her lip to keep from crying out.

"Rose!" he called again, his voice a mixture of anger and desperation.

He reached the bottom of the stairs, and for a moment, Rose thought he might pass by. But then he paused, his gaze fixed on the small space beneath the stairs.

"Rose! Rose! Don't make me come looking for you now. Where the hell..." His voice trailed off as he turned away.

Relieved, Rose exhaled quietly as she watched him ascend the stairs. Her mind raced—she needed a new hiding place. But moments later, her stomach dropped as she heard his footsteps return to the base of the stairs. Suddenly, he stopped.

His eyes narrowed, locking onto a tiny pair of red shoes sticking out from beneath the stairs. A sinister smile spread across his face, slow and deliberate. He moved with predatory intent, crouching low as if ready to strike, each step measured and silent, calculated not to startle his quarry.

Rose held her breath as his hand extended cautiously toward the curtain. When his grip tightened, he yanked it back in one swift motion, revealing... nothing. Only a pair of her shoes lay in the shadows.

Rose had escaped from under the stairs, trying to keep one step ahead. She had eventually found refuge in a small cupboard in the kitchen.

His anger had now erupted into rage. "Where the fuck are you, you little shit?"

She could hear him frantically searching, each crash and bang sending tremors through her body. She knew, deep down, that he wouldn't give up. This wasn't the first time—she had been here before. But usually, it was her mother who bore the brunt of his rage.

Then, for a fleeting moment, there was silence. The only sound was her own ragged breathing, heavy and fast with fear. Her heart pounded in her chest as she strained to listen. The quiet was shattered when she heard him stir again.

Rose carefully cracked the cupboard door open just enough to see him.

"I need a drink," he growled.

She watched as he pushed himself up from the chair, his movements heavy and unsteady. He staggered toward the drinks cabinet, his frustration mounting as he knocked over her mother's sewing table on the way. Rose prayed he would find solace in the bottle, that he would drink himself into a stupor and forget about her.

For now, in her cramped hideout, she felt a sliver of safety. But for how long? She knew punishment was inevitable. If only she could hold out until her mother returned.

In the oppressive darkness, she clasped her trembling hands, whispering desperate prayers that he would drink himself to sleep. But her prayers went unanswered.

"Where the fuck has all the drink gone?" he growled, slamming the drinks cabinet door shut with a force that sent a cascade of glasses tumbling. They shattered on the floor; a glimmering sea of shards. Rose's breath caught as she watched a single glass teeter on the edge of the cabinet, pirouetting defiantly. It danced, hesitating as though defying gravity, then it gave one final spin and crashed to the floor, splintering into pieces.

In the tense silence that followed, Rose's eyes flicked to the kitchen clock. Its steady tick-tock seemed to sync perfectly with the pounding of her heart: *tick-tock—thump-thump—tick-tock—thump-thump*. From her hiding place, she peered out, noticing that her father was no longer rooted to the spot. Her stomach twisted as she watched him slowly lift his head, turning toward the kitchen—the very room where she was concealed.

Panic surged through her as she quickly but quietly closed the cupboard door, her ears straining against the sharp crunch of glass underfoot. His footsteps were slow and deliberate, a menacing march in her direction: *tick, tick, thump, thump, crunch, crunch*.

Rose clenched her eyes shut, her heart hammering as she prayed he hadn't heard her. But her fragile hope shattered as the refrigerator door thudded open.

"Nothing," he cursed, slamming it shut. His fury reignited; she could hear him ransacking the cupboards.

Rose's silent tears flowed over her rosy cheeks as she tried to remain hidden.

"Isn't there anything to drink in this fucking place?" he roared. "Rose! Rose! Please tell Daddy where Mommy put my beer."

Rose's foot slipped at that moment, nudging her hiding spot's door ajar. She hoped he didn't see it, but the door creaking drew his attention. He turned towards the sound, smirked, and slowly advanced.

Rose's breath hitched as the handle turned. The door swung open, and her father loomed above her. "Ah! There you are," he smiled. Rose thought of Red Riding Hood, fearing she was now face-to-face with the Big Bad Wolf.

"You shouldn't hide from Daddy," he crooned, his voice deceptively soft. His gentle demeanor was a thin disguise for the terror he was about to inflict. He grabbed her arm and yanked her from the cupboard. Her birthday dress tore, exposing her pale thigh. He paused, a strange look crossing his face, and stroked her hair gently.

"You're so pretty, Rose," he murmured.

Could it be he was coming to his senses? Rose dared to hope. She forced a smile and moved to embrace him. "I love you, Daddy," she whispered.

A tense silence hung in the air before he erupted. "You lying little whore," he roared. "You're just like your mother. Like mother, like daughter. I'll show you."

He dragged her up the stairs, her knees scraping painfully against the wooden steps. Blood trickled down her legs as she tripped and stumbled, but he didn't slow down. He dragged her into the bedroom, slamming the door behind them.

An eerie silence fell over the house, the clock seeming to stop in anticipation of the horror. Time stretched painfully before shattering with Rose's scream—a closed door contained the unfolding horror within. Another scream echoed, this one more beastly, grunting rhythmically, then silence.

A moment later, the bedroom door burst open; Rose bolted out, her father close behind, in a state of undress. He tripped, hitting the banister hard. Blood flowed from his lip; sitting in a daze, he cried out, "Rose, Rose, I'm sorry." These were empty words from a man devoid of remorse.

"Rose! Rose!" The principal's voice snapped her back to the present. "Answer me, Rose. Do you want June to take you home?"

"What? Sorry!" she stammered, still a little disoriented.

"Would you like June to take you home?" he repeated gently, a touch of concern in his voice.

"No, I'll be fine. I have my car," she replied, gathering her belongings before glancing back at him. "I'm so sorry about all this, Mr. Henderson."

"John," he corrected, softly.

"Sorry?" she asked, blinking.

"My name's John. Please, call me John," he said, kindly. "And don't worry, Rose. I'll keep in touch with the captain to stay informed on any updates, and please, reach out to me if there's any news. We'll find Jack, Rose."

Rose managed a small, grateful smile. She didn't know the principal as well as Jack did, but she wished she did—he seemed kind, unexpectedly compassionate, in her moment of worry.

The door creaked open, and June appeared, holding it ajar for her. After a firm handshake with John, Rose stepped out, and he closed the door quietly behind her.

ONCE ALONE, John slumped back into his chair, shaking his head. He took a deep breath, his mind heavy with unanswered questions. What had really happened to Jack?

SEVENTEEN
SOLITARY CONFINEMENT

WILL'S mind drifted to Jack's mysterious disappearance, wondering where he could have gone after locking up the school. He silently vowed to continue his search for Jack as soon as his shift ended. But right now, he had a pressing job to do. The water pressure had dropped significantly and needed urgent attention, and he was the only one who could fix it.

Will took a deep breath, steeling himself, as he descended the long, echoing stairwell into the school's forgotten depths—a place that sent a chill through him every time he stepped foot in it. The old boiler room was down there, buried in a part of the building few dared to visit. This was where the old prison cells lay, silent reminders of a time when the lower depths of the building had held condemned prisoners awaiting their fate. Even after all these years, the air hung thick with an unsettling stillness, as if the walls themselves held onto the misery of the condemned souls who had once languished there. The quicker he got the work done, the better.

As he reached the boiler room, he noticed the light was already on. He hesitated, trying to recall if he'd left it on during his last visit, but the thought slipped from his mind as he heard an eerie sound. It started as a low, mournful wailing, almost like a pack of wolves howling in sorrow, echoing behind the heavy steel doors down the corridor. Then came a rattling noise, like a cage full of restless baboons, their frantic calls reverberating through the halls. Will took a deep breath, unfazed—he recognized these sounds as the strange effects of air pressure building up in the boiler system. They needed to be released and quickly.

Forgetting, for now, the odd mystery of the lights being on, Will swung open the heavy boiler room door, gripping his wrench tightly, and got to work. He wrestled with the ancient pipes for ten long minutes, muttering curses under his breath. "Darn it... Motherfucker" he grumbled, giving the stubborn bolts a good dose of Kroil and finally managing to release the built-up pressure. With a loud hiss, the system stabilized, and gradually, the strange noises quieted. The mournful howling of the 'wolves' faded, and the frantic rattling of the 'baboons' stilled, leaving the corridor shrouded in an eerie silence.

Will straightened up, wiping his brow, and let out a sigh of relief. But just as he turned to leave, a faint, rhythmic tapping echoed through the room, coming from somewhere deeper within the pipes. It wasn't mechanical—this was something else. He froze, listening, the sound sending a chill down his spine.

Heart pounding, Will moved cautiously toward the far side of the boiler room, drawn by the persistent tapping. It led him to a wall lined with old storage lockers and forgotten rusted equipment. The sound continued, slow and deliberate, as if someone—or something—was signaling from beyond. His eyes followed the wall to an area crudely bricked up; an old doorway sealed off years ago.

Above the bricked-up entrance, a grimy metal sign riveted into the wall caught his attention. Taking a deep breath, he reached up and wiped away decades of dust and grime, revealing the words beneath. His blood ran cold as he read, 'Solitary Confinement.'

EIGHTEEN
THE DYING OF THE LIGHT

MEANWHILE, barely conscious, Jack had heard Will, and he banged the pipe with his broken torch.

Will leaned his head closer to the pipes, a little too close, touching the hot pipe with his ear. He yelped and cussed, then tried again, taking more care.

Jack could muster no more strength and began to drift back into unconsciousness. Will heard nothing, shrugged, and put it down to old plumbing. He picked up his tools and carried them out of the boiler room. As Will turned and locked the door, he looked to his left and saw another door. Will walked over to the door. Instinctively, he reached into his pocket for the keys he carried. He looked at several keys but realized that the only key that fitted the lock was on Jack's set.

Will placed his ear to the door and listened.

Jack, in his dazed state, could hear Will behind the door and tried desperately to gain his attention but could not muster enough strength to move or even to whimper, let alone lift the broken torch by his side.

Will, still standing outside the door, frowned. He stood silent for a few more seconds, looked at his watch, and realized he had to be elsewhere. He needed to help continue the search for Jack, he reminded himself.

Jack looked up at the thin sliver of light, his only anchor to the world beyond. He watched helplessly as a shadow passed over it, drifting away. Unable to move, he stared at the faint crack of light—his last constant, his fragile thread of hope for rescue. Then, without warning, it went dark. Will had unknowingly extinguished more than just a light; he had snuffed out Jack's final glimmer of hope and left him alone in the suffocating darkness. The boiler was fixed and wouldn't need attention for at least another week. As for the storeroom, there was no reason to check it; it was unused, so what would be the point?

Jack lay alone, his life slipping away with each labored breath. His thoughts turned to peace and deliverance from the demons that had tormented him for so long. As his consciousness wavered, he could feel Death's firm grip tightening, brought on by the concussion and dehydration that ravaged his body. He knew he had only a few hours left—to escape Death's relentless hunger, someone needed to find him, and soon.

The room around him was eerily quiet, the oppressive silence broken only by the relentless rhythmic dripping of water from the leaking pipe. Each drop smacked against the tiled floor, marking the relentless passage of time like the ticking of a distant clock. The sound echoed hauntingly around the room, each drip a stark reminder of how little time he had left. Jack's mind drifted in and out of focus, fragments of his life flashing before him—a chaotic swirl of fleeting joy interspersed with the far more frequent memories of pain and suffering.

He tried to move, but his body felt heavy and unresponsive. Panic surged through him as he realized how truly helpless he was. He had no strength left to call for help, no voice to shout out his desperation. His only hope was that someone, anyone, would find him before it was too late.

As the minutes dragged on, Jack's vision blurred, the shapes around him dissolving into an indistinct haze. The room seemed to close in, darkness creeping at the edges of his sight, a suffocating shroud that grew thicker with each passing moment. Once sharp and clear, his thoughts became muddled, the boundary between reality and hallucination melting away like snow under a cruel sun. Faces from his past, both friend and foe, flickered in and out of existence, merging into a grotesque tapestry of torment.

His breathing now grew shallow, each breath a painful struggle. The weight on his chest felt like a vice, squeezing the last remnants of life from him. In his final moments of clarity, Jack made a silent plea—for forgiveness, peace, and an end to the suffering that had defined his existence.

Jack's body trembled, a cold sweat breaking out across his skin. He closed his eyes, surrendering to the encroaching darkness. As his consciousness faded, a sense of calm washed over him, a serene acceptance of his fate. The demons were silent for the first time in years, their whispers and taunts fading into oblivion.

In those final breaths, Jack found a fleeting moment of peace; his last thoughts were a desperate hope that the torment would not follow him into the void. And as the light of his life dimmed, the Oubliette, with all its horrors, was about to claim him.

NINETEEN
REVENGE IS BITTERSWEET

ROSE MADE her way across the car park, her heart heavy with worry. Where was Jack? Was he injured? Had someone hurt him? The thought haunted her—what if he was out there somewhere, calling for her, just as he had done as a child? She had always been there for him. Now, in his moment of need, she felt lost, helpless. As these anxious thoughts raced through her mind, a voice suddenly brought her back to the present.

"Mrs Brooks?"

Rose turned to see the girl from earlier. "It's Miss... or Rose, if you prefer," she offered with a gentle smile. "Monica, isn't it?"

"Rose, I think I can help you find Jack. I believe Brad Marshall has something to do with it," Monica said, her voice urgent.

Rose recalled overhearing Monica's conversation with the principal. On any other day, much like the principal, she might have dismissed such accusations as mere youthful exaggeration. But this wasn't just any other day. This was about Jack. And there was something in Monica's eyes—a genuine fondness for him—that made Rose pause, her instincts urging her to listen carefully.

"I think Brad did something to Jack," Monica insisted, her voice trembling. "I overheard them talking about him—they said he got what he deserved."

Rose clenched her fists, holding back the anger rising within her. "So, what can we do?"

Monica leaned in, lowering her voice. "The principal said he has a meeting with Brad and his mother this afternoon, so they'll be out of the house. I can sneak in and see if there's any evidence linking Brad to Jack's disappearance. I know where they live, and you can drive me there."

THE DRIVE WAS QUICK, and soon they found themselves parked across the road from Brad's house, engine running as they waited. They didn't have to wait long. Moments later, the front door opened, and Brad's mother stepped out, calling after him as he pushed his motorbike down the drive.

"You need to come with me, Brad. We have to get this sorted," she urged, her voice edged with frustration.

Brad didn't respond. He simply pulled on his helmet, turned the key, and kicked the bike into gear. With a roar, he sped off down the road, leaving his mother standing alone in clear despair. She watched him go, visibly torn, before heading back inside to gather her things. Moments later, the garage door lifted, and Brad's mother pulled out. As the door closed behind her, she sped away, leaving the house empty and silent.

Rose took a deep breath, feeling the anticipation rise. "Ready?" she asked, glancing at Monica.

Monica nodded; her determination unmistakable. This was their chance.

Rose turned off the engine. "I'll keep a lookout. Climbing through windows isn't my thing. If you find anything, we'll take it straight to the principal. Don't take too long—Brad could come back at any time."

Monica nodded, then slipped out of the car, shutting the door firmly behind her. As she crossed the street, her heart pounded with a mix of fear and resolve. She tried to appear casual, her steps steady despite the adrenaline coursing through her. She approached Brad's house, glancing around to ensure no one was watching, and then made her way up the driveway. She spun around, scanning the surroundings, then quickly ducked behind the fence. Cautiously, she peered above each window ledge, checking every room at the front and back of the house. Relief washed over her when she confirmed that no one was home.

"Shit," she muttered under her breath when she found all the doors locked. *Of course, they're all locked, stupid,* she chided herself. Just as she was about to give up, she spotted a window slightly ajar, tantalizingly out of reach. Desperately, she searched for something to stand on and found an old wooden fruit box filled with rusty chains and bike parts. She tipped out the contents with a clatter and positioned the box under the window.

Standing on the balls of her feet, she grasped the ledge, using it to hoist herself up. The window was stubborn, stuck halfway open, and the clasp scraped painfully against her back. Gritting her teeth, she pressed on, driven by her desire for revenge. She knew Brad was involved somehow, and she was determined to uncover the truth.

With awkward tugs and pushes, Monica finally hauled herself through the narrow window, landing hard on the floor inside. Her foot caught; her shoelace ensnared by the window latch. She yanked and twisted, desperate to free herself, but the heavy window suddenly came crashing down onto her ankle. The pain was excruciating, and she stifled a scream, biting her lip so hard she tasted blood. Clenching her teeth, she absorbed the agony, eventually managing to free her foot.

She attempted to stand, but a sharp stab of pain shot through her ankle, making it difficult to bear her weight. As she steadied herself, she accidentally banged against a side cabinet, knocking over a vase of freshly cut red roses. She glanced at the scattered blooms and shards of glass on the floor. A fleeting thought crossed her mind—perhaps Brad had bought them for his mother, a hint that maybe he wasn't entirely bad. But the thought vanished as quickly as it had come. She had no time to worry about the mess she'd made; there was something far more pressing at hand.

Limping slightly, she began moving through the rooms, her eyes scanning every corner, every surface, searching for any clue that could link Brad to Jack's disappearance.

Nothing. The frustration mounted as she found nothing of significance. Her gaze drifted upward. *His bedroom*, she thought with a surge of hope.

She hobbled toward the stairs, but the sudden roar of a motorbike outside sent a jolt of panic through her. "Damn," she whispered, heart racing. Halfway up the stairs, she paused to peer out of a small window, hoping against hope it wasn't who she feared.

Through the glass, she saw Rose exiting the car, clearly concerned. Frantically, Monica waved her hands and shook her head, signaling for Rose to stay put and not to disrupt the search. Rose caught on, quickly retreating back into the car.

Monica took a shaky breath and glanced down toward the driveway. Her worst fear was confirmed—Brad was back. Heart racing, she turned to the doorway at the bottom of the stairs and to the roses and scattered glass across the floor, but there was no time to clear it up. She hoped Brad wouldn't notice. She forced herself up the remaining steps, each one sending a sharp stab of pain through her ankle.

At the top of the stairs, she spotted a door slightly ajar and moved towards it, but her ankle finally gave out. She collapsed against the door, falling to her knees. "Shit," she hissed through gritted teeth, the pain so intense it immobilized her.

Suddenly, the front door slammed, the sound reverberating through the house, followed by Brad's voice. "Mom, is that you? I'm sorry! I will go to the meeting."

Panic surged through her veins. Had he heard her? Or worse, had he noticed the mess she'd left by the door? But as she strained to listen, she realized she might have been lucky. The door had swept most of the scattered glass and roses aside, leaving the floor clear enough to avoid immediate suspicion. She took a slow, silent breath, praying he wouldn't look too closely.

She knew she had to move—now. Desperation fueling her, she scurried through the slightly ajar door, leaving it just as she'd found it, hoping it wouldn't catch Brad's attention. She scanned the room frantically for a place to hide. With no strength left to stand, the bed was her only option. She crawled underneath, her breath coming in shallow, rapid bursts, praying she wouldn't be found.

She listened, heart pounding, as the stairs creaked under Brad's weight, each step louder and closer. Glancing around the room, she noticed a calendar on the wall; Miss May, in a provocative swimsuit, smiled down at her. Her eyes flicked to the dressing table, where a half-finished Harley model stood. This was definitely Brad's room. The final, repugnant clue came when her head brushed against a pair of soiled Y-fronts, their stench making her gag.

The footsteps stopped outside the door. Her heart pounded wildly; each beat a desperate attempt to break free from her ribcage. Her breaths came in ragged, shallow gasps, each one a struggle to feed her oxygen-starved lungs. She knew she had to calm herself; any sound, even the faintest panting, would give her away.

Suddenly, an overwhelming urge to pee added another layer to her mounting anxiety. She clenched her muscles, trying to maintain control. Just as she took a final, shaky breath to steady herself, the door swung open with a loud creak. The noise startled her, making her jump and lose her tenuous grip. A warm, humiliating trickle began to seep through her clothes, pooling beneath her.

She lay frozen, eyes wide with fear, as the trickling stream meandered across the varnished floorboards from under the bed. There was nothing she could do to stop it. Any movement, even the slightest shift, would alert Brad to her presence. She had no choice but to let nature take its course.

As the little stream neared the edge of the bed, she managed to halt the flow. She silently thanked God that she hadn't finished her cold glass of milk at breakfast, fearing the puddle would have been much larger. Her body trembled with a mixture of fear and shame, her only hope being that Brad wouldn't notice the incriminating evidence in the puddle of piss at his feet.

Brad threw his rucksack on the floor, landing perilously close to Monica's face. The heavy thud sent a shiver through her, and she could smell the faint scent of sweat and leather from the bag. He sat on the bed with a creak of springs. Monica inhaled slowly, the breath catching in her throat as she accidentally bit her lip. The sharp pain brought tears to her eyes, but she dared not make a sound. She felt like a pressure cooker on the verge of exploding. Blood mingled with the sweat that dripped from her brow, and she recoiled at the bitter taste of fear, blood, and sweat that lingered in her mouth.

Just as she felt she could no longer contain herself, the shrill ring of the telephone cut through the tension. Brad jumped up, his footsteps thudding heavily as he hurried downstairs to answer it.

As he left the room, Monica exhaled forcefully, like a whale venting stale air. She inhaled deeply, filling her lungs with fresh air before reaching out to pull the rucksack closer. Her hands trembled as she rummaged through it—finding only an ounce of weed and some cigarette papers. A sly smile crept across her face. If she couldn't get him for what he had done to Jack, she could at least get him for this.

She pulled herself up from beneath the bed and moved silently to the door, listening intently.

"What?" Brad shouted; frustration evident in his voice. There was a pause, as if someone was explaining something to him. "Fuck," he cursed. The conversation continued in muffled tones. "Yes, I have. They're in a safe place. Okay, okay, I will." Brad slammed down the phone, the sound reverberating through the house. He wasn't happy, and Monica instinctively knew it had something to do with Jack.

Monica hurried back to her hiding spot as Brad's footsteps pounded up the stairs. She just managed to pull her foot under the bed as the door swung open. Brad went straight to one of his drawers, yanking it open to retrieve a set of keys. Monica realized that the phone conversation must have been about these keys. He picked up his rucksack, stuffed the keys inside, and placed the bag on the bed before heading to the bathroom.

As soon as he was out of the room, Monica reached out and dragged the rucksack towards her. She swiftly removed the keys and replaced the bag, her heart racing.

When Brad finished in the bathroom, he returned to his room, grabbed his bag, and stormed out. Monica lay silently under the bed, holding her breath, until she heard the roar of his motorbike fade into the distance. Only then did she crawl out, her heart still pounding. She looked at the keys more closely—they were Jack's. She instantly recognized the yellow smiley face key ring she'd picked out for him at the five-and-dime on his last birthday.

Without wasting a moment, she darted downstairs and out the door, nearly colliding with Rose, who was coming in from the opposite direction.

"Find anything?" Rose asked, her voice steady but her eyes full of hope.

Monica didn't answer, only lifted her hand to jangle the keys. Rose's eyes widened as she recognized them immediately. She understood their significance—these weren't just physical keys; they were a clue, the key to unlocking the mystery of where Jack was.

TWENTY
OUBLIETTE

MRS. MARSHALL SAT in June's office, waiting anxiously for her appointment with the principal. She had been sitting for ten minutes before Brad finally joined her. Relief softened her face as he approached—maybe he had had a change of heart. Perhaps this would be the moment he acknowledged his mistakes and started taking responsibility for his actions. She patted the seat beside her, and Brad sat down.

BRAD LOOKED UP, meeting June's gaze with a smirk. June stared back, her eyes burning with quiet rage. She reached up, unconsciously rubbing the small tag on her necklace—Mungo's tag. Her beloved cat had been murdered by the very boy smirking at her now. Her fingers tightened around the tag as hatred simmered inside her, but her thoughts were interrupted by the crackle of the office intercom.

"June, please send in Mrs. Marshall and Bradley."

June didn't speak; she simply gestured toward the door; her expression unreadable. As they entered, her eyes fixed on Brad's back, smoldering with the quiet fury of someone who had yet to see justice.

The moment didn't have time to settle as the office door swung open and in marched the police, Rose, Monica, and Will. The officer took command. "Is the principal available?"

"Yes, of course—I'll call him," June replied, her hand hovering over the intercom. But before she could press it, the officer interrupted, "Is Bradley Marshall with him?"

"Yes, he is, Officer," June confirmed, her voice taut with anticipation. Without wasting another moment, the officer crossed the room to the principal's office door and knocked sharply.

"Enter," came the principal's voice from inside. The door swung wide, and the principal looked up, eyes widening as he took in the unexpected crowd. Mrs. Marshall and Brad turned in their seats, and as Brad caught sight of the officer, panic flickered across his face. His gaze shifted to the right, landing on Monica, who stared back with a look of steely triumph. Her expression said it all: she had vowed to get him back, and she had done just that.

In a matter of seconds, Brad was cuffed, the metal clinking harshly against the tense silence. Mrs. Marshall, torn between horror and disbelief, pleaded with him to cooperate, urging him to reveal Jack's whereabouts. Under the mounting pressure, Brad finally broke, his defiance cracking he said he would take them to Jack. The officer handed Will Jack's set of keys, and as they prepared to leave, Rose turned to Monica, pulling her into an embrace.

IT WAS MONICA'S DETERMINATION, her refusal to back down, that had brought them to this moment. In the young girl's unwavering gaze, Rose saw a reflection of her own fierce resolve.

They moved quickly, following Brad's lead as he took them down the narrow, shadowed corridors of the building, where the air grew colder, and the walls pressed closer. Rose followed behind him, her gaze locked onto his back, simmering with barely contained rage. Brad must have felt the intensity of her stare; he glanced over his shoulder, catching her glare with a mocking smirk.

The sight of his smug expression shattered her last shred of restraint. With a feral cry, Rose lunged at him, her nails clawing, her fists striking, every ounce of her fury unleashed. It took two officers to pull her off, their firm grip the only thing keeping her from tearing into him. But Brad only laughed, his voice low and sinister, taunting her with a chilling calm.

"Oubliette—Oubliette," he drawled, repeating the word with venomous glee, the twisted meaning lost on all but him. The sound of his laughter echoed through the cold, empty corridors as they drew closer to Jack's prison, each step a reminder of the horrors that lay just beyond.

Will could not contain himself any longer, like Rose, he was filled with rage; he turned and squared up to Brad. "You little fuck! If my friend is hurt down there, I swear to you, your life won't mean squat, ya hear me?"

Brad just smiled back at Will and repeated his taunting, "Oubliette."

"What the fuck are you talking about?" Will growled.

"Dumb motherfuckers," Brad chuckled. The principal stepped in and held Will's arm.

"Will, calm down. Let's just find Jack," the principal sternly spoke. Brad, defiant to the end, just smirked, and turned to the officer holding him.

"Are you gonna let this psycho freak speak to me like that? I thought you were here to protect me."

"Just get moving and keep your mouth shut," came the reply from the young officer. As they carried on, Rose promised Brad, "You're gonna get yours, you little creep. I'll see to that." Brad turned his head.

"Fuck you, bitch, and your brother," he replied. Once again, she lunged, this time, scratching his face. It began to bleed. The officers once again dragged her off, kicking and screaming. The principal was losing his patience. He held Rose firmly by the shoulders and pleaded with her.

"For God's sake, Rose, calm down. We have to find Jack. Don't listen to him. He's not worth it." He too looked at Brad, who was now wiping the blood from his cheek.

Brad licked his hand then leered back at Rose.

"Rose, listen to me. He's just trying to goad you on. Don't let him get to you, okay?"

Rose was calm now and looked up at the principal.

"Okay?" he repeated.

Rose just nodded her head.

"Shall we move on, people?" the officer asked. They carried on down the corridor into a maze of pipes and wiring. Every now and then, a squeak or a rat was heard, then a faint murmuring of old pipe work.

They finally got to the room where Jack had been imprisoned for almost three days. Jack hadn't much time left.

WILL WAS FILLED WITH SHOCK, then anger. He was angry with himself for not checking this room earlier, but how could he have known? He fumbled at the lock, trying several keys, each time getting angrier and angrier with himself. He kicked and punched the door.

Rose began to cry and became hysterical as she begged, "Please, open the door! Jack's in there. He needs me. Jack, can you hear us?"

Will frantically tried each key until one finally turned the lock. The door swung open, slamming against the wall. Light flooded into the room, though the figures in the doorway cast long shadows.

UNAWARE OF HIS IMPENDING RESCUE, Jack lay unconscious, lost in the depths of his past.

In his unconscious mind, he was eight years old again, crumpled on a moldy, flea-bitten mattress in the cellar where his father had imprisoned him. Broken and defiled he felt utterly forsaken. If he had fully understood the teachings of Jesus, he might have questioned why he was subjected to such a vile act. If he had had the strength to pray, he would have pleaded for deliverance, for any sign of salvation.

At that moment, the cellar door creaked open, and a bright, almost divine light pierced the darkness.

"An angel," Jack whispered.

The figure swooped down, lifting him with an almost ethereal gentleness. Jack looked up, an overwhelming sense of peace washing over him. Though the face remained indistinct, he felt safe, as if wrapped in a cocoon of warmth. With frail arms, he clung to the angel, the scent of fresh roses enveloping him. At last, he was free from his tormentors.

When he opened his eyes, it was Rose holding him, her tears falling softly onto his face. "Rose," he whispered, his voice barely audible. With trembling fingers, he reached out, cupping her face gently. "Thank you," he murmured, a faint smile touching his lips before his body went limp in her arms.

"WE NEED MORE LIGHT IN HERE!" Rose cried out. Will flicked the switch, but it was in vain. They called for Jack—nothing. The police shone their torches as they made their way down the steps behind Rose, who stumbled down each step in the dim light. There was still no sign of Jack, no cry for help.

"Jack, where are you?" Rose called desperately. Frantically, she searched amongst the mess of the storeroom. "Jack, Jack, please, where are you?" she pleaded. Her attention was grabbed by a slight movement in the corner of the room. Several rats squeaked and ran for cover like escaping convicts as the searchlights swept over them. She investigated and almost fell on top of Jack, as he was under several tailor dummies that had fallen on him. He was barely alive. More rats scurried around him, squeaking, biting, and scratching away at his clothes and face.

"Quickly, over here!" Rose shouted, and one of the officers came over and looked down.

"Oh, my God, quick, call a paramedic!" the officer called out.

"It's on its way, Sergeant," another officer replied.

Brad, hands shackled, was taken into custody while Jack was taken to the hospital. He was suffering from dehydration, concussion, and hypothermia and had lost a lot of blood, which had caused him to slip into a coma. He needed immediate medical attention if he was to survive.

TWENTY-ONE
EMOTIONAL DEBRIS

IT WAS TUESDAY, the day Jack would finally leave the hospital, exactly five weeks since the harrowing incident that had nearly claimed his life. Now, he sat upright in bed, looking remarkably well despite the ordeal he had endured. Rose stood steadfast by his side, having been there every moment during his six-day coma, sleeping in a small side room and providing unwavering support throughout his recovery and subsequent rehabilitation. She carried a deep sense of guilt over the accident and had become fiercely protective of him. With Jack now out of the coma and intensive care, making steady progress toward a full recovery, Rose's longing to bring him home grew stronger with each passing day.

The room where Jack had been recuperating was the epitome of comfort and care, a testament to the quality that money could buy. It was adorned with vibrant flowers, heartfelt get-well cards, and a slightly deflated helium balloon from the kids at Lincoln High. Despite sagging slightly, the balloon still hung cheerfully, bearing the message: *Get Well Soon, Mr. Jack!* On the reverse side, it proudly declared, *Go Cardinals*, a nod to the school's team spirit.

Rose gently pulled back the sheets and helped Jack to the edge of the bed. She let him take the lead as he pushed himself up, then opened the suitcase she had placed at the foot of the bed. Inside were Jack's leaving clothes: a perfectly starched and ironed shirt, neatly folded jeans, and a boxed pair of CK low rise briefs—the kind he liked. She also handed him his favorite baseball sneakers and a new pair of ankle socks.

Gesturing toward the en-suite, Jack acknowledged her silent instructions and slowly made his way to the bathroom. Rose had ensured that no expense was spared; the bathroom was elegantly appointed and fully equipped for his comfort and convenience. Jack took the clothes, made his way inside, and quietly shut the door behind him.

Rose was certain she could care for Jack better at home. He was eager to leave as well, missing his cat Spot, his model trains, and the comfort of his familiar routine, including his job. However, despite being fully insured and being able to ensure that all his needs were met, Rose couldn't ignore the reality that the expenses had been significant. She knew her insurance premiums would likely increase next time, so having Jack home made sense both financially and spiritually.

Jack had undergone a thorough check-up and a psychiatric evaluation and was declared fit to leave, so Rose was following the hospital's advice. She checked her watch—11:30 a.m.—and noted that they had half an hour before the car arrived to take them home. Just then, the door opened, and Jack emerged, looking as dapper and handsome as ever. Rose couldn't help but smile, relieved and happy to see him up and about. Tapping her watch, she reminded him, "The car will be here at noon, so let's start packing up."

Jack nodded and began gathering his get-well cards. He spotted the helium balloon from the kids at Lincoln High, still floating albeit slightly deflated. With a playful glint in his eye, he untied the string and put the end of the balloon in his mouth, inhaling the remaining helium.

"Really? Feeling better?" Rose teased, raising an eyebrow.

Jack grinned and, in a comically high-pitched voice, tried to mimic Arnold Schwarzenegger's iconic line, "I'll be back."

Rose laughed, shaking her head. "I see someone hasn't lost their sense of humor," she remarked, amused, as she zipped up the suitcase.

Jack, enjoying the lighthearted moment, took another deep breath of helium. Just then, the door swung open, and Dr. Warrick walked in.

Caught off guard, Jack instinctively greeted the doctor with a high-pitched "Hello!" that sounded somewhere between Pee-wee Herman and Elmo. He tried to apologize, but the words came out in a squeaky, cartoonish voice more reminiscent of Mickey Mouse than Patrick Swayze. He blushed, and before he could make it worse, Rose jumped in.

"Dr. Warrick, nice of you to come see us off," she said smoothly, offering the doctor a warm smile. Her intervention provided a momentary distraction, allowing Jack to compose himself.

Dr. Warrick chuckled, clearly amused by the scene. "Well, it seems you're in good spirits, Jack," she said with a grin. "Just wanted to wish you both well. You've been a model patient, and I'm sure you'll continue to recover nicely at home."

Jack, still chuckling from the helium-induced mishap, nodded appreciatively. "Thank you, Dr. Warrick. For everything," he managed to say, his voice finally back to normal.

With the formalities wrapped up and goodbyes exchanged, Rose and Jack finished packing the last of their things. As they prepared to leave, Rose felt a mixture of relief and anticipation. The last few weeks had been long and challenging, but the thought of bringing Jack home filled her with hope. Despite the obstacles and the looming financial considerations, she was grateful for this moment—a new beginning for both of them.

One last thing remained before they could leave: signing out. They all made their way to the front desk, which was far from the typical reception area of a district hospital. It more closely resembled the lobby of a fancy hotel. The polished marble floors gleamed under soft lighting. Sharp-dressed doctors strolled by, their lab coats pristine, and their expressions composed. Nurses in starched white uniforms bustled about, clipboards in hand, exuding a sense of professionalism and efficiency. At the entrance, uniformed security guards stood vigil, ensuring the smooth flow of people in and out of the facility. The atmosphere was one of quiet elegance and order, making the process of leaving feel almost ceremonial.

AS ROSE BEGAN SIGNING the numerous release papers, Dr. Warrick approached Jack for a final conversation. Despite the outward signs of recovery, she had sensed a deeper turmoil within him over the past weeks and recommended counseling. Dr. Warrick had grown fond of Jack during his recovery and felt compelled to offer him more than just medical care.

While the medical team agreed on his physical readiness to leave, Dr. Warrick reiterated the importance of therapy, handing Jack a business card. Before he could take it, Rose quickly intercepted and tucked it into her purse, her actions betraying a tinge of jealousy.

"You don't need counseling, Jack. You look fine," Rose interjected, attempting to dismiss the doctor's suggestion and curtailing the growing rapport between Jack and Dr. Warrick.

"I disagree, Mrs. Brooks," Dr. Warrick replied, maintaining her professional stance.

"Miss," Rose corrected sharply, setting a clear boundary.

"Apologies, Miss," Dr. Warrick acknowledged, not missing a beat. "Jack has been through a traumatic experience. While the body heals, the mind often lags behind, holding onto traumas. It's crucial to address these issues, to clear out the emotional debris and replace it with positive, focused thoughts."

"But doctor, aren't some demons better left locked away?" Rose countered, her voice faltering as she seemed to realize the depth of Dr. Warrick's insight.

"That's a dangerous misconception. Unaddressed, these demons can cause long-term psychological harm," Dr. Warrick explained, her tone firm yet compassionate.

Recognizing the doctor's expertise, Rose chose to step back from the argument, silently conceding the point.

Jack, overhearing their exchange while packing his belongings, chimed in, "What about real demons, Doctor? What if they can't be destroyed?"

"There are no real demons, Jack. They're constructs of our minds," Dr. Warrick replied gently, noting Jack's unease. "So, Jack, will we see you next week?" she asked softly, hoping to encourage him to seek help.

"I think Rose is right, Doctor. Some things are best left locked away," Jack replied diplomatically, avoiding a firm commitment.

Rose smiled at the doctor, offering her hand and a polite thank you. Dr. Warrick shook her hand warmly, watching them as they left. There were unresolved issues that the doctor felt needed addressing. Though she understood Rose's protective instinct, she couldn't help but think it might be detrimental to Jack's recovery to forego therapy. Dr. Warrick lingered momentarily as Jack and Rose walked away, wondering if she would ever see Jack again.

TWENTY-TWO
CARA CARE BEAR

DR. WARRICK RETREATED to her private office, a secluded corner of the hospital complex. Instead of returning it to the cabinet, she opened Jack's file and slipped it into her briefcase. With a sigh, she picked up the phone and dialed her solicitor; her voice tinged with weariness and frustration as she navigated the complexities of her ongoing divorce. Despite her efforts to separate her personal and professional life, the strain was visible to those around her. Colleagues offered their support, but she steadfastly declined, fiercely protective of her independence, which she had cultivated over years of self-reliance.

The only true love in her life now was Sigmund, named after one of her intellectual heroes, a man whose brilliant mind she deeply admired —Sigmund Freud. 'Sig,' as she affectionately called him, was a shaggy Afghan stray she had accidentally injured with her car a few years back. Compelled by an overwhelming sense of duty to nurse him back to health, she paid for his treatment and, in the process, found herself growing fiercely attached to the scruffy mutt. This impulsive, albeit costly, act confirmed the affectionate nickname her father had called her from an early age, 'Cara Care Bear.' Her mind drifted back to her childhood; she missed her father deeply.

It was he who had inspired her to pursue a career in psychiatry. As a young teenager, she had watched helplessly as he descended into despair, diagnosed with PTSD from his years as a marine in the Vietnam conflict. She witnessed the illness ravage him, tearing apart both his spirit and their family, until it finally culminated in his tragic decision to end his life with a single, devastating bullet to his head. Too young at the time to understand the depth of his suffering—or the complexities of the human mind—she now, as a trained psychiatrist, fully grasped the relentless grip of his anguish. With this understanding, she had become resolute in her mission to help others struggling against the same inner demons that had consumed him. She made a promise to herself, and as a tribute to her father, she would work hard to bring solace to those haunted by the demons of misery that linger in the mind, metaphorically speaking, of course.

She wasn't immune to the pull of despair herself, often beset by moments of overwhelming hopelessness and grief at losing her father at a young age—and right now, she felt one of those moments closing in.

"I need a drink," she muttered.

A phone call with her solicitor awaited her, and as she listened to his careful but grim updates, the misery deepened. She had learned she would not only lose the house but might also risk losing custody of Sig. Her ex-husband, David, had argued that her demanding work schedule rendered her incapable of properly caring for the now elderly dog and that removing Sig from his home would be cruel. The house she could reluctantly concede, but Sig was a battle she was determined to fight.

Her solicitor, however, was less optimistic. With David likely to secure the house, the courts might also favor his case for custody of Sig. Frustrated and angry, Cara exchanged a few sharp words before ending the call with a slam of the receiver. The thought of losing Sig brought stinging tears to her eyes. In a moment of defeated resolve, she pulled open her desk drawer, revealing a glass and a bottle of George Dickel whiskey. There were other Tennessee whiskies, but none hit the spot quite like a straight Dickel. She knew it wasn't the healthiest way to cope, but tonight, she thought, *what the hell*.

Slumping back in her chair, she poured herself several glasses, the alcohol helping to numb her spiraling thoughts. As the last sip slid down her throat, she contemplated another refill. She lifted the bottle off the floor, only to find it empty. "I guess not," she murmured to herself. "Oh well," she sighed.

Cara placed the glass on the table and tossed the bottle into the bin. She switched off the harsh overhead light and turned on a stylish lamp beside the couch, casting a softer glow in the room. As she settled onto the couch, exhaustion finally overtook her, and she drifted off to sleep, hoping to escape her troubles, if only for a while.

A few hours had passed when she awoke abruptly, a sense of dread seeping into her consciousness. It was as if a presence hovered just beyond her line of sight, watching her intently. Her eyes strained in the dim light, and that's when she heard it—a soft creak, the unmistakable sound of a door easing open. She sat up sharply, her heart hammering against her ribs, her breath shallow and quick.

"Who's there?" she called out, her voice a mix of fear and authority. She stumbled to turn on the light, colliding with furniture like a pinball in a machine. It was a reminder of her inebriated state, though the adrenaline coursing through her veins was quickly sobering her up. The light snapped on, flooding the room with a harsh brightness that made her squint. The sudden illumination caused the room to spin, overwhelming her senses. She felt a wave of nausea rising, her stomach rebelling against the whiskey she had consumed.

Desperately, she looked around for a place to purge. Spying the wastepaper bin beside her desk, she rushed over and, with a fleeting glance at the mocking empty whiskey bottle inside, began to retch. The sound echoed in the quiet room as she heaved, bile burning her throat.

After a few agonizing moments, she sat back in her office chair, drained. She grabbed a Kleenex from the box on her desk and wiped the sweat from her brow and the vomit from the corners of her mouth and chin. Relieved that the worst was over, she reflected briefly that maybe having eaten something would have mitigated the effects of the alcohol.

Composing herself, she knew she needed to clean up before leaving; the night cleaners were notorious for gossip, and she didn't want her personal mishap to become hospital lore. She tied a knot in the plastic waste bag, securing the evidence of her indiscretion. As she did, her eyes caught sight of the open office door. A frown creased her forehead. *I'm sure I shut the door earlier*, she thought, though her memory felt hazy. She couldn't be entirely certain, given her state when she had drifted off. The feeling of being watched lingered, unsettling her even more. She quickly dismissed it as a product of her anxiety and fatigue, but a small part of her remained wary, scanning the shadows for any sign of an intruder.

As she made her way to close the door, she heard the clattering of doors in the corridor outside. Curiosity piqued, she peered into the hallway, her head poking out from the side of the door frame. Just as she looked, she caught a glimpse of a shadow moving swiftly, disappearing around the corner. *Who could be roaming at this time of night?* she wondered. She reached for the phone to call security, but the line rang out. It dawned on her why there was no answer—this part of the building wasn't in use at night, and the security guards were likely patrolling elsewhere. For now, she was alone. The clock read just past nine; she should be home in bed, fast asleep, she pondered.

Gathering her courage and momentarily forgetting about the mess she left behind, her curiosity got the better of her. She decided to pursue the shadowy figure. With her belongings hastily gathered, she left her office and closed the door behind her. Slowly, she walked down the dimly lit corridor, her earlier bravery starting to wane. As she turned the corner, she glimpsed the shadow once more before it vanished again. A swinging door at the end of the hall indicated the specter's direction. She followed cautiously, not wanting to catch up too quickly; she was in no condition to confront anyone, let alone a potentially dangerous individual. She was brave but not foolish.

As she advanced, she noticed that only her own footsteps echoed in the hallway. *Strange*, she thought. The realization that she was blindly pursuing an unknown entity made her uneasy, but she continued, nonetheless. Eventually, she reached the end of the corridor and passed through a small annex into an older part of the hospital. There, a large, reinforced door blocked her path. She tried the handle—it was locked. Confused, she looked around. The figure had to have come this way; there was no other exit. The darkness seemed to close in around her, with the only light coming from an exit sign overhead, casting a flickering glow reminiscent of an old out-of-town motel.

She fumbled for the light switch on the wall, but nothing happened. Her heart sank as the switch clicked uselessly, the bulb above her head remaining dark. The faint, erratic flicker of emergency lights barely held the shadows at bay, as if they were alive, creeping closer with each passing second. The fog of her earlier inebriation had fully lifted, replaced by an icy, creeping dread that tightened her chest. Her eyes were drawn to the faded sign above the door: 'High-Security Mental Ward.'

A shiver ran down her spine. She hated this part of the building. It had been closed for years now, the patients long relocated—well, all those who remained after the incident four years ago. She could still remember it all too clearly; she had been a junior doctor back then, wide-eyed and unprepared for the nightmare that would unfold. Eight patients, all of them found hanged in their rooms one night, with no sign of struggle, no warning. All except one: a John Doe coma patient they had nicknamed George. George, who had lain unmoving in his bed, comatose for nearly eighteen years.

The incident had been swept under the hospital's pristine white rug, spoken of only in murmurs and half-finished sentences. There had been whispers of malpractice, suspicions of a cover-up, and hints of something darker lurking in the ward's abandoned halls. It was a story buried in the hospital's past; a memory too haunting to resurface.

Now, standing here alone in the silence, she felt the weight of that past pressing in, thick and suffocating. The shadows seemed to pulse as if something within them was waiting, watching. As she pondered what to do next, an unsettling scent wafted past her—stale cigarettes and alcohol. She raised her right hand to her mouth and breathed out, then sniffed. *It's probably just the whiskey*, she thought, recalling the half bottle she had consumed earlier. A brief grin crossed her face, like a guilty child caught with their hand in the cookie jar. But her smile quickly faded. She suddenly felt an overwhelming presence behind her, a chilling sensation that made the hairs on her neck stand on end.

She stood rigid, whispering, "This is not happening," as a mantra to steady herself. All the self-defense training she had ever received seemed futile in this moment of paralyzing fear. She was frozen to the spot, unable to go forward because the door was locked, hemmed in by a wall on one side and a window on the other. There was no escape. The oppressive darkness behind her seemed to close in, a shadowy presence that sent chills down her spine. With every ounce of willpower, she slowly reached into her bag, fumbling for the can of mace she had hoped never to use.

The shadow loomed larger, almost upon her. Her breath caught in her throat as she gritted her teeth, bracing for whatever was to come. With a swift motion, she swung around, the can of mace held aloft, ready to fire. "Hold it, creep!" she shouted, her voice shaky but determined.

To her immense relief and embarrassment, she found herself face-to-face with Jo, the hospital security guard. "Whoa, whoa, Dr. Warrick, it's Jo. Hold your fire," he exclaimed, hands raised protectively in front of his face.

Stunned, she lowered the mace, her heart still racing. "What the hell are you doing down here, Doctor? This part of the building has been closed off for years. There's nothing down here now," Jo continued, his tone puzzled but calm.

Quickly regaining her composure, she forced a laugh and lied, "I thought I saw a cat down here and didn't want it to get locked in."

Despite knowing Jo for many years, she couldn't bring herself to tell him the truth—that in a drunken state she had followed a shadowy figure into this abandoned part of the hospital, only to find it seemingly vanish into thin air. Given the circumstances, and the whiskey she'd consumed, the 'lost cat' explanation seemed like the safest, least crazy excuse.

Apologizing again, she started to make her way back up the stairs, Jo following closely behind, casting occasional concerned glances her way. Unbeknownst to them, the shadowy figure reappeared behind them, watching silently. It lingered for a moment, then, like a mist caught in a draft, it seemed to dissipate into the darkness, leaving no trace behind.

Jo escorted her out of the building and asked, "Do you want me to call you a cab?"

"No, I'm fine. I drove in," she replied, trying to sound casual. Jo hesitated, clearly concerned.

"Are you sure you don't want a cab?" he pressed gently. Realization dawned on her—he must have smelled the alcohol. Embarrassed, she conceded.

"Maybe a cab would be a good idea."

TWENTY-THREE
ONE MISSISSIPPI

WITH JACK now home from the hospital and beginning to settle in, Rose hoped for a return to some semblance of normalcy in their lives. Feeling the weight of the recent stressful events, she reluctantly decided to take a few hours for herself and have a quick drink with Scott. Jack, ever supportive, insisted that a night out would do her good and that he would be fine on his own. Despite initially hesitating, she agreed, promising she wouldn't be gone long. She made it clear to herself and Scott that this wasn't a date, just a casual evening to unwind and catch up.

The night stretched on longer than Rose had anticipated. She had arrived late to her date, apologizing to Scott and explaining that she had a few things to sort out. Although the evening was pleasant enough, Rose couldn't lower her guard; her mind was elsewhere, her defenses firmly in place, and she could sense Scott's disappointment. But now wasn't the time for her to be distracted—she had Jack to look after, and her priorities were clear.

As they strolled back to her apartment block, she tried to explain her reasoning, offering what reassurance she could. The evening ended in the dimly lit foyer with an awkward goodnight hug, a fragile moment lingering between them. But before either could say another word, a voice sounded from behind, breaking the silence.

"Get a room already."

It was Bella, the tiny, slippered Jewish lady from apartment number ten. She peered over the top of her glasses with a mischievous grin then she pushed the glasses back into place.

Rose and Scott chuckled, the tension easing slightly. They exchanged a quick smile, and a silent agreement to leave things as they were, for now. Scott turned and headed off to his shift while Rose made her way up to her apartment, her mind still elsewhere.

As Rose passed Bella, she noticed Spot, Jack's cat, snuggled comfortably in her arms. While Jack was in the hospital, Bella had been looking after Spot, and it seemed increasingly unlikely that the cat would be going home anytime soon. Rose paused briefly to exchange pleasantries with Bella, thanking her for caring for Spot.

"I'll check in on him soon," she assured Bella with a smile, though her thoughts were already drifting back to her responsibilities and the hope that Jack was managing okay in her absence.

After a quick, polite goodbye, Rose continued toward the elevator. As she waited for the doors to open, she felt the day's weight settle back on her shoulders, her mind racing with everything still left to do. The elevator dinged, and she stepped inside, giving Bella one last wave before the doors closed.

A few moments later, Rose stepped into her darkening apartment. The space was eerily quiet, with only a faint sliver of moonlight slipping through the curtains, casting a soft, pale glow across the room. She hesitated to turn on the lights, not wanting to disturb Jack if he was resting. Carefully, she navigated through the dimly lit space, feeling relief and a tinge of guilt for having taken some time for herself, even for a little while. An uneasy feeling settled in her chest as her eyes adjusted to the darkness. Something felt off, but she tried to dismiss it, attributing it to the unsettling quiet and the night's events. *Perhaps it was just one too many whiskey sours*, she thought, trying to rationalize the twist in her stomach.

She collapsed onto the couch with a weary sigh, attempting to relax. Her eyes wandered across the room, and she noticed an upturned chair next to Jack's crumpled jacket. A chill ran down her spine. Instinctively, she knew something was wrong. Her heart began to race, and a knot of dread tightened in her stomach.

"Jack?" she called out, her voice edged with rising concern. The silence that followed only amplified her anxiety.

"Jack, I'm home," she called again, louder this time. She quickly rose from the couch and pressed the light switch, but nothing happened. Panic began to creep in as she tried another switch, but still, there was no response. Fumbling in the dark, she bounced from one piece of furniture to the next, catching her hip on the hallway table and knocking off her bag, which she had placed there earlier. "Shit," she muttered as its contents scattered across the floor. Undeterred, she pressed on, wincing as she stepped on her keys. Despite the pain and her growing frustration, she continued toward Jack's room, her pulse quickening with every step.

"Jack!" she shouted, her voice now tinged with urgency. Still no reply. Remembering the flashlight in the kitchen cupboard, she quickly changed course. Rummaging through the cabinets, she realized it wasn't there. All she could find was a pack of candles. "These will have to do," she muttered, pulling open the kitchen drawer and rummaging for some matches. She eventually found them and, once again, set off for Jack's room.

Not wanting to worsen her bruised hip and now bleeding foot, she struck a match to light the candle. But before igniting the wick, she tripped over something soft and large. Instinctively, she knew it was Jack. She knelt, her arms outstretched, feeling the familiar shape of his body. The pungent smell of alcohol hit her nose. "Jack?" she whispered inquiringly, though she knew it was him.

Frantically, she searched for the dropped matches and managed to light a candle, revealing her worst fears: Jack lay unconscious on the floor. Desperately, she shook him, trying to rouse him, but in her panic, the flame from the candle caught the edge of his shirt, setting it on fire. Her heart racing, she quickly patted out the flames, her hands trembling as she tried to control her growing fear.

Rose cried out, her anxiety escalating as she shook him, but there was no response. She feared Jack had relapsed and slipped back into a coma. She couldn't lose him; he was all she had. She rushed to the phone and dialed 911.

"911, what's your emergency?"

"Please, you've got to help me! It's my brother. He's unconscious on the floor. Please come quick!" Rose's usually calm demeanor dissolved into frantic urgency.

"Ma'am, please take a deep breath and try to calm down. What's your name?" the operator asked calmly.

"Rose," she managed to say, taking a shaky breath.

"Okay, Rose. We need you to stay calm. Can you tell me where you are?"

Rose quickly provided her address, and the operator assured her that help was coming. "Stay with me now, don't hang up the phone, okay?"

"Okay," Rose replied, her voice trembling. "Please hurry."

The operator continued to guide Rose, instructing her to place Jack in the recovery position and to check the fuse box. With careful movements, she made Jack as comfortable as possible before hurrying to locate the fuse box. The operator's intuition had been spot on—it was only a blown fuse. She quickly reset it, and the lights flickered back to life, casting a soft glow over the room.

Rose rushed back to Jack's side, gently cradling his head in her lap. Gradually, his eyes fluttered open, and he began to murmur, his voice weak and disoriented.

"Rose, don't let them hurt me," he mumbled, fear and confusion bleeding through his slurred words.

"I won't, Jack. You're safe now," she whispered, holding him close, her hand lightly stroking his hair as a single tear slid down her cheek. In that moment, she was overwhelmed by the fierce protectiveness she'd felt for him as a child—a need to shield him, not from their father this time, but from the darkness he wrestled with inside himself.

She had saved him before, and she was determined to save him again.

A loud knock at the door jolted her back to reality. Scott arrived with the paramedics and pushed open the unlocked door. "Rose, are you okay?" he called out urgently.

Rose called out, "Over here!"

Scott hurried through the apartment, immediately noticing a trail of blood on the floor. Unaware that it was from Rose's injured foot, he quickly followed the trail, with the paramedics close behind.

As Scott turned the corner, he found Rose propped up against the wall, cradling Jack in her arms. Her face was a mix of fear and desperation while Jack lay semi-conscious, the faint smell of burnt fabric lingering in the air. The paramedics swiftly moved in to assess the situation as Scott and Rose stood back, helpless and concerned.

"What happened, Rose? Are you okay?" Scott asked, his eyes darting between Rose and Jack.

"It's Jack," she pointed to where the paramedics were attending to him. He was now sitting up and more alert.

Rose heard a faint voice emanating from her phone and remembered the 911 operator. She picked up the phone and quickly thanked the operator for her help. The operator responded soothingly, "You're welcome." Rose ended the call.

Scott stayed close, wrapping his arms around her in a comforting embrace. Rose didn't flinch or pull away for once, finding solace in his support. Meanwhile, the paramedics administered oxygen to Jack, and his condition began to stabilize. They confirmed that he hadn't slipped back into a coma but had blacked out, likely exacerbated by alcohol consumption. Relieved but still shaken, Rose leaned against Scott, absorbing the weight of the night's events.

With the paramedics gone, Rose and Scott helped Jack to his room. Rose removed his muddy shoes, which she found odd, and remembered the crumpled-up jacket. Where had he been? She wondered and would ask him later, but not now. She pulled back the covers, and Jack turned away from them, curling up on his side. Rose thanked Scott, who gave her a reassuring squeeze on the shoulder.

"Anytime, Rose. You know where I am if you need me," he said warmly.

Rose nodded, grateful for his support. She watched Scott leave, then closed the door softly behind him. Returning to Jack, she sat by his side, her voice soft and gentle. "Jack, what happened?"

Jack remained silent, so she tried a different approach. "Did you faint, trip, what?"

"You said you would only be gone briefly," Jack said, quietly. "Why were you so long?"

"I'm sorry, Jack, we lost track of time. It won't happen again, I promise. But please, Jack, tell me what happened tonight?"

"They switched off the lights."

"Who, Jack? Who switched off the lights?" she pressed, but he didn't respond.

"Jack, Jack," she whispered, but he had fallen asleep. She stood up quietly, intending to leave, but Jack spoke again.

"Rose, don't let them hurt me," he pleaded.

"I won't, Jack. You're safe now. I'll protect you. No one is going to hurt you ever again."

Leaving the door slightly ajar and the hallway light on, Rose retreated to the living room, the evening's events still weighing heavily on her mind. She poured herself a generous glass of whiskey, noticing the bottle was nearly empty. And she knew why.

As she held the glass in her hand, a sinking feeling settled in her stomach, a cold realization creeping over her—Jack had started drinking again. It had been years since he'd quit, the hard-won progress she had thought he'd never undo. She took a deep breath, knowing she would need to approach the topic carefully with him the next day.

With a weary sigh, she took a long sip, but the familiar warmth of the whiskey did little to quell the worry churning inside her. Her mind drifted to the events of the past few weeks, each memory darkening her thoughts. She couldn't shake the anger festering inside her toward Brad, the root of Jack's suffering, the one who had pulled him back into this spiral.

Quietly, she turned towards Jack's room, her gaze softening as she watched him sleep, just as she had so many times when he was younger. His face looked peaceful now, a stark contrast to the turmoil she knew was simmering beneath the surface. In the stillness of that moment, memories of years past—the nights she'd spent watching over him, protecting him—flooded her, and she was struck by how fragile he seemed, even now.

Before long, her own exhaustion overtook her, and she drifted off to sleep, the empty glass still in her hand, her final thoughts a tangled mix of love, anger, and resolve.

TWENTY-FOUR
A MURDER OF CROWS

JACK QUICKLY FELL into a restless sleep in his room, slipping into vivid dreams. He first dreamed of happier times, waking up in a familiar room, clean from a hot bath and dressed in fresh pajamas. The scent of fresh roses filled the air, and he realized he was in his sister's room. The morning sun streamed through the lace curtains, casting a heavenly glow. Outside, a large tree swayed gently in the breeze, its shadow dancing on the walls. Two birds landed on a branch, chirping and hopping like Irish dancers.

But as the dream progressed, the atmosphere shifted. The door to the room, slightly ajar, slammed shut with an unnatural force. Jack turned, puzzled; the breeze wasn't strong enough to have caused it. When he tried to open the door, the knob turned uselessly in his hand. The window, which had been open and letting in the morning breeze, suddenly slammed shut, shaking the glass panes. A dark, ominous cloud rolled in, blotting out the sun. The once-friendly branches of the tree now clawed at the window, skeletal and menacing. The room grew cold and dark, the air thick with foreboding.

A murder of crows replaced the chirping birds, their red eyes glowing ominously. They lined up on the branches, watching Jack with a predatory stillness. The tree creaked under their weight, and the air buzzed with tension. Jack felt trapped, terror rising in his throat.

A lightning bolt split the sky, illuminating the room in a blinding flash. The crows took flight, their wings flapping frantically. The thunder followed almost immediately, shaking the house. Jack instinctively counted the seconds between the lightning and thunder. "One Mississippi, two Mississippi." The storm loomed dangerously close. Suddenly, a brilliant flash of lightning tore through the sky, illuminating the scene in a stark, eerie glow. The bolt struck the now frantic tree with a deafening crack, sending a shower of fiery embers into the air. The lightning cleaved through a massive limb, splitting it violently and sending it crashing to the ground with a resounding thud that echoed through the stormy night. The impact scattered leaves and debris, adding to the chaotic, electrifying atmosphere. Jack's dream had turned into a nightmare. Fearing the next strike would hit the house, he dove under the covers.

He felt a chill run down his spine as the room fell into a strange silence. The storm seemed to pause, the only sound being the heavy drumbeat of his heart. Jack knew he couldn't stay hidden forever. He peeked out from under the covers, only to be greeted by the sight of shadows creeping along the walls. They moved with a life of their own, stretching and twisting in the moon's pale light.

"Come with us, Jack," they whispered. "You belong with us," they moaned. "We've come for you, Jack. Let go; you belong to us." The voices melded together, a weird chorus echoing in the dark.

"JACK!"

Jack spun around, his heart pounding in his chest. In the dimly lit corner of the room, a figure sat hunched over—a figure that looked eerily like his father. But was it? The resemblance was there, yet distorted, twisted into a grotesque version of the man Jack barely remembered. The face was a cruel caricature, features exaggerated and warped into something almost monstrous. Shadows clung to the figure, making it hard to tell where reality ended, and the nightmare began. Maggots crawled from open wounds, and rotting flesh clung to the bones. Once a familiar blue, the eyes were now glowing red, bulging grotesquely, with thick, crimson veins snaking across the whites.

Jack's breath caught in his throat. He screamed, "NO! NO! NO!" and crumpled to the ground, overwhelmed by terror. The room spun around him; the nightmare too real to bear. As he collapsed, darkness swallowed him, and everything went silent. It was over.

TWENTY-FIVE
THE EASY WAY OUT

BRAD LAY awake in his bedroom, unable to find sleep. Since his arrest, restful nights had become a distant memory. He wasn't the big shot he once thought himself to be; his friends had abandoned him, and even his mother had disowned him. Now, out on bail, he faced an impending court hearing just weeks away. The outcome felt inevitable; he was convinced he was headed for juvie, with the only question being how long he'd be there.

The thought of juvenile detention terrified him. He had heard chilling stories about the beatings and assaults that occurred there. One of his so-called friends, who had spent time in detention, had shared harrowing tales. Though his friend claimed these things had happened to others and not to him, he still warned Brad to comply with everything to avoid further beatings. "It doesn't matter how tough you are. There's always someone tougher," he had cautioned.

As Brad reflected on his life, all he could see was the trouble he had caused. He hadn't cared about school, had made enemies almost as a pastime, and was now despised by his own mother. His future seemed bleak; there was no light at the end of the tunnel. The only person he had ever felt a connection with was his father, an alcoholic. While Brad had cherished moments of camaraderie with his father, they often ended in violent outbursts fueled by alcohol. With no prospects and a deep sense of despair, Brad decided he couldn't go on. He made up his mind.

As he hastily packed his rucksack, strange sounds outside his window caught his attention. He tripped and fell against the bedpost, hitting his head hard. A lump quickly formed, and with eyes watering, he cursed and kicked the shoes that had caused his stumble. Struggling to regain his footing, he moved to open the stubborn window. Peering out into the backyard, he saw a trash can moving slowly, seemingly on its own. It toppled over, revealing a large rat, sending a shiver down his spine. The smell of rot wafted up, almost suffocating him. Unnoticed, a dark shadow loomed behind him, cast by the overhanging roof's eave.

As the night clouds parted, moonlight illuminated the upturned bin and scattered trash. Across the road, under a streetlight, stood an old man holding a brown paper bag. He had long gray hair and appeared to be of Native American descent. Brad felt an irrational surge of anger at the man's piercing gaze.

"What are you looking at, creep?" Brad shouted, frustration and anger bubbling up inside him. The old man remained silent; his piercing gaze unbroken. "Hey, Cochise, go back to the reservation," Brad sneered, throwing out the taunt in a mix of bravado and insecurity. The old man, undeterred, simply raised his brown paper bag to his lips, ignoring the insult. His silence and unyielding stare only intensified Brad's irritation, making him feel even more unsettled.

Frustrated, Brad climbed back through the window and closed it, trying to shut out the stench and the old man's unsettling presence. For added security, he drew the curtains. Suddenly startled by a shadow, he spun around, only to realize it was an overcoat hanging from his door. He switched on his bedside lamp and checked behind a large chair in the corner of his room. Finding nothing, he turned off the light and climbed back into bed.

But the room had gained a new smell, not the thick smell of the joint that Brad had smoked earlier but a new smell. Brad returned to the window to ensure it was properly closed. It was locked, yet the old man had vanished. Shivering from the eerie encounter, he sniffed the air, trying to locate the source of the odor. He searched under his bed, in his trash bin, and behind his dressing table for rotting food or dirty socks. A creaking sound caught his attention, but he dismissed it as the old plumbing in the hundred-year-old house.

Sitting at the end of his bed, Brad stared into the emptiness of his bleak future; the reality of the situation now taking hold, suffocating and relentless. *I won't end up like my father,* he thought, though the conviction felt hollow. *It's over for me.* Slowly, he reached into his drawer, pulling out a pen and a scrap of paper. With a trembling hand, he began to write, each word heavy as though dragging him deeper into the abyss of his despair.

As he whispered each word under his breath, a shadow rose behind him, creeping along the wall, growing darker and more solid, an eerie presence taking form in the dim light. The air thickened, and the room grew colder as the shadow loomed closer, almost palpable, as if his despair itself had summoned it. He could feel it behind him, an oppressive weight pressing in, feeding off each word he scribbled on the page, each syllable a silent invocation.

TWENTY-SIX
THE ALGEA

THE NEXT MORNING, Mrs. Marshall called up to Brad's room. It was getting late, and he had an appointment with his court-appointed solicitor at 8:30 a.m. After several unanswered calls, she decided to bring breakfast up to him. The air felt thick with unease as she ascended the stairs. She knocked on his door but received no response.

"Brad," she called out. Still nothing. She placed the tray on the floor and retrieved the spare key from her bedroom. Unlocking the door, she picked up the tray and backed into the room, pushing the door open with her hip as she entered.

"It's no use hiding away in here. You have to face the world sometime." As she moved towards the dressing table, her tone remained firm yet hopeful. "Come on, Brad, it's time to—" Her words froze as her gaze shifted to the mirror, viewing the horrific scene within its frame.

Brad hung motionless from the doorway of the en-suite bathroom, his face a ghastly shade of blue, eyes bulging in a grotesque expression of final agony. Veins protruded starkly against his skin, winding like dark vines across his throat and temples. A desperate flicker of hope surged within her, and she rushed toward him, praying for a sign of life. But as she drew closer, that hope dimmed.

His mouth was stained with dried blood, his half-severed tongue hanging grotesquely by a thin sinew. Thick, congealed threads of mucus and blood stretched from his mouth, marking his final breaths. The droplets had long since ceased, pooling thickly on the bathroom floor, a silent testament to his final, desperate moments.

In a frantic attempt to save him, she tried to lift his weight, her hands fumbling as she struggled to loosen the noose. Her feet slipped in the blood pooling beneath them, her frantic efforts thwarted as her strength began to fail. Desperate, she grabbed a dull knife from the breakfast tray nearby. Climbing onto the bedside stool, she began to saw at the rope, each stroke slow and agonizing, as though time itself had thickened to resist her every movement. Finally, with a last, painful push, the rope frayed and gave way.

Covered in blood, she collapsed to the floor, cradling Brad's lifeless body, her entire being racked by sobs. The finality of his choice that night was devastatingly clear—his despair had led him to an irreversible end. She let out a scream, raw and piercing, a sound so anguished it seemed to echo into eternity. The air grew heavy, darkening as if the heavens themselves had heard her cries. Clouds thickened, blocking out the sunlight, casting the room in a chilling shadow.

And within that shadow, something shifted—dark, menacing, a presence that seemed to reach out as if in response to her anguish. She held Brad tighter, unwilling to release him, her grip fierce as the shadow loomed closer. For a fleeting, harrowing moment, she thought death itself had come to take her son's soul, to finish what despair had begun.

Then, as quickly as it had gathered, the darkness dissipated, and sunlight pierced through the clouds, flooding the room and chasing the shadow back to wherever it had come. But no light could penetrate the cold void that now consumed her, no warmth could console the endless sorrow of a mother holding her dead son in her arms, the echoes of despair lingering long after the darkness had retreated.

TWENTY-SEVEN
THE CRIME SCENE

IT WASN'T long before the police arrived, their presence quickly attracting a small crowd around the Marshall house. Like ghouls drawn to a morbid spectacle, onlookers tried to catch a glimpse of the tragedy unfolding inside. A local news camera crew was already on the scene, reporting live on the breaking news.

"I'm John Sable, and this is SCN, bringing you news as it happens," the reporter announced, his voice steady despite the chaotic scene unfolding around him. "Here we have the latest in a tragic story at the Marshall residence." His words faded slightly as the camera panned over the scene, capturing the flashing lights, the line of officers, and the tense energy surrounding the cordoned-off area.

Just then, a car screeched to a halt nearby, drawing attention. A young, clean-cut man stepped out from the passenger side, his movements sharp and purposeful. With a quick flash of his gleaming detective's badge from his jacket pocket, he ducked under the police tape. Moments later, another man climbed out of the driver's side—a slightly older, rumpled figure with a bit of a paunch. After presenting his badge to the officer at the perimeter, he followed close behind, trailing the younger detective with a steady, knowing stride.

"Hi, John, can you tell us the latest?" a distant voice crackled over the reporter's earpiece, cutting through the background noise.

"Well, Ray," John replied, focusing his gaze on the scene, "what we know so far is that it's currently being treated as a suicide. However, the arrival of two plainclothes detectives suggests there may be more to this story than we initially thought." His tone was measured, hinting at the complexities unfolding behind the scene he was reporting on.

The camera zoomed back in on the detectives as they approached the house. Their expressions were determined, perhaps indicating questions and layers to the tragedy that had yet to be uncovered.

The two detectives entered the house and made their way to the scene upstairs. As they reached the top of the stairs, the younger detective—Clean Cut—glanced to his right and saw Mrs. Marshall. Her face and arms were encrusted with dried blood, and fresh tears streaked down her cheeks, mingling with the crimson stains. She clutched a once-white handkerchief, now stained with a mix of blood and tears, sobbing deeply as a female officer tried to console her. Clean Cut sensed his partner, Harper, coming up behind him. He caught Harper's eye and gestured for him to handle the situation. Harper approached Mrs. Marshall and gently instructed the young officer to give them a moment.

The young female officer brushed past Clean Cut, exchanging a soft, empathetic look with him before moving on. The detective continued to the scene upstairs, pulling a pair of rubber gloves from his pocket. He tore open the packet, removed the gloves, folded the empty packet neatly, and placed it back in his pocket. Standing in the doorway, he snapped the gloves on with a crisp *crack*, the sound cutting through the room's commotion. Muffled voices, distant sirens, and garbled radio chatter filled the air, occasionally punctuated by the clicking of cameras.

Clean Cut cautiously entered Brad's room, pushing the door open and stepping inside deliberately to avoid disturbing the scene. Nothing Clean Cut did was left to chance; he had made detective by twenty-five, following in the footsteps of his father and grandfather, both high-ranking officers. His pedigree ensured a bright future, but Clean Cut had his sights set higher: the FBI.

Inside the room, Clean Cut spotted a familiar face, one he hadn't seen in a while—a stout man with graying hair and a well-worn expression, his badge reading *O'Brien*. The man looked close to retirement age; his rank of sergeant displayed prominently. He was deep in conversation with a forensic officer, his thick Irish accent cutting through the quiet hum of activity in the room.

"Hey, Bill!" Clean Cut called out, addressing him by his familiar nickname.

Surprised, Officer O'Brien turned and grinned, his eyes lighting up with recognition. A hint of a smile broke through his otherwise serious expression as he acknowledged the man's greeting. "Well, if it isn't JJ," he replied, stepping over, his voice carrying a warmth that softened the grim atmosphere around them. "Look at ya, that's a nice suit you've got there —all clean cut and sharp. In fact, 'Clean Cut' is my new name for ya."

He preferred JJ, but accepted the compliment with an easy smile, taking it as it was intended.

Bill's voice softened as he laid a large, steady hand on JJ's shoulder. "How's your Da doing?" His tone held genuine concern, layered with nostalgia, a reminder of the close ties between their families

"Fine, he's doing fine," JJ replied.

"It's terrible about... well, ya know, the big C. But if anybody can beat it, it's the captain. You tell him me and the boys will be around soon. It's been a while. I miss takin' all his money at poker. He's a lousy bluffer." Bill chuckled, reminiscing about the old days. "Sad to hear about Grace, you have her smile. I remember your ma, she was a looker, she was."

Both men were lost in fond memories for a moment, then they got back to business.

"So, where ya been lately, son? Haven't seen ya around the precinct much," Bill asked.

JJ smiled. "Been away, doing this and that."

Before JJ could continue, Bill interjected, "Don't tell me—FBI." There was pride in his voice.

"Well, I've got a few tests to take—aptitude, physical stuff, you know the drill. I just hope I've got what it takes," JJ replied modestly. "So, what's the story here, Bill?"

"We've got a note, a motive—nothing too unusual. The boy was apparently depressed about an upcoming court case," Bill explained.

JJ interrupted, "That's right! I remember now. This is Chad Marshall's boy, Bradley. He locked his school caretaker in a cellar for a few days. The man nearly died. I read about the case a few months ago and did a bit of legwork on it. He was due in court soon."

"Today," Bill clarified.

"The boy would've probably got three years in juvie, maybe more. That couldn't have been much to look forward to," JJ mused.

"Yeah, those places can be pretty rough for a blond, pretty boy like him," Bill added.

JJ glanced over to the bed, his eyes catching on something partially hidden beneath it. He took a step closer, squinting. "It seems he was also partial to a drop of the good stuff," he remarked, reaching down carefully. With the tip of his pen, he lifted an empty whiskey bottle, holding it up to the light before slipping it into a clear plastic evidence bag. He marked it with an 'A' in thick black marker, sealing it with practiced precision.

"Look, son, it's open and shut. You don't want to bother yourself with this. You've got real crimes to solve. Leave this to us old guys," Bill suggested, respectfully.

"Thanks, Bill, but I think I'll stick around for a bit, speak to the boy's mom, tie everything up," JJ replied.

"Alright, JJ. Say hi to your Da for me. You're looking good, son. Stay safe."

"Yeah, you too, Bill. The streets are a scary place," JJ said with a smile as Bill tipped his hat and headed downstairs to deal with the waiting press and cameras.

With personnel still milling around, JJ surveyed the room. Moments later, the coroner arrived. Before they took the body away, JJ quickly examined it, noting the signs of asphyxiation and the gruesome state of Brad's severed tongue. The body was placed in a black bag and removed.

JJ meticulously inspected the room, stepping over the chalk outline where Brad had fallen. He walked over to the dresser, his gaze catching on a folded piece of paper lying there—the suicide note. It was brief, a final apology scrawled in hurried script, the ink smudged in places as if written with trembling hands. The words were laced with despair, yet amidst the bleakness lay a flicker of warmth, a tender acknowledgement of his mother's love that seemed to linger in the carefully chosen phrases.

He unfolded the note fully and read it, his lips moving silently over each word, absorbing the sorrow embedded within.

Sorry, Momma, for everything. You and everyone else don't deserve my shit. If I could change it all, I would, but I can't. Goodbye.

A moment passed as he held the note, feeling the pain of a child's last words and its finality. Then, with a measured breath, he slipped it into an evidence bag marked 'B', sealing it with the care reserved for something fragile, almost sacred.

JJ methodically opened each drawer, carefully sifting through its contents, his movements deliberate and precise. When he closed the last drawer, his attention shifted to the open window. A few steps later, he was peering into the yard below, his eyes narrowing as he spotted an upturned trash can—an odd detail that piqued his curiosity.

As he studied the scene, something caught his eye—a faint, metallic glint nestled in the window frame. Moving closer, JJ noticed a key lodged in the crevice. Without hesitation, he reached into his jacket pocket, retrieving a set of tweezers. Handling them with practiced caution to avoid smudging any potential fingerprints, he expertly extracted the key, his focus sharp and unwavering. Once the key was free, he carefully bagged it, marking the evidence tag with a bold 'C'.

Just as he finished, the door creaked open, and Harper entered the room. Oblivious to the delicate nature of the scene, he nearly stepped into a small, dark puddle of blood—the chilling remnant of Brad's severed tongue.

JJ's eyes flicked to the puddle, a silent reminder of the grim reality they were unraveling. "Whoa! Watch out," JJ called, stopping Harper in time.

Harper sidestepped the blood and asked, "So, what's the story, buddy? We got a suicide?"

"It seems that way," JJ replied, though his tone lacked conviction. He moved to the back of the door where Brad's rucksack lay crumpled. He examined its contents and continued, "How's his mom?"

"Not well, but that's understandable," Harper replied, glancing around the room.

"Yeah, I suppose," JJ murmured, checking the rucksack. A spare set of clothes, motorbike keys, an address book, a bag of weed, a large bag of potato chips, a pen knife, and a *Playboy* magazine were all neatly placed in the bag.

"What have you found there, Columbo?" Harper asked.

Still holding the rucksack, JJ stood up and opened it, revealing its contents to Harper. He carefully placed them into a larger evidence bag marked 'D'. JJ then straightened up and looked at Harper, his expression one of disbelief.

"What suicide victim do you know packs an overnight bag and a copy of *Playboy*?" JJ asked; his tone laced with skepticism.

Harper, caught off guard by the question, could only shrug his shoulders in response. He had no answer, and the implications of JJ's observation were clear: this might not have been a suicide after all.

As they stood there, a female officer entered the room carrying a box. JJ methodically transferred everything he had collected from the scene into it, his movements steady and precise. Once all the items were inside, he removed the self-seal strips and secured the box tightly. He then signed the officer's clipboard, formally documenting the chain of custody.

JJ nodded and offered a small, appreciative smile as the officer turned to leave. She departed, leaving the door slightly ajar. It was then that JJ noticed Brad's mother, Mrs Marshall, lingering quietly just outside, her face a mixture of grief and exhaustion.

He approached her with a careful respect, understanding the sensitivity of the moment. Gently, he asked, "Mrs. Marshall, may I ask you something? Did your son drink alcohol?"

She looked at him, momentarily confused. "What?"

"Alcohol. Whiskey," JJ clarified softly.

She shook her head, her voice cracking slightly. "No, he hated it. The smell made him nauseous. And... well, he despised it because of his father, Chad. He couldn't stand it when his father drank."

"Thank you, Mrs. Marshall," JJ replied, his voice quiet with sympathy. "I'm truly sorry for your loss."

She nodded, her eyes distant, and then turned slowly, heading to the bathroom to wash her hands and remove the remnants of her son's blood from her skin, needing to shed the last painful traces of the morning.

"Why did you ask her about the whiskey?" Harper inquired, watching JJ closely.

"I found a bottle under his bed," JJ replied, his tone edged with quiet curiosity.

Both detectives stood in contemplative silence as the investigation began to wind down. The low hum of voices, the click of cameras—all had faded as the room emptied, leaving behind a stillness, a somber quiet.

There were loose threads, questions lingering unanswered, and JJ couldn't shake the uneasy feeling that something about this scene wasn't right. The whiskey bottle beneath Brad's bed seemed out of place, clashing with his mother's insistence that he despised alcohol. It was a small, almost innocuous detail, but JJ remembered his father's words: *Small details have a way of unraveling deeper truths.*

He exchanged a glance with Harper, both of them sensing that they had barely scratched the surface of whatever lay hidden beneath the tragedy.

TWENTY-EIGHT
JUST ONE MORE THING

IT WAS STILL EARLY MORNING, and Rose had just brewed a fresh pot of coffee. The rich aroma of the roast wafted through the air as she prepared the tray. Standing upright, she paused in thought, the popping sound of the toaster breaking her reverie. The enticing scent of fresh coffee made her smile. Life was almost back to normal. With a slight skip in her step, she made her way to Jack's room. Quietly, she eased open the door and entered. Not wanting to wake him, as he needed the rest, she tiptoed to the window and opened it slightly to let in some fresh air. As the morning light softly filled the room, she noticed the bed was empty. Surprised, she looked around and called out, "Jack, are you up?" She glanced toward the en-suite and caught a glimpse of feet protruding from the doorway.

"Jack!" she cried as she rushed over. He was fully clothed in jogging bottoms, sneakers, and a hoodie. "Oh my God, not again," she muttered, kneeling by his side and shaking him gently. He slowly came around, looking dazed.

"Is there a fire?" he mumbled, still disoriented.

"Jack, where have you been? Why are you dressed?" Rose asked, her concern evident. Jack seemed more puzzled than Rose, but before he could respond, the doorbell rang.

"Who could that be at this time in the morning?" Rose wondered aloud as the doorbell rang again.

"Whoever it is, they're very impatient," Jack added groggily.

"Stay there, I'll be back in a second. Are you sure you're okay?" Rose asked.

Still confused, Jack nodded, and began pulling himself onto the bed, wincing as though he had a pain in his side. He lay back.

The doorbell's now-annoying chime rang out repeatedly.

"For God's sake, okay, I'm coming," Rose muttered, losing her patience. She hurried to the door, wondering who it could be so early in the morning. Peering through the peephole, she recognized one of the figures as the detective who had taken her statement regarding Jack's case. She opened the door.

"Hi, Detective..." Rose paused, struggling to remember his name.

"Jackson, ma'am," the detective replied.

"That's right, Detective Jules Jackson," Rose said, her voice jubilant as if expecting a reward for remembering. Jules seemed a fitting name for the detective's smooth, clean-cut image, but he appeared slightly uncomfortable with Rose's emphasis on it.

"JJ, ma'am," he corrected, offering a small smile.

"What?" Rose snapped, momentarily taken aback.

"JJ, ma'am. My friends call me JJ," he clarified, extending an olive branch.

"So, Detective, what can I do for you?" Rose asked, her tone shifting to something more businesslike. She stepped aside, allowing them to enter. "I've just made some coffee. Would you like a cup?" she offered. Once they had settled in the living room, Rose excused herself to the kitchen, swiftly preparing the coffee. She returned moments later, placing a tray on the coffee table. The detectives took their seats, and a quiet tension filled the room, anticipation building as they readied themselves to discuss what had brought them there so early.

JJ, with his coffee cup and saucer in hand, rose from his seat and casually walked over to the sideboard.

Rose shifted in her chair, uncomfortable as she watched the detective.

He picked up a silver frame, studying a recent photo of Rose and Jack.

"Is there something I can help you with, Detective?" Rose asked her voice tight with unease.

After a moment's pause, JJ carefully placed the frame back, his gaze drifting thoughtfully around the room. His movements were deliberate, almost leisurely, reminiscent of his literary hero, Columbo. His attention lingered over a few more photographs on the sideboard.

"So, it's just you and Jack, then? I don't see any pictures of other family members," JJ remarked, his tone casual but probing.

Rose's response was guarded; instead of answering directly, she countered with a question of her own. "I asked what brings you here, Detective?"

JJ turned back to her, offering a small, unreadable smile.

Her discomfort was growing more apparent. Seemingly unbothered, Detective Jackson took a slow sip of his coffee before finally breaking the heavy silence. "How is Jack?" he asked, his tone deceptively casual.

"Fine," Rose replied quickly, eager to regain control of the conversation. "So, why are you here? Is there a problem?"

Detective Jackson returned to his seat next to Harper, carefully placing his cup on the table.

Rose glanced nervously between the two detectives as an uneasy silence settled between them.

Harper gestured towards the biscuits on a side plate. "Do you mind if I...?"

"No, please, help yourself," Rose said, her tone polite but strained.

"And you, Detective?" Rose trailed off, waiting for a reply.

"Not for me, thanks. It's the sugar—'once on the lips, twice on the hips,' as my mother would say," JJ responded, glancing at Harper, who had already devoured one sugary treat and now seemed uncertain whether to have another.

Rose placed her cup back on the table, stood up, and went to her bag. After a brief rummage, she pulled out a pack of Marlboros. Lighting a cigarette, she took a deep drag, closing her eyes as she slowly exhaled a thick cloud of smoke, savoring the moment. She returned to her seat and sat down.

Detective Jackson spoke again. "Brad Marshall—remember him?"

Rose, caught off guard, let her cool, calm demeanor slip, replaced by a flash of fiery anger that visibly unsettled the detectives. "Remember him? The little shit. I'll never forget that creep, and neither will Jack." Her voice grew more agitated with each drag of her cigarette, the tip glowing bright red with every long inhale. As she exhaled a thick plume of smoke settled around her. She continued, "So, what's the little creep been up to now? Don't tell me he's still terrorizing decent people. He should be locked up."

"When was the last time you saw him?" Detective Harper asked.

"Not since they arrested him. And if I had, I'd have strung him up for what he did to Jack."

The two detectives exchanged glances before turning their attention back to Rose. "Well, you won't have to," JJ said, waiting for her reaction. "Seems he beat you to it. He hung himself last night."

At that moment, Jack entered the room.

"Hi, honey," Rose quickly extinguished the cigarette and walked over to Jack, still ignoring the detective's news.

"Who's hanged themselves?" Jack asked.

"Nobody important, Jack. Go back to bed, and I'll bring you some breakfast in a moment," Rose replied.

Detective Jackson pressed further, "How about you, Jack? When did you last see Brad Marshall?"

Jack looked directly at JJ. "I haven't seen him since the day he tried to kill me, Officer. Why, has he gone and hung somebody now?" he quipped.

"Yes, Jack," JJ paused for dramatic effect, "himself."

The detective waited for a reaction, possibly even a confession. But Jack's face showed only remorse, if anything. He slumped into a chair behind him, running a hand through his unkempt hair. "My God! Poor boy. How's his mom taking it?" Jack seemed genuinely concerned, but Rose was having none of it.

"Poor boy?" she snapped, her voice boiling over.

"Nobody deserves to die, Rose. It's not Christian."

Rose shook her head in disbelief at Jack's sympathy. "Not Christian?" she hissed through gritted teeth. "An eye for an eye, that's in the Bible. Don't talk to me about being Christian. I've read the book, got the T-shirt. Did anyone check the creep's scalp? You'd probably find '666' etched into it. The boy was the Antichrist, and you're saying, 'Poor boy.' He's done us all a favor, especially the taxpayers. He would have ended up in jail eventually. My Christian charity ran out when he tried to kill you."

"He didn't try to kill me. It was a prank that went wrong, that's all. Yes, he deserved to be punished, but not this way."

The room fell silent, the tension thick enough to cut with a knife.

Detective Jackson broke the silence, "Okay, we won't keep you any longer." The two detectives stood, followed by Jack.

Rose had lit another cigarette and took a deep drag. This did not go unnoticed by JJ, and he wasn't sure whether she was a chain smoker or there was something troubling her. He smiled. "Thanks, Rose, for your time. We won't bother you again. Take care now."

Rose barely acknowledged their departure with a forced smile.

As they reached the door, Jack spoke, "Look, Detective, I'm sorry about Rose. She doesn't mean it. She just gets a little protective now and then."

"That's okay, Jack. You take care," Detective Jackson replied as Jack closed the door behind them.

Jack made his way into the kitchen returning to the living room, a piece of toast in one hand and a glass of milk in the other.

NOW'S AS *good a time as any,* she thought, steeling herself for the conversation she'd been avoiding.

"Jack, where have you been? And why are you dressed?" she asked, her voice firm but laced with worry.

He rolled his eyes, shrugging. "I couldn't sleep, so I went for a walk. Is that a crime now?" His tone was edged with sarcasm, a defensive barrier that felt strangely foreign.

"You're drinking again, aren't you?" she pressed, refusing to let it go.

"Jeez, give it a rest, Rose! You're not my mother," he shot back, his voice laced with irritation.

The response took her aback. His attitude seemed off, almost as if he were someone else entirely. She held her gaze steady, refusing to let his defensiveness throw her. "Have you been taking your medication, Jack? You know what happens when you miss it."

"Yes, yes," he replied dismissively, already making his way back to his room.

Rose sank back into her chair. She hoped, with silent desperation, that he wasn't slipping again—that his demons weren't creeping back to haunt them both. The house seemed heavier somehow, thick with an anxiety she hadn't felt in years.

TWENTY-NINE
CHARLIE SMILER

AS THE DETECTIVES walked down the corridor and made their way out of the building, Harper couldn't help but chuckle. "So, Columbo, is it open and shut suicide, or do we have a murder on our hands?"

Detective Jackson frowned. "That woman has some issues, jeez! And did you smell something when Jack opened the door when we left?"

"Yeah, whiskey," Harper replied. "So he likes a shot first thing. It's not a crime, you know."

"True," JJ agreed. "But why was he dressed in a tracksuit and sneakers? If you're going for a jog, you don't polish off half a bottle of whiskey."

"Come on, JJ, you're clutching at straws. There's no crime here."

"Maybe," he muttered, still unconvinced. They got into the car and drove away.

That afternoon, JJ pored over the Brad Marshall case file, his eyes tracing every detail for the third time that day. He wasn't ready to let it go—something about the case didn't sit right with him. Leaning back, he tapped his teeth with the end of a pencil, deep in thought, before sipping his coffee, grimacing at its coldness. With a sigh, he tossed the file into his empty inbox, a silent signal that he wasn't done with this yet. He couldn't shake the instinct that something was off.

With a sudden burst of energy, he spun around in his chair, letting the spring propel him to a standing position, executing the move with practiced precision. Striding briskly to the coffee machine, he poured himself a fresh cup, raising it as he called over his shoulder, "Harper! Want a coffee?"

"No thanks, I gotta pee," Harper replied, veering off toward the restroom.

The day pressed on, and the precinct descended into its usual state of organized chaos. Drunks, prostitutes, and pimps filled the holding seats, a steady hum of noise echoing through the station, adding to the relentless cacophony of noise.

In the afternoon, JJ returned to his desk, casting a weary gaze over the scene, letting out a tired sigh. The job had become too predictable, too routine. He yearned for something more—a challenge that would push him, force him to rely on his instincts and wits. A high-stakes bank heist, perhaps, or the pursuit of a cunning serial killer—something that would make him feel truly alive in his work.

His mind drifted to Quantico, where he would soon begin his training at the FBI Academy. He pictured himself excelling there, passing with distinction, and finally escaping this dreary precinct for the adrenaline-charged streets of Washington or LA. This small city was fading into the past, but he couldn't shake the feeling that one last mystery here needed his attention—and he couldn't leave it unsolved.

But before his thoughts could fully settle on his ambitious future, a commotion erupted at the front desk, pulling him harshly back to reality. Irritated, JJ stood to investigate, spotting an elderly Native American man swaying unsteadily, clearly under the influence.

Something about the man immediately caught JJ's attention. His thick, wiry gray hair, pulled back by tiny multicolored beads, and his deeply creased face, resembling weathered stone, suggested a hard life. JJ noted the man's large, calloused hands, dirt embedded under his fingernails—some blackened—and an ornate bracelet hanging loosely from his wrist. But something didn't sit right. His clothes, while wrinkled and a bit stained, were relatively clean for someone supposedly living on the streets.

The usual signs of a vagrant were absent—no string holding up his trousers, no half-empty bottles bulging from his pockets. His shoes, though simple, were neat and polished. Despite the coolness of late summer nights, he wore only a thin yellow cotton shirt beneath a wool pullover and a tasseled waistcoat. JJ doubted this man was homeless.

One glaring detail confirmed JJ's suspicion: the absence of fingerless gloves. Anyone living rough, especially in this weather, wouldn't be without them. JJ's instincts sharpened—this man, despite his clear inebriation, wasn't just another drifter. *Something else is at play here*, JJ thought. Was his imagination running wild, or did he secretly hope something was unfolding? Or was it his sharp reasoning and honed powers of deduction kicking in?

JJ smiled to himself. It was all of those things, but most importantly, it was a gut feeling. He thought of his father, his hero, alongside the legendary detective Columbo, whose powers of observation and deduction JJ had always admired. He recalled snippets of his father's advice: *Always trust the unconscious signals that transmit through the gut —never dismiss them until you have all the facts.*

JJ resumed his scrutiny of the old man, searching for those facts, and noting his nervous, edgy demeanor. At first, JJ had thought the man was harmless—just a little too inebriated. But then he caught sight of the man eyeing the young officer's gun, prominently displayed on his hip.

As the situation unfolded, JJ realized the man might be more dangerous than he first thought. The rookie officer at the front desk had made a critical error by not handcuffing the man upon arrest. The old man grew more agitated, prompting JJ to instinctively reach for his own weapon, undoing the safety strap. His instincts were on high alert, ready for action.

In an instant, the old man shoved the rookie aside and snatched the gun from his holster. He spun around, frantically waving the weapon at anyone in his path, including a young woman and Detective Kowalski, who was too distracted exchanging phone numbers to notice the chaos unfolding. As JJ stormed past them, the severity of the situation became clear. The woman turned, staring down the barrel of the gun, and screamed, her cry piercing through the noise and grabbing the attention of the entire precinct.

Kowalski shielded the woman with one arm while unclipping his holster with the other. He froze momentarily, torn—drawing his weapon could escalate things further. Instead, he acted swiftly, pulling the woman behind the desk to safety while keeping a careful eye on the armed man.

JJ, now with his gun drawn, held off on neutralizing the armed man, opting for de-escalation and pointed his weapon down to the ground. He noticed the safety was still engaged, giving him hope of resolving the situation peacefully without a shot being fired. He tracked the man's movements, keenly aware of the civilians in the room. Just then, Detective Harper, oblivious to what had just transpired, appeared, still adjusting his belt from a visit to the restroom. "Hey, JJ, maybe a coff—" Harper noticed what was happening and instinctively drew his weapon.

JJ quickly held out his arm and gestured for him to hold, shaking his head. Harper, knowing JJ's methods, trusted him and relaxed his stance.

The room fell silent as the standoff reached its peak. JJ, keeping his gun slightly lowered, spoke calmly, "What's your name, friend?" The old man stared back, fear in his eyes.

"They're here," he muttered.

"Who's here?" JJ asked.

"The dark ones, the evil ones Mnedo," the man cried, his voice trembling.

JJ exchanged a puzzled look with Harper, who shrugged, just as confused. The man continued, his voice rising, "nshka, nshka" he chanted, swaying as if in a trance.

JJ knew he had to keep the man talking. "Look, what's your name, friend?"

The man snapped out of his trance. "Charlie, Charlie Grinning Wolf. Folks call me Charlie Smiler." He grinned, showing a surprisingly full set of teeth.

The rookie officer's slight movement caught Charlie's eye, causing him to aim the gun at the rookie.

JJ spoke again, trying to draw Charlie's attention back, "Charlie, look at me. Hey, Charlie, look at me. Calm down. Nobody is going to hurt you. I want you to put the gun down."

Detective Harper inched closer, weapon drawn, safety off, ready for the situation to escalate.

"I'm not going to let them get me like they got the boy," Charlie muttered, his voice trembling with fear.

"Who, Charlie? Who got the boy?" JJ asked, trying to keep him focused, his voice low and steady.

"The shadows, the dark ones," Charlie whispered, his panic rising with each word. "They took the boy, hanged him." His eyes flickered with a desperate gleam as he began to chant, "Mnedo, Mnedo." The name rolled from his lips with a shiver of fear and reverence. Clutching the gun tighter, he glanced around wildly. "I need the gun."

"No, Charlie," JJ coaxed, moving forward, slow and careful. "You don't need the gun. Let me have it."

But Charlie was slipping, the remnants of his sanity fragmenting as he teetered on the edge.

Harper, closing in from the side, gestured to the rookie whose weapon Charlie had snatched, preparing to take action. The movement caught Charlie's attention; he turned, raising the gun to his own head. A collective gasp echoed through the room.

"You don't want to do that," JJ urged, voice firm but calm. "That way, they'd win."

Charlie managed a sad smile. "You're right. Have you seen them? You'll have to kill me. That way, I win." Without warning, he swung the gun towards JJ, eyes flashing with grim resolve.

Harper, quicker than a heartbeat, fired twice. Charlie crumpled, bleeding from two wounds to the chest. Harper rushed forward, kicking the gun out of reach, his face taut with adrenaline and anger.

"Are you crazy?" he yelled at JJ. "He could have killed you! Why didn't you shoot him?"

JJ exhaled slowly; his voice steady but weary. "The safety was on. He was too drunk to notice."

Harper's face went pale as he checked the gun, his fingers trembling slightly as he confirmed it was indeed still on safety. "Fuck," he muttered under his breath, the realization sinking in.

The medical team arrived swiftly, and despite the critical injuries, they managed to stabilize Charlie and rushed him to the hospital.

"JJ, what's your interest in this guy?" Harper asked, still puzzled.

"I'm not sure yet," JJ replied, "but I think he witnessed a murder."

"Whose?"

"Brad Marshall's."

"The kid that hanged himself? JJ, it was suicide, open and shut," Harper insisted, his patience wearing thin with JJ's obsession.

JJ called out to Frank, whose heroic act hadn't gone unnoticed by the woman he'd protected. He had resumed his flirting and, after handing her his card, made the familiar 'call me' gesture as she turned and left.

"Frank, when you're done feathering your nest, I need you to do some legwork," JJ said, eyeing him from across the desk.

Frank smirked. "What's that?"

"I need you to check this guy out. Where he lives, where he eats, drinks—everything," JJ instructed.

"Okay, on it, JJ," Frank replied, turning to head out.

"And Frank," JJ called after him, "I want a guard on Charlie around the clock."

Frank nodded in acknowledgement as JJ grabbed his jacket, preparing to head for the door. Just as he was leaving, an officer approached him—Joseph, whom JJ knew to be Potawatomi.

"Hey, Joseph, were you here when Charlie was shot?" JJ asked.

"Yes, poor guy, he was really shaken," Joseph replied with a somber nod.

"Did you hear what he was saying?" JJ asked, curious.

Joseph's expression darkened slightly. "Yeah. It creeped me out a bit."

JJ struggled to recall the word Charlie had muttered. "So, what does it mean—mondo, mendosi…?" He fumbled with the pronunciation.

Joseph stepped in to help. "Mnedo," he said, his tone lowering. "It means 'evil one.' Or 'demon.' My parents used to tell me stories of Mnedo—a bad spirit that brings nshka, a deep sadness, or misery. Really bad medicine."

JJ exhaled. "Cheers, Jo, I really appreciate that."

Joseph nodded, his expression respectful but grave, before continuing on his way.

JJ lingered a moment, processing the new layer of mystery, his mind racing with questions.

JJ turned to Harper. "Let's go."

"Where we going?" Harper asked, catching his eye.

"To the hospital. Coming?"

"Someone's got to keep you from making an ass of yourself," Harper quipped, grabbing his jacket with a grin.

THIRTY
TOUGH OLD BOOT

THE JOURNEY to the hospital was a quiet one. Both detectives sat in contemplative silence, the weight of the earlier incident lingering. JJ was preoccupied with thoughts of what Charlie might know, while Harper remained skeptical about the whole situation, leaning towards the likelihood of a straightforward suicide.

Upon arriving at the hospital, they quickly inquired about Charlie's room—number 221. JJ wandered down the sterile corridors, noting the typical hospital smell of disinfectant. Finally, they reached the right ward, and JJ said, "Two-two-one, this is it."

But something was off. The guard who should have been posted outside the room was nowhere to be seen. Instead, an empty chair and a half-eaten doughnut were all that remained. A wave of irritation surged through JJ as he swiftly turned, his eyes scanning the corridor for any sign of the missing guard.

As they walked down the corridor, they encountered a young, uniformed officer, Miles, who appeared around the opposite corner, coffee in one hand and a magazine in the other. Oblivious to the detectives' presence, Miles sat down and began reading. JJ doubled back and confronted the officer, his voice firm but controlled.

"What's your name, officer?" JJ snapped, startling the young cop, who quickly stood upright, nearly spilling his coffee.

"Miles," the cop answered swiftly.

"Well, Miles, if you ever leave this door unattended again, I'll have you on school crossing duty before you can blink," JJ warned, maintaining his composure.

The young officer nodded, clearly understanding the gravity of the situation.

Harper interjected, trying to lighten the mood, "He ain't going nowhere, JJ. No need to chew his balls off. Why do you need the guard anyway?"

"To protect him, if he did witness a murder," JJ replied.

"Suicide," Harper interrupted.

"Whatever he saw, he saw something; murder or suicide, I need to put my mind at rest. If it was murder, then the killer might not want Charlie to tell us who he is."

"Or she," Harper added.

"Unlikely, but I suppose," JJ conceded. "But unlikely."

Their conversation was cut short as a woman in scrubs walked by. "Excuse me, nurse," JJ called out.

"Doctor," the woman corrected, her tone sharp.

"No, I'm a detective—Detective Jackson," JJ replied with a polite smile, catching Harper smirking at his partner's quick recovery.

"I'm a doctor, and he's a nurse," she clarified, gesturing towards a large, tattooed man in green scrubs.

THE MAN, Hispanic in appearance and resembling a bouncer rather than a nurse, pushed a wheelchair occupied by a pale, sickly child. Yet the child was laughing softly, sharing a gentle moment with him—a jarring contrast that caught Harper off guard. His hand instinctively rested on his weapon, a reflex born of decades on the force, though he couldn't tell if it was unconscious bias or seasoned instinct preparing him for danger.

Harper's gaze shifted to the man's face, immediately drawn to a snake tattoo curling around his neck, slithering onto his cheek, and encircling his left eye. A strange sense of déjà vu gripped him, stirring something unsettling deep in his gut. Before he could act on the thought or dissect the feeling, the doctor's voice pulled him into the conversation with JJ.

JJ HAD REMAINED focused on the doctor as the nurse passed them both "Sorry, Doctor... Warrick," he read from her ID. "Can you tell me how long until I can speak to the man in room two-two-one?"

"No, I cannot," Dr. Warrick replied curtly.

JJ persisted, "Dr. Warrick, I'm in the middle of a murder case, and this guy may hold the key to that murder."

"Suicide," Harper interjected. JJ shot him a sharp look, prompting Harper to mutter an apology.

"That man may be a witness to a serious incident," JJ corrected himself, continuing, "I need to speak to him as soon as possible. His life may be in danger."

"The only danger to him I see is from you two," Dr. Warrick retorted, walking away, leaving JJ open-mouthed in disbelief.

"I can't believe this place," JJ muttered, still stunned by the doctor's bluntness. "Can you believe she wouldn't help me?"

"You're wrong, JJ. She said she couldn't help you, and if you'd looked more closely at her badge, you'd know why," Harper explained.

"What do you mean?" JJ asked, puzzled.

"She's a psychiatrist," Harper clarified.

"Shit, Harper, she must think I'm a real asshole. Why didn't you help me out?"

"You were doing fine being an asshole all by yourself," Harper quipped, laughing.

JJ, still slightly embarrassed, joked, "Funny."

"Hey, JJ, I think she likes you," Harper teased.

JJ glanced back, catching Dr. Warrick smiling his way. "Did you see that? She smiled at me."

"No, she smiled at me. She was laughing at you," Harper corrected.

"Harper, I think she likes me."

"No, she thinks you're rude, arrogant, and ignorant. But hey, don't let that stop you," Harper shot back with a grin.

Eventually, JJ found the attending doctor. "So, Doc, can I see him?" JJ asked.

"You can, but he's in and out of consciousness," the doctor replied as they approached the door to Charlie's room.

"Is he gonna make it, Doc?" Harper inquired.

"Well, he's stable for now. He lost a lot of blood, but he's fit for his age, so that's good. But you never know. The next couple of hours will be critical," the doctor explained, not sounding overly optimistic.

The doctor led them into the room, where the rhythmic beeping of the cardiac monitor and the steady hiss of the oxygen ventilator filled the air. One of the bullets had punctured Charlie's lung, making mechanical ventilation essential for his survival.

JJ looked down at Charlie, who lay there barely alive, tubes attached to various parts of his body. The scene reminded JJ of his mother during her final days in the hospital, connected to machines, fighting for life, not from a gunshot but a fall down the stairs, she hung on for a few days before she passed, hopefully Charlie would make a full recovery.

Harper, standing by the bed, sighed, "Poor old guy. If only I'd noticed the safety catch was on."

"It wasn't your fault. You did what had to be done. He'll be okay. He looks like a tough old boot," JJ reassured his partner.

After checking Charlie's vitals, the doctor seemed satisfied and, before leaving, opened the window slightly to let in some fresh air. Charlie was stable for now, but only time would tell if he would pull through.

THIRTY-ONE
JUST PASSING BY

THE AFTERNOON SUN filtered through the hospital windows as Jack wandered into the building that had saved his life and nursed him back to health—a place that would forever hold a special place in his heart. He carried a large basket of meticulously arranged flowers in his hand, with a thank you card in the center. After exchanging pleasantries with the familiar, smiling staff who had gathered around, Jack turned to the receptionist and inquired if Dr. Warrick was available.

The receptionist, recognizing Jack, mentioned that he hadn't made an appointment. But the flowers, combined with his fond memory of Jack as a kind and considerate patient, prompted him to bend the rules slightly.

"Good news, Jack, she's available and said she can see you."

"Thanks," Jack replied, glancing at the name tag on the receptionist's uniform, "Ben."

"You're welcome," Ben responded warmly before directing Jack. "Go to the end of the corridor, turn left, and her office is on the right."

Jack thanked him and followed the directions, soon finding himself standing outside Dr. Warrick's office. He paused and took a moment to prepare himself before gently knocking on the door.

"Enter!" came the prompt reply from inside.

Jack stepped into the room, greeted by Dr. Warrick's welcoming smile. "Jack, how are you?" she asked, genuinely pleased to see him.

Summoning the courage that had eluded him for weeks, Jack had finally made the visit. He was really here. "I'm fine. I was just passing by and thought I'd drop in," he replied, closing the door softly behind him.

Dr. Warrick smiled. She knew there was no reason for Jack to be 'just passing by' since the hospital was clear across town. But she didn't press him; she was simply glad to see him. He had been one of her more memorable patients, and although he hadn't scheduled an appointment, her schedule was free for the next hour. She considered this visit part of her non-chargeable lunch break; one of her Cara Care Bear moments.

"So, what's happening in your life, Jack? How are the trains?" she asked, recalling his passion for model trains.

"Fine, though I don't get much time for it now because…" Jack began, his words trailing off into unfinished silence. The pause lingered, waiting, expectant, as they stood facing each other.

Noticing the tension, Dr. Warrick gently pressed him. "So, is this just a social visit, or is there something you'd like to talk about?" she asked, her voice soft yet probing.

"No, as I said, I was just passing by," Jack repeated, his voice calm but his eyes restless, drifting over every corner of the room.

"Okay," Dr. Warrick pressed gently, her curiosity unwavering. "But something must have brought you here. Do you want to talk about it?"

Jack turned slowly toward the window, his back tense, his expression unreadable. Dr. Warrick observed him, her steady gaze silently evaluating him. *You can learn so much by simply watching*, she reminded herself.

"I brought flowers," he murmured, his voice almost swallowed by the stillness as he reached the window. The afternoon light spilled through the partially drawn Venetian blinds, painting a delicate checkerboard of light and shadow across his face, accentuating the hint of vulnerability in his features. He turned his head slightly, his eyes meeting hers for a fleeting moment. "As a thank you for looking after me and helping me heal," he added softly, the words carrying a sincerity that made his voice tremble ever so slightly. Then, as if the moment had become too much, he turned back to the window, retreating into the quiet solace of his thoughts.

Dr. Warrick smiled warmly. "That was very thoughtful of you, Jack."

He returned her smile, and for a brief moment, the doctor found herself noticing the strength in his features—the tanned skin, the fullness of his lips. She quickly dismissed the fleeting thought, reminding herself of her oath and the ethical boundaries that governed her profession. Yet, Jack was no longer her patient; he had been discharged. The memory of his deep blue eyes, which had captivated her from the first moment they met, lingered. Her thoughts wandered briefly until Jack's voice brought her back.

"Nice dog," he commented, nodding toward the ornate silver frame on her desk.

"Yes, he's a great friend," Dr. Warrick replied, seizing the opportunity to steer the conversation. "Do you have many friends, Jack?"

She was trying to draw him out, to peel back the layers of whatever burden he was carrying.

Jack hesitated before answering.

"No, well, some. Actually, just one," he said, making his way over to the couch. Then, after seating himself, he instinctively laid back.

The lunch break was officially over. 'Cara Care Bear' was gone, and Dr. Warrick was back, along with the professional rules she had to follow. She felt a slight pang of guilt for not explaining that the session would now be charged; after all, she did have an expensive divorce to pay for. She also didn't want to interrupt the delicate balance of the moment. Satisfied with her reasoning, she continued.

"And who might that be?" she asked, her curiosity piqued as she sensed more beneath the surface.

"Max" Jack replied, his tone flat.

"Tell me about him," she pressed, leaning in slightly, hoping to uncover more.

Jack shrugged, his eyes drifting away. "Not much to say. He likes trains. We were school friends," he said, letting the words hang in the air before falling silent.

The doctor studied him carefully. She sensed that this 'Max' wasn't significant in Jack's life, just a surface detail, a deflection from what mattered. But there was someone else—someone who held real weight in his heart. She knew who this was, but she needed Jack to open up about her.

"What about Rose? How is she?" she asked, her voice softer, more deliberate.

Jack hesitated, then met her gaze with a question of his own, one that caught the doctor off guard. It wasn't the response she expected, and the shift in the conversation left her with a growing sense that something deeper was at play.

"Do you believe in demons, Doctor?"

Dr. Warrick remained composed. "I've told you before, Jack, they're all in the mind," she replied, standing and moving to perch on the edge of her desk, facing him. She gestured for him to continue.

"So you say," Jack murmured, his voice tinged with doubt. "But just because they're in my mind doesn't mean they're not real to me."

"True," Dr. Warrick conceded, "but sometimes what we think is real is just a trick of the mind. They're not a physical manifestation, and you can defeat them. We need to talk about them; that's how you strip them of their power." She reached for her tape recorder. "Do you mind if I record this conversation?"

Dr. Warrick moved an analyst's chair directly opposite Jack's on the couch. She settled in with a practiced ease, her eyes never leaving his as she reached for the recorder.

Jack shook his head, offering silent consent, aware that this meant the session would be billed. There was a brief moment of mutual understanding—the kind that had formed over the many sessions they'd shared during his recovery.

With a soft click, Dr. Warrick turned on the recorder, her fingers deftly adjusting it as she spoke. "Recording now. Session with Jack, noting the time and date," she stated, her tone steady and clear. She set the device aside, its tiny red light glowing softly, a quiet observer of their conversation.

"Talk to me, Jack. What's been troubling you?" she asked, her tone gentle but attentive, ready to listen and document.

"I'm having nightmares. I hear voices, then I black out."

Dr. Warrick returned and leaned back in her chair; her gaze steady as she encouraged him to continue.

"They got him."

"Who, Jack? Who did they get?"

"The Miseries. They killed him."

"Killed who, Jack? You're not making sense. Who's dead?"

"They tried to get me, but Rose protected me. She's always protected me."

Jack reached into his pocket, pulled out a red handkerchief, and pressed it to his nose, inhaling deeply as if the scent offered him some comfort.

"That's nice, Jack. Who gave you that?" Dr. Warrick inquired gently.

"Rose. She says it's to protect me. She says that God will protect me as long as I have it with me."

The doctor's eyes fell on the intricate gold cross embroidered in one corner of the handkerchief. "Did Rose embroider this?" she asked.

"Yes," Jack replied. "They're a pair. She's very good at that sort of thing."

"So, Jack, tell me, what do you need protection from?"

"You know, Doc. You've seen them. They live in the shadows. They get you when you're down, drive you to drink, and make you see and hear things."

Dr. Warrick's curiosity was instantly piqued. Her mind couldn't help but drift back to the night she had stayed late when she had followed a shadowy figure deep into the bowels of the hospital. Was Jack referring to that eerie night, or was he just waxing lyrical? The connection sent a shiver down her spine, blurring the line between professional detachment and personal unease.

"Who are these demons you talk about, Jack?" she asked, her voice a careful blend of curiosity and concern.

Jack's eyes darkened, and a warning crept into his tone. "You need to be careful, Doc. They can make *you* do things, too."

Dr. Warrick felt a ripple of unease at his uncharacteristically ominous tone. She shifted slightly in her seat, her professional facade wavering just enough for her to wonder, for a brief and unsettling moment, *who was really analyzing whom*?

"Do these demons have a name, Jack?" she asked, steadying her voice and holding his gaze, even as the tension in the room grew.

Jack's once vivid blue eyes now seemed distant, clouded by a fear that made him look almost terrified. Dr. Warrick noticed the shift and felt a pressing need to defuse the moment.

"Jack, speak to me. Who's trying to get you?" she prompted, her voice gentle but urgent.

Jack's lips curled into a faint, humorless smile. "Me, Doc? They're not after *me*. They're after *you*."

Dr. Warrick's pulse quickened. "Who's after me, Jack? Tell me," she urged, leaning forward, her professional calm barely concealing the sense of dread creeping up her spine.

Jack fell silent, his gaze drifting back to the window. The doctor felt a twinge of anxiety. She needed to know if she was in any real danger.

"Tell me, Jack. Who is after me? Am I in danger?" she asked, her voice calm but firm.

Jack's eyes flicked to the window, where shifting light cast long, restless shadows that seemed to gather in the room, as if preparing for some dark revelation. Jack's voice broke the heavy silence. "Not *who*,' he said, his words hanging ominously in the air. He paused, then turned and locked eyes with her, his gaze intense. "*What!*"

"Okay, *what* am I in danger from?" She asked. A sense of fear was beginning to grip her.

Jack's eyes still locked onto hers, unblinking, and with an intensity that sent a shiver down her spine. "The Miseries," he whispered, the fear in his voice so raw, it was almost tangible.

Dr. Warrick watched as Jack's gaze flicked anxiously around the room, his body tense and wary. She noticed his eyes settle for a moment on a shadow in the corner, cast ominously by the coat stand as if he expected something to emerge from it.

Dr. Warrick felt a wave of relief wash over her as the realization dawned—Jack had given his demons, his depression, a name. *The Miseries*. She knew she wasn't in any immediate physical danger, but that didn't ease the tension that was lingering in the room. She understood, both through her professional training and her own painful experiences, just how devastating misery and despair could be. Memories of her own struggles and the echoes of her family's battles with the same misery of despair surfaced momentarily. She fully recognized the reality of Jack's internal war, knowing how relentless and consuming those unseen demons could be. His pain was undeniable, and his struggle was all too familiar.

"You mean depression, Jack."

"No, Doctor. I mean the demons that live in your head. We all have them, but some people are strong enough to keep them locked up, while others let them out. That's when they strike. You can't destroy them; you can only keep them chained. Don't let The Miseries get you, Doc. Stay strong." Jack's voice trailed off; his thoughts seemingly scattered.

The doctor offered a nervous smile, trying to lighten the moment, but Jack's vacant expression remained.

Suddenly, a knock at the door interrupted the tense silence. Dr. Warrick was momentarily startled but quickly regained her composure.

"Enter," she called out.

It was her secretary.

"Dr. Warrick, your 2 p.m. appointment has arrived."

"Thank you, Ben. Give me two minutes."

"Yes, Doctor. Anything else?" Ben glanced at Jack, as he quickly rose and returned to his position by the window, staring out blankly.

"No, that will be all." Dr. Warrick replied.

She watched Ben leave, and after the door closed, she turned her attention back to Jack. She opened her drawer and took out her diary, opening it, and she began flicking through the pages.

"Look, Jack, we need to talk again. I have a slot free next Tuesday at 2 p.m." She tapped the page. "Shall I book you in? That way, we won't be disturbed. Okay?"

Jack turned to face her and smiled, the familiar, gentle expression returning. It was the Jack she remembered from his recovery—a sweet, hopeful man, not the troubled soul he appeared to be now. But who could blame him? There was a lot of work ahead to help him pull back from the edge, but she still had hope for him. She stopped the recorder, removed the tape, and placed it in her drawer for later analysis. Jack was now officially her patient again, and she was determined to help him.

Jack agreed to the appointment time but mentioned he would confirm with Rose. He gently clasped the doctor's hand, smiled warmly, and left the room.

Dr. Warrick watched Jack leave, exhaling a deep breath as the tension began to lift. She turned back to her desk, bracing herself for her next client—a sex addict. She liked this client, and the case would be something a little less taxing, and she hoped it might even lighten her mood. Just then, she noticed the red handkerchief Jack had left behind.

She grabbed the handkerchief, quickly hurrying after him, but he was already long gone. The hospital corridor was nearly deserted, with only a few orderlies pushing wheelchairs quietly down the hall. She looked down at the handkerchief in her hand, her fingers tracing the delicate gold-embroidered cross. Drawn by its sweet, familiar scent, she raised it to her nose, inhaling deeply as she lost herself in thought. A wave of sadness washed over her as she wondered whether she could truly help Jack; only time would tell.

Shaking off the melancholy, she reminded herself that her next client was waiting. As she turned to head back to her office, her eyes fell on the basket of flowers Jack had given her, now proudly displayed on the front desk. The sight brought a small smile to her face. She carefully tucked the handkerchief into her top pocket, knowing she would have the chance to return it to Jack at his next appointment.

As Dr. Warrick made her way back to her office, she crossed paths with the two detectives she had briefly met earlier that day. JJ acknowledged her with a slight nod; his expression tinged with embarrassment from their earlier exchange. He knew he had acted poorly, and she was aware of it, too. Yet, when their eyes met, and she noticed the flush of embarrassment on his cheeks, she offered him a gentle smile—a quiet gesture of forgiveness. He smiled back, relieved, and in that shared moment, the matter was silently resolved.

No words were exchanged; there was no need. The understanding between them was unspoken, the connection clear. After the exchange Dr. Warrick continued on her way, leaving behind a moment of reconciliation that hung quietly in the air.

THIRTY-TWO
POKER FACE

JJ and Harper hurriedly left the hospital, Harper struggled to keep up with JJ's brisk pace. Noticing this, JJ eased back slightly, allowing Harper to catch up.

"What's next, JJ?" Harper asked, slightly out of breath as he fell into step beside him.

"There's nothing we can do right now. We'll just have to wait until Charlie comes around," JJ replied.

As they chatted, JJ noticed Jack at the bottom of the steps.

"Hey, Jack!" JJ shouted. Jack either didn't hear him or was trying to avoid them. JJ's curiosity got the better of him, and he decided to follow.

Harper, uninterested, headed in the opposite direction.

"I'll catch you later, JJ. Call me with an update," Harper said, walking away.

JJ didn't turn; he raised his hand in acknowledgement and continued pursuing Jack. He was just a few yards behind him when he called out again.

"Jack!"

This time, it was impossible for Jack to ignore him.

Jack turned and forced a smile. "Hi, Detective. What brings you here?"

"A case I'm working on. In fact, it's something you might be interested in. But what brings you here?" JJ asked, his tone casual but his eyes sharp.

"Nothing important. I come back now and then for a check-up. So, what case might I be interested in?" Jack's curiosity was piqued.

"The Brad Marshall case."

"I thought that was a cut-and-dried suicide case."

"Yes, that was the initial finding, but now it seems he might not have committed suicide after all."

Jack remained poker-faced, showing no reaction, though sweat began to form on his brow.

"You mean it could be murder? Why would anybody want to kill a young boy?"

"I don't know, Jack. You tell me." JJ was looking for a reaction, but Jack stayed calm, pausing to choose his words carefully.

"What's that got to do with you being here at the hospital?" Jack asked, deflecting.

"That's where our witness is right now. He had an unfortunate accident and got himself shot. Some old Indian guy—seems he saw everything."

Jack paused again, apparently considering his next move. "Well, I hope he pulls through. We don't want murderers roaming around, do we?" Jack's tone was casual, but JJ sensed something beneath the surface.

"You're right there. Anyway, I'll let you go. Got a few leads to run down. Say hi to your sister for me," JJ said, turning to leave.

Jack forced a smile. "Will do."

JJ walked down the steps, glancing back as he reached the bottom. Jack was still standing in the same spot, wiping his brow again, watching JJ leave.

JJ knew he had no real leads and wasn't even sure about the witness, let alone the murder case. Mentioning the old guy wasn't just idle chat; JJ never did anything idly. He had his reasons—a gut feeling, a sixth sense, that Jack knew something. Jack's reaction only fueled JJ's inquisitive, and sometimes overly imaginative, mind.

THIRTY-THREE
MARLBORO MAN

JACK SLOWLY CLOSED the door behind him, wandered into the living room, and gently sat down, though he didn't fully relax. Sitting upright, he ran his hands through his hair and exhaled heavily. His eyes landed on an unopened packet of cigarettes on the table in front of him—Marlboro, his sister's preferred brand, and once his, too. He stared at the tempting pack of death sticks. He reached out and held them in his hand for a moment before he began picking at the plastic wrapper, searching for a way in.

Eventually, he found the thin cellophane strip and peeled it back. Once it was removed, he stared at the packet, almost unsure how to proceed or whether he should. He turned it on its side and read the warning, 'Smoking kills.' He shrugged, "Oh well, we all gotta die someday." In one swift motion, he flipped the lid open, flicked the bottom of the packet, and a single cigarette popped up. Before it could retreat, Jack's lips had encircled it, and a match was struck, sealing its fate. Jack took his first drag, his cheeks hollowing as he inhaled deeply. It had been years since Jack had smoked, and though he had secretly craved this moment, the reality was harsher than expected. Before he could savor it, he heard his sister's voice, startling him and causing him to cough violently.

Between gasps, Jack cursed, "Are you trying to kill me?"

"No, the cigarettes will do that for you," Rose quipped, picking up the packet, extracting a cigarette for herself, and lighting it. She drew back on her cigarette.

Jack spoke. "I thought you were out with your friends tonight?"

"They canceled," she replied, her eyes narrowing as she studied Jack curiously. "So why have you started smoking again, Jack? I thought you quit?"

"I don't know, I just felt like having one."

"Well, it's your life. Does this mean you'll stop nagging me now?" Rose asked, placing her hands on her hips with a smirk.

Jack just frowned and took another drag.

Rose made her way back into the kitchen. As she left the room, she called out, "So, what have you been up to today?"

Jack had two choices: lie and say 'not much' or tell her the truth about visiting the doctor and getting an hour-long lecture.

"Not much," he replied, not in the mood for a lecture.

Drawn by the smell wafting from the kitchen, Jack joined Rose.

"Smells good," he said, leaning against the doorway.

"It should. I've been cooking it all day. It's your favorite—rabbit bake, just like Momma used to make." Rose paused, her gaze drifting and Jack guessed that memories of their mother flooded her thoughts. For a moment, she appeared lost in the warmth of those recollections.

Jack smiled, though he was too young to remember exactly how their momma used to make it—he had been six when she left. All he knew was how Rose made it; to him, it was perfect. The comforting aroma that filled the room, the tender meat, the way Rose carefully prepared it—all of it spoke of love, just as their mother's cooking must have done.

Rose was still lost in her daydream, the memories of their mother swirling in her mind when Jack's soft voice broke through.

"Rose, why did Momma leave us?" he asked, his tone gentle yet tinged with the weight of a question he had long held inside.

She turned to face him, her eyes glazing over. "She had her reasons, but one thing's for sure—she loved you very much."

Jack smiled wistfully. "I wish I could remember her."

"You were so young, Jack, and it was so long ago." Rose's voice was tinged with sadness. "Anyway, what do you want for dessert—chocolate sponge or apple pie?" she asked, quickly changing the subject.

"Apple pie," Jack replied, but his mind was still on their mother. "Don't you ever wonder why she never came back?"

Rose's answer was short and final. "No."

"I mean, she must still be alive somewhere out there."

Rose didn't answer this time; instead, she focused on removing the large pan from the oven.

"Maybe we should put out an ad? 'Desperately seeking Mary Brooks.' She might read it and come home."

Jack's voice was hopeful, but Rose remained silent.

"What do you think?" Jack persisted.

Rose, with her back to Jack, seemed oblivious to his conversation.

"What do you think, Rose?" he pressed.

"No, Jack," Rose replied more sharply this time, banging the potato knife down on the table. Jack didn't notice the tear that had formed in the corner of her eye. She quickly wiped it away, but he knew he had upset her. Rose walked out of the kitchen into the front room and lit another cigarette. She sat down and patted the sofa, beckoning Jack over.

"Look, Jack, sit. It's about your mother," Rose began as he sat beside her.

"Our mother, Rose," Jack corrected softly.

"Yes, Jack, you see she..." Rose paused, wondering whether Jack should hear what she had to say. She stood up and sat on the arm of the chair, facing him. She took another drag of her cigarette and thought for a while. The suspense was too much for Jack.

"Come on, what about Momma?"

Rose had started something she couldn't take back. She had to tell the truth or...

"She wasn't very well when she left. That's why she left," Rose finally said.

"What do you mean 'not well'?" Jack asked, concern growing in his voice.

Rose hesitated, and Jack wondered if there was something she was holding back. She seemed a little edgy as her eyes darted.

"Cancer, Jack. She was terminally ill with the cancer..." Rose gathered her thoughts and took another drag of her cigarette.

Jack sat in stunned silence, waiting for her to continue.

"I woke up one morning, and she was gone," Rose continued, her voice distant.

Jack remained silent, unsure what to say, what to feel. He waited for more, but Rose had said enough—enough to dampen Jack's interest in finding their long-lost mother, at least for now. Though Jack felt sure there was something he was missing, something more she wasn't saying.

With a final draw of her cigarette, Rose leaned forward and crushed it among the other discarded ends in the ashtray. She scooped up the ashtray and made her way back into the kitchen.

Jack just sat there, more upset that Rose hadn't told him sooner than by the revelation that his mother might be dead. He had few memories of his mother—he was just a baby when she left. He wasn't emotionally attached to the revelation, but it was clear that Rose was deeply affected by it. Sensing her vulnerability, Jack decided not to push the issue any further. Instead, he followed her into the kitchen, where he softly apologized for pressing her to reveal such a painful truth.

Rose gave him a gentle smile, a silent acknowledgment that she appreciated his understanding, before turning her attention to the food. She began to serve, the familiar routine bringing a sense of calm. Jack, recognizing the need to shift the conversation, quickly changed the subject as Rose poured thick, dark gravy over the steaming plates in front of them.

They sat together at the table, and for a brief moment, a comforting sense of normalcy wrapped around them as they tucked into their meal.

"I saw Detective Jackson today," Jack mentioned, trying to keep the conversation light. Rose, still focused on pouring the gravy, raised her eyebrows in acknowledgement, encouraging him to continue.

"Is that right? What did he have to say for himself?" she asked.

"Apparently, they think Brad Marshall was murdered, and they have a witness."

Rose suddenly dropped the gravy pot on the table. The hot, thick liquid splashed up like a geyser, engulfing her right hand. She recoiled, knocking over a glass of Merlot she had poured earlier. The glass crashed to the floor, shattering into a million fragments, its contents splashing against the kitchen wall. Jack jumped to her side, grasping her arm and rushing her to the sink. Snatching at the cold-water tap, he frantically turned it on, releasing a high-pressure stream of icy water. He plunged her hand into the cold torrent. Rose winced in pain, but she knew she had to endure it to lessen the inevitable blistering.

"Are you okay?" Jack asked, his voice laced with concern.

"Yes, it's just a little scald. Don't worry. Go on with your story about the detective..." Rose said, trying to recollect the detective's name. "What's his face?"

"Jackson..." Jack filled in, relaxing slightly now that the situation was under control. He cleared the broken glass, brushed the tiny pieces into a dustpan, and discarded them in the trash. He then grabbed a cloth to clean up the wine from the wall. For a moment, as he looked at the dark red liquid splattered against the wall, it felt like he was wiping away blood from a crime scene. The way it meandered down the wall and pooled at the base... Before his imagination could run away with him, he rubbed hard and refocused on his conversation with Rose.

"Anyway, they've got some old guy in the hospital. He's been shot and is in pretty bad shape. Apparently, he's supposed to have witnessed the whole thing, and when he comes around, they're going to question him."

"Who's going to listen to a drunken old Indian guy who's seeing things?" Rose retorted.

"How did you know he was an Indian?"

"Just guessed. Downtown is full of them, drunk and causing trouble."

Jack frowned momentarily, but quickly continued, "Well, the detective seems pretty sure the guy knows something."

"Brad made a lot of enemies in his short, pathetic life. Maybe he got what he deserved," Rose said coldly.

Jack didn't reply. There was no point; he knew Rose had no intention of forgiving Brad for what he had done.

Once he'd finished tidying up, Jack returned to the table and poured them both a generous glass of Merlot. He wasn't particularly fond of wine, especially red, but it would be a shame to let it go to waste. As he sat down, he sensed a tentative truce had settled between them. The discussion about Brad, their mother, and the detective was over—for now.

THIRTY-FOUR
COMING DOWN WITH FLU

THEY FINISHED their meal around 9 p.m., and after clearing away the dishes, Rose made her way to the study. A few minutes later, she returned, holding a cardboard tube that held dress designs she had worked on.

"Jack, I'm heading out for a little while," she announced, her tone casual but with a hint of distraction.

Jack looked up, surprised. "I thought you were staying in tonight."

"I changed my mind," Rose replied with a light shrug. "Candice is back from her holidays and wants to show me her photos—really boring stuff. Plus, I've sketched out some designs for a summer dress she asked for." She held up the papers as proof, offering a brief smile. "Will you be okay?"

"Yes, I'll be fine," Jack reassured her, nodding. "I'm planning to hit the hay soon anyway. The summer sports day is coming up, so I need to prepare the grounds. You go enjoy yourself. Say hi to Candice for me."

"Will do," Rose replied with a quick nod. She placed the papers on the table, buttoned her coat, and lit another cigarette with a practiced flick of her wrist. She took a deep drag, exhaled slowly, and then with a final glance at Jack, she headed for the door.

A soft click echoed in the quiet room as the door closed behind her. Jack watched her go, feeling a faint sense of unease, though he couldn't quite pinpoint why—shaking off the feeling. Before turning off the light, Jack began the usual hunt for the TV remote. This time, however, he spotted it immediately on top of the TV—a truly remarkable occurrence, he thought with a smirk. He pressed the red button, and the screen flickered to life.

The words, "Jerry, I have come here tonight to tell my wife I am in love with her brother," blared from the television, cutting through the quiet of the room. Jack shook his head in disbelief, smirking. Television had become a cesspool of empty entertainment—politicians spinning their webs of deceit, preachers hawking salvation for ten bucks a pop, comedies that couldn't manage a genuine laugh without the crutch of canned laughter, and Hollywood blockbusters more concerned with explosions than substance. But the worst offenders, by far, were the so-called reality shows. Jack's preferred medium was the radio, with jazz as his chosen musical genre.

Jack once again shook his head in disappointment as the reality show on his screen descended into chaos, with shouting matches erupting and fists flying. "You call this reality," he muttered under his breath, his tone a blend of frustration and reluctant amusement. Yet, as absurd as the spectacle was, it wasn't so far removed from the bizarre twists his own life had taken in recent weeks, blurring the lines between reality and fiction. That was enough for Jack. He pointed the remote at the TV and began channel surfing, flipping from one station to the next in a futile search for something remotely interesting. If only he had a remote for the last few months, he thought, he could hit rewind and avoid going down into the school storeroom on that fateful day.

After flicking through channels offering the same dull repeats and sugary family soaps, he finally hit the red button, plunging the room into silence.

Now, the only illumination came from the pale, silvery glow of the full moon. It dominated the heavens tonight, appearing almost close enough to touch, an illusion magnified by the expansive window framing it.

As Jack got up to head to bed, something caught his attention—Rose had left the designs for Candice's summer dress on the table. Knowing it was too late to catch her, he decided to leave them as they were, confident she would find them in the morning. He wondered, for a second, if that had really been where she was going, but he pushed the thought away.

Before drawing the blinds, Jack stepped out onto the balcony. The night air was crisp, and a cold breeze sent a shiver through him; the summer was coming to an end, he thought. He gazed up at the sky, awestruck by the stars twinkling like distant diamonds and the moon's commanding presence. It seemed to hold the darkness at bay, bathing everything in a gentle, ethereal light. But as he admired the scene, a sudden dizziness hit him. He gripped the railing for support, a sharp pain slicing through his skull with alarming intensity. The pain was fierce, as if an invisible vice was squeezing his brain.

Jack rubbed his temples, trying to alleviate the discomfort, but the nausea only intensified. It felt as though his head was being pounded from the inside, the pressure building relentlessly behind his eyes. "Must be something I ate," he muttered to himself, before recalling his sister's cooking and reconsidering. "Maybe I'm coming down with the flu," he mused, trying to settle on a plausible cause. As the wind began to pick up, Jack decided it was best to retreat indoors before he caught a chill.

"What's best for the flu?" he muttered to himself as the headache continued to hammer away. He made his way to the bathroom, opened the medicine cabinet, and reached for the painkillers. To his dismay, the packet was empty, every last pill gone. The harsh light of the bathroom only intensified his discomfort, causing him to squint and recoil as he switched it off.

The sudden darkness brought a slight relief, easing the throbbing in his head. He stumbled into a chair, holding his head in his hands. The pain was relentless, not worsening but refusing to abate. Leaning back, Jack tried to think of remedies for his sudden illness. "Sweat it out," he thought, recalling Rose's usual advice. "Hot water and whiskey, then wrap up in bed—that should help." He sighed, feeling the weight of fatigue settle in, hoping that some rest and a simple remedy would see him through this unexpected bout of discomfort.

He made his way to the drinks cabinet and spotted a half-full bottle of whiskey. Grabbing the bottle and a glass, he headed to the kitchen. He flicked on the kettle and leaned against the counter, waiting for it to boil. As the quiet hum of the heating water filled the room, he poured a generous measure of whiskey into the glass, the amber liquid swirling gently. He hoped the hot drink would ease his discomfort and help him settle for the night.

THIRTY-FIVE
MAKE IT A LARGE ONE

ROSE PULLED into the car park of the Cattle Drive, a seedy bar on the outskirts of town. It wasn't the sort of place she would normally go. As she peered out of her open window, a rowdy scene spilled into the street. Pounding music erupted into the night air as the bar's door swung violently open. Two drunken men staggered out, fists raised, looking for a fight. They tumbled over each other down the steps as a group of equally inebriated women followed—the kind who had likely sparked the altercation in the first place, their laughter shrill and echoing.

After raising the window, muting the drunken chaos spilling from the bar entrance, she killed the engine and glanced at the passenger seat. That's when she realized she'd left the designs for Candice behind. Not that it mattered—she had no intention of sitting through hours of someone else's holiday photos, enduring forced smiles and awkward laughter. The designs had been a convenient prop, a lie to sell her story to Jack. She needed to get away, to find a place where she could breathe, even if just for a moment.

The Cattle Drive was as gritty as its name suggested: dimly lit, thick with cigarette smoke, and saturated with the pungent blend of stale sweat and spilt beer. The flickering neon sign outside cast an eerie glow, cutting through the dark and making the shadows seem to shiver. Rose stepped inside, unfazed by the oppressive atmosphere. She made her way to her usual spot—a battered stool at the far end of the bar, where she could watch the world unravel around her.

She sat down, releasing a heavy sigh that seemed to expel all the troubles weighing her down. Perhaps it was Jack dredging up the past, forcing her to relive the trauma of waking up one morning to find her mother gone—a pain he only half-understood. Maybe his words had cut deeper than she cared to admit. Or perhaps the relentless strain of looking after Jack, of juggling a demanding career while trying to hold together a fractured family, was finally catching up with her. Then again, maybe she simply needed a stiff drink. Whatever the reason, only Rose knew, and tonight, her only solace was George—the liquid kind.

She checked her watch, then glanced up, as if anticipating the next moment. Before she could utter a word, the bartender had placed a glass in front of her. Rose offered a tired smile and a nod. The bartender poured her a large whiskey "Hi, Danny."

"Long day?" he asked, his voice warm with familiarity.

"Long life," she replied, her tone tinged with regret, echoing a lifetime of struggles. Without so much as a flinch or a sharp exhale, she knocked back the drink in one smooth motion, slamming the empty glass onto the bar with practiced ease. Here, in this dimly lit corner of the world, Rose always felt she truly belonged—among her kind, her *real* kind. It was a stark contrast to the polished, high-powered life she led as an executive magazine editor.

A good bartender knows when to talk, when to pour, and when to walk away. Danny had known Rose for most of her drinking life, and he wasn't just a bartender; he'd owned the Cattle Drive since the sixties. He knew how to keep secrets—he could write a book filled with the ones he'd kept for Rose alone. But Danny also knew when to keep those secrets safe, buried deep under layers of quiet understanding.

"This one's on me," Danny said, pouring her another round before moving on to attend to another customer, giving Rose the space she needed.

Rose watched him leave, the second glass waiting patiently in front of her like an old friend. She wrapped her fingers around it, feeling the cool, familiar weight. For a brief moment, she let herself sink into that comfort, allowing the heaviness of the day—no, the weight of her entire life—to slip away. The past, with all its burdens and unspoken regrets, seemed to fade, if only for this moment, leaving her alone with the quiet solace of the present.

After finishing her fourth glass, Rose looked up and nodded to the bartender.

"Danny, make it a large one," she said. He quickly filled her glass.

Amidst the crack of pool balls, barroom banter, the occasional rough cough, the shuffling of drunken feet, and the distant drawl of country music—definitely, not her favorite style, though the idea of requesting some jazz amused her—a slurred voice cut through the noise.

"Do I know you?"

Her eyes shifted slowly to the right, GI Joe-style, before returning forward, expressionless. She had no interest in small talk, especially from a half-drunk, slightly overweight guy with an unoriginal pick-up line. She decided to tell him as much.

"That's original," she said with a frown.

"No, I mean—I do know you, can't think where though. It was on a train, not long ago. I'm sure of it," he insisted.

Still looking straight ahead, she replied, "Sorry, buddy, I don't take trains." She sipped her whiskey and nodded again to the bartender.

"I'll get this one," the man offered, pulling out a money clip bulging with notes. Probably dollar bills, Rose thought. He peeled off a crisp twenty-dollar bill. "Keep the change."

If he was trying to impress Rose, it didn't work. Even the bartender seemed unimpressed as he scrutinized the note before placing it in the till.

Rose slightly raised her glass—not enough to give him the wrong impression, just a small gesture of thanks.

"Wait a minute, you're right—it wasn't a train."

"Look, buddy, I've never seen you before—not on a train, a boat, a plane, or a goddamn camel drive. So if you don't mind..." She didn't finish her sentence; she didn't have to. He got the gist of what she was saying. But it didn't deter him.

"That's it, now I know where I've seen you before."

"Come on, thrill me," Rose said, trying hard not to offend the guy, but she was close to telling him to leave her the hell alone.

"On the plane from New York—you were sitting across the aisle, and you had a train for your son, if I remember rightly. No, wait, the train was for your brother." He smiled, pleased with himself for being so astute.

Rose turned to him, a half-smile creeping across her face.

"That's right, now I remember," she said, her smile broadening, but it was a trap. Behind the smile lay a cutting remark. She was waiting for the perfect moment to strike. As the man beamed back, feeling confident, Rose delivered the final blow.

"I ignored you, didn't I?"

"Yes, that's right," he chuckled, thinking she might be more receptive this time—a big mistake.

Still smiling, she struck like a cobra. "So why the fuck can't you get the message this time?"

Bullseye. His smile remained fixed, masking his deep embarrassment. If it weren't for his face turning a bright shade of pink, no one at the bar would have been any the wiser.

He reached into his pocket, again pulling out his money clip, and threw another twenty on the bar. "You need to relax, lady," he said, turning to the bartender. "Get her another drink—in fact, get her several," he added before swaggering to the end of the bar. His pride was a little dented, but he wouldn't let Rose completely ruin his night.

Rose checked her watch—11:30 p.m. *Shit*, time had flown by. She needed to make a move; she'd promised Jack she wouldn't be late, but she hadn't yet found what she had come to this particular bar to find. With a sigh, she picked up the twenty-dollar note the not-so-nice gentleman had left behind earlier and handed it to the bartender.

"You heard the guy—get me several." The bartender fetched a bottle from under the bar and left it with her.

"Danny, you're a star. You really know how to treat a woman," she slurred, the alcohol taking effect. So much so that she even started tapping her feet to the music.

She glanced around the room, not casually but with purpose. She was searching for something—or someone—specific, her gaze sweeping over the usual mix of bottom feeders, petty criminals, and the salt of the earth. Despite her expensive clothes, Rose blended in seamlessly. In a place like this, it wasn't about what you wore; it was all about attitude, and Rose had that in spades. She carried herself with a confidence that spoke volumes, an unspoken message that she belonged, that she wasn't to be messed with.

Rose also understood that if she needed something done outside the bounds of legality this was the place to find it. Here, favors were traded as easily as drinks, and secrets were as valuable as cash. It was a world she navigated with ease, her polished exterior hiding a deeper understanding of how things really worked beneath the surface.

Her wandering gaze halted abruptly. "Bingo," she muttered under her breath. Rose's eyes locked onto the pool table, and with a confident stride, she made her way over. She slapped down a twenty-dollar bill, her eyes glinting with the thrill of a new challenge, a spark of excitement cutting through the smoky haze of the bar.

"Any takers?" she declared, her voice cutting through the low hum of the bar. A tall, slim man dressed all in black stepped forward, a menacing snake tattoo coiled around his throat, its head poised to strike near his left eye. His expression was cool, bordering on cocky, as he sized up the challenge. Rose hadn't seen him around the bar before, but she could already feel the thrill of taking him down.

Unfortunately for him, he had no idea who he was up against. He hadn't seen Rose play before—was completely unaware of her reputation. Her sharp eye and the ruthless precision with which she wielded a pool cue were legendary in these parts. As the game began, she could see his overconfidence on full display, a mistake she was more than ready to exploit.

After she had wiped the floor with him, he was ready to give up when she leaned in and said, "Double or quits."

"Lady, I'm all out of cash. You've wiped me out," he moaned.

"Okay, not for cash then," she replied smoothly. "For a favor. You win, you get all your money back. You lose, and you owe me a favor."

He considered her offer, rubbing his chin thoughtfully. He had nothing left to lose—at least, not money-wise—and perhaps the favor would be something... intriguing. "You got a deal, lady," he said, a glint of hope in his eyes.

THIRTY-SIX
RABBIT BAKE

JACK HAD TAKEN his hot whiskey flu remedy and lay in bed, half-asleep, still wrapped in his clothes. He wasn't feeling any better, but he hoped that sleep would bring some relief by morning. The wind outside howled, rattling the windows he had forgotten to close. The strong breeze blew against the thin curtains, making them dance eerily.

Suddenly, a loud crash from the kitchen jolted Jack awake. He sat bolt upright in bed, his heart pounding in his chest.

"No, not again," he whispered, fear creeping in. He feared The Miseries had returned, the terror that had haunted him before. Muttering under his breath, he repeated the doctor's words like a mantra, "It's all in the mind, it's all in the mind," desperately hoping for that to be true.

As he looked around the room, more strange noises emanated from the kitchen. Still groggy, Jack tried to stand but had to steady himself against a chair as beads of sweat formed on his forehead. His nausea hadn't subsided; in fact, it seemed to have worsened. He took deep breaths, trying to keep down the remnants of the rabbit bake and apple pie that threatened to resurface.

Once he felt somewhat stable, Jack gingerly made his way to the bedroom door. He opened it slowly, peering out into the hallway—

nothing. But the noises from the kitchen continued, growing louder. Rustling sounds, like something moving. Jack moved cautiously toward the kitchen, not daring to enter, and leaned against the wall, his hand searching for the light switch.

Before he could reach it, something brushed against his leg. He froze, his heart skipping a beat. After a few tense seconds, he resumed his search, finally feeling the ridge of the switch beneath his fingers. He quickly pressed it, flooding the kitchen with light.

Spot, his cat, just as startled as Jack, shot out from under the table, knocking over more pans and crockery as he bolted out of the kitchen. Jack clutched his chest, trying to calm his racing heart, relieved that his earlier fears had been unfounded.

He bent down to pick up the upturned pan and swept the broken cup pieces to the side of the bin, being careful not to step on any loose shards. As he was cleaning up the last remnants of the mess, the kitchen radio suddenly burst into life. Jack shot up, staring at the radio, which emitted nothing but white noise. His head, already throbbing, now pounded with renewed intensity, each beat like a hammer against his skull. He squeezed his eyes shut, desperately trying to will the pain away, but it only seemed to deepen. The earlier whiskey cure had backfired, not dulling the ache as he'd hoped, but instead, intensifying it, leaving him regretting every sip.

"This isn't happening," he muttered, wiping the sweat from his brow with a trembling hand. Just as suddenly as it had turned on, the radio fell silent. Jack opened his eyes, hoping he had imagined the whole thing. Maybe it was just food poisoning, or an electrical fault. He clung to that explanation, refusing to let his imagination get the better of him.

To be sure, he walked over to the radio and unplugged it from the socket. Then, he finished cleaning up the mess Spot had made. As a final precaution, he emptied the pan containing the rabbit bake into the trash. He glanced at his watch—11:45 p.m. Where was Rose? She wasn't usually this late. Then again, she hadn't seen Candice for at least a month, so she probably had a lot to catch up on.

Jack boiled the kettle and made himself another whiskey cure, this time doubling the amount of whiskey. *This'll either kill or cure me*, he thought grimly. With his cup of medicine in hand, he turned off the kitchen light and headed back to the bedroom. As he stepped out of the kitchen, the radio began to play again.

This time, it wasn't just white noise. The familiar tune of 'Puppy Love' by The Osmonds filled the room. Jack recognized it instantly from Rose's old record collection. But before the song could fully play out, a DJ's voice cut in, fast and jarring. Jack knew all the local DJs past and present, but this one eluded him. He couldn't quite put his finger on whose voice it was. But then it came to him.

"That's it," Jack whispered, his voice barely audible, "Jamming James Freeman." But that couldn't be right—Freeman had shot himself six years ago after a downward spiral into drugs, booze, and crippling depression. The tragedy had been sparked by the death of his wife in a car crash—a crash where Freeman had been behind the wheel. The guilt had consumed him, especially because he had been high at the time of the crash.

Jack's mind raced, struggling to make sense of what was happening. How could this be? Confusion tightened its grip on him as he tried to comprehend the moment. It wasn't just the fact that the radio was inexplicably playing without being plugged in—something else was off, something that made his skin prickle with unease.

The DJ's voice crackled through the speakers, casually announcing that The Osmonds were topping the charts. Jack's breath caught. 'Puppy Love' had topped the charts in 1972. His pulse quickened as he tried to piece things together, the impossibility of it all gnawing at him.

Then, before he could fully grasp the situation, another voice filled the airwaves—this one with a tone of urgency. It was a news report breaking into the broadcast, and Jack instinctively leaned in, a cold dread settling over him as he waited to hear what would come next.

"Four more arrests have been made in connection with the break-in at the Watergate Hotel."

Jack's heart skipped a beat as he recognized Michael Beaumont's unmistakable voice—the voice of the Lincoln Mauler. It sent a shiver down his spine, the same way it had when he first heard it as a teenager during a sleepover. They had watched a *60 Minutes* exposé on the notorious serial killer, and the memory of it had haunted him ever since; a deep, unsettling disturbance that gnawed at him. This wasn't the voice of fun Micky he had known as a young boy, but the voice of the evil he had later become.

The Mauler's voice had a distinct, sinister timbre, one that etched itself into Jack's mind and refused to fade. He could hear it now, clear as day, reverberating in his head like an unwanted echo from the past. There was no mistaking it—Jack's memory had always been sharp, and his instinct told him this was no coincidence.

But then another realization hit him, a thought that felt like a punch to the gut: *Watergate.* He remembered the scandal being mentioned in that same report. It had stuck with him because it had been part of his history exam in school—a key event that had shaped the political landscape of the 1970s. The connection seemed odd at first, out of place, but something about it gnawed at him. Why would the two be mentioned together? What had the Mauler to do with a decadesold political scandal?

The unsettling pieces began to align in Jack's mind, but the full picture remained elusive, hovering just beyond his grasp, sending a chill down his spine.

But this wasn't breaking news—this was decades old. How could these voices be coming through the radio as if they were fresh headlines? His mind reeled, struggling to reconcile the present with what he knew to be historical fact. The lines between past and present blurred, leaving Jack grappling with a deepening sense of unease. Something was terribly wrong.

Then, another announcement: "A man has been found hanged in his family home." The realization hit Jack like a ton of bricks. Could they be reporting his father's suicide back in 1972? Was this some twisted coincidence, or were they doing a year-in-review broadcast? He clung to the hope of a rational explanation, but then the voice changed again.

"Brad Marshall?" Jack cried out in disbelief, recognizing the voice that now filled the room.

"That's right, Jackie boy," the voice replied, but this time it was clear, and it came from behind him. Jack froze, realizing he wasn't alone. He turned sharply—nothing. But then the voice spoke again, "Over here, Jackie boy." He spun around again but still saw nothing.

Panic set in as Jack slammed his glass down on the kitchen table, his head pounding with such intensity that he staggered back, clutching his skull. The pain was overwhelming as if a herd of cattle were stampeding through his mind. The song 'Puppy Love' reverberated through the room once more, but Jack knew he wasn't imagining this—everything felt too real.

He slumped into a chair, leaning forward as he vomited violently. The voice continued, mocking him. It was Brad.

"That's it, Jackie boy, better out than in. You didn't think you could get rid of me that easily, did you?"

The voice was coming from the radio again. Jack screamed at it, "Leave me alone!" He grabbed the nearest object—a large book—and hurled it at the radio, smashing it to pieces. Sparks flew, and the radio crackled as it died, yet it hadn't been plugged in at all.

For a moment, there was silence. Jack dared to hope it was over, that he had destroyed whatever demon had been taunting him. But the answer came quickly and terrifyingly as a dark mass began to form in front of him. The voice returned, emanating from the darkness—Brad's voice.

"Goosey goosey gander, where shall I wander?" The voice was deeper now, more throaty, demonic in its resonance. It filled the room, rattling glasses and shaking picture frames. The noise built to a crescendo, like a banshee's wail.

Terrified, Jack threw a saltshaker at the shadow that had formed in the corner of the room, but it was only a coat stand. Still afraid, he cried out, "Leave me alone! I know you're not real!" Tears welled in his eyes.

"Oh, we're real, Jack," the voice hissed through the crackling radio, sending a shiver down his spine. But now the voice had changed—it wasn't the Mauler anymore or Brad. It was his father's voice. His dead father's voice.

Jack's breath caught in his throat, and for a moment, he felt as if the ground had shifted beneath him. The familiar tone, the subtle inflections—there was no mistaking it. It was the voice he feared as a child, now echoing out of the old radio, twisted by an otherworldly presence.

His heart pounded in his chest as the reality of the situation hit him full force. This wasn't just a distortion of time; this was something much darker, something that defied the boundaries of the living and the dead. The voice—his father's voice—was real, and it was here, reaching out to him from beyond the grave.

"Don't be such a wimp, Jack. You know what happens when you cry."

Jack lunged at the radio, smashing what was left of it against the wall, but he knew it was futile. He had to do something, anything to make it stop.

"You're not real! I made you up! You're just a bad rabbit bake!" Jack shouted before vomiting once again. The voice mocked him, laughing cruelly. Jack felt like he was losing his mind.

"Come on, Jack, you know why we're here. We've come to collect you—it's time."

"No! No! No! Leave me alone!" Jack cried, banging his hands against his head, trying to block out the voices. He staggered toward the balcony, desperate to escape, but before he could get far, he stepped on a piece of wood that had broken off the radio. Yelping in pain, he fell back against the wall, lifting his foot to see blood soaking through his sock as he removed it. The splinter had gone deep. He wrapped the sock around the wound, trying to stem the bleeding.

More voices surfaced, hissing and screeching, blending into an unrecognizable cacophony. And if the voices weren't enough, then came the shadows.

The first one appeared in the corner behind the chair, the next by the window. Their laughter filled the room, mocking him. A third shadow rose from the coffee table, pointing an oversized, twig-like finger directly at Jack.

"Just joining us in the studio, ladies and gentlemen, please welcome Jack Brooks! Howdy, Jack! What's new in sad town?"

It was Jamming James Freeman's voice again, but why? What did all this have to do with him? Jack, now completely confused, tried once again to escape, but the spindly, over-stretched fingers of the shadows lunged at him, trying to grasp him. He felt a sharp, icy swipe across his arm—the figures had no substance, but they were no less menacing. He finally made it to the corner of the room, sliding down the wall as the shadows closed in.

Jack felt light-headed, dizzy. His eyes rolled back in his head as he struggled to stay conscious, desperately clinging to what was left of his sanity. The shadows moved closer, reaching, grasping, sometimes merging together into deeper darkness. They swirled and reformed into two-headed beasts, then three. Their arms, snake-like, hissed at Jack, snapping at him as they drew nearer.

Overcome by shock and fear, Jack finally passed out.

THIRTY-SEVEN
SHACKLED

ONLY A FEW ORDERLIES, the night doctor, and a lone nurse wandered the quiet hospital ward where Charlie lay. It had been a relatively uneventful evening—just a couple of shootings, both fatal—but nothing out of the ordinary. The nurse had started her rounds, methodically checking each room. Charlie's was the last on her list.

Charlie remained unconscious, shackled to the bed, while the window in his room rattled incessantly. The gentle breeze from earlier had strengthened, causing the blinds to slap against the window frame. As the nurse made her way down the corridor, she noticed the empty chair outside Charlie's room. The guard was missing, but a book lay face down on the chair, its title, *The Art of Surveillance*, clearly visible. She couldn't help but smile at the irony. She continued down the corridor, but the persistent rattling from within Charlie's room pulled her back. Doubling back, she opened the door and stepped inside.

A dim lamp cast a soft glow over the room, the only illumination aside from the rhythmic green pulses of the monitors, their steady beeps a reassuring sign of life. The nurse scanned the room for the source of the noise, her eyes landing on the open window. Shivering slightly, she walked over to close it, rubbing her arms against the unexpected chill. Unbeknownst to her, Charlie had begun to stir. His hand twitched, and his eyelids fluttered, his head turning just enough to watch her. She twisted the latch to seal the window, then opened a smaller pane above to keep the room ventilated, completely unaware of the quiet movements behind her. Charlie's arm lifted weakly, but the nurse remained oblivious, too focused on the window and the whisper of the cold air beyond.

She turned back to Charlie, who had drifted back into unconsciousness. "Poor old fella," she muttered as she approached the bed, her eyes falling on the handcuffs binding Charlie to it. "What could an old man like you have done to deserve this?"

She had no knowledge of the earlier incident that had led to Charlie being restrained; her only information came from the charts—two gunshot wounds, one to the chest and one to the lower abdomen. The sight of the frail, unconscious man shackled to the bed tugged at her heartstrings.

As she adjusted Charlie's bandages, she noticed how tight the handcuffs were. She considered asking the young officer to loosen them. "Who would want to shoot a poor old man like you?" she whispered softly.

Suddenly, the door flew open, startling her. The young guard had rushed back, alarmed by the sound of her voice, fearing someone might have broken into the room.

"Shush!" the nurse hissed, pressing a finger to her lips.

"Sorry, nurse, I heard voices and thought…"

"Thought what, officer? That I was here to help your prisoner escape? Hardly!" she replied with a touch of sarcasm, though her smile softened the words.

As they exchanged hushed words, Charlie's hand moved again, but neither the nurse nor the young officer noticed—they were too absorbed in their brief flirtation. The nurse turned to leave, and the officer held the door open for her. As she passed under his arm, she looked up and smiled, and he returned the gesture, a blush creeping into his cheeks. Just before leaving, she remembered the handcuffs.

"Any chance you could loosen these cuffs? They seem a little tight," she asked, her tone gentle.

The officer hesitated, weighing his decision. The nurse gave him a pleading look. "Look, he's in no shape to make a quick getaway... please?"

With a resigned nod, the officer stepped forward and inserted the key into the locks, carefully loosening both cuffs to give Charlie some relief. He intended only to ease the restraints slightly, but what he hadn't realized was that he had completely freed Charlie from his shackles. There was no distinct click to alert him to his mistake.

The nurse smiled warmly at the officer, and he felt his cheeks flush a deeper shade of red, a small surge of pride swelling within him. As they walked out of the room together, he glanced back checking over Charlie, unaware he had freed him. He softly closed the door behind them.

For a few moments, the nurse and the young officer lingered in the corridor, chatting idly before glancing at her watch; realizing she was behind on her rounds, she quickly made her excuses, heading back to the front desk to pick up her charts. As she passed the officer again, she told him she'd be back in half an hour.

"HARPER, WHAT TIME IS IT?" JJ asked, breaking the silence in the car.

"Ten after midnight," Harper replied, glancing at his watch.

The two detectives were parked in a narrow alley, pulling the late shift. They passed the time with idle chatter and the occasional card game. It had been a quiet night so far, apart from a drunk relieving himself against the wall in front of them.

Harper sipped his coffee, while JJ was engrossed in a book titled *Criminal Psychology*—required reading if he wanted to become an FBI agent. Harper knew his partner had what it took and supported him every step of the way, even though it meant losing a great partner and close friend. They had been partners for five years, their bond forged through trust and shared experiences. Harper, however, had no ambitions of becoming an agent. He came from a long line of cops stretching back to the days of the Texas Rangers. According to his Pop,

Harper's great-grandfather was a famous gunslinger in the frontier days. While Harper took these stories with a grain of salt, he liked the idea of having a gunslinger in the family. After all, he was pretty fast on the draw himself—Charlie had found that out earlier that day. It was the only time he had ever let JJ down, though JJ insisted he had done the right thing. Still, Harper couldn't shake the feeling that he needed to make up for it.

"How's the studying going?" Harper asked, breaking the silence.

JJ looked up from his book with a grin. "Great! I've got a test next week. That's why I'm reading this—it's fascinating stuff. You should give it a try. It really opens your eyes to how the criminal mind works. There are things in here I never even considered, and I've been a cop for years."

As JJ spoke enthusiastically, Harper found his mind wandering, contemplating the prospect of breaking in a new partner.

"Isn't that amazing?" JJ asked.

"What is?" Harper replied, snapping back to reality.

"You haven't listened to a word I've said, have you?" JJ teased, smirking.

"Sorry, buddy, I was just thinking about who my new partner might be."

"I heard it might be Frank."

"Frank 'Hard Head' Kowalski? You've got to be kidding me!"

JJ couldn't help but laugh. "He's not a bad guy, just needs some of your guidance to keep him focused."

Harper gave him a skeptical look. "You're pulling my leg, right?"

JJ's smirk widened. "Yep, but it made you smile."

"Yeah, real funny."

"Look on the bright side—if he didn't get you shot, he'd at least get you laid," JJ quipped with a grin.

"You're not as funny as you think. Read your damn book," Harper grumbled, taking another sip of his now-cold coffee.

CHARLIE BEGAN to stir as the detectives joked and bantered in the alley. His eyelids fluttered open, and the first thing he registered was the cold breeze wafting through the room. The blinds by the window swayed gently, catching the draft. Weak and disoriented, he tried to lift his arms. As he did, he noticed the handcuffs; somehow, the restraints slipped free, falling away from his wrists. But it hardly mattered—though the cuffs had been unlocked, his body still lacked the strength to respond. His limbs felt like lead, and every movement was an exhausting struggle.

A nagging thought crossed his mind as he lay there, trying to make sense of his surroundings. He distinctly remembered the nurse closing the window earlier, shutting out the chill. Yet now, it stood wide open, letting in the cold night air—confusion mixed with a growing sense of unease.

His gaze shifted, and he became aware of a tall, shadowy figure lurking behind the curtain on the opposite side of the room. It stood still, shrouded in darkness. Charlie's heart raced as his mind scrambled for an explanation—he hoped, *no*, he prayed it was just a doctor's coat hanging on a coat stand. But as much as he tried to convince himself, he couldn't take his eyes off the ominous figure. Time seemed to stretch as the shadow remained motionless.

The strain of holding his head up became too much, and Charlie had to let it drop back onto the pillow, his strength fading rapidly. But curiosity gnawed at him, and he summoned the last of his energy to lift his head again. The shadow was gone. Panic surged through his veins. He was trapped, immobilized, his eyes frantically scanning the room for any sign of the vanished figure. Terror gripped him, and he tried to cry out, but the oxygen mask smothered his voice. All he could produce was a weak, muffled whimper that barely broke the silence, leaving him helpless and alone in the sterile, shadow-filled room.

His heart monitor began to beep frantically, the sound echoing through the room as fear surged through his veins. Charlie fought in his weakness, each struggle futile, his strength slipping away with every desperate effort. Exhaustion washed over him, and with one final burst of will, he managed to lift his head. His gaze swept across the room—and then he saw it. The shadow had reappeared, lurking in the far corner, still and silent, its presence oppressive and unyielding. It was watching him, waiting. *But for what?* Charlie's mind raced with the question.

Then, as if responding to his thoughts, the shadow began to inch closer, gliding forward with a deliberate, almost taunting slowness. It crept to the edge of his bed, dark and menacing, just as Charlie's exhausted eyes fluttered shut. The world around him faded, and he slipped back into unconsciousness, leaving the silent shadow looming over him in the pale glow of the monitors.

THE NURSE HAD FINISHED her rounds and was now standing outside Charlie's room, watching the young officer, who had dozed off in his chair. She began to turn the handle but paused, noticing that the book lay open on a section titled 'Vigilance.' She smiled to herself. Once again the irony was not lost on her as she entered Charlie's room, keeping the lights dim to avoid disturbing him.

As she stepped inside, she felt a chill and noticed that the window had been reopened. She hesitated, a sense of unease creeping over her. *How had it opened?* It couldn't have been Charlie, so perhaps the guard had done it? She considered asking him but decided to close the window first. She made her way to the foot of Charlie's bed and picked up the chart hanging there. Taking out a gold pen—expensive and shiny—from her top pocket, she began to note the readings on her clipboard.

Charlie opened his eyes, but the nurse again didn't notice. He was too weak from his earlier struggles to do more than twitch a finger, a movement too small to catch her attention. The shadowy figure remained in the room, hidden behind the curtain, watching. Whatever it intended to do, it could wait a little longer. It stood motionless, silent, biding its time.

HARPER AND JJ were still parked in the alley, Harper had drifted off to sleep while JJ neared the end of his book. As JJ finished the last page, he closed the book with a snap and playfully smacked Harper on the back of the head, waking him abruptly.

"What's happening?" Harper mumbled, rubbing his eyes.

"I've finished my book," JJ announced, grinning.

"So? Read another one," Harper muttered, trying to settle back into his nap.

"I've got a better idea," JJ said excitedly, a gleam in his eye. Harper knew his rest was over.

Sighing, Harper stretched and yawned. "What's your new idea?"

"I want to go to the hospital and see if Charlie's regained consciousness," JJ replied, his enthusiasm evident.

Harper was now fully awake, staring at JJ in disbelief. "Are you crazy? It's 12:45 a.m.—they won't let you in now."

"Wanna bet?" JJ shot back, already starting the car before Harper could protest.

THE NURSE HAD FINISHED CHECKING on Charlie and returned the chart to the foot of the bed. Charlie, drifting in and out of consciousness, lay still. She leaned over the bed to make sure he was comfortable and tucked the covers around him. As she leaned over, her gold pen slipped from her top pocket and rolled under the bed. Unaware of her loss, the nurse turned to leave, gently closing the door behind her to avoid disturbing Charlie or the sleeping guard outside.

AS THE DOOR closed the shadow once again began to stir inside the room, gliding silently toward Charlie's bed. This time, there would be no interruptions. This time, it would finish what it had come to do —whatever that was.

THIRTY-EIGHT
MNEDO

THE GUARD HAD ONCE AGAIN LEFT Charlie, his earlier chastisement a distant memory. Besides, he could see the door, he would notice if there was anything wrong.

Charlie drifted: conscious moments punctured with sleepiness. At that moment his eyes began to flutter, his fingers made slight movements, his breathing deepened. Moments later his eyes fluttered open, only to be met with the terrifying sight of a shadowy figure looming closer. Panic surged through him as he struggled with every ounce of strength he could summon, but his efforts were futile—his body refused to cooperate. Even if he could scream, the oxygen mask strapped to his face would stifle his cries, and the guard, too preoccupied with flirting, was oblivious to his plight.

A cold, paralyzing fear gripped Charlie as the figure drew nearer, its presence radiating a malevolent intent. He knew, deep in his soul, that this phantom had not come to offer mercy, but to claim him in the most sinister way imaginable. Trapped in his own body, Charlie could do nothing but await his fate, his heart pounding with the terrible realization that there would be no escape.

As the figure loomed closer, Charlie's eyes locked onto those of the phantom. It was a tall, slim figure. A beast with long, greasy jet-black hair that draped over its shoulders. The figure was dressed entirely in black, and Charlie's gaze was drawn to a tattoo that curled menacingly around the figure's neck—a snake, its head appearing from the figure's cheek, poised as if ready to strike.

In that moment, with terror suffocating him, Charlie's muffled voice began to chant in his native Potawatomi, the words slipping through the oxygen mask: "Mnedo, Mnedo," then ending with, "Gzhemnédowen nwi zhewebak."

Charlie had made his peace, and was ready for death.

THIRTY-NINE
SHOTS FIRED

THE TWO DETECTIVES had barely made it halfway to the hospital when the police radio crackled to life.

"Ten-ten shots fired the Cattle Drive 115 N 5th Street Springfield. All units in the vicinity respond."

"That's close by, JJ. Should we call in?" Harper asked, his voice tinged with the anticipation of action.

"It's probably a twenty-minute detour, but Charlie can wait a little longer. He's not exactly going anywhere," JJ said, grabbing the radio. As he transmitted their location, he flicked on the siren, the wail slicing through the air as he pressed the accelerator, making the speedometer climb swiftly.

"This is car six, en route. ETA three minutes. Do we have backup?" Harper called out, releasing the switch. A burst of static crackled over the airwaves before another unit came through.

"Car nine here, en route. ETA one minute. Looks like we'll beat you there, JJ. You're our backup."

Hearing the response, Harper shot JJ a look. No words were needed—JJ understood perfectly and pressed harder on the accelerator.

"Okay, Frank, we'll see about that. Oh, by the way, Harper, your new partner told me to remind you to take it easy," JJ teased.

"What? What was that?" Frank asked, irritation clear in his voice.

"Nothing, just be careful," JJ replied, a smirk playing on his lips.

"Hardy, ha ha! There goes another rib," Harper muttered, unimpressed by JJ's humor.

JJ just grinned.

Moments later, JJ spotted Frank's flashing lights up ahead. It looked like they really would be backup after all. Just as that thought passed through his mind, a car coming from the opposite direction suddenly veered into their lane, cutting them off as it turned at a stoplight. Only JJ's quick reflexes and expert driving saved them from a head-on collision. Tires screeched as he slammed on the brakes, bringing the vehicle to a jolting halt.

"Goddamn, son of a..." Time seemed to slow as JJ's eyes locked onto the car speeding past. He glimpsed at the car for a split second, missing the driver but catching a familiar face in the back seat. It was Rose—or at least, he thought it was. His heart raced as he turned to Harper, shaken.

"That was Rose," he said, his voice wavering.

"What?" Harper asked, impatient to continue toward the scene. "Who?"

"I swear that was Rose—the one I nearly ran into," JJ insisted.

"Did you get a plate?" Harper pressed.

"A plate? I didn't even see what kind of car it was. It was old and black, that's all I've got," JJ replied, frustration thick in his voice. The acrid scent of burning rubber filled the vehicle, a sharp reminder of their sudden stop. On any other day, they would have pursued the reckless driver, but they had a more serious issue ahead.

Before they could dwell on it, the radio burst to life. Frank's voice crackled through, panicked and desperate. "Where's our backup?!"

Gunshots echoed through the transmission, cutting through the tension like a knife. Frank's terrified cry came next, unfinished and chilling: "Mother fu—" The radio went dead.

In an instant, their conversation ended. JJ and Harper exchanged a grim look before JJ hit the gas, the car lurching forward. Their brothers were in trouble, and there was no time to waste.

Moments later, they screeched to a stop, the tires screaming as they halted near the scene. Frank and his partner were pinned down behind their squad car, exchanging fire with unseen assailants. JJ and Harper exited their vehicle, keeping low as they made their way over.

"You okay? What's the deal?" Harper asked, breathless.

"Am I okay? Do I *look* okay? Where the hell were you?" Frank snapped, eyes wide with adrenaline.

"We got held up. Doesn't matter now," JJ replied, scanning the area. "So, what's going on?"

Before Frank could answer, another squad car arrived, blue lights pulsing and sirens wailing. More adrenaline-fueled officers poured onto the scene, weapons drawn and ready for action. The air was thick with tension, adrenaline, and testosterone along with the smell of gunpowder, as the battle unfolded in a flurry of chaos.

"So, witnesses said there was a fight earlier," Frank explained quickly, his breath coming in short bursts. "Two guys picking a fight with a couple who were just enjoying their night out. The guys left but came back looking for trouble. Things got heated, and a fight broke out with the owner. Shots were fired. Everyone else ran, leaving just the owner and a bartender. Apparently, the owner was shot in the leg, and now they're holding them both hostage."

As Frank finished his explanation, the gunfire ceased, and a tense silence fell over the scene. The wailing sirens were cut off, replaced by an uneasy quiet.

A voice called out from inside the building, calm yet dripping with arrogance. "Hey, you guys, I hope you brought something to the party. We're about to have some fun with Grace. Danny, on the other hand—well, let's just say he's checked out early." The threat was punctuated by a grotesque, pig-like snort of laughter that echoed through the stillness. The chilling words lingered, laden with menace, leaving no doubt about the gravity of the situation.

The tension was palpable, visible on everyone's faces as officers gripped their weapons tighter and exchanged anxious glances. They all held their breath, waiting for the next move.

JJ's instincts kicked in, honed by years of training and experience. He peered into the window of the bar, spotting one gunman holding a young, terrified woman hostage. JJ immediately asked, "Where's the SWAT team?"

"They're tied up with another shooting downtown," Frank's partner explained. "No telling when they'll get here. We've been told to sit tight."

"Damn it!" JJ cursed. "Our guys inside are likely wasted. You know what that means," JJ said to Frank.

"Don't do anything stupid, " Frank replied.

JJ looked at Harper.

Harper shook his head. "You're going to do something stupid, aren't ya?" Harper answered his own question.

JJ sank low behind several parked cars, followed by Harper, crouching the best he could. He moved towards the bar. Frank's voice became distant in the background as they made their way around the back.

"JJ, it's too dangerous. Wait for SWAT. It's not worth it, it's—" JJ didn't hear the last part of the conversation. He had made up his mind.

Harper knew a little thing like danger wouldn't deter JJ. He was a brave son of a bitch, and the hostage's only hope. Harper gestured to Frank, signaling what they were about to do. Frank, though not pleased, knew they had to back them up. He and his partner moved to Harper's position, where Harper quickly briefed them.

JJ tried the back door—it was locked. He re-holstered his gun, then pulled out a small pouch from his inside jacket pocket, revealing a pair of lockpicks. As he worked the lock, the stench of rotten food wafted up from the dumpsters, where a few rats were feasting on the spoiled mush. Occasionally, one of the larger rats looked up at JJ, curious about his activities.

"What's your problem?" JJ muttered, glancing down at the rat. The rat stood on its hind legs and squeaked as if issuing a warning. JJ chuckled softly. "Just carry on with your business, boys. I won't be long." A moment later, the lock clicked open. JJ pushed the heavy door ajar, grateful for the store's lax security. As he slipped inside, the largest rat sneaked in behind him, disappearing into the darkness.

JJ found himself in a back office that doubled as a storeroom. He drew his pistol, flicked off the safety, and listened intently, his heart pounding in his chest. No amount of training could suppress the adrenaline rush that came with hostage situations. Moments like these reminded him why he loved being a cop.

He heard distant voices and moved toward a small window on the left side of the office, which offered a clear view of the bar area. Climbing onto a crate of beers, he opened the window wider to better hear the conversation. He caught a name—'Sonny Joe'—and made a mental note. The voices grew quieter, replaced by the soft sobs of the young girl.

Suddenly, JJ became aware of another presence in the room. He remained still, waiting for them to reveal themselves. A shadow moved, and JJ realized it was Harper.

"Pssst! Harper!" JJ whispered, trying to get his attention.

Harper, startled, looked around before spotting JJ. He quickly moved over to his position.

"Well, what's the plan?" Harper asked, glancing through the small window. The hostage had stopped crying, sitting frozen with fear. The two gunmen were now in view—one, tall and gaunt, with a rough ponytail, ripped jeans, and a leather vest that revealed a large tattoo of Jesus on the cross with the word 'LOSER' beneath it. The other, shorter and muscular, had a shaved head and a menacing scar on his neck, carrying a shotgun.

"They're getting agitated," Harper observed.

"Here's the plan," JJ said. "I'll take the guy with the shotgun; you take the other."

"That's your plan? Fuck, JJ, how did you pass the FBI tests?" Harper muttered, shaking his head.

JJ just smiled and began to climb down from the crates. He quietly opened the door leading to the side of the bar, motioning for Harper to follow.

"Please, let me go," the bartender sobbed. "I know the combination to the safe. There's money in it, I'll show you. It's in the back." She pointed in the direction of the detectives.

"I'm gonna check it out. You stay here, Sonny," the taller gunman said.

"Okay, but I need a drink," Sonny replied, looking at the terrified girl. She quickly stood and began to pour him a drink. She looked over at Danny, her boss, unconscious with blood oozing out of a leg wound. After she finished pouring the drink, she was grabbed by the arm. "Alright, cutie, take Poppa to the cash," the short man sneered and dragged her toward the back office. The detectives, realizing they were headed their way, moved quickly. Harper rolled under a table while JJ circled around to a stage area behind a set of speakers, keeping both gunmen in his sights.

HARPER LAY STILL under the table. It wasn't the most comfortable position, but it would have to do. Heavy footsteps thudded closer, and Harper turned his head to see a pair of large boots just inches from his face. He could smell the leather—and the man's socks, which reeked of rotten eggs. Harper wrinkled his nose in disgust, trying not to gag.

Then he spotted the bartender's flat-heeled shoe as she was shoved along. She stumbled, falling to the floor, and her eyes widened when she saw Harper hiding under the cabinet. He quickly pressed a finger to his lips, mouthing, "Shh." Luckily, she managed to stifle any reaction. Before she could even return a look of gratitude, she was yanked back to her feet and dragged into the back room.

Harper edged his way out from under the table to get a better view of JJ's position. He could just make out JJ's leg but couldn't risk making any noise to gain his attention. Slowly, he rolled from under the table and crouched behind a jukebox. Now he had JJ's gaze. They signaled their plan of attack—Harper would grab the girl and take out the first gunman, while JJ would take out the second.

They were both ready to move. But just then, the large rat that had slipped in earlier decided to make its presence known. It scurried across the floor, unnoticed by Harper and JJ—but not by the second gunman. At the sight of the rodent, he panicked and opened fire. The rat, sensing danger, bolted, darting past JJ as a shotgun blast ripped into the corner of the speaker he was using for cover. Wooden splinters exploded around him in a burst of sharp debris. JJ barely managed to shield his face from the blast, the fragments stinging his hands and forearms.

"Fuck, that was close," JJ muttered.

All hell broke loose. The second gunman burst out of the back room, dragging the girl with him. Harper tried to move, but Frank and his partner burst in through the front, grabbing both gunmen's attention. The situation had escalated fast.

The gunman pulled the girl close, pressing the shotgun to her head as she screamed and sobbed uncontrollably. Harper ducked back behind the jukebox, which provided little protection against a shotgun blast. He dived back under the table, where he found himself face-to-face with the rat. The rat cowered as if sharing Harper's fear—they were in this together. Harper hated rats but, for once, didn't mind the company.

Several more shots rang out; Frank and his partner retreated, and then an uneasy silence filled the air, the smell of gunpowder mixing with the smoke from the shotgun. In the chaos, one gunman was down. JJ had managed to take out the first gunman just in time, unseen.

The remaining gunman tightened his grip on the shotgun, pressing it harder against the girl's temple.

JJ called out, "Harper, you okay?"

"Yep, but my friend Fievel here is pretty scared," Harper replied, referring to the rat.

"What are you talking about?"

"Never mind. But our guy's got the girl."

"That's right, cop. And if you come any closer, this pretty girl ain't gonna look so pretty anymore. You get my drift?"

"I hear you, Sonny Joe," JJ replied, trying to calm the situation.

"That ain't my name. That's my brother's name."

"Well, you might as well have it. He doesn't need it anymore," Harper quipped.

JJ shot him a discerning look.

"What? What?" Harper shrugged, smirking.

"You killed my brother, you motherfuckers!" the gunman shouted, his voice trembling with rage.

"Look, you don't have to go the same way. Let's talk about this. You haven't shot anyone yet, so things still look good for you. Just put down the weapon and let the girl go. Come on, what do you say?" JJ's voice was firm but measured, his hostage negotiation skills coming into play.

But the gunman's response was swift and brutal. Two more wild shotgun blasts ripped through the bar, exploding bottles and beer glass rained down like hail.

It was no good. JJ knew he had to take the gunman out. He moved closer, eventually finding Harper—still with the rat.

"Is this your friend?" JJ gestured to the rat.

Harper just smiled.

"JJ, meet Fievel. Fievel, this is JJ," Harper joked. The rat twitched its nose, then scurried off, making a quick getaway. "Seems you have the same effect on rats as you do on women," Harper quipped.

JJ smirked. "We've got to get closer," he insisted. They signaled their plan and began to move in. The gunman caught sight of JJ and fired off a couple more rounds, just missing him but shattering the mirror behind the bar.

"Fuck, that was close," JJ muttered, letting out a thankful sigh. He noticed blood trickling from his hand—one of the shards had lodged itself in his skin. It wasn't serious, but it stung like hell. He quickly wrapped a handkerchief around it as a makeshift bandage and peered over the bar.

"You okay?" Harper called out.

JJ nodded, both of them now having a clear view of the gunman. The problem was the girl was far too close—they couldn't risk taking a shot. Before they could think of a new plan, Harper's eyes caught a familiar sight: Fievel, the brazen rat, scurrying back into the chaos. Harper couldn't believe the rodent's sheer disregard for danger, and apparently, neither could the young bartender.

Her eyes widened, and she let out a scream, frantically kicking at the floor. Her sudden outburst caught the gunman by surprise, distracting him just long enough. In the chaos, she managed to break free, scrambling away and diving behind the pool table for cover, leaving the gunman momentarily exposed.

JJ and Harper didn't waste a second. They seized the opportunity, springing into action, ready to turn the tables.

"Drop it," Harper commanded, his voice cold and steady.

JJ moved in from the opposite side and yelled, "Get down on the floor!" The gunman froze for a split second, staring down the barrel of Harper's gun.

Harper, his voice firm and unyielding, barked, "Do yourself a favor." The gunman, realizing he was outgunned and out of options, slowly placed the shotgun on the floor. He then lay flat, spread-eagle on the ground.

Harper swiftly cuffed the man, glancing up at JJ with a grin of accomplishment. With the gunman secured, Harper hauled him up and marched him out of the bar, not before announcing his presence. "Coming out, everything secure?"

Two uniformed officers rushed in and took the gunman into custody; it was over.

Thankfully, only one fatality resulted from the chaotic scene—the first gunman. Frank and his partner, though a little shaken up, were fine.

"You okay, JJ?" Frank asked, concern etched on his face. JJ nodded. Frank's gaze dropped to JJ's crudely bandaged hand.

JJ raised it, shaking his head. "Just glass," he explained, then approached the EMS team that had arrived to get a bandage. The medics were busy loading the bar owner, who was now conscious, onto a stretcher.

As one medic carefully bandaged JJ's hand and another attended to the bar owner's injuries, JJ's mind drifted back to the earlier encounter with the woman he had almost collided with. *Rose*, he thought, her face vivid in his memory.

"What's your name?" JJ asked the bar owner.

"Danny," the man replied, wincing slightly.

"Look, Danny, I wonder if you could help me out," JJ continued. "A woman was speeding up the road earlier, and it seemed like she was in a hurry. Her driving was all over the place, and she was probably a little drunk. Since this is the only bar nearby, I thought she might've come from here. I almost ran into her. Attractive, around forty, with long black hair. Do you know her? Was she drinking here this evening?"

Danny's reply came quickly—too quickly. "Nope, not someone I recognize," he said, his voice defensive.

JJ's instincts pricked at the response, but before he could dig deeper, the EMT ushered him away from the ambulance, shutting the back doors firmly. Moments later, the vehicle sped off, sirens wailing into the night, leaving JJ with a nagging suspicion that the guy was hiding something.

JJ made his way back to Harper, then glanced at his watch. "Let's go," he instructed.

"Where?" Harper asked, raising an eyebrow.

"The hospital," JJ replied.

"At this time? Are you crazy?" Harper exclaimed.

"Why not? Nothing else is going on. Besides, I think my bandage wasn't wrapped properly—it might need looking at," JJ said, holding up his hand as if to prove his point.

Harper shook his head, a grin breaking through despite himself. "It's your head that needs looking at," he retorted.

JJ responded with that familiar, *trust me* look, one Harper knew all too well.

"Okay, okay, let's go," Harper conceded. "We have an hour left of this shift anyway." A moment later they were in their car heading towards the hospital.

FORTY
THE ROOKIE

AT THE FRONT desk the young rookie guard leaned across the counter, brushing a wisp of hair from the young nurse's face. She blushed.

"Shouldn't you be looking after our dangerous criminal in room 241? Protect and serve, isn't that your motto?" she teased.

The rookie grinned. "How about I protect and serve you over dinner sometime?"

"Maybe," she replied, playing hard to get.

"There's a new club just opened called Thursdays. It's supposed to be great."

"Actually, it's called Fridays, and you're right—it is a great club. I've been."

"So is it a date?"

"Maybe."

"Give me your number, and I'll call you this weekend."

The nurse rolled her eyes, debating whether dating a cop was a good idea. She looked back at him—he was kind of cute, she thought, finally smiling.

"Okay, one date. And if you're nice to me, maybe another." She reached into her top pocket for her pen, only to find it missing. The cop offered his pen, but she declined—hers was special, a gift from her father, and it had to be found.

"Where did you have it last?" he asked.

She retraced her steps in her mind, then suddenly lit up. "Charlie's room!" she exclaimed with a smile. They began heading in that direction, but their progress was leisurely. They frequently paused to chat, sharing laughter and playful looks, unaware of the urgency they should have felt. Charlie's situation was growing dire, but they had no idea of his impending danger.

They finally stopped outside a room marked with a plaque that read 'Private.' They exchanged a look, momentarily distracted, and a smile spread between them as they blushed, the urgency briefly slipping to the back of their minds.

The rookie cop thought, perhaps optimistically, that this might not be as hard as he'd imagined. With that thought, he pushed open the door, and the nurse stepped inside. The rookie glanced around the room quickly, taking in his surroundings, before following her in.

FORTY-ONE
MISSING

IT WAS 2:15 a.m. when JJ and Harper parked their car and hurried toward Ward 9. The hospital corridor was dimly lit, with only a few flickering lights casting long shadows on the sterile walls. JJ was the first to notice the empty chair outside Charlie's room, and his eyes narrowed with frustration.

"Shit, that rookie left the room unattended again. I'm gonna have his badge, the son of a bitch," JJ muttered, his anger bubbling to the surface.

"Calm down, JJ. There's probably a good explanation," Harper said, trying to calm him. But as the words left his lips, the door marked 'Private' swung open. The rookie stepped out first, looking sheepish, followed closely by the nurse, her face flushed. She adjusted her belt, brushed her hands through her tousled hair, and then froze, spotting the detectives.

"Great explanation," JJ sneered.

"Good enough for me—she is kinda cute," Harper chuckled, unable to resist a grin.

JJ paused, shot Harper a disapproving look, and shook his head. "What did I say, boss? What did I say?" Harper scoffed, amused.

JJ didn't answer. He half-smiled, shook his head again, and quickened his pace down the corridor. Harper followed, still grinning, though at a more leisurely pace.

The rookie, now aware of their approach, paled. He knew he was in deep trouble but hadn't yet grasped how deep. Sensing the tension, the nurse hurried toward Charlie's room, trying to act casual.

JJ let loose on the rookie. "What the hell were you thinking, leaving your post? You're supposed to be watching a key witness, not chasing skirts!"

A sharp cry pierced the air before Harper could say much to defuse the situation. "Oh my God!" The nurse's voice trembled, and the corridor fell silent. JJ and Harper rushed to the door of Charlie's room, JJ shoving the nurse aside as he barged in.

Charlie's bed was empty.

Harper turned to the rookie cop; eyebrows raised in disbelief. "You know that shit you were in? It just got deeper."

JJ rushed to the open window, peering outside. "He didn't escape through the window, that's for sure. We're two stories up, and he was too ill to climb down." His eyes scanned the room, locking onto a pair of handcuffs dangling from the bedframe. "How the hell did he get out of these?" he demanded, grabbing the cuff and thrusting them in the rookie's face.

The nurse quickly intervened; her voice shaky. "That's my fault. I asked Greg—" She hesitated, then corrected herself. "I asked Officer Blake to loosen them. They seemed tight, and I—"

"They seemed tight?" JJ roared, making the nurse flinch. "They're supposed to be tight to stop him from escaping. For God's sake, Greg!" He turned his glare back to the rookie. "Officer Blake, what the hell were you thinking?"

The nurse, tears brimming in her eyes, tried again. "He was an old man—he wasn't even conscious. He couldn't just walk out of here!"

"I've got news for you," JJ snapped. "That old man may have been our only witness to a murder. And unless I'm mistaken, he didn't just float out of this building."

Harper sensed JJ had gone too far and stepped in. "You're right, JJ. He couldn't have just floated out of here." JJ continued to glare at the nurse, who turned and fled the room, tears streaming down her face.

"That was big," the rookie muttered under his breath.

"Don't push it. Now get the hell out of here—and I suggest you dig out your outdoor uniform. You're writing tickets tomorrow," JJ barked. The rookie left, slamming the door behind him.

As the door slammed shut, Harper tried to ease the tension. "Look, JJ, he's an old guy. He can't have gone far. The sooner we start looking, the quicker we'll find him."

JJ took a deep breath, trying to calm his temper. His eyes swept the room, and something on the floor caught his attention. He crouched down, examining the mark closely.

"What is it, JJ?" Harper asked, stepping forward.

"A footprint," JJ replied, his voice taut with focus.

"Probably the rookie's," Harper said dismissively, peering over JJ's shoulder.

"Maybe?" JJ moved toward the window, pushing aside a few medical trolleys. He noticed a ledge about two feet up where another print was visible. "Then again, if it was the rookie, I don't think he would have climbed in through the window." He gestured for Harper to come over and take a look.

Harper moved closer and peered down. JJ was right—the footprint was facing inward as if someone had climbed in. JJ climbed out onto the ledge and then onto the fire escape, simulating the motion of entering through the window. Harper spoke up, "Do you think our guy, whoever he is, climbed in, grabbed Charlie, and carried him down the fire escape?"

JJ followed the fading footprints, his movements mirroring those of the intruder, almost as if transporting himself back to the moment. "Our guy went over to this coat stand, probably to grab a jacket."

"Doctor's coat," Harper interjected.

"Maybe," JJ replied, scanning the room. "Where's the wheelchair Charlie came in on?" He glanced around, his mind racing. "I need to see the CCTV footage. Whoever took him wheeled him straight out of the building."

He quickly pulled out a packet of surgical gloves from his pocket and slipped them on. "Get Forensics in here ASAP and close this area off."

"Okay, JJ, but don't you think we should try to find Charlie first? If he did manage to walk out, he can't have gone far."

"He's been gone for one hour and thirty-eight minutes. Even if—and that's a big if—he walked out, he's long gone by now."

Harper turned to JJ, hands on his hips, confused. "How the hell can you be so precise?"

"What time is it?" JJ asked.

"Two thirty-one a.m."

"Well, now he's been gone one hour and thirty-nine minutes." JJ pointed to the medical equipment next to the bed. Harper moved closer, his brow furrowed, still trying to grasp JJ's logic.

"Okay, I'm looking. What am I supposed to see?" Harper asked, clearly baffled.

JJ had gathered a pile of paper that had spilled from the EKG machine, tearing off a section near to the end. He handed the strip to Harper. As Harper unrolled it, JJ gestured toward the now-silent heart monitor, which had been switched off.

"This is an EKG—it monitors the heart," JJ explained, watching Harper study the strip of paper. "See these steady blips? They rise and fall evenly." JJ pointed.

"Yeah, I see them," Harper replied, his eyes following the rhythmic pattern of peaks and troughs.

"Now, look at the distance between the peaks and the height of the peaks. See how they gradually get higher, and the spaces between them get shorter?" JJ continued, his finger tracing the increasing frequency of the blips. JJ turned and headed to the door, leaving Harper behind him.

"Uh-huh," Harper nodded, starting to catch on. Then he noticed that JJ was heading out of the door.

"Good. Now, notice where the blips suddenly stop, and the line goes flat." He continued as he walked, "Look at the time printed at the top, right where the flat line begins. What does it say?"

Harper squinted at the timestamp on the footage. "Twelve fifty-two a.m.," he read aloud, comprehension slowly dawning on his face. As he looked up, he noticed JJ already on his phone, arranging for a forensic team to head to Charlie's room.

JJ ended the call, slipping his cell phone back into his pocket. He turned back to Harper, picking up where they'd left off in their conversation.

"Twelve fifty-two a.m. was the moment he left," JJ continued, his tone measured and calm. "Before that, his pulse was racing, which means he was scared—more than a little."

"Or he died," Harper suggested, a hint of skepticism in his voice.

JJ shook his head. "Not likely. Why would someone go through the trouble of stealing a dead body?"

"Good point," Harper conceded, mulling it over. "Maybe he had help to escape."

JJ paused, taking a deep breath as his mind raced through the possibilities. "Maybe," he replied, nodding slowly. "But either way, we've got to act fast."

They arrived at the front desk, where JJ asked the receptionist for directions to the CCTV room. She pointed to a small room off to the side, and without wasting a moment, JJ and Harper made their way over. Knocking on the door, they didn't wait for a response before stepping inside.

After a brief look at the footage, which yielded no conclusive clues, they emerged from the room carrying the last two hours of tape. The images were grainy, but JJ knew there might be something hidden in the details. First thing in the morning, he would take it to Forensics to have the footage cleaned up, hoping it would reveal the answers they desperately needed.

As they left more uniformed officers arrived to secure the area. This was now an active crime scene, and JJ was determined to get some answers.

FORTY-TWO
A WALK IN THE PARK

ROSE SLIPPED her key into the door, turning it slowly to avoid making a sound. The lock clicked softly, and she gently pushed the door open, carefully closing it behind her with a quiet click. She stood, listening for any signs of movement, desperately hoping she hadn't woken Jack. The apartment was silent, save for the faint hum of the refrigerator and the ticking of the wall clock.

She crept towards her room, slipping off her shoes as she went. Her bare feet moved quietly across the polished wooden floor, the cool surface grounding her—a small comfort as she steadied herself. The whiskey still buzzed through her veins; she'd had a bit too much to drink. As she tried to walk in a straight line, she wobbled slightly but managed to keep her balance. Her mind drifted back to the near miss with the police car earlier. Thankfully, they hadn't given chase; she was in no fit state to drive, and an encounter would have completely ruined her plans.

Her eyes flicked to the clock on the wall—it read 3:38 a.m. A knot of anxiety tightened in her stomach. It was later than she'd intended.

As she removed her gloves and set them on the side table, a foul smell suddenly assaulted her nostrils. She froze, taking a deeper breath, and the stench seemed to claw its way into her insides, nearly making her retch. With a sense of unease, she moved further into the room, each step bringing her closer to the source of the odor. The smell grew stronger and more overpowering, filling her senses with a sickening dread.

Suddenly, a searing pain shot through her heel as she stepped on something sharp. Instinctively, she tried to balance on one foot but stumbled backwards, her back crashing into the kitchen wall. The impact stopped her fall, but she slid down slowly, her palms scraping against the wall to control her descent. The pain pulsed up her leg, radiating from her foot in hot, relentless waves. She grimaced, her teeth clenched tightly, and carefully reached down. Her trembling fingers frantically felt around the floor, searching for the offending object that had pierced her skin.

As her hand swept across the floor, she felt it land in something thick and lumpy. Panic flared in her chest. She instinctively brought her hand to her nose to identify the substance, but halfway there, a realization struck her—vomit. She recoiled, a wave of nausea hitting her as she frantically wiped her hand on her pants, her stomach churning from the foul stench that now filled her nostrils causing her to retch.

Jumping to her feet, she winced as she stepped on something sharp again. This time, her cry was louder, more desperate. Limping, she reached for the wall to steady herself, her fingers fumbling for the light switch. When she finally flicked it on, the room was suddenly flooded with harsh, bright light. She blinked against it, her eyes adjusting, and then she saw it—the room was a disaster.

Furniture was overturned, broken pieces of shattered plastic from what looked like the radio, or what was left of it, littered the floor like tiny daggers. Her heart raced as she looked around, her gaze finally landing on the puddle of vomit smeared across the kitchen floor. Panic surged through her veins like ice. What had happened here? And where was Jack?

Her mind raced with possibilities—an intruder, a fight, some terrible accident. She could feel her pulse pounding in her temples as she limped forward, avoiding the radio guts. She needed to find Jack. She needed to know he was safe. The silence that had seemed so comforting moments before now felt heavy and oppressive, like the calm before a storm.

"Jack?" she called out, her voice trembling. There was no answer, only the echo of her own voice in the chaos of the room. She swallowed hard, fear gripping her tighter with every passing second.

She quickly made her way to his room, trying to avoid the pieces of shattered radio. Blood oozed from her feet, leaving a trail of red footprints across the floor. She reached Jack's door, pushed it open, and flipped on the light—his bed was empty. Frantically, she searched the apartment, calling out his name, her voice growing more desperate with each unanswered call. But Jack was nowhere to be found.

She slumped to the floor, her breath coming in ragged gasps. Before she could gather her thoughts, she heard a key turning in the front door. Her heart leaped into her throat. She struggled to her feet, shouting, "Jack?" The door swung open, and relief washed over her—it was Jack.

"Are you okay? What happened here tonight? Where have you been? Are you okay?" She fired questions at him in rapid succession, her voice frantic.

Jack didn't respond at first. His face was pale, and he looked dazed. Rose reached out, touching his forehead. He was cold and clammy. She helped him out of his jacket, guiding him to a chair as he rubbed his hands through his disheveled hair.

"What happened here tonight, Jack?" she demanded.

"Food poisoning," he muttered, avoiding her gaze.

"What are you talking about?" Rose asked, her confusion deepening.

"I think the rabbit bake was off. I started feeling sick, so I came out of my room. The cat knocked over some pans. I knocked over the radio. I tried to get a drink, but then I threw up. Still felt awful, so I went out for some fresh air. Simple as that—okay?"

Jack's voice was defensive, his explanation hurried and unconvincing. He omitted the part about the monsters he'd seen or the voices he'd heard—especially their father's voice.

Rose already sensed something was off. His story explained the mess, and he did look genuinely ill, but something didn't sit right with her. She decided not to press him further, at least not yet.

"So, where did you go?" she asked, her tone softening.

"I needed some air," Jack replied. "Went for a walk around the park."

She wrinkled her nose. "You reek of booze," she said, a note of worry creeping into her voice. "For God's sake, Jack, please don't tell me you're drinking again," she pleaded, her eyes searching his face for the truth.

"It was just medicine for my flu," he protested weakly. He began to take off his jacket.

"I thought you said food poisoning," Rose interjected.

"Whatever it was, I thought a drink would help me sleep," he said defensively. "But it didn't—it made things worse."

"What do you mean?" Rose asked, her eyes narrowing. "And what happened to the radio?"

Jack followed her gaze to the broken device. "It's evil," he whispered, his voice cracking. "Possessed. The voices… Pop's voice, Brad's voice, the monsters—they were all screaming at me," he cried.

Rose's expression softened, her initial shock giving way to concern. She stepped closer and placed a gentle hand on his shoulder, trying to steady him.

"Jack," she said softly, her voice filled with worry, "we'll figure this out. I promise. Did you take your medication today?" she asked carefully.

Jack said nothing, his expression distant and troubled. His eyes flicked to the clock on the wall: 3:52 a.m. "So, where have you been until now?" he demanded, suspicion threading through his voice.

Not ready—or willing—to answer, Rose leaned in closer, catching a whiff of his clothes. "What's that smell? Hang on, that's weed," she said, her tone hardening. "Since when did you start smoking marijuana? No wonder you were hearing voices!" Her voice cut through the room, sharp and accusatory. Her eyes widened, locking onto his, and the concern that had softened her expression moments ago was swiftly replaced with anger, demanding an explanation.

Jack looked up. "It wasn't the weed," he protested, shrugging his shoulders. Rose stared at him, waiting for an explanation that never came. Frustrated, she let out a sigh. She had bigger concerns at the moment; the pain in her feet was flaring up again, demanding her attention. For now, the interrogation would have to wait. The unanswered questions lingered in the air, but she knew they would have to be addressed later, when she had the strength—and when Jack could remember.

Jack helped Rose to the couch and fetched a warm bowl of water to soak her feet. Carefully, he tried to remove the shards of plastic embedded in her foot, but his woozy hands only made things worse, causing her more pain.

Rose winced but offered him a gentle smile. "It's okay; I can finish this," she said, taking the bandage from him. "You get off to bed. I'll clear all this up." She smiled softly. "We can talk about what happened tomorrow, when we're both in a better frame of mind."

"You mean today," Jack said, glancing around at the mess. He looked at the clock—it was now 4:33 a.m.

Rose followed his gaze and nodded. "Indeed, it is today. Don't worry, I'll sort it out," she reassured him.

Jack gave a tired smile. "If you're sure?"

"I'm sure," she replied with a small nod. After sharing a brief smile, Jack turned and made his way to bed, leaving Rose alone.

Once Jack had gone, Rose quickly tidied up the chaos left behind. She made her way to the cupboard and retrieved a pill bottle labeled 'Jack.' Opening it, she peered inside, her lips moved silently as she counted the pills. Realization dawned on her: he had been skipping his medication. It wasn't food poisoning or the flu causing his erratic behavior—it was something far more serious. A wave of concern washed over her. She would have to keep a closer eye on him and make sure he took his medication regularly.

But that worry was for tomorrow, or later, she thought, glancing at the clock. The time made her yawn, exhaustion setting in. With the apartment now quiet and the earlier commotion fading into stillness, she finally made her way to her room. Closing the door behind her, she allowed herself to relax, though the dull throb from her foot lingered as a reminder of the night's events.

FORTY-THREE
THE BLUE PILL

JACK, still a little groggy, woke up a little later than usual, and Rose was still fast asleep. After all, they had both endured a pretty traumatic night and early morning. He wasn't ready to face the difficult conversation he had promised to have with her—about the voices in his head, the monsters, his drinking, and the joint he had discovered in his pocket and smoked. The memory of how he'd gotten it from Max resurfaced suddenly.

"Max!" he said, jolting upright. He'd promised to call and tell him about the train Rose had bought him months ago, which he had yet to add to his model railway collection, and the intricate landscape he had spent so much time constructing. Just as this thought drifted away, he heard the creaking of a door. Rose was awake.

Panic bubbled up inside Jack. The last thing he wanted was to dive into an awkward conversation about his demons. He knew he'd forgotten to take his medication, and that was likely the reason for his delusions returning. Desperate for a distraction, he dressed, and quickly made his way to the kitchen where he began preparing breakfast, hoping to delay the inevitable discussion just a little longer.

"Morning," came a voice from behind him.

Jack turned to see Rose reaching into the cupboard and pulling out two identical pill bottles. The only difference between them was the name: 'Jack' on one and 'Rose' on the other.

"I checked yours last night," she said, her voice firm. "I counted the pills, Jack. You've been missing your dose. You know what happens when you don't take them." She walked to the sink, filled a cup with water, and tossed his pill bottle to him. Jack sighed, opened the bottle, and retrieved two blue pills. Rose gestured for him to take them. He placed the pills in his mouth, swallowed, and then took the water from her, washing them down.

Rose wasn't completely satisfied. She locked eyes with him, waiting for proof. Jack opened his mouth, wiggling his tongue playfully. "Satisfied?" he said with a grin.

"Jack, you *need* to take them. You know what happens when you don't." Her voice carried an edge of worry. Jack nodded, but deep down, he knew the truth. The recent events were more than just missed doses. He had only skipped a couple, and yet, what he was experiencing felt disturbingly real. He could feel things, hear things.

"So, am I forgiven?" he asked, his voice lighter.

"For what?" she replied, a small smile tugging at her lips.

"For earlier."

Rose's smile widened. "You're forgiven," she said, placing two blue tablets in her own mouth and swallowing them quickly, chasing them with a gulp of water. Her mood reset, the tension between them softening as the morning light filled the room.

"So, you got back late," Jack said, a hint of suspicion in his voice. "Must have been a great night with Candice."

Rose felt her stomach tighten but forced a cheerful smile. She hoped he'd forgotten the exact time she came in, but Jack never forgot anything. *Keep the mood light*, she reminded herself. "We went for a quick drink at the Cattle Drive and got a bit carried away," she replied, letting out a forced chuckle.

Jack raised an eyebrow. "I figured you might've had a drink or two —you were pretty wasted last night."

"Just a little," she said, laughing again, trying to brush it off.

Jack turned back to the stove. "I was just about to make breakfast," he announced over his shoulder.

Rose saw this as the perfect opportunity to shift the conversation. "No way," she said, determined to take control. She opened the refrigerator, pulled out ingredients, and playfully gestured for him to step aside.

Jack knew better than to argue over who would cook. With a small, knowing smile, he conceded, stepping back to set the kitchen table as Rose took over breakfast duty.

The tension from earlier lingered, but for now, the kitchen was filled with the warmth of playful banter and the familiar routine they both needed.

As he laid out the plates, he spoke matter-of-factly. "I'm gonna call the doctor. Something's wrong, and I think she can help."

Rose looked up, a little startled by his announcement. "Jack, you don't need the doctor, you need to make sure you take your medication," Rose replied.

"I know, but maybe they missed something, or perhaps something has changed since I left the hospital..." Jack hesitated, his voice trailing off before adding quietly, "Or maybe the doctor was right."

"It's probably just after-effects of the coma. They did all the tests, remember? They gave you a clean bill of health."

Rose placed a plate of bacon, eggs, sausage, and hash browns in front of him, with a side of toast. The delicious smell wafted up and Jack instantly dug in. The conversation paused, with Rose waiting expectantly. But Jack remained silent, the moment slipping away.

"What exactly did the doctor say, Jack?" she asked, her tone more insistent now, eyes fixed on him.

Jack shrugged, absent-mindedly buttering a slice of toast and dipping it into the eggs, cooked sunny-side up, just how he liked them. "She mentioned something about the demons in my head." He paused then took a bite of his toast. "Maybe I am going mad."

"You're not going crazy," Rose said firmly. "You just got out of a coma. You nearly died, Jack. Don't even think like that. What you need is a night out. Call Max, go do something fun. You haven't even unwrapped the train I bought you."

She offered her untouched plate to Jack, who eagerly accepted. Rose managed a smile despite her worry. "See? You've got your appetite back. You'll be fine once you're back at work next week. Fresh air will do you good."

Jack frowned but nodded, obviously not wanting to upset Rose any further. "Maybe you're right, but I'd feel better after a check-up."

"If you insist, I'll call Dr. Amen," Rose offered, referring to their family doctor.

"No," Jack said firmly. "I want to see Dr. Warwick. She understands what I've been through. I'll make an appointment for this afternoon."

Rose wasn't happy with his decision, but she knew arguing wouldn't change his mind.

"So, what are you up to today?" she asked, trying to change the subject.

Jack wiped his plate clean with the last bit of toast, then shrugged. "I haven't decided yet. What about you?"

"I've got some work to do for the magazine. One of the new designers messed with the artwork without my consent, so I need to straighten that out."

Jack kissed her forehead as he got up. "Give 'em hell. I'm sure you will."

Rose smiled as she watched him head into the study. "Your train is by the table," she called out. "I hope it's the one you wanted."

Jack's face lit up as he spotted the brown paper bag. "It's perfect," he said, grinning like a kid on Christmas morning.

For a moment, everything felt normal again.

FORTY-FOUR
746 LONG STRIPE J

AS ROSE BUSIED herself in the kitchen, Jack rummaged through the study, his movements hurried and distracted. He tripped over a magazine rack, sending a few publications tumbling to the floor. With an annoyed grunt, he bent down to pick them up, sifting through the scattered magazines until he found what he was looking for—last month's *Model Railroader*. He placed it on the table, then reached for the phone and dialed a number. After a few rings, he was met with an answering machine's familiar yet frustrating voice. "Thanks for calling. Sorry, I'm not here. Leave a message."

"Damn answering machines," Jack muttered under his breath. He hung up without bothering to leave a message, making a mental note to call Gary back later. He wanted to inform him of his new acquisition —and maybe gloat a little, just for good measure.

Dialing again, he waited until the call was answered. "Hi, yes, this is Jack Brooks. I'd like to speak to Dr. Warrick... Oh, she's not available? Well, can I make an appointment for this afternoon? No? How about tomorrow? Two-thirty? Great."

After placing the receiver back on its cradle, Jack quickly jotted down the appointment time, tore off the note, and slipped it into his pocket. Satisfied and holding his 746 Long Stripe J model train in hand, he made his way to the spare room, where his pride and joy awaited him. He pushed the door open wide, revealing a meticulously crafted model of the Old West. The room was filled with a sprawling display: papier-mâché mountains towered over winding railway tracks, and a carefully arranged frontier town stretched across a massive table that took up nearly the entire space, leaving only narrow paths to navigate around it.

Jack's eyes sparkled with anticipation as he carefully placed his new train on the tracks, aligning it perfectly. With a flick of a switch, the train roared to life, its wheels clattering rhythmically along the rails. It raced through the miniature town, weaving between tiny saloons and stables, narrowly avoiding an attack from a group of Indian horsemen strategically poised on the edge of a ridge.

The scene burst into motion; every detail animated before his eyes. For a moment, Jack was completely absorbed in the miniature world he had painstakingly created—a world where he controlled every twist and turn, every story and outcome. It was his perfect escape, a place where he could lose himself in the thrill of the adventure, leaving the outside world and all its complications far behind, even if for a short while.

He only had five days left of his rehabilitation, and Jack couldn't wait to get back to the real world—most of all, to his beloved garden. Even though the garden technically belonged to the school, he had always thought of it as his own private sanctuary; a place where he could escape the chaos of everyday life and find peace among the plants. The thought of returning to his little patch of paradise was what kept him going through the long, grueling hours of therapy.

But as much as he longed to return, a small worry nagged at him. He just hoped Will had taken good care of the garden in his absence. Will was the backbone of the maintenance team—solid, dependable, and always ready to lend a hand. But gardening wasn't exactly his specialty. Jack had left him with detailed instructions on how to care for the plants, going over every detail: how to prune the rose bushes, water the delicate flower beds, and maintain the soil. Despite his confidence in Will's abilities, he couldn't help but worry that the garden might not receive the same care and attention he had always given it.

He could already picture stepping back into the sunlight, feeling the earth between his fingers, pruning the overgrown branches, and repairing the grounds in preparation for autumn, which was just around the corner. The anticipation of returning to his garden filled him with a sense of purpose, a reminder of the life waiting for him outside these walls.

FORTY-FIVE
SACRIFICE

JJ WOKE EARLY THAT MORNING, a sense of purpose driving him that had been building for days. As he sat at the breakfast table, he retrieved his notepad from the jacket hanging on the back of his chair. Flipping through the pages, he replayed recent events in his mind. Where had Charlie gone? Had he escaped, been kidnapped, or perhaps even rescued? Each possible answer seemed to open up more questions than it solved.

He glanced at the clock and then checked his diary: at 1 p.m. there was a note: 'Forensics.' *I need to call Harper and get him to meet me there*, he thought. Reaching into his jacket pocket, he pulled out his cell phone. With a flick of his wrist, the mouthpiece snapped open, and he made the call.

"You up?" JJ asked. He pulled the phone away from his ear as a muffled, somewhat irritated voice came through the speaker. "Do you kiss Maggie with that mouth?" JJ joked, grinning. "Yeah, I know it's early. Just wanted to let you know I'm popping over to the Cattle Drive first to follow up on last night. Maybe I can figure out whether I really did see Rose."

JJ paused, listening to Harper's muffled reply before cutting in.

"No reason, just making inquiries, that kind of—" He was interrupted by another garbled request from Harper. JJ chuckled. "I will, but you know those things are gonna kill you, right?" he quipped.

"Don't forget, one p.m. at the lab," he reminded Harper. "We've got a meeting with Dr. Zhang. See you then." Ending the call, JJ returned his focus to his notebook, his mind already racing ahead, piecing together the clues.

He checked another entry in his diary: 'Sherlock, 4 p.m.' This meeting was crucial. Here, he would learn about all the evidence gathered from Bradley Marshall's house. JJ knew something wasn't right; there were too many red flags, and his resolve hardened. Brad's death was more than it seemed, and JJ was determined to prove it.

As soon as he arrived at the station, he planned to approach the division captain and request a formal murder investigation. He knew his evidence was circumstantial at best, but the captain had always trusted his instincts. Still, it would help if he could present something more concrete—anything to strengthen his case and justify the overtime request.

Convincing Harper would be easier. His partner trusted JJ's hunches, even when the proof was thin.

After pouring himself a strong, sweet coffee, JJ leaned back on a stool and closed the worn leather notebook he had pulled from his jacket pocket. The initials *DJ* were inscribed on the cover: Dug Jackson. It had once belonged to his father and had been passed down to JJ when he graduated from Rookie School.

Inside, written in his father's bold, familiar handwriting, were a few simple yet powerful words: *To my son, JJ—Protect and serve*. It was signed *Captain*—a title that had belonged to JJ's father, a legacy JJ carried with pride and a sense of duty.

JJ stared at the notebook, feeling a wave of pride mixed with sorrow. His father, once a strong man, was now in the final stages of a battle with cancer. The doctors were not optimistic, and his father, always the realist, had accepted the truth. He wasn't afraid to face death; he just didn't want the cancer to define his final days. JJ only wished he had half of his father's courage.

He moved into the living room, his gaze drifting to a small, framed photo beside the phone. In the picture, a young, attractive woman clung to his neck, both of them smiling, their eyes bright—a snapshot from a time when life felt full of promise. JJ's lips curved into a bittersweet smile as the memory floated to the surface, now edged with a deep, lingering regret. He had made countless sacrifices for his career, and she was one of the biggest.

They had been divorced for five years now, but he still missed her, especially during the long, lonely nights. He remembered the love they had shared—the spontaneous trips to North Carolina to visit her parents, the way they laughed and held hands on their drives, their shared love of camping under the stars. But JJ had always been torn between two loves: Christina and the police force. His badge had demanded long hours, a hardened heart, and a commitment that left little room for anything else.

He often wondered if they had made the right decision to part ways. In quiet moments like this, the silence around him pressing in, he wasn't so sure. Alone with his thoughts, he questioned if his dedication to the job had cost him his chance at true happiness. The life he chose was a constant tug-of-war between duty and love, and as the years passed, he found himself increasingly uncertain about which one truly mattered more. He sighed deeply, the weight of his choices pressing down on him, knowing that some sacrifices never stop hurting.

The room around him was a testament to his dedication—a couple of plaques and marksman trophies gleamed in a small display cabinet, while framed commendations and a newspaper clipping took pride of place on the wall. JJ remembered the day he earned his first commendation. His father had been so proud. Becoming a cop wasn't just about living up to his father's expectations; it was something deeper, something innate. It was in his blood. It was his destiny.

JJ's eyes drifted to the package sitting on the counter: the CCTV footage from the hospital. He'd need to drop it off at Forensics on his way to the Cattle Drive, making sure his friend Sherlock would review it in time for their crucial meeting at 4 p.m.

Glancing at his watch, he realized how much time had slipped away. Cursing under his breath, he quickly grabbed his jacket, his keys, and the package. In a few swift strides, he was out the door, leaving his apartment behind as he hurried down the steps. His mind was already racing with the possibilities of what the day might reveal —and what he might uncover next. But first, he had to get to the Cattle Drive.

FORTY-SIX
BACK TO NORMAL

MEANWHILE, BACK AT THE BROOKS' apartment, the phone rang in the kitchen, its shrill tone cutting through the silence. Jack had turned off the one in his study to avoid distractions. After several rings, Rose emerged from her bedroom, slipping on her shoes as she hurried to answer.

"Hello—Hi, Max. Yes, he's here. I'll go get him." She hadn't spoken to Max since the night of Jack's disappearance, and though it had been a while, she still felt the need to apologize for her behavior. "Look, Max, about that night..." she began, but Max quickly reassured her, cutting the apology short. Relieved, she placed the phone on the kitchen worktop and went to fetch Jack, placing her other shoe on as she walked.

She eased open the door to the study. Jack was fully engrossed in his hobby, meticulously painting the face of an Indian horseman with an artist's precision, his right eye scrunched behind a jeweler's eyepiece for better detail. Absorbed in crafting his imaginary world, he didn't notice Rose enter. She watched quietly for a moment, not wanting to disturb him during such a delicate task. She waited until he dipped his paintbrush into a small paint pot before speaking.

"Jack," she called softly, careful not to startle him. He turned to face her. "Max is on the phone."

Jack smiled, setting down the paintbrush and wiping his hands on an old rag. He followed Rose into the kitchen.

She clipped on her earrings, grabbed her jacket, and asked, "Do you need anything from town?"

Jack shook his head. "No, I'm good," he replied, picking up the phone.

Rose smiled, feeling a sense of normalcy returning. "See you later," she said, heading for the door.

Jack waved goodbye as he began his conversation with Max.

"Hi, Max. Yeah, all good… Monday, hopefully. Right, can't wait to get back to work." Jack paused, listening for a response. "Are you coming round?" He checked his watch. "Okay… how's eleven thirty a.m.?" Another pause. "Alright, meet you at the Cattle Drive."

Jack's voice brightened. "Hey, before you go—remember the train I told you about? The one coming up for auction?" He listened, then nodded. "Yeah, that's the one. A little expensive, but worth it."

He hesitated, then added, "One more thing—Rose has got some tickets for The Catz Club on Friday. You up for it?" Another pause. "Great, I'll let her know. See you then. Bye."

Jack hung up, feeling his mood shift entirely. The thoughts of demons and eerie voices from the radio were momentarily pushed aside. Maybe it was the pills taking effect, maybe it was hearing from Max, his old school friend and fellow train enthusiast, or perhaps it was the comfort he'd found in spending time with his train collection, escaping into his world of imagination.

Or maybe it was all those things combined, each one a hopeful sign that life was slowly returning to normal.

FORTY-SEVEN
QUID PRO QUO

AFTER DROPPING off the CCTV footage at forensics and handing it over to Sherlock—one of the few people he trusted—JJ explained what had happened before they parted ways. Moments later, he was back in his car, heading out of the city toward the Cattle Drive. Twenty minutes later, he arrived at the scene of that morning's shooting.

The area was being put back together: workmen were boarding up shattered windows, police tape was being wrapped up, and the crackle of a lone police unit's radio drifted through the air. The bright morning sun and clear blue sky masked the chaos that had erupted just hours earlier, but the acrid smell of gunpowder still lingered.

JJ made his way into the building and spotted the owner. "Danny, isn't it?" JJ called out. Danny looked up from where he was sweeping broken glass, limping as he moved. Other staff members bustled around, cleaning up the mess.

"How's the leg?" JJ asked.

"In and out," Danny replied. "I was lucky." He paused, his expression sincere. "I didn't get a chance to thank you guys. It could've been a lot worse."

JJ nodded. "Yes, they were pretty high on something. Shame one of them had to die."

Danny's expression shifted. "Was it?" he replied.

"Maybe not," JJ said, studying him carefully. He needed answers, and he didn't have much time. "Look, we spoke last night about women."

Danny handed his broom to a staff member mopping up the dried blood and gestured for JJ to follow him to a nearby table. They sat down, Danny looking uncomfortable.

"Yes, we did," Danny said. "And I told you—I don't remember any women named Rose."

JJ kept his cool, though he knew Danny was lying. JJ had only given a description, never the name. The fact that Danny mentioned it unprompted confirmed his suspicions.

"I know," JJ replied, his tone casual. "And I believe you." He didn't, of course, but he wanted to give Danny one last chance. Reaching into his jacket pocket, he pulled out a folded magazine clipping. He opened it and tapped the image. "I just want to be sure. This is the woman I was referring to."

Danny glanced at the photo, far too quickly. "Nope, never seen her before," he said, avoiding JJ's eyes.

JJ smiled; the lie obvious to him. Why was Danny hiding the truth? "Alright, no problem, Danny. I'll get out of your hair."

JJ stood, and Danny tried to get up, but the pain from his gunshot wound made it difficult. JJ reached out a hand but pulled back, noting Danny's discomfort. "That's okay. I'll see myself out. That must hurt like hell," he said, gesturing to Danny's injured leg.

Danny sank back into his chair. "Yeah, it does," he muttered.

JJ tucked the magazine clipping back into his pocket. "You have a nice day, Danny."

Danny just nodded, watching as JJ left. As JJ stepped outside, he caught Danny's gaze through a pane of broken glass propped against a post. Danny's eyes followed him, and everything about their conversation felt off. JJ knew one thing for sure: Danny was lying.

As JJ made his way back to the car, he noticed a woman approaching the entrance of the bar. It was the bartender from the incident. Before she could enter the building, JJ intercepted her.

"Hey, how are you? Shouldn't you be taking the day off? Last night was pretty intense," JJ said.

"It was," she replied, "but it's not the first time. It gets pretty rowdy in there some nights." JJ couldn't help but admire her toughness.

"I didn't catch your name," he said.

"Grace," she replied, offering a small smile. "And I didn't get a chance to thank you for saving me."

"Saving Grace," JJ quipped, but the reference seemed lost on her. He pressed on, "Since I saved your life, maybe you can help me out—a bit of quid pro quo?" Again, the reference didn't land, but she looked curious.

"How can I help you?" she asked.

JJ had already pulled out the magazine clipping from his pocket. He unfolded it and showed her. "Do you know this woman?"

Grace glanced at the image and shrugged. "No, she looks fancy," she said.

"Take another look," JJ urged. "Have you ever seen her here, at this bar, before?" Grace studied the image more closely this time.

"Actually, now that you mention it," she said, a hint of recognition lighting her eyes, "I have seen her here once or twice. I've only been working here a couple of weeks, but she was here last night, right before the fight and shooting started." She thought for a moment. "She was playing pool with some guys."

JJ took out his notebook and pen. "Do you remember any of those guys, Grace?" he asked.

"Hmm, let me see," she said, thinking. "There was Jake, Tony, and another guy... tall, dressed in black, with a tattoo on his face. Kinda creepy." She paused, then added, "Luke, I think his name is."

JJ wrote down the names and thanked Grace. She gave him a quick nod and headed back into the bar. JJ watched her go, feeling a new lead beginning to take shape. The day was looking promising, but there was one surprise still waiting for him.

As he was about to leave the car park, he stopped to let a car pass. As it rolled by, he noticed the driver—it was Jack. JJ caught his eye and called out through the window. "Hey, Jack! How are you?"

Jack rolled down his window fully, a hint of curiosity in his expression. "Hey, Detective. What brings you here?" he asked.

JJ gave a casual smile. "I was just about to ask you the same thing."

Jack chuckled lightly. "Well, I'm meeting a friend here. Your turn."

JJ's smile faded slightly. "There was a shooting here last night," he replied. "I'm just following up and making a few inquiries."

Jack's eyebrows shot up in surprise. "Really? What time?" he asked.

"Around one a.m.," JJ said, narrowing his eyes. "Why do you ask?"

Jack hesitated. "Well, Rose never mentioned it, that's all."

"Maybe she'd already left by then," JJ offered, studying Jack's reaction.

"Yes... maybe," Jack said. A troubled look crossed his face, and JJ noticed.

"What's on your mind, Jack?" JJ asked, interrupting his thoughts.

"Nothing," Jack replied, forcing a smile. "Well, you have a nice day, Detective Jackson."

"You too, Jack. Tell your sister I said hi."

"Will do," Jack said, and they drove off in opposite directions.

As JJ rolled up his window, he reflected on his morning's investigation. It was confirmed: not only had Rose been at the bar last night, but she and Jack also frequented the place. Still, something didn't add up. Why would Rose drink at a dive bar like the Cattle Drive? And who was driving her home? The more answers JJ uncovered, the more questions seemed to emerge.

FORTY-EIGHT
DOUGHNUTS

1 P.M. FLASHED on the clock in the car, its glow casting an eerie light on a small Roswell alien figurine perched at the base of the dashboard. The alien's little gray head bobbed with every bump in the road, wobbling as if in disapproval with each turn JJ made. He had expertly navigated the afternoon rush hour and secured a prime parking spot in front of the white, boxy municipal building. The sign outside read: 'Springfield Forensics Lab.' Once a shared facility with the Springfield Police Department, the building now served the entire state of Illinois after the SPD moved to new uptown headquarters.

With the car parked, JJ waited for his partner, idly glancing around the parking lot. His cell phone rang with a jaunty jingle, prompting him to retrieve it from his blazer pocket. Flipping it open, he spoke while scanning the area. "No, I can't see you… No, I'm by the sign at the bottom of the steps… Okay, I see you." He raised his arm out the window, waving as he spotted Harper entering the car park.

Harper, who had opted to walk the short distance from his nearby home, returned JJ's wave. The walk, though brief, had taken longer than expected, and Harper—carrying a few extra pounds—arrived slightly winded, with an appetite that made his sweet craving all the more urgent. He hoped JJ had remembered his promise to bring a snack. As Harper approached, JJ exaggeratedly tapped his wrist, pretending to check a non-existent watch.

Harper grinned, catching on to the playful hint. "What did I miss?" he called out as JJ rolled up the car window.

JJ stepped out of the car, slipping on his jacket. Harper crossed his arms, irritation creeping in. "So?" he demanded.

"So what?" JJ replied, feigning confusion.

Harper rolled his eyes. "*Balls of freshly baked dough filled with red jammy goodness!* You promised to pick some up for me," he reminded, his voice almost pleading.

JJ reached back into the car and pulled out a brown paper bag, handing it over to Harper. "Here you go," he said, slamming the car door shut with finality.

Harper's face lit up, his grin spreading from ear to ear as he eagerly opened the bag. But as he rummaged inside, his smile quickly faded. The anticipation turned to disbelief. There were no sticky buns, no jam-filled dough balls—just a brown baguette stuffed with chicken and salad. His face twisted in disappointment, and he began to bark in frustration.

"You've gotta be kidding me, right? How am I supposed to get through the day with a *chicken salad*? You promised me doughnuts!"

JJ shrugged, completely unfazed. "Didn't have time," he said, patting Harper's stomach with a teasing grin. "Besides, I think you need to lose a bit of weight."

Harper glared, clutching the disappointing sandwich, as JJ winked at him, slipped on his Ray-Bans, and sauntered up the steps to the forensic building. Harper was left fuming, clutching his poor substitute for a doughnut while JJ disappeared inside, the sound of Harper's grumbling echoing behind him.

Harper scowled, waving the baguette menacingly. "You may be a smooth, soon-to-be FBI agent, but just remember I can still kick your butt, overweight or not, you son of a bitch!"

JJ WAS ALREADY DEEPLY CONVERSING with Dr. Zhang, the pathologist, as Harper finally reached the lab. Dr. Zhang was an attractive, slim, petite woman who wore her dark hair pinned loosely. Her striking green eyes were full of intelligence. She exuded a quiet, professional confidence.

JJ greeted him with a smirk. "Glad you could finally make it," he said sarcastically. Harper mumbled a half-hearted excuse, still slightly out of breath. JJ turned back to the pathologist. "Dr. Lian Zhang, this is my partner, Detective Harper."

"Hi, Detective Harper," she said, extending her hand.

"Lou," Harper corrected, shaking her hand eagerly, maybe a little too eagerly.

They all made their way over to the corpse. JJ took in the scene as Harper chatted to the doctor. He always felt uncomfortable in places like this—a destination we all inevitably face, devoid of hope. Glancing around, he thought every morgue he had ever been in looked the same.

The morgue was sterile and cold, illuminated by overhead fluorescent bulbs that buzzed faintly, casting stark shadows on the tiled walls. The air was heavy with an antiseptic scent, mingling with the unmistakable, metallic odor of death. The temperature was kept deliberately low, and JJ shivered as the chill bit through his skin. He watched one of the medical staff move quietly, their footsteps echoing softly off the linoleum floor.

In the center of the room, a single stainless steel table was positioned under a focused light, its surface reflecting a ghostly sheen. On it lay the lifeless body of a young boy, his fragile frame a stark contrast against the sterile metal. It was Brad—barely fifteen, with a whole life ahead of him. JJ had read his file; sure, he was troubled and had some issues to answer for, but people could change and turn their lives around. Hell, he thought of himself at fifteen—if it wasn't for his father, he too might have gone down the wrong path. JJ looked at the boy's body. His pale, bluish skin was mottled with the early signs of livor mortis, and his face showed the unmistakable signs of asphyxiation.

A deep, purplish ligature mark encircled his neck, the skin above and below slightly swollen, the edges rough and uneven where the rope had bitten into his flesh. The mark was a cruel reminder of his final moments, the desperate struggle for breath etched into his taut skin. His eyes, half-closed, were glazed over with a milky haze, and his lips, tinged with dark blue, were slightly parted as if frozen mid-gasp, seeking air that would never come.

The boy's small body lay still, his pale skin contrasting with the sterile, gleaming metal of the table. His hands, once full of youthful promise, now lay motionless at his sides, fingers curled inward, almost as if they were still gripping the rope in a final, desperate attempt to survive. A solitary tear had dried on his cheek—a silent testament to a life cut tragically short and a mystery that still demanded answers.

Dr. Zhang stood between them as they stood over the body. After donning her surgical gloves, she carefully inspected the boy's neck, explaining the telltale signs—the fractured hyoid bone, the broken capillaries around the eyes, the petechial hemorrhages that speckled his cheeks and the whites of his eyes—each one a silent testament to his agonizing final moments.

"Cause of death is consistent with hanging," she murmured to JJ, who stood beside her, nodding as he took notes on his notepad. "No signs of defensive wounds or struggle beyond the initial trauma. It looks like a straightforward case of suicide, but..." Her voice trailed off, a slight frown creasing her brow as if contemplating something unseen.

JJ glanced up. "But what?"

Dr. Zhang hesitated, her eyes narrowing as she leaned closer to the boy's neck, her breath visible in the cold air. She adjusted an overhead spotlight on a flexible arm, bringing it closer to highlight the area around the neck. "This mark... it's strange. Most suicides by hanging leave a different pattern—a more defined suspension mark, upward and diagonal. This one... it's more horizontal, like strangulation."

JJ stepped closer, peering at the bruising. "What about the claw marks?" he asked.

"Clawing is not uncommon," Dr. Zhang explained. "When someone hangs themselves, they usually don't try to grab the noose. By the time they've jumped, they're committed. However, instinct might compel them to grab at the ligature—or it could be a hesitation, perhaps a last-minute attempt to save themselves."

"Or maybe his mother scratched him when she found him," Harper suggested.

"Unlikely," Dr. Zhang replied. "These marks were made before rigor set in. You can tell by the slight bruising here. There wouldn't be any coloration if they were made after death."

JJ considered this. "Or he could have struggled against someone trying to strangle him," he offered.

"Theoretically, both are possible," she conceded. "But it's all conjecture at this point."

"What else can you tell us?" JJ asked. "Do you think someone could have done this to him?"

"It's possible," she replied cautiously. "Or it could have been staged to look like a hanging. We'll need to run more tests—the initial blood work and toxicology didn't show much. There were some narcotics in the boy's bloodstream, but not enough to incapacitate him or raise any major concerns. Physically, he was fit and healthy."

"What about alcohol? Did you find any traces?"

"There were no signs of alcohol in his system."

"So, whose bottle of whiskey did I find under his bed?" JJ mused aloud.

Dr. Zhang shrugged. "That, I can't answer. That's your department."

JJ nodded. Having completed her assessment, Dr. Zhang began to cover the body. The room fell silent, save for the faint hum of the refrigeration units lining the walls. The stark, clinical atmosphere was heavy with unspoken questions, each demanding answers to uncover the truth behind the tragic death of the child.

The silence was abruptly broken by the rumbling of Harper's stomach, drawing curious glances from JJ and Dr. Zhang. Harper just smiled sheepishly, his cheeks reddening slightly.

"It was nice meeting you, Doc," Harper said, his voice a bit hurried as another rumble came from his stomach, betraying his eagerness to satisfy his craving.

"It was nice meeting you too, Lou," Dr. Zhang replied.

"Thanks, Doc. I may need your help again sometime," JJ said, extending a firm handshake.

"You have my number," she reminded him softly.

JJ nodded, offering a brief, polite smile before heading to the door, Harper following closely behind.

Harper was the first to break the silence as they walked down the corridor. "So, are you going to call her?"

"Who?" JJ replied, feigning ignorance.

"The doc," Harper clarified, a teasing tone in his voice.

"If I need more information, yes," JJ answered curtly.

"No wonder you're single," Harper retorted with a grin.

JJ didn't rise to the bait; he knew what Harper was hinting at, but as usual, more pressing matters were on his mind.

Changing the subject, Harper asked, "So, where to next?"

"The lab," JJ replied. "Remember the key we found on Brad's desk?"

"Yep," Harper said.

"I want to see if there's anything there, and Sherlock called me—he has checked the CCTV footage and he has something to show us." JJ explained.

"Okay, I'm with you," Harper agreed, then added hopefully, "But can we please stop at Mo's? I could really use a hot espresso and a jam-filled doughnut."

JJ glanced at Harper, knowing he wouldn't win the battle against Harper's cravings. With a resigned sigh, he nodded. "Fine. We'll stop at Mo's first."

Harper grinned triumphantly. "Thanks, partner. I promise I'll make it quick."

JJ rolled his eyes but couldn't help but smile a little. Despite everything, Harper's appetite for life—and doughnuts—never seemed to wane.

FORTY-NINE
THE FAMILY

AS THEY MADE their way to the forensics lab, JJ kept his promise to stop at Mo's. As Harper drove, JJ had time to mull over the case and get his facts in order. He was building a case—one that even the captain couldn't dismiss as anything less than compelling. Yet, JJ knew that despite their evidence, glaring gaps remained in his understanding of what had happened.

A case box on the back seat was beginning to fill; Harper had retrieved the CCTV tapes from the hospital, and perhaps something on them would help fill those gaps. JJ flipped open his notepad, revisiting the strange conversations with Jack and Rose, the shooting of Charlie and his bizarre rantings before his sudden disappearance, the coroner's report—and then there was Brad's rucksack.

He turned the pages thoughtfully. Why had Brad packed an overnight bag if he planned to kill himself? Why had he struggled so desperately to remove the noose from around his neck? And what about the empty bottle of whiskey found under his bed? Most puzzling of all, what exactly had Charlie witnessed that night?

These unanswered questions swirled relentlessly in JJ's mind, poking at his thoughts and torturing his analytical instincts. Individually, they might have seemed insignificant, but together, they kept him from sleeping.

JJ slipped the notepad back into his jacket pocket and thought of his father, who had not only been a cop but had finished his career as a captain. He was proud of his father's achievements—Captain Jackson was a hero, not just to JJ, but to the entire community—a bona fide local legend.

He recalled the old, antique mahogany cabinet that stood proudly in his father's house. Among JJ's football trophies and other sporting achievements was a selection of gold stars and silver crosses hanging from colored silk ribbons—medals that were a testament to his father's forty years of dedicated service. The walls were adorned with framed commendations for bravery under fire, for saving a child from a burning school, and—what was the most significant medal of all in JJ's eyes—for the apprehension of the Lincoln Mauler. Or, as his father put it, 'For burying the truth.'

JJ's father, a respected cop, had always been a source of inspiration. However, his cryptic comments about the Mauler case had always troubled JJ. As he grew older and joined the force, those words took on a new significance. Occasionally, JJ would ask what his father meant by 'burying the truth.' His father would only respond with vague remarks like, 'Some details just didn't sit right,' or 'Tell me, son, what turns a promising young student into a cold-hearted murderer and rapist?' These words had a profound impact on JJ's approach to his career.

JJ was too young at the time to connect his father's words to anything concrete, but as he got older and joined the force himself, he stumbled upon Case 666LM. He couldn't help but muse at the unfortunate case number and wondered if the clerk who filed it added 'LM' at the end as a charm to ward off evil spirits, just in case they ever had to handle the file again.

After reading through Case 666LM, JJ came to the same unsettling conclusions his father had. Like the case with Brad, there were gaps and leads, but JJ was resolute in his determination to follow every lead and close every gap. In the Mauler case, there was evidence that contradicted the prevailing narrative that had been set aside. Potential leads remained just that—potential. They caught the guy, he confessed before his death, and that was enough to declare it 'CASE CLOSED'—soon-to-be forgotten. But JJ could see it clearly now: buried in the margins and the overlooked details was a truth waiting to be uncovered.

JJ came from a family with three generations of cops, so it was no surprise that he became one himself. His rise to detective had been swift, and now he hoped his acceptance into the FBI would be a mere formality, having already passed all the necessary tests. His thoughts drifted briefly to Harper and what would become of him. Just as that thought lingered, the car came to a stop.

After parking, they quickly made their way to Mo's. The cerulean sky had turned a smoky gray, and a light rain had begun to fall. A few steps away from cover, the heavens opened up, and the drizzle turned into a downpour just as they darted inside.

"That was close," JJ said, brushing off the few raindrops that had landed on him.

"Yes, it was," Harper chuckled. "I swear, they must get their weather forecasts from fortune cookies." He headed straight for the counter, focused on one thing: doughnuts.

JJ took in the familiar surroundings and removed his jacket. Mo's was a classic cop hangout and had been since his father's days as a beat cop back in the fifties. The decor, the smell, the black-and-white photographs of Hollywood starlets—Sophia Loren, Marilyn Monroe, Natalie Wood—pouting from their frames on the walls, seemed frozen in time. JJ's gaze lingered on Natalie Wood's photograph. Now, that would be a great case to crack, he thought, recalling her tragic death by drowning. Why didn't Robert Wagner call for help? What was the argument really about with Walken? There are so many unanswered questions and too many loose ends.

JJ had fond memories of Mo's; whenever he got the chance, he would stop in for lunch. It was exactly as he remembered it from childhood, unchanged since the fifties. The only thing different now was the absence of Big Mo, the original owner, who had passed away years ago. The only remnant of him was his apron, signed and mounted around a life-size cardboard cutout of Big Mo, framed and placed on the entrance wall. JJ remembered the night they hung it up, a tribute to a man who had served the cops as loyally as they served the city.

He glanced at his father's signature on the apron and noticed a large photo to the right of Big Mo's shoulder. JJ lingered on the image, recalling some familiar faces: Big Phill, one of his father's partners before the infamous Mauler case—what had happened to him? And there was Rosetta, his father's secretary. JJ had fond memories of her, too; she had passed away recently, and he had attended her funeral with his father. Everyone from the precinct had been there because, whether you were a cop or worked at the station, you were considered family.

Then JJ's eyes were drawn to another figure in the photograph, slightly out of focus. All he could make out was a striking tattoo on the man's left arm—a death's head skull dagger. Despite the distinct tattoo, JJ couldn't place him. He wasn't a cop—too young—and the apron he wore confirmed he must have been a student working at Mo's. JJ wondered what had happened to him. Behind the tattooed man was another image, a young woman, slightly blurred, with her arms around his waist and her head turned to kiss his cheek, obscuring her face. She was probably a student from the high school, he guessed.

JJ's thoughts wandered to his future with the FBI. He couldn't wait to get his hands on the latest technology in the FBI lab, imagining what he could do with that old photo to uncover more details. But for now, he snapped back to reality, back to Big Mo—gone but not forgotten. The diner was now run by his son, Little Mo, who was anything but little. A chip off the old block, though a rather large chip at that, JJ thought with a smile, wondering who had started calling him 'Little.'

JJ continued to survey the room, soaking in the nostalgia of a place like a second home, filled with memories of a past that was still alive for him.

The black-and-white checkered floor gleamed, a testament to the daily dose of elbow grease it received. Heavy-set beat cops spilt over the red faux leather seats, perched on chrome stools that lined the counter, ten in a row. Except for their swivel, the stools stood rigid before a long black Formica bar. Above them, opaque pendant lights hung from the high vaulted ceiling like tulip buds on long stems. A red

'55 Chevy half-protruded from the back wall, its chrome shining like new. A sign above it read, 'If you don't own it, don't touch it,' perhaps contributing to its pristine condition over the years.

JJ glanced over at the small stage area in the left-hand corner of the diner. He smiled wryly, his gaze landing on what he sought—the neon-lit, original Wurlitzer jukebox. It flashed and beckoned him to feed it, and he reached into his pocket to fish out a couple of dimes. As he made his way over, he passed the ex-Chief of Police, Jo Bertram—larger than life in both stature and character. With his imposing frame, bald head, and snowy white beard, JB, as everyone called him, resembled a black onyx-carved Buddha.

JB had come up from Decatur, Atlanta, to take over the precinct when JJ's father retired after the Mauler trial. He was on garden leave due to ill health and had been for a few weeks. With retirement approaching, JB had also decided to run for mayor once he left the force, but it was family time for now. Seated with him was one of his six daughters, Clarissa, whom JJ recognized as the youngest and who is still living in Atlanta. JJ had met her once or twice before. Sitting next to her was a young boy, about five years old, sporting a fine afro and a brilliant white smile, which JJ noticed just before the boy stuffed his face with a 'Mo Burger.' His grandfather, JB, had opted for 'Big Mo's Monster Breakfast.' JJ nodded respectfully in JB's direction.

"Sir," he greeted him.

JB looked up and craned his neck, a smile spreading across his face. He began to rise from his chair, his girth matching his height, and JJ couldn't help but think of a line from a favorite childhood book his father read to him: *Fee-fi-fo-fum...*

"JJ, nice to see you, son." JB dipped his head in mock chastisement. "And don't be calling me 'sir'—I ain't sitting behind my desk. How are you, son? How's your Pa? And how's Quantico?"

"I'm fine. He's fine. As for Quantico, I'm just waiting for the results," JJ replied, glancing around the table. "Don't let me disturb your breakfast."

"That's okay, son." JB placed a firm hand on JJ's shoulder and gestured to his guests. "You've met my daughter Clarissa, and this here's her young' un, Luke."

JJ smiled at Clarissa, who returned the smile with a warm southern drawl, "Nice to meet y'all again, JJ."

"Likewise," he replied, then looked down at the young boy, who was enthusiastically slurping his malt shake. JJ ruffled his hair. "How ya doing, Luke? Enjoying your shake?"

The boy stopped slurping and answered respectfully, "I'm good, sir. Thanks for asking. Are you a cop?"

"I sure am... Are you?" JJ teased.

"Yes, I am, sir," the boy replied, still chewing his Mo Burger, mixing it with his shake. He reached into his back pocket and, after a bit of tugging, pulled out a toy badge with a gleeful grin. The gold star gleamed in the sunlight streaming through the large window, the rain having momentarily stopped.

"So, you're the sheriff of these parts, huh?"

"Sure am, sir! And one day, I'm gonna be captain like my grandpa."

They all chuckled.

"Well, you better finish your burger, then. Maybe try one of Mo's biscuits and grits to make you big and strong," JJ suggested, but the boy's face soured at the thought.

"I think I'll stick with my burger and fries."

They all laughed again.

JB patted JJ on the back. "I heard about your little incident at the precinct. You can brief me when I'm back next week, okay?"

"Will do, JB." JJ nodded.

"Well, take care, son. Tell your Pa it's about time we had another game. It can't be fun cooped up all day at home; he wants to be careful The Miseries don't get him."

"I'll let him know. Y'all take care now." They smiled back, and JJ looked at the boy. "Sheriff," he said with a playful salute.

The boy stood up and saluted back, his face beaming. JJ ruffled his hair once more and then turned to make his way to the jukebox, acknowledging a few familiar faces along the way.

"Dave."

"JJ."

"Mac."

"JJ, how the devil are ya?"

"I'm good, thanks. How's Liza?"

"She's good, she's good. It's Bobbie's birthday on Saturday, and she'd love for you to come over. Can I put you down for some jelly and ice cream? We've got a clown who makes balloon animals."

JJ smiled. "Okay, save me some jelly and ice cream. How old is Bobbie now?"

"He's six. He's gonna be so happy his favorite uncle is coming."

JJ chuckled. He wasn't actually related to the boy, but in the cop world, they were all brothers, sisters, and uncles—they were all family.

Finally, JJ reached the jukebox and glanced down at the track selection. Each 45 in the jukebox told a story, each song an epitaph of a fallen officer. If you were killed in action, a track was posthumously chosen for you. If you had been decorated, you could select your song, which would be added to the playlist upon your death. JJ hadn't yet earned this honor; he hadn't been killed in action, and though his bravery was undeniable, it had yet to be formally recognized by his fellow officers—the family. Harper, however, had earned the distinction after saving Libby Langford from the clutches of the Lincoln Mauler, a story Harper never tired of telling—about his bravery, the bullet wound in his thigh, and the Medal of Valor he received for it. JJ often teased him about the story—not his bravery, which was never in doubt, but whether it had been the Lincoln Mauler. The shooter was never caught; no gun was found, but it was Harper's story, and who knows—maybe it was the Mauler.

Harper's track and JJ's father's track were locked in the safe in Mo's back office, and JJ hoped both songs would stay there for many years. On the day of a funeral, everyone would return to Mo's, and the honored song would be played. JJ scanned the track list. There were so many songs for so many brave cops. The jukebox, though original, had been modified over the years and now could hold thousands of songs —a thought that unsettled JJ.

At the top of the hit parade was Doug Urbanowski. During the Illinois Gambling Raids in the fifties, he was shot by Fat Freddie Graziani. Doug had been a big Sinatra fan, so the Family thought 'My Way' was fitting. At number two was Bob O'Connor, who had several commendations and a posthumous Medal of Valor. He was shot dead during a robbery at the Bank of Springfield in '57. His chosen song, 'Not Fade Away' by Buddy Holly, was a favorite of his. But JJ had only one song on his mind: 'Under Pressure.' It was his favorite tune and belonged to a legend on the force—Jules McBride. He had been his father's first partner and JJ's godfather. JJ was honored to have his name, and he, too, had received numerous commendations, including the Medal of Valor. JJ had fond memories of him growing up and still took time to visit his wife, Mary, who lived in Springfield. Jules died in eighty-six, having finished his career as mayor of Springfield.

Armed with a dime, JJ flicked the coin into the air, caught it, and slid it into the machine. The Wurlitzer arm whirred to life as if consciously agreeing with his choice. It plucked the 45 from its slot, maneuvering it into place; the steel rod pushed the record up to the needle arm. The hiss and crackle gave way to that distinctive bass intro: Bum... Bum... Bum... ba ba bum bum. The sounds of 'Under Pressure' filled the air, and everyone stopped to listen.

JJ turned on his heel, noticing almost everyone in the room nodding along to his chosen tune, pleased with his choice. Satisfied, he made his way over to Harper, who was seated in a booth in the far corner. Once more, JJ took in the room. Off-duty cops sat with their families in separate booths, dads wolfing down the house special, 'Big Mo's Monster Munch,' while little Jimmies slurped tall shakes. Beat cops were having breakfast, and retired cops were getting free refills on their coffee as they read the *Register*, catching up on local news. Everyone here was Family, save for a few tourists who stuck out with their fanny packs, head visors, and 'I Love Abe' T-shirts. At times, it was annoying but never unwelcome.

JJ made his way over to the booth Harper had claimed, where a large plate of doughnuts and two steaming cups of black coffee sat waiting on the table. Harper was engrossed in the *Register*, his brows furrowed in concentration, as JJ paused for a moment, observing his first and only partner. Harper had taught him everything he needed to know about the streets. One day, JJ would thank him properly. He'd wanted to do it sooner, but the timing was never quite right. Still, he promised himself that one day he'd find the perfect moment.

Harper glanced up from the newspaper, catching JJ staring at him.

"What are you looking at?" he grunted, still a little disgruntled at JJ forgetting his doughnuts and saying he was fat.

"Nothing," JJ replied, a smile tugging at his lips.

JJ leaned back in his seat, relaxed. He added sugar to his coffee. As he stirred, he asked, "Am I the best partner you've ever had?" His tone was teasing.

Harper's response was blunt, his voice muffled behind the newspaper. "No."

JJ grinned, undeterred. "I must be in the top three, then? So who was it?" he pressed, curiosity dancing in his eyes.

Harper lowered the newspaper slightly, meeting JJ's gaze. "Who was what?" he asked, pretending not to follow.

"Your best partner," JJ repeated, pulling the newspaper down further to look Harper directly in the eyes.

Harper sighed, a hint of a smirk appearing as he answered. "The Captain," he said simply.

"My father?" JJ asked, surprised.

Harper raised the newspaper back in front of his face. "Yep, you're a close second," he confirmed.

JJ chuckled, shaking his head. "Well, at least you're keeping it in the family," he said, sliding into the booth. Harper's eyes peeked over the top of the newspaper, a smile ghosting his lips as they settled into the familiar, easy camaraderie that had defined their partnership for years.

JJ continued to study Harper. He knew everything about the man, not just from their time together but also from the stories his father used to tell him. Harper wasn't just brave—he was a different kind of brave, the kind that would take a bullet for you, and he had done so on more than one occasion, even saving JJ's father's life a couple of times. JJ loved Harper like a big brother. Harper was a rare breed, one who had held onto his marriage where others had failed, including JJ's own, which had only lasted a few years. Harper and his wife, Maggie, had been together for over forty years.

Suddenly, JJ remembered something: Harper and Maggie's anniversary was coming up soon, and that also meant it was Sophie's birthday—Harper's daughter, who shared the same special day. Those were always lively celebrations, especially when Harper inevitably forgot and had to scramble to make things right. JJ figured he'd better give him a gentle reminder.

"So, what did you get Maggie?" JJ asked, raising an eyebrow.

"What?" Harper grunted from behind the newspaper.

JJ grabbed the paper, folded it, and set it on the table. "Your wife, Maggie. What did you get her for your anniversary?"

Harper's face fell, realization dawning on him. "Damn it!" he cursed. "I forgot." He rubbed his forehead. "And by extension, Sophie's birthday... Damn."

JJ tried to hold back a laugh. "Any ideas?" Harper asked.

"You're asking me? I'm separated, remember?" JJ chuckled.

"Good point," Harper muttered. "I'll figure something out by the weekend."

"It better be good," JJ quipped. "You're retiring soon—you need all the points you can get, or your last few years will be miserable." He leaned back. "Sophie's turning eighteen, right? Planning to follow in your footsteps?"

Harper's face softened with pride. "Yep, she's going to be a cop, just like her old man. Her tests are this week, but she'll pass. She's a chip off the old block," he said, chuckling.

JJ sat back, taking in the moment and reflecting on the idea of family. It wasn't always about blood—it was about the bonds forged through the force. To be a cop was to be part of something bigger, a band of brothers and sisters who lived and died by the code 'Protect and Serve.' The family he had within the department was all he had apart from his father. His mother had died when he was fourteen. He had a sister, but she moved to Europe ten years ago and he had only seen her a few times in those years. They were close but had separate lives. He had few memories of his mother but cherished every one. He carried her picture in his wallet and wore a gold cross around his neck—a gift from her on the day she passed. His father never remarried, and when JJ once asked why, his father had simply said, 'Your mother was a God-given gift, and it would be rude to ask for another.' JJ never questioned it.

He glanced at his watch, realizing how quickly time had passed. He took a final sip of his coffee, while Harper polished off another doughnut.

"Let's go," JJ said, standing up.

"Where to?" Harper asked, still savoring his snack.

"Forensics, remember?" JJ reminded him. "The CCTV footage and the evidence from the Bradley Marshall scene. Sherlock called—he's got something that might give us the answers we need to open a murder case."

"What about my doughnuts?" Harper asked.

"Bring them with you," JJ replied with a grin.

Harper wiped his hands on a napkin and stood.

The morning banter faded, and they shifted back into detective mode, ready to chase down the truth.

Harper quickly stuffed the last morsel of his doughnut into his mouth, savoring the sugary treat. He licked each finger clean before carefully placing the remaining doughnuts into a brown paper bag. As they made their way to the door, the song playing on the jukebox, 'Under Pressure,' came to an end. The final notes echoed through the diner, adding an ironic soundtrack to their exit.

FIFTY
SHERLOCK

IT WASN'T long before they arrived at the SPD forensic lab. JJ often dropped by, sometimes just for the fun of it, enjoying the easy banter and camaraderie with his old school friend who worked there. But today was different. He wasn't here for banter—he was here for answers. And he knew that if anyone had them, it would be Sherlock.

Of course, *Sherlock* wasn't his real name. The nickname had stuck over the years, given to Robert by JJ as a playful nod to his uncanny ability to solve puzzles that left even the most experienced detectives baffled. It also paid homage to JJ's love for the adventures of Sherlock Holmes. Robert had an extraordinary talent for peeling back the layers of a mystery, cutting through the smoke and mirrors to uncover the truth hidden beneath.

Unlike Dr. Zhang, the pathologist who specialized in the science of death, Robert was more of a human puzzle master. His expertise lay in distinguishing the obvious from the elusive, spotting details others overlooked, and making connections that transformed chaos into clarity. His sharp, analytical mind made him an invaluable asset to the force—and to JJ.

Beyond his work in the lab, Sherlock's brilliance extended to the chessboard, where he was known for always being several moves ahead of his opponents. Anticipating every strategy before it unfolded, he was virtually unbeatable. Even JJ, a formidable chess player in his own right, had never managed to beat him.

Today, JJ hoped that Robert's brilliance would shine through once more, as he needed every bit of insight to make sense of his mounting collection of circumstantial evidence and finally pull it all together so his can get an official go-ahead to open a murder case.

JJ had known Sherlock since they were kids; they had grown up together in the same neighborhood, shared the same classrooms, and formed a bond over their mutual love of problem-solving and chess. Though he lacked charm in the conventional sense and often had an awkward demeanor around strangers, Robert was undeniably handsome with his rugged but well-groomed appearance, short, cropped hair that always seemed perfectly in place and piercing eyes framed by thick, black horn-rimmed glasses, giving him an almost *Superman* vibe. His gaze had a way of making people feel like he could see right through them, discerning their secrets with just a glance.

JJ hoped that one day Robert would join him at the FBI and become his partner. What a team they would make, JJ would say to him. But Sherlock would just laugh it off, never saying yes but never saying no either. In the meantime, he was content to share in the adventures they faced together as it stood, solving cases and cracking puzzles, knowing that with Sherlock by his side, there wasn't a mystery in the world they couldn't solve.

After a quick hug they were off down the corridor heading to Sherlock's office. Harper clutched his bag of doughnuts tightly in his chubby fingers while JJ fished his notepad from his jacket pocket, his mind already running through the list of questions he needed answers to. "So, you mentioned you found something odd about the key, and you managed to lift prints off the whiskey bottle?" JJ asked, his tone a mix of curiosity and urgency.

"Indeed," Robert replied with a slight nod as he pushed open the door to his office.

As they stepped inside, JJ's eyes immediately caught sight of a video player on the desk and a large TV mounted against the wall. His brow furrowed slightly. "Before we dive into that, there's something else I think you'll find just as intriguing," Robert continued, gesturing to the chairs in front of the TV. "Take a seat."

Harper and JJ settled into the chairs, Harper still clutching his precious brown bag of doughnuts. Meanwhile, Robert moved to a metal evidence locker and pulled out a large box of evidence collected from the crime scene. He carefully extracted the whiskey bottle, still sealed in its evidence bag, and placed it on the desk with a deliberate motion. Then came the key, also in its original bag. He reached back into the box and pulled out a rugged-looking rucksack, followed by the preliminary autopsy report and, finally, a CCTV tape from the hospital. He arranged everything neatly on the table, his movements methodical and precise. Just like everything else in the room, ordered and deliberate.

"Pop, anyone?" Robert asked, breaking the tension as he opened a mini retro Coca-Cola fridge by the water cooler. His voice was casual, but his eyes gleamed with anticipation.

"No, I'm good," JJ replied, his focus still on the array of evidence in front of him. "Harper? You want a Coke?"

Harper shook his head. "No thanks," he said with a smirk. "Fizzy sugar water? That stuff'll kill ya." He dipped his hand into the brown bag, fishing out the last doughnut and taking a big, satisfied bite.

The irony wasn't lost on JJ and Robert. They exchanged amused glances. Robert chuckled softly as he cracked open a can of Coke for himself, the sound hissing through the otherwise quiet room.

"Alright," Robert said, sipping his drink before setting it down. "Let's get started." He slid the CCTV tape into the video player and sat on the corner of the desk as the TV screen flickered to life, casting a pale blue glow across the room. The grainy footage began to roll, and the tension immediately thickened, an almost tangible presence in the room.

JJ leaned forward, his eyes narrowing as he focused on the screen. "What are we looking for?" he asked, his voice low, almost a whisper.

Robert leaned back in his chair, his gaze never leaving the screen. "Just watch," he said. "I think you'll know it when you see it."

The footage showed a series of nondescript hallways, dimly lit and mostly empty except for the occasional figure passing through. As the seconds ticked by, the tension in the room grew. Each of them leaned in closer, their eyes fixed on the screen. Suddenly, a figure appeared on the screen pushing a wheelchair, moving quickly but deliberately, head down, face obscured with a surgical mask.

"There," Robert pointed, his voice a soft command. "Notice anything odd?"

JJ squinted, studying the figure's movements on the screen. "It's an orderly pushing a patient," he deduced from the man's uniform. But something felt off. The orderly's movements were too deliberate, almost as if he was trying to appear casual but a little too stiff and careful. The camera angle made it hard to see the patient clearly; the figure in the wheelchair was covered entirely with a blanket, obscuring any detail.

"Keep watching," Robert instructed, his tone calm but insistent.

JJ leaned in closer, his eyes fixed on the screen. As the orderly continued to push the wheelchair down the hallway, something caught JJ's attention. An arm suddenly slipped out from beneath the blanket, hanging limply over the side of the wheelchair.

"Rewind that," JJ said quickly, his voice tight with urgency.

Robert nodded, reversed the footage a few seconds, and then hit play again.

This time, JJ watched with heightened focus, his eyes narrowing as he scrutinized every detail. Again, the arm fell out from under the blanket, dangling lifelessly. "Stop! Pause it!" JJ commanded. "Can you zoom in on that?"

Robert shook his head slightly, a faint smile tugging at his lips. "I can do better than zooming in. I've already prepared some enhanced images," he said as he pulled two large photographs from the box, his expression turning serious. These could be the final pieces JJ needed to open an abduction case—or possibly a murder investigation. Robert laid the first image on the table, and JJ and Harper rose from their chairs to look closer.

JJ picked up the photograph and brought it closer to his eyes. It was a close-up of the arm hanging limply over the side of the wheelchair. The details were striking: an ornate bracelet around the wrist, one that JJ instantly recognized. "That's Charlie's bracelet," he murmured, his voice barely more than a whisper, his mind racing. He'd seen Charlie wearing it the day he was shot, noticing it as he cuffed him.

Robert nodded. "Interesting. And that's not all," he said, laying down the second image. It was a side view of the orderly pushing the wheelchair. The man wore a surgical mask, but it didn't completely obscure his face. A distinct tattoo—a snake—was visible, curling from beneath the mask and wrapping around his eye. The snake appeared to enter the mask from the bottom left and reemerge at the top, coiling around the man's left eye socket.

Harper's face tightened with a mix of recognition and anger. "I know that tattoo," he muttered under his breath. "That's Zane—Zane Cardoso, he even left his name tag on his scrubs. The guy's got a rap sheet a mile long: armed robbery, assault, gun for hire—you name it. Not a guy you want to mess with."

Robert nodded grimly; his expression serious. "Your memory's close, Harper, and the name tag threw me too but that's not Zane. It's Lucas, his twin brother. I also recognized the tattoo from a case I worked on about a year back. They both have the same tattoo, but Zane's is on the right side, and Lucas's is on the left. I couldn't remember which one had which, so I ran their details through the NCIC database. Bingo—Lucas has the snake tattoo over his left eye. Here's the kicker: Lucas doesn't work at the hospital, but Zane does. That's how Lucas got his hands on the uniform."

Robert paused, allowing the gravity of the situation to sink in. "If Lucas is involved, this isn't just a straightforward abduction. We're dealing with something far more complex—and a lot more dangerous. Zane might be part of it, or maybe he's not, but he's always been under his brother's control. Lucas is the real threat we need to worry about."

Harper's eyes narrowed. "So, Lucas is the one calling the shots, using Zane to get into the hospital. This is way bigger than we thought."

Robert nodded, his face set in a grim expression. "Exactly. We need to act fast. If Lucas is involved, there's a mastermind behind the scenes pulling the strings. Whoever orchestrated Charlie's extraction from the hospital didn't want him dead. If death was the goal, Lucas could have easily ended it with a single bullet. No, Charlie knows something—

something important—and someone out there is desperate to find out what."

JJ's jaw clenched as his mind raced through the possibilities. "Lucas wouldn't take on a job like this unless there was a big payoff involved. We need to find out what that payoff is and who's funding it—and figure out where he might be holding Charlie."

Harper nodded, his face set with determination. "We've got to move fast. we're already behind the curve."

JJ tossed the car keys to Harper. "Get to the hospital and see if you can track down Zane," he instructed.

"Will do, boss," Harper replied, his tone brisk as he moved toward the door. As it slowly shut behind him, his footsteps echoed down the hallway, leaving JJ and Robert alone.

The silence that followed was thick with tension, the weight of their predicament settling over them like a dense fog. JJ glanced at Robert; both men were lost in their thoughts, minds racing with the implications of what they had just uncovered. The air was charged with a palpable urgency, each passing second pressing down on them, heavy with unspoken fears and unanswered questions. The clock on the wall ticked loudly, a reminder that time was slipping away and that every moment counted.

JJ turned back to Robert. "Can you get any more details from the footage? Maybe track their movements outside the hospital?"

Robert nodded, his eyes narrowing with determination. "There's another tape from the front of the hospital. It should have caught them leaving. If we're lucky, we might be able to track their next move from there. I'll see what I can pull up," he said, moving swiftly toward the tape recorder. Moments later, the footage flickered onto the TV screen. With the remote in hand, Robert began cycling through the frames, his gaze sharp, searching for any clue.

The footage showed the moment Charlie was wheeled out of the hospital doors, the frame freezing just as they turned a corner. The camera then caught a brief, crucial moment: Charlie being roughly lifted from the wheelchair and forced into the back of a car. It was a black Lincoln Continental—common enough to blend in, nothing immediately identifiable. Worse, the car was angled side-on to the camera, obscuring the license plate from view.

Robert leaned in, scrutinizing every detail. "What's odd is Lucas got into the back seat with Charlie," he pointed out, his tone edged with suspicion. "That means there was someone else driving. If I had to bet, I'd say it's his brother, Zane."

JJ's face hardened. "That definitely complicates things. If both brothers are involved, we're up against more than just an abduction. We're looking at a calculated operation."

JJ ran a hand through his hair, thinking aloud. "So, we have the abduction of Charlie, a getaway car, and two suspects. That's a start, but I need that to tie in with Brad Marshall's supposed suicide. What else do you have?"

"I think I might have your final connection. Let's start with the key," Robert suggested, holding up a bagged piece of evidence.

"Do you have any prints?" JJ asked, leaning in with anticipation.

"Better than that. The key confirms it. Someone else was in the room," Robert replied, a small smile playing on his lips.

JJ raised an eyebrow. "Go on then, Sherlock. Whose prints are on it?"

Robert's smile widened. "No prints," he clarified.

"Damn it!" JJ exclaimed, frustrated. "How does that tell me who was in the room with Brad?"

"I didn't say it would tell you who. I said it confirms someone was there," Robert explained. "You mentioned the key was nestled in the window frame, right?" He paused, waiting for JJ to acknowledge.

"Yes," JJ confirmed, thinking through Robert's words. Robert gave him a moment to catch on, and JJ's eyes widened with realization. "Of course—the key had been wiped clean. Whoever wiped it was planning to take it with them. It must have fallen out of their pocket as they climbed back out the window."

"Exactly," Robert agreed. "That's my guess."

JJ's mind was racing. "So, do you want to know who was in the room?" Robert asked, his voice teasing.

"You're kidding me, right? Did you find prints? Where?" JJ asked, eyes narrowing with curiosity.

Robert glanced down and gestured toward the whiskey bottle sitting on the table.

"You got prints off the bottle?" JJ asked.

"Partial prints," Robert replied, "but more importantly, we found saliva and got a DNA match."

JJ let out a low whistle. "Jeez, Sherlock, you sure know how to build suspense. Come on, you're killing me here. If we can rescue Charlie and catch our murderer before lunch, I might just get to add my song to the jukebox," JJ joked, trying to lighten the mood.

Robert looked puzzled, not catching the reference.

"Never mind," JJ said with a dismissive wave. "So, who's our murderer?"

Robert leaned forward; his expression serious. "If you can find Charlie, you might just kill two birds with one stone."

JJ frowned, confused. "What do you mean?"

Robert pushed the folder closer to JJ. "Charlie's partial prints were on the whiskey bottle, and the DNA confirms it. He was in the room at some point. I'm not saying he murdered Brad, but it raises a lot of questions about what he was doing there."

JJ slumped back into his chair, a heavy sigh escaping his lips. "Yeah it sure does." His mind raced with possibilities, trying to piece together how Charlie fits into this twisted puzzle and what his connection to Brad's death might be.

Robert grabbed his jacket from the hook on the door. After slipping it on, he turned to JJ. "You want a lift?"

"Where to?" JJ asked, glancing up from the files he was sorting through.

"Well, unless you plan on walking to the hospital to meet up with Harper," Robert said with a wry smile, "I thought you might like me to drop you off there."

JJ nodded and stood up, quickly gathering the images and the case file from the table. "Yeah, these are going to come in handy—not just for showing the captain but also when we're interrogating Zane."

Robert moved to open the door but paused, watching as JJ carefully placed the documents, images, key, and bottle into the evidence box.

The entire case was now packed into that single box—every clue, every vital piece of the puzzle.

"Let's get moving," JJ said, his voice steady but laced with tension. He stepped through the open door, his gaze focused straight ahead, ready to face whatever awaited him at the hospital. Robert followed closely behind. He was now an integral part of the case and fully grasped the urgency to find Charlie and bring him home. The lingering question gnawed at him: Was Charlie a victim caught in something far beyond his control, or was he the villain making his escape?

FIFTY-ONE
SNAKE EYE

HARPER STOOD CASUALLY in the hospital break room, his eyes fixed on Zane, who sat in a white molded chair, still in his orderly uniform. The fluorescent lights overhead buzzed and flickered, casting a harsh, cold glow across the room. Other orderlies moved about, opening and shutting lockers, doing their best to appear busy and ignore the palpable tension simmering between Harper and Zane.

As the last person left, Harper moved over to the door, intending to lock it and ensure privacy. But before he could turn the lock, there was a knock. He opened the door to see JJ standing there, his expression serious but calm.

Harper turned back to glance at Zane, then stepped out into the corridor to talk to JJ.

"Look," JJ began, keeping his voice low, "you start. Use your 'man of the street' charm on him, soften him up—that sort of thing, okay?"

"You mean… bad cop, good cop?" Harper offered, raising an eyebrow.

JJ nodded. "Yeah, that's right."

Harper's face lit up, almost serious. "So, like Starsky and Hutch?"

JJ sighed but couldn't help a small smile. "If that's what helps you, sure," he said. "Starsky and Hutch."

Harper smirked, rolling his shoulders back and getting ready to play his role. With a nod of understanding, he stepped back into the room, ready to set the scene and get some answers from Zane.

Harper entered the room and muttered, "Starsky and Hutch" but didn't ask JJ which one he was to be, so just started the conversation simple and unassuming.

"Nice tattoo," Harper began, nodding toward the intricate design peeking out from under Zane's collar—a cobra coiled around his neck, its body winding up toward his cheek with its fangs poised as if striking at his right eye. "Your brother—your twin, right—has the same one on his left eye, doesn't he? Must've hurt like hell getting it done."

Zane's lips curled into a faint smirk, his dark eyes narrowing slightly. "Yeah, it did," he replied, his voice low, carrying a hint of amusement. "But pain's part of the process, isn't it, cop? You didn't come here to talk about tattoos, did you?"

Zane sat calmly in the hospital break room, commanding attention despite his casual demeanor. He was muscular, his broad shoulders and defined arms filling out his orderly uniform. His skin was tanned, a deep bronze that hinted at his Spanish-American heritage, and it seemed to glow under the harsh fluorescent lights.

His dark hair cropped short in a near-military style framed his face, emphasizing the sharp angles of his features. A faint shadow of stubble traced his strong jawline, lending a rugged edge to his appearance. His dark eyes, intense and piercing, held a mixture of defiance and suspicion—always watching, always assessing. He had a certain charisma about him, the kind that came from a life spent on the edge, navigating trouble and learning to survive on his wits and his fists.

The serpent tattoo was a mark of danger and a nod to his reputation on the streets. Despite the tension in the room, Zane's body language remained relaxed, almost casual, but there was a coiled energy beneath the surface, like a predator ready to strike. His gaze was steady, clearly a man who had seen his share of battles and wasn't afraid of facing another.

The small talk was over before it started. Harper decided to shift gears. "So, when was the last time you spoke to your brother, Lucas?"

he asked, keeping his tone light and almost conversational. Harper watched Zane closely, looking for any sign of hesitation or surprise. He'd been a cop for forty years—long enough to know when someone was lying.

Zane shrugged, his face carefully composed, betraying nothing. "It's been a while," he said flatly, his gaze dropping to a scuffed spot on the linoleum floor. "Lucas does his own thing. We don't talk much anymore. Not like we used to."

Harper nodded, feigning understanding. "Yeah, I get that. Family can be... complicated." He leaned back against a table, his posture relaxed as if they were just two old friends catching up. "So, no calls, no texts recently? Nothing at all?"

Zane shook his head, his voice steady. "Nope. Like I said, we live separate lives. I've got my job here; whatever he's doing, that's up to him. That's just how it is."

Harper could tell he was getting nowhere fast. Zane wasn't about to give up his brother easily, and Harper knew he needed something more substantial to break through the wall of silence. His frustration simmered beneath the surface, but he kept his face impassive, trying not to show how stuck he felt. He needed leverage, something to push Zane out of his comfort zone.

It was time to bring in Hutch—or was it Starsky? Before Harper could decide, the door swung open, and JJ walked in, his expression determined. He had the case file tucked under his arm and two steaming cups of coffee in hand. He handed one to Harper, who took it gratefully, and motioned for him to come over.

The two exchanged a few whispered words, with JJ quickly filling Harper in on the latest developments. Harper's eyebrows shot up in surprise, and a new spark of hope lit his eyes. He nodded, understanding immediately. It was time to change tactics.

With their new information, they were ready to turn up the heat on Zane. Harper knew that this time, they might just have the leverage they needed to make him crack.

In a hushed tone, Harper leaned toward JJ. "So, are you Hutch or Starsky?"

JJ shook his head, a playful grin spreading across his face as he held out his upturned hands. "I'm the good-looking one," he quipped.

Harper rolled his eyes, unimpressed. "That doesn't help me," he muttered, waving JJ off. But beneath the banter, both men were ready to move forward, their partnership seamless as ever as they prepared to take their shot at Zane.

JJ turned back to Zane, stepping closer with a more intense presence than Harper's laid-back demeanor. The room had emptied, the other orderlies, instinctively sensing the rising tension, had discreetly vanished. With deliberate calm, Harper strode to the door and turned the latch, locking it with a soft click. No interruptions.

JJ set the case file on the table, placing both hands flat in front of Zane, leaning in just enough to invade his personal space. "Alright, Zane, let's cut the crap," he said, his voice firm and unyielding. "Do you know Charlie?"

Zane's eyes flicked between Harper and JJ, feeling the shift in the room's energy. He hesitated for a moment, then shrugged. "Charlie who? I don't know any Charlie."

JJ, undeterred, leaned in a bit closer. "What car is Lucas driving these days? What color?"

Zane's jaw tightened, and his eyes narrowed, a flicker of defiance crossing his face. "I don't know what you're talking about," he replied coolly. "I don't keep tabs on Lucas. He's not my responsibility."

JJ's voice dropped to a low, almost menacing whisper. "Listen, Zane, we both know you're not under arrest, and you're right—you've kept your nose clean. But here's the thing: Lucas is in over his head, and we know you know more than you're letting on. You have two choices, either help us find him and maybe protect yourself from whatever shitstorm he's bringing your way, or you can play dumb and see how far that gets you."

Zane's expression remained steady, but Harper noticed a fleeting flicker in his eyes—whether it was fear or uncertainty, he couldn't tell. Still, it was enough to know he had rattled him. Still, Zane wasn't giving in. "Look, I told you, I don't know what my brother's up to," he said, his voice steady and calm. "I'm just here doing my job, trying to stay out of trouble."

JJ exchanged a glance with Harper. They were running out of time and needed to break through Zane's defenses.

JJ reached into the case file and pulled out a stack of photos, spreading them on the table in front of Zane. "You want to know who Charlie is? That's him in the wheelchair," he said, tapping the first photo. Then he pointed to another image, a close-up of the man pushing the wheelchair. "And if I'm not mistaken, that's your brother."

Zane glanced at the photos, his face unreadable, but his voice was defiant. "That could be anyone. He's wearing a mask, and the picture's not clear. You're grasping at straws, cop."

Harper decided it was time to switch tactics. He took a deep breath and softened his tone, making it sound almost pleading. "Zane," he began, "we both know that's Lucas in the footage. Let's not play games. Here's the situation: the man he's pushing—that's Charlie. Charlie's not well, and Lucas has taken him somewhere. He used your uniform, with your name tag, to help him get out of the hospital. If anything happens to Charlie—if he dies—you could be looking at serious charges: accessory to kidnapping, maybe even murder."

Zane's face remained stony, but Harper could see the wheels turning in his mind. For a brief moment, it looked like he might break.

Harper pressed on. "Look, Zane, listen," he said, leaning in. "You've done time. A lot of time. And I can see you've turned your life around. You're clean now, got a solid job. But this could drag you right back into that hellhole of a prison, and for a long time."

Harper's words seemed to hit a nerve.

Zane's expression shifted as memories of those years in prison flooded his mind. He had barely made it out last time. The Miseries—the dark, crushing despair that haunted inmates—had almost claimed him. He remembered seeing others succumb: men hanging themselves in the shower block, in the recreation room. One inmate had even jumped headfirst over the top rail, the sickening snap of his neck echoing through the cell block. And then there were the screams, the sounds of men losing their minds, haunted by shadows and dark creatures that only they could see.

Zane's jaw tightened. He didn't want to go back to that nightmare. But this was his brother's mess, not his. He wasn't about to snitch, even if it meant risking everything. He drew a deep breath and shook his head, his resolve firm. "I've got nothing to say," he muttered. "If you have nothing to charge me with, I'm done here."

He stood, walked to the door, and unlocked it. As he opened it, JJ's voice cut through the tension in the room, stopping Zane in his tracks.

"We'll be in touch, Zane. You know this isn't over, right?"

Zane paused in the doorway and glanced back over his shoulder. "The next time you talk to me, it'll be through my lawyer," he said. With three swaggering steps, he was gone, the door slowly closing behind him.

Harper turned to JJ as the door clicked shut. "We're running out of time," he said quietly. "We need to find Lucas—and fast."

JJ nodded, lost in thought, his mind racing with their next move. JJ turned to Harper. "We'll find him," he said with a steely determination. "One way or another, we'll find him."

Harper glanced at the door Zane had just walked through, his expression thoughtful. "What about Zane?" he asked, hoping JJ had the answer.

JJ paused, weighing the question. "I get the feeling he's pissed that Lucas pulled them both into this mess," he said. "Zane's not the type to give up on his brother easily, but he's definitely not happy about being dragged into whatever disaster Lucas has stirred up." The big question is, who drove them away? I checked with hospital security—Zane has an alibi. He worked the late shift, clocked in at ten p.m., and didn't leave until eight-thirty the following day."

Harper frowned, absorbing the information. "So, if Zane wasn't the driver, then there's got to be someone else involved. Another player we haven't identified yet."

JJ nodded. "Exactly. Lucas isn't working alone. He's got help; the question is who. Zane might be able to lead us to them whether he wants to or not. That's why having Frank tail him is critical. If Zane's pissed, he might slip up and go looking for Lucas—or whoever else is helping them."

Harper nodded slowly, his mind working through the possibilities. "Maybe we should put a tail on him and see if he leads us to Lucas," he suggested, his voice low and cautious.

JJ allowed himself a slight smile. "Already ahead of you," he said. "I checked Zane's schedule earlier. His shift ends in an hour. Frank's on the late shift tonight and owes us a favor. He's agreed to watch Zane and see where he goes after he clocks out."

Harper raised an eyebrow, clearly impressed by JJ's foresight. "Smart thinking. If Zane makes a move, he could lead us straight to Lucas—and hopefully Charlie. But do you think Charlie had anything to do with Brad Marshall's death?"

JJ's expression darkened. "Hard to say. The evidence points to Charlie being there, but only he can explain why and what really happened that night," he replied, his face tightening with resolve. As he gathered the photos, JJ added, "Let's hope Zane takes us to him. If not, we'll find another way."

The two detectives exchanged a glance filled with understanding and resolve. They could feel the pressure mounting; time was running out, but they drew closer with every passing minute. It was only a matter of time before they had Lucas, the mystery driver, and Charlie —and they hoped to find Charlie alive.

FIFTY-TWO
BACK ON THE RES

AS THE MYSTERY surrounding Brad Marshall's death and Charlie's disappearance deepened, JJ and Harper knew they needed concrete evidence to move the case forward. Finding Charlie was crucial, not just to save his life—he was in poor health and in urgent need of medical attention—but also to uncover the truth about what he had witnessed the night Brad Marshall supposedly hung himself. Determined to piece the puzzle together, JJ and Harper sought answers, starting with Charlie's last known address: Springfield's Potawatomi Indian Reservation, where he had been staying at the John Eliot Mission.

They headed east on I72, the landscape stretching out before them after passing Clear Lake. JJ's mind wandered to Charlie's life on the reservation. He imagined the bleak reality of growing up there. Back in Charlie's day, the reservation had been a place where opportunity was scarce—no jobs, barely any government support, and an ever-present shadow of discrimination from the outside world. Access to education was limited, and hope seemed like a distant dream for most. It was a harsh environment where many, overwhelmed by despair and trapped by circumstance, turned to alcohol to numb their pain or simply gave up, lost in the weight of their struggles.

But the times they had changed. Today, many reservations are thriving. A new middle class had emerged from the shadows of the past, finding a way to balance the old ways and traditions with the demands of modern life. Totem poles and ceremonial wigwams stood proudly alongside new developments—casinos, theme parks, and museums—that showcased the rich history of their ancestors.

The Native Americans were determined to tell their own stories and claim their place in the broader narrative of the nation. Education had become a cornerstone of their resurgence. Children were taught their heritage and the skills to thrive in the modern world. This strategy had paid off; the reservations had become vibrant centers of culture and commerce. Families were no longer leaving—they were returning. The reservations had become a melting pot of cultures—Native American, White, African American—creating a unique community governed by the Bureau of Indian Affairs.

Yet, all this change had come too late for Charlie. He was still missing, still wanted for questioning in the mysterious death of Brad Marshall. Was Charlie merely a witness, or was he involved somehow? So many questions remained unanswered. It didn't take JJ long to build a profile of Charlie Harris. He had a record—nothing serious, mostly minor offenses like drunk and disorderly conduct and vagrancy. Certainly not a hardened criminal and not someone you'd peg as capable of murder. But JJ knew all too well that a desperate man could be driven to anything, so he didn't dismiss the possibility outright.

Charlie's last known residence was the John Elliot Mission, and JJ suspected some answers might lie there. He contacted Pastor John, and after a brief conversation, they agreed to meet at the mission.

The road ahead twisted and turned through a forest, or what remained. The skeletal trees, stripped bare by the autumn winds, lined either side of the highway. Their branches reached out like gnarled hands, seemingly trying to reconnect across the asphalt that divided them. The trees creaked and swayed with each gust, a symphony of wooden groans echoing through the otherwise silent forest. As they drove deeper, the clear blue sky began to darken, and unseen gusts pushed the car from side to side as if nature was trying to steer them away.

Harper, always one to lighten the mood—or, in this case, send a shiver down JJ's spine—launched into one of his tales about evil spirits and bad medicine lurking in the woods.

"Hey, do you remember the stories from the old folks?" Harper asked, his tone conspiratorial.

JJ's curiosity was piqued. "What do you mean?"

"Well, way back—and I mean *way* back," Harper began.

"You mean before you were born?" JJ joked, a smirk playing on his lips.

Harper didn't bite. He was determined to get his story across. "Yes, *way* back when the first settlers came. The German ones."

"Oh, you mean when Springfield was just getting started," JJ said, his interest growing. "I've read some of the history, so what's this story I missed?" He kept a firm eye on the road but leaned in just enough to show he was listening.

Harper's voice grew serious, almost somber. "You wouldn't have heard this one. Your family's roots don't go back that far, but mine do. My great-grandfather told me a story about these demons they brought over from the old country. They called them *Leidmahler*. When the settlers came, they wanted the land that the Potawatomi occupied. So, in desperation, they summoned these demons."

JJ shot Harper a sideways glance, one eyebrow arching in skepticism. "Summoned demons?" he repeated. "And what, they just... came over on the boat?"

Harper ignored the sarcasm. "No, listen," he continued. "To summon the Leidmahler, they needed someone for the demons to possess. So they kidnapped a young squaw, a Potawatomi girl, and treated her terribly—drove her to the brink of madness. Because that's when the demon takes you, when you're at your lowest, full of despair."

JJ's grip on the steering wheel tightened, his face mixed with disbelief and discomfort. "And you believe that nonsense?" he asked, turning his gaze back to the road.

But Harper's words lingered, and JJ's mind couldn't help but drift back to the day Charlie was shot. He remembered how Charlie had raved, his voice wild and broken, muttering about demons and *the evil ones that bring misery*. The coincidence gnawed at JJ, no matter how hard he tried to brush it off as mere superstition.

Harper continued, undeterred. "Once she was possessed, they sent her back into the Potawatomi camp. The tribe took her in, and within a week, most of them were dead—killed themselves in one way or another. The rest fled, never to return, because of the *bad medicine* that had cursed the land."

JJ swallowed, his skepticism wavering. "So, where was this patch of land?" he asked.

Harper's voice dropped, almost conspiratorial. "The land Lincoln High School is built on," he revealed. "It stretches all the way into Alexander. Even now, the Potawatomi won't go near that land. They refuse to send their kids to that high school—still convinced it's cursed with *bad medicine*."

"Get out of here," JJ chuckled, though his laughter had a nervous edge. "Joseph went to Lincoln High, and he's Potawatomi."

Harper shrugged. "Maybe his family didn't believe. But a lot of them still do."

JJ's curiosity finally got the better of him. "Alright, so what do these demons look like?"

Harper's expression grew grim. "No one knows," he said. "Only a few who've encountered them survived. But rumor has it they're described as towering, skeletal figures with limbs impossibly long and thin. They wear tattered, shadowy cloaks that seem to blend into the mist and darkness around them. Their faces are hollow, mask-like visages, with sunken, empty eyes that glow faintly when they sense despair. And their grins..." Harper shuddered. "Twisted and unnatural, a grin that reflects the anguish they devour."

JJ felt a chill run down his spine, and the hairs on the back of his neck stood up. He forced a laugh, trying to dispel the creeping unease. "You've really got a way with ghost stories, Harper."

Harper offered a wry smile. "Just passing down what the old folks said," he replied, but his voice held an undercurrent of sincerity that left JJ feeling anything but reassured.

JJ threw another glance sideways at Harper, momentarily shifting his focus from the road. "You're full of it, and I know you're just winding me up," he added with a half-smile, his tone hovering between humor and disbelief.

Before Harper could respond, he suddenly shouted, "Watch out!" JJ whipped his head back to the road just in time to swerve around a small Native American child standing in the middle of the highway, dressed in full tribal regalia. The car screeched to a halt, tires smoking as they left dark marks on the pavement. A thick, acrid cloud of burnt rubber filled the air around them. Both men sat frozen, their hearts pounding in their chests, their eyes locked on the rearview mirror, hoping to catch a glimpse of the child. But there was nothing.

They bolted from the car. JJ dropped to his knees, scanning underneath, while Harper sprinted to the rear, frantically searching both sides of the road. They found nothing. Slowly, they shook their heads in disbelief, their breath visible in the cool air as they exhaled. Harper couldn't resist bringing up the demon again. "Leidmahler," Harper said, but JJ dismissed it with a wave, though he couldn't help but wonder where the child had come from—and where it had gone.

Back in the car, they continued down the road. Moments later, they emerged from the forest, and the sky cleared. The wind died down to a gentle breeze. Ahead, a small town lay nestled among fields of corn and pastures dotted with grazing cattle. As they passed a camp of tepees and tethered ponies, they saw children in traditional tribal clothing playing near a few smoldering campfires. JJ's thoughts drifted back to a time long before, when life here was simpler, driven by the rhythms of hunting and the seasons. His daydream was abruptly interrupted when he spotted a child playing with a remote-controlled truck, and through the open flap of a tepee, the unmistakable sound of a television blaring the latest episode of *The X-Files* filled the air. A wry smile crept across JJ's face as they entered the town.

"What was the name of the road again?" JJ asked, snapping back to reality.

Harper fumbled with a crinkled piece of paper. "Fitzgerald," he replied, scanning the road signs. "John Eliot Mission, just off Fitzgerald... There!" He pointed to a small swinging sign above a solid oak door—'The John Eliot Mission.' The building stood out, its cedar latticework and brick frame reminiscent of an old Puritan mission. The small brick spire and slightly sagging terracotta roof gave it the quaint look of a cottage, though larger in scale. A bronze bell hung in the spire, waiting to toll. The mission looked out of place among the modern bars and diners surrounding it, a solitary guardian of a bygone era.

JJ's gaze was instinctively drawn to a black Lincoln idling further up the road as they parked. Its tinted windows were always a red flag for JJ, but it wasn't enough to cause alarm—yet! After parking, they ascended the mission's stone steps. JJ couldn't shake the feeling of being watched and instinctively glanced back over his shoulder at the Lincoln still there, its engine idling.

A surge of adrenaline rushed through him. Was it a getaway car? Unlikely, no bank was in its vicinity, and there were no high-class jewelers. In fact, nothing worthy of being robbed. The Lincoln was parked in front of a pet store—not exactly a high-stakes target. Unless it was a bizarre case of dognapping, there was no immediate threat. JJ turned back to the mission door just as Harper raised his fist to knock. But before he could, the door swung open, revealing a tall, bespectacled man in a long black robe with a priestly collar and a round, brimmed hat.

"Can I help you, gentlemen?" the man asked, his voice was a Midwestern drawl with a hint of Irish.

"Father John?" JJ asked. "It is Father, isn't it?"

The man chuckled softly. "You can call me whatever you like, son, if it brings you closer to God," he replied with a friendly smile. "Or Pastor, if that suits ya. But my name's John." He reached into his pocket, pulled out a set of keys, and walked over to an old bicycle chained nearby with a large wicker basket that looked like it belonged in the English countryside. He bent down to unlock it and added, "So, how can I help you gentlemen today?"

"Detective Harper," Harper said, flashing his badge. "And this is Detective Jackson. So, you're John Elliot?" he enquired, glancing at the sign swinging above the entrance. JJ shook his head at Harper's blunder, but the pastor quickly responded with good humor.

"Not quite. John Elliot died in 1690, and we're still mourning the loss," the pastor joked with a chuckle. "I'm Pastor O'Brien." JJ couldn't tell if Harper was joking or just clueless, so he jumped in, just in case.

"Pastor, we spoke on the phone. You mentioned you might have some information regarding Charlie," JJ explained, steering the conversation back on track.

"Ah, yes, I remember now," the pastor said with an Irish inflection. After unlocking his bike, he leaned it against a nearby post.

"I see you don't have much trust in people, Pastor," Harper joked while glancing at the heavy lock in the pastor's hands.

"I put all my trust in God, but my bike, only chains and a heavy lock can keep it out of the hands of a thief." The pastor, though a man of God, was a realist—a rare find, Harper mused.

JJ stepped forward. "Charlie had a room here, and we'd like to take a look around if that's alright with you."

"He did, but we haven't seen Charlie in nearly a month," the pastor replied. "We offer rooms and meals to those in need, but if they're gone for more than a week, there's always someone else waiting. And if they're gone for a month, we rarely see them again. What's Charlie done to warrant two detectives coming all the way out here from Springfield?"

As Harper explained the situation, JJ's eyes darted back to where the Lincoln had been. It was gone. He exhaled, relaxing slightly. There had been no heist, robbery, or dognapping. Still, his instincts told him there was more to this.

"Well," Pastor O'Brien continued, "since Charlie hasn't returned, his room has been given to someone else. But I do have a few of his things if you want them. Not much, but you're welcome to them."

"That won't be necessary, Pastor—" Harper began, but JJ quickly cut him off.

"Yes, that would be very helpful," JJ said.

Pastor John wheeled the bicycle back toward the mission door, JJ and Harper followed close behind as he disappeared inside. Moments later, he returned with a small, battered brown suitcase and a black sack. "I don't know what's in the suitcase; it's locked. But the sack contains some clothing," he explained as he handed them over.

JJ took the suitcase, nodding for Harper to grab the sack. A sour smell wafted from it—old, unwashed clothes. Harper grimaced, deciding he'd rather not open it if he could avoid it. They both thanked the pastor, and as they turned to head back to the car, the pastor mounted his bike. Just before he set off, he called out, "I hope you find Charlie, and I hope he's not in any trouble. He wouldn't harm a soul." The comment confirmed JJ's own assumptions about Charlie.

A moment later, with a slight wobble, the pastor pedaled off down the road.

"There it is again," JJ muttered, eyes narrowing.

"What?" Harper asked, glancing over.

JJ had spotted the Lincoln once more, parked slightly concealed down an alley. "The Lincoln. Something's not right about that car," he replied, his gaze fixed on it.

"Look, it's getting late, and if I'm not home soon, Mrs. Harper's going to be pissed," Harper said, tossing the black sack into the trunk. JJ handed him the suitcase, and he placed it beside the sack. "This sack is gonna stink up the whole trunk. Maybe we should just toss it?"

Ignoring Harper's complaints, JJ started toward the Lincoln, his focus sharpening as the car sat further down the road. Harper sighed, momentarily contemplating whether to follow, but before he could make a decision—and before JJ had taken more than a few steps—the Lincoln's engine roared to life. JJ quickened his pace, breaking into a jog, but the car lurched into reverse and screeched away, tires squealing as it sped down the road.

JJ halted, watching the vehicle disappear into the distance. He muttered the license plate number under his breath, quickly pulling out a notepad to jot it down. Harper, meanwhile, remained by the trunk, shaking his head. A foot chase after a speeding car was never a good idea, and as for a car chase—there was always a time for that, but now wasn't it.

Slightly out of breath, JJ returned to the car, where Harper still stood, the trunk open. "What's that smell?" JJ asked, wrinkling his nose at the sour odor seeping from the black sack.

"That sack is going in the bin, no doubt," Harper replied, wrinkling his nose.

As they got back into the car, JJ's mind raced. There was something about that Lincoln—something off. He knew he had to dig deeper, not just into Charlie's disappearance, but also into whoever—or whatever—was now shadowing them.

FIFTY-THREE
SECRETS

ROSE PACED in the kitchen of her apartment; the phone pressed tightly to her ear. Her voice, usually smooth and commanding, now had a sharp, nervous edge. She bit her bottom lip, frustration seeping into every clipped word.

"Is he alright?" she hissed, barely keeping her voice in check. The voice on the other end of the line was muffled, but Rose's growing agitation made it clear that the conversation wasn't going in her favor. Her hand tightened around the phone as the demand came through loud and clear.

"More money?" she echoed, incredulity hardening her tone. "I've already given you the car." She paused, listening, and then let out a bitter laugh. "Are you trying to blackmail me?"

Rose leaned against the kitchen counter, her free hand tapping an impatient rhythm. The person on the line was trying to shake her down, and she knew she had no choice. She squeezed her eyes shut, exhaling slowly through her nose.

"Fine," she snapped, her voice dropping to a harsh whisper. "You'll get your cash, but I want something in return." She paused, waiting for an answer. "Keep an eye on Jack, and I'll give you the money. Five grand, and that's it—we're done."

A question came back, and for a moment she hesitated before replying, "Take care of it."

Before the conversation could continue, the sound of footsteps made Rose's eyes snap open. She swiveled around just in time to see Jack standing in the doorway, his gaze narrowing as he took in the scene.

"Who were you talking to?" Jack asked, his tone casual but his expression questioning.

Rose forced a smile, her mind racing. "Oh, just sorting out some car repairs," she lied, her voice steady but lacking its usual warmth. "It's nothing."

Jack's eyes lingered on her face, searching for a crack in her composure. He wasn't entirely convinced, and Rose knew it. But she ended the call swiftly, slipping her phone into her pocket with a forced nonchalance.

"All sorted," she added, brushing past him. "I'm off to the bank. Don't forget your appointment."

Jack didn't respond immediately. He watched her, a gnawing unease forming in his gut. It wasn't like Rose to lie. And lately, she had been acting strangely distracted and guarded. He still hadn't questioned her about her night out and why she had come home so late. Where had she been?

But he glanced at his watch, the minutes ticking away faster than he liked. He had an appointment with Dr. Warrick and couldn't afford to be late. His suspicions would have to wait—at least for now.

"Right," Jack muttered, grabbing his jacket. "Let's get moving. Can you drop me off?" he called out, his voice trailing off as she emerged from the living room.

"Of course," she replied as she made her way to the door. Jack watched her leave, a deep sense of unease settling over him. He couldn't shake the feeling that whatever secrets she was keeping, they involved him.

FIFTY-FOUR
CONNECTING THE DOTS

HARPER AND JJ sat at their desks in the precinct, with JJ deep in conversation with the captain. In a spontaneous moment, JJ moved behind a seated Harper and dramatically mimed a strangulation, catching Harper off guard as his expression showed surprise. After the performance, JJ handed the coroner's report to the captain and pointed to various sections, building his case. Slightly flustered, Harper adjusted his tie as the dull hum of ringing phones and scattered chatter filled the background, adding to the odd scene.

The captain nodded at JJ's convincing performance and the possibility that JJ had uncovered inconsistencies in the original verdict. While the evidence was, at best, circumstantial—perhaps little more than a series of coincidences—the captain acknowledged there was more to the case. He gave JJ and Harper the green light to dig deeper into Brad Marshall's supposed suicide.

Though not officially classified as a murder case, it was now up to them to connect the dots and solidify the case before making any bold moves or public statements. They needed everything to be airtight.

JJ signaled to Harper, and together, they headed to a side room. A worn, faded sign above the door read 'Case Room.' As Harper flicked the light switch, the fluorescent tubes buzzed to life, casting a cold glow over the neatly arranged space. JJ had been busy—he had already assembled the evidence earlier that day, files meticulously laid out, everything JJ had collected to make his case, all in anticipation of the captain's go-ahead.

"Someone's been busy," Harper remarked, his eyes sweeping over the documents and diagrams that lined the surfaces.

JJ met his gaze with a knowing smile, offering no words but communicating everything with that one look—he was ready to crack the case wide open.

In the corner, a large chalkboard dominated the room, its surface cluttered with pinned photographs, Brad Marshall's hastily scribbled suicide note, and crisscrossing red strings stretched across it like a makeshift spider's web. The strings linked scribbled notes with times of death and names, weaving a chaotic map of the investigation. At the heart of this tangled web was a photograph of Brad Marshall, staring out like a ghost haunting the case. His death, though officially ruled a suicide, had never sat right with JJ—he'd never believed it. Now, even Harper was beginning to see it, too. Too many pieces didn't fit, and the mounting evidence was now impossible to ignore.

"Rose," JJ began, pointing to a torn-out page from a glossy magazine; Rose's own publication featuring an image of her in a padded, power-shouldered pinstriped suit beside an article titled 'Power Play,' with the subtitle 'Rose to the Top.' The article had impressed him, portraying her as a formidable figure—a woman who not only knew her brief but mastered it, blending beauty with unflinching ruthlessness. JJ had experienced that ruthlessness firsthand when they met; her cold, commanding presence was impossible to ignore. But there was something more—something simmering beneath the surface, a pressure behind the eyes, a subtle tell. It was as if Rose, while maintaining control over the events around her, was barely holding her emotions in check—like a coiled cobra, ready to strike. If JJ was going to uncover who Rose truly was, he'd have to get under her skin. And he knew exactly how to do it: through Jack.

He laid out his assessment of her character with a tone of certainty.

"She openly threatened to kill Brad Marshall—or, at the very least, wanted him to face more severe consequences after nearly getting her brother killed. When she heard about his death, there wasn't a shred of sympathy."

JJ paused, his finger lightly tapping on her image as if deep in thought. Then his eyes shifted, scanning the board, before landing on another photograph.

"Charlie Harris." His picture was a mugshot; Charlie had a record. "The DNA evidence places him in Brad's room either before, during, or after Brad's death. Now he's missing. He claimed to have seen something the night Brad died, but he wasn't clear about who—or even what. We can only assume he was talking about Brad."

Harper, sitting on the edge of the table, chimed in. "What did he call them, the shadowy figures he saw?"

JJ reached into his inside pocket and pulled out his notepad. He flipped through a few pages, his brow furrowing as he searched for something specific. Finally, he stopped, his eyes scanning a particular entry. "Mnedo," he said. "The Evil Ones. But Charlie was drunk at the time," he added with a shrug as if that single fact could easily dismiss the wild claim. Yet, the unease in his voice suggested he wasn't entirely convinced himself.

Harper's expression grew serious, and he spoke softly, almost as if he feared that speaking too loudly might invoke something sinister. "You mean Leidmahler."

JJ let out a frustrated sigh. "Seriously?" he said, his voice edged with irritation. "Focus." He tried to redirect Harper, but the name lingered in the air, heavy and unsettling, as if the spirits themselves were listening.

"Next, we have Jack," JJ said, pointing to a picture of Jack pulled from his employment records at the school. "He's the only one with a legitimate grievance against Brad. That prank he pulled almost got him killed."

Harper, still perched on the table's edge, offered his opinion. "Yeah, but Jack doesn't strike me as the vengeful type. He seemed genuinely shocked when we broke the news about Brad's death."

"True," JJ agreed, his gaze lingering on Jack's photo a little longer.

"But there's something else about him. I can't quite put my finger on it, but something doesn't sit right." His voice trailed off as he sank into his thoughts, that nagging feeling pulling him back to Jack. There was more beneath the surface—JJ could feel it—something Jack wasn't saying, something that didn't add up.

The room fell into a heavy silence, broken only by the soft hum of the strip lights above. The tension was thick as JJ and Harper studied the board intensely. A sudden, hard knock at the door startled them both, and before JJ could even respond, the door swung open with a creak. Frank strolled in, his usual no-nonsense demeanor giving away little.

He walked to the evidence board without a word, taking in the crisscrossing threads and photos. He finally spoke, his tone dry. "Geez, you guys have been busy. Unfortunately, I don't have much to add to... whatever this is." He gave a glance towards Harper.

"Harper."

"Frank," Harper replied, acknowledging him with a brief nod.

Frank turned his attention back to JJ. "The guy you had me tail—Zane. I've got nothing. Did some asking around, and it looks like he's turned over a new leaf. Been out of trouble for a while now. He was telling the truth—he hasn't seen his brother Lucas in months."

JJ frowned, his gaze steady and focused. "What about Lucas? Anything at all?"

Frank shook his head. "Nothing. Nada. He's practically vanished off the face of the earth." He paused, tapping his top pocket before pulling out a small notepad. Flipping through a few pages, he found the note he was looking for. "The last anyone saw of him was when he left a bar—the Cattle Drive," he said. "Got into a black Lincoln."

JJ's eyes narrowed, the gears in his mind turning. "Well, we know Rose goes to that bar," he said thoughtfully. "And so does Jack. It's very interesting that Lucas also frequents the same place."

The coincidence felt too strong to ignore, and JJ's suspicion deepened, a sense of connection forming between all three of them.

"Anyway that's all I got" Frank said

JJ sighed, clearly disappointed, but nodded. "Thanks, Frank. I appreciate the effort."

Frank glanced once more at the chaotic board, smirking slightly. "Well, I hope you catch your guy, girl, or whatever the hell you're after," he said, gesturing vaguely at the collage of photos and notes.

He turned to leave, walking past Harper on his way out. With a half-smile, he offered the same parting words as before.

"Harper."

"Frank," Harper echoed, sharing a brief, knowing glance before Frank disappeared through the door.

JJ turned to Harper, his voice buzzing with excitement. "There's that Lincoln again," he said, recalling Frank's earlier conversation. "Could it be the same Lincoln that took Charlie? And the same one that was watching us at the reservation?"

Harper nodded slowly. "It could be," he replied, his tone cautious. "But we won't know for sure until we get a registration." Despite the measured response, his voice had an unmistakable spark of intrigue, matching JJ's rising anticipation.

"What's the info on the plate you got from the res?" Harper asked.

Frustrated, JJ answered, "Still waiting. I did, however, find out what make of car it was; it was an old Lincoln Continental Mark IV. Frankie's dad has one, and she said they are quite rare, especially in the condition I described. It's from the early seventies, so it's almost a classic. The database has yet to be updated to go that far back, so we need to do some further digging. Joanna from DMV is looking into it."

"Okay, so we have the players. Let's look at the evidence," JJ said, moving towards the table. Both slipped on surgical gloves as they surveyed the scattered items before them. Each piece of the assembled evidence told part of the story, but the whole picture remained elusive.

The key, with no fingerprints, was found stuck in the window ledge. The grainy CCTV photos show what could be Charlie's abduction—or was he being helped to escape? Was Charlie the murderer, or had he simply witnessed something that put him in danger? Brad Marshall's rucksack, packed like an overnight bag, offered more questions than answers. Last but not least, Charlie's battered brown suitcase, retrieved from Pastor O'Brien, is still unopened. JJ had waited for the proper warrant to crack it open, respecting Charlie's rights despite his disappearance, and with the warrant finally in hand, the time had come.

JJ leaned over and pulled the old suitcase towards him. The lock was fragile and worn with age. The latch gave way with a quick push and tug, popping open with ease. Inside, nestled among personal items, was a set of car keys with a faded tag. The registration number, though worn, was still legible. JJ squinted as he slowly read it aloud: "Two-eight-two two-six-two."

His brows furrowed as he grabbed his notepad, scanning his scribbled notes. He read aloud again, more slowly this time: "Two-eight-two two-six-two." The numbers clicked into place, and JJ's expression shifted.

"The license plate matches," he muttered, his voice a mix of frustration and realization.

"It's the same car that's been following us. It's all tied to Charlie." Harper leaned in, peering at the keys in JJ's hand. "You're sure?"

"Positive," JJ replied, his voice steady but laced with urgency. "The Lincoln that's been tailing us must belong to Charlie—he has a spare set of keys in his case. And although it's not confirmed yet, it's likely the same Lincoln that Charlie was placed in when he was abducted."

Before the weight of the revelation could fully settle, a soft knock at the door broke the silence.

"Come in," JJ called.

Joanna from the DMV entered, a folder tucked under her arm and two steaming cups of coffee, one balanced in each hand.

"Thanks, Jo," Harper said, reaching out to take one of the coffees.

"Black, two sugars, right?" she asked with a smile.

Harper took a sip and nodded. "Perfect."

Joanna set the other coffee on the table for JJ, then retrieved the file from under her arm, waving it slightly. "Took a bit of digging, but I finally got a name on the registration."

In unison, both JJ and Harper responded, "Charlie Harris."

Joanna smiled faintly, shaking her head. "Close, but no cigar. It's registered to Bartholomew Harris and still is. Do you think they're related?"

JJ and Harper exchanged stunned looks, the weight of the new information sinking in. The name—Bartholomew Harris—hit them both with unexpected force.

For Harper, it dredged up memories of an old, unsolved case from years ago: the infamous Lincoln Mauler case. Bartholomew Harris had been the missing, presumed-dead student and possible final victim of the Mauler. Though the Mauler case was now closed, the missing teenager case had gone cold. It had never disappeared from the department's collective memory and remained an open case.

For JJ, the revelation carried a deeper, more personal weight. His father had not only spoken about the Mauler case but had played an active role in the investigation. JJ remembered the grim details his father would recount during their late-night conversations, each etched into his memory. Bartholomew Harris's name had come up often, becoming synonymous with the case that had haunted Springfield—and, by extension, JJ—for years.

With this unexpected revelation, their current case had taken a chilling, unexpected turn that tied it directly to JJ's new case. "Thanks, Joanna. Much appreciated," JJ said, taking the file from her and flipping through it.

As Joanna left, JJ moved swiftly to the evidence board. With a determined hand, he jotted down Bartholomew Harris in his notebook, then tore the page out and pinned it to the outskirts of the board, reserving it for now—until he had more information that could directly link him to the case. Grabbing a length of blue elasticated band, he carefully connected the note to Charlie's photo.

There was every indication that Bartholomew was related to Charlie. The question now was how deep that connection went—and what it meant for the investigation.

"We've got a possible new suspect," JJ said, his hands resting on his hips, voice dropping to a low, serious tone. "Bartholomew Harris—a missing student, presumed dead, and somehow tied to all of this."

The room fell silent as Harper stared at the board, his mind racing to piece it all together. The case had just swerved, and the truth seemed even more elusive. The two steps forward they had just taken suddenly went a step back, throwing the case wide open.

They turned back towards the table, contemplating what else might surface and what new clues could emerge to drive the case deeper into a mystery that even Sherlock Holmes might struggle to unravel. As they sifted through the contents of the battered suitcase, the familiar scent of aged paper and old memories filled the room. They pulled out a half-empty bottle of whiskey identical to the one found under Brad Marshall's bed. JJ placed it next to the evidence bottles, possibly confirming Charlie's presence in the room alongside the DNA sample. A selection of yellowed photographs and faded letters lay scattered before them, each a glimpse into a life unknown to both Harper and JJ. As JJ carefully spread them out across the table, a flicker of sadness crossed his face, the weight of these forgotten lives pressing down on him.

The suitcase held fragments of Charlie's life—faded memories tucked away in mundane snapshots of Charlie, his wife, and their son. As JJ continued sifting through the photos, one, in particular, caught his eye. It was a picture of a young couple and a boy. JJ flipped it over and read the names written on the back in a neat, careful hand: *Charlie, Rosetta, and Bart.*

JJ looked up at Harper, holding the photo. "Well, we can confirm who Bartholomew is and how he is connected to Charlie."

"Who?" Harper asked, glancing over.

"His son, Bart," JJ said, passing the photo to Harper. "How the hell did I miss this?" JJ cursed; frustration etched across his face.

Harper took the photo, studying it carefully. "Don't beat yourself up," he said, offering a reassuring nod. "You've done well so far, piecing all of this together."

JJ sighed, running a hand through his hair. "Considering the fact that his son went missing, presumed dead... it's no wonder Charlie spiraled into despair and booze."

The revelation cast a somber light over the case, and for JJ, it deepened his understanding of Charlie's pain, making it easier to empathize with the man and the path that had led him here.

JJ continued looking at the photos, all capturing moments from happier times. But as JJ's hand hovered over the final image, something caught his eye, and his expression shifted to one of quiet shock.

"There she is again," JJ murmured, sliding the photo across the table towards Harper.

"I've seen her and the boy together in an old photo on Mo's wall." He didn't immediately recognize who she was.

Harper squinted at the photograph. It showed an older Charlie standing beside his wife while a teenage Bartholomew, around seventeen or eighteen, stood to the right, his expression distant and brooding. Not the sweet young boy from the earlier images; his demeanor had shifted, his face now obscured by a full, dark, bushy beard. A dagger tattoo stretched along his right forearm, giving him a hardened, almost menacing look. Draped casually over his shoulder was a teenage girl—Rose.

"It's her," Harper said, his breath catching. "Rose. A young Rose, I'll grant you, but no doubt. That's her." He studied the image more closely, adding, "She was quite the looker back then, too."

"Still is," Harper replied

JJ leaned in, confirming his suspicion. "Goddamn! You're right—that's Rose." His mind raced. He'd always felt she was hiding something; she was involved somehow. Until now, she had hovered on the edges of the case, a peripheral figure but never fully in focus. But with this new evidence, Rose was suddenly at the heart of it all. She hadn't just crossed paths with Charlie; she had been romantically involved with his missing son. The photograph was undeniable proof, yet it only thickened the layers of mystery surrounding her.

Without hesitation, JJ grabbed the photograph of Bartholomew, marched over to the chalkboard, and replaced the scribbled scrap of paper bearing Bart's name with the picture, pinning it between Charlie and Rose. He then swapped the blue elastic band for red, signaling a significant shift in the investigation. Bartholomew was no longer a minor figure, presumed dead or missing—he was now central to the investigation; the question is how. The connections between them all were becoming clear, but the questions were multiplying just as rapidly.

JJ's eyes narrowed in thought. They had to bring Rose in for questioning. He hadn't done so before because he didn't have the right questions. But now, he had plenty.

Harper studied the photograph again, his face thoughtful. "Do you think she's connected to Brad's death and Charlie's disappearance?" he asked, his tone measured as if weighing the possibilities.

JJ didn't respond immediately, running his hands through his hair before resting them on his hips, his mind darting between possibilities. He glanced at Harper, then spoke, his tone measured and deliberate. "Hear me out," JJ began, outlining his theory. "Rose confronts Brad in his room about the prank he pulled on Jack. In a fit of rage, she strangles him, then stages the scene to make it look like a suicide and slips away. Charlie sees the whole thing, rushes in, and tries to save Brad..."

Harper let out a short chuckle, shaking his head. "That's one theory. But don't you think this might be a bit of a reach? You're connecting so many dots that your picture's starting to blur. What about Charlie? Has she kidnapped him? Does she even own a Lincoln Continental Mark IV? And, more importantly, why would she kidnap Charlie? How could she know he might—might—be a witness?"

JJ froze, his mind flashing back to a conversation he'd had with Jack earlier in the week. He had mentioned Charlie—perhaps unintentionally, perhaps with the deliberate aim of gauging Jack's reaction. The reasons now didn't matter; however, the full weight of his actions hit him like a freight train.

JJ slumped into the chair beside the table, the weight of his impending confession pressing heavily on him. His voice was strained with guilt as he finally spoke, the words tasting bitter as they left his mouth. "I told Jack that Charlie might be a witness," he admitted, his eyes clouded with regret. "I think I might be the reason Charlie was abducted."

The realization landed heavily between them, the gravity sinking in. Harper's eyes widened; the implications were clear to them both. JJ's earlier hypothesis, which focused on Rose, could just as easily fit Jack. And now, they had two suspects to consider.

They had made progress that afternoon, but while they had made some connections, it only opened up more questions. What was becoming clear was that the case had grown far wider, potentially reaching back twenty years. Who was driving Bartholomew's Lincoln?

And why was it still registered in his name after all this time? And who was now behind the wheel?

Now, four potential suspects stood in the shadow of Brad's death—Jack, Rose, Charlie, and possibly even a teenager who had gone missing and was presumed dead two decades ago. The next step was clear: they had to bring Jack and Rose in for questioning. However, without enough evidence for a search warrant, any interrogation must be voluntary. And knowing Rose, as JJ did from their tense first encounter, that wouldn't be easy.

FIFTY-FIVE
THE CHECK UP

THE NEXT DAY arrived quickly for Jack. During a brief conversation with Rose, she excitedly told him she had secured tickets to *The Catz Club*, a local jazz bar. The plan was for all of them to go—Rose, Jack, Max, and Scott. Though Jack tried to share in her enthusiasm, his mind quickly drifted to the day's more serious matters.

While he was genuinely happy about the upcoming night out, his thoughts remained heavy. The hallucinations, the nightmares, and the ever-present fear that he might be losing his grip on reality continued to haunt him. But for now, he wanted to be present for Rose. He didn't want to cloud the evening with his worries. Maybe, just maybe, this night out would offer a brief escape, a chance to relax and lighten the burden pressing on him.

If only for a while, he was willing to let go and enjoy the distraction.

As Rose headed into the kitchen, Jack took a deep breath and followed her. "By the way," he said, his voice steady but serious, "I have an appointment with Dr. Warrick this morning." He watched her carefully, hoping she would understand and support him, even if he couldn't fully explain the reasons behind the visit.

Jack watched Rose, hoping to judge the mood. The spring in her step was suddenly gone and as she turned to him he noticed her expression had shifted, he sensed the concern on her face. "If you think it's going to help and you're sure, then let's go," she said, her voice soft but guarded.

Jack braced himself. "Actually, I'm going alone," he said, his words carefully chosen. "You've got things to do—maybe go shopping for a new dress for tonight," he offered with a small smile.

Rose raised an eyebrow, then broke into a playful grin. "Jack, I have a million dresses," she joked. But she saw the seriousness in his eyes and paused, finally accepting his decision. "Fine, if you're sure?"

Jack exhaled, relieved. "I'm sure," he replied, a smile spreading across his face. *That wasn't so bad*, he thought.

"Okay, I'll call you a cab," Rose said, pulling out her phone and starting to dial.

"There's no need," Jack began, but his words were interrupted by the sharp buzz of the doorbell. "I've already called one. In fact, that's probably it now," he added, grabbing his coat and preparing himself for the day ahead.

Moments later, Jack stood at the open door, ready to leave, but before he left he turned back to see Rose standing in the hallway, her earlier excitement now fully replaced by unease. She smiled at him but the sparkle in her eyes had dimmed, and the cheerful anticipation of their evening plans was gone. He could see he had upset her, and that realization twisted something in his chest.

Jack knew Rose liked to have control over every situation—she needed to. She thrived on predicting outcomes and managing every detail with precision. But this moment wasn't about her; it was about him. This was something he had to face alone, without her guiding the conversation or steering the narrative.

He understood that his decision left her in unfamiliar territory, a place where she couldn't pull the strings. But as much as he hated causing her discomfort, he knew he had to do this on his own. Both of them had secrets buried deep, but maybe—just maybe—some of those secrets needed to come into the light if he was ever going to heal.

The thought of revealing those truths, of exposing the things he'd kept hidden, made Jack uneasy. But worse still was the knowledge that the idea terrified his sister even more. He could see the fear lurking behind her composed facade, a fear that mirrored his own, and he silently hoped that they could both find a way to face it—together.

FIFTY-SIX
LET ME TELL YOU A SECRET

AN HOUR LATER, Jack found himself outside the hospital, exchanging a few polite hellos with the staff as he made his way down the corridor. Soon, he stood in front of Dr. Warrick's office. After a gentle knock, a soft voice invited him in.

"Enter," she called.

As Jack opened the door, Dr. Warrick rose from her chair, her face lighting up with a warm smile. She crossed the room to greet him, offering a firm but friendly handshake. "Hi, Jack," she said, gesturing toward the couch. Jack returned the smile, and as he walked over to sit, she continued, "I'm really glad to see you and even happier that you decided to take me up on my advice."

Jack settled into the worn leather couch, its familiar creak taking him back to another time, another place. "Well," he replied, shifting slightly in his seat, "you convinced me. I need to get to the bottom of my issues."

"Hold that thought," Dr. Warrick said as she moved to her chair. She placed a recorder between them on the table. "So, Jack, we're here to talk about you—your life. We're going to leave no stone unturned. Are you ready for that?"

Jack took a deep breath, his shoulders lowering as he leaned back into the couch, his eyes momentarily glazing over with a mixture of fatigue and hesitation. The room, though welcoming, triggered memories of his childhood—those quiet sessions after his father's death, sitting with Dr. Amen, being asked about his feelings. He was young then, too young to understand how to express his feelings. Back then, he had simply been relieved that his father was gone, no longer able to hurt him or his sister. But the memories, even now, carried an uncomfortable weight. He had never told Dr. Amen about his father's abuse; the dark secrets Rose had told him to keep hidden. And yet, sitting here, with Dr. Warrick's expectant gaze on him, he could feel those secrets inching closer to the surface, just waiting to be unearthed.

"Let's do it," Jack said, his voice steady but laced with an undercurrent of uncertainty.

Dr. Warrick pressed the record button, the soft click filling the air. Her eyes met Jack's, steady and calm. "Whenever you're ready," she said softly, her voice professional but not without empathy.

Jack nodded, knowing that this was the moment—one that could unravel everything he had kept buried for so long. It was time to face his nightmares and confront the truth.

"I've been having the hallucinations again. Worse this time."

Dr. Warrick nodded, already expecting the familiar theme to return. "What kind of hallucinations, Jack? You mentioned your father before."

Jack's lips tightened as he shifted uncomfortably, avoiding Dr. Warrick's gaze momentarily before speaking. "I saw him last week... or at least it looked like him, it sounded like him." He hesitated, searching for the right words. "It was his voice, but his face... it wasn't right. It was decomposing, and there were maggots." Jack's breathing quickened, his pulse visibly rising. "He doesn't say much. He keeps telling me he's here to collect me."

He was barely holding it together, but there was more, and he needed to say it. "Then there's the radio," Jack continued, his voice strained. "I heard voices, but the radio wasn't even on. Wasn't plugged in or anything." His words came faster, rushing out now. "It was like some old broadcast from 1972. The music, the news... then Brad

Marshall's voice started mocking me. After that, Jammin' James Freeman. And..."

Jack faltered, his mind teetering on the edge of a thought he couldn't articulate.

"Who else was there, Jack?" Dr. Warrick pressed gently, her fingers resting lightly on her notebook, though her recorder captured every word.

Jack swallowed hard, his voice barely above a whisper. "Beaumont. The Mauler. Michael Beaumont."

Dr. Warrick leaned in slightly, her brow furrowing in concentration. The pieces of Jack's fragmented reality were troubling, yet it was clear that Jack believed in every haunting detail.

"And The Miseries?" Dr. Warrick asked softly, pushing him a bit further. "Are they still around?"

Jack turned his head slowly to meet her gaze, his eyes dark and distant. "I think... I think *they* are The Miseries," he said, his voice trembling. "My father... he always said they'd come for me."

Jack's words chilled the atmosphere in the room, and a heavy silence settled between them.

Dr. Warrick studied him carefully, her trained eye noting the tension in his jaw, the haunted look in his eyes. Whatever this fear was —whether a figment of his imagination or rooted in something real—it had deeply embedded into Jack's psyche, shaping how he viewed the world. Now, she had to navigate through the terror of his mind to unearth what was real and what had been buried beneath layers of pain and memory. There was a secret that Jack was holding on to, and she needed to know what that was if she was going to fix whatever was going on in his mind, a chance she never got with her father.

Jack felt some ease now, as though a weight had been lifted just by sharing the demons that had haunted him for so long. Even though he knew how unbelievable his story sounded, at least Dr. Warrick had listened without judgement; her calm, sympathetic presence offering a fragile comfort. Maybe, just maybe, she had the answers he needed.

His hands fidgeted nervously with the cuff of his sleeve, his voice dropping to a softer, more vulnerable tone. "I've seen them all my life, but they were mostly in my nightmares. I could handle them... they weren't as bad." He swallowed hard, eyes distant as if replaying something he didn't want to relive. "But since the incident, since being locked in that cellar, it brought me back to when my father…" Jack hesitated, his voice trembling, the words lingering on the edge of confession. "I think I'm starting to lose it."

Dr. Warrick's gaze remained steady; her face calm yet alert. Jack's words were heavy on her mind, especially the mention of his father. What he was about to say felt crucial, but she knew from experience that pressing too soon could cause him to retreat. Instead, she let the silence settle between them, a gentle space for him to fill if he was ready. She hoped her quiet patience would encourage Jack to continue, to let out whatever he had been holding onto for so long.

Jack wasn't sure if she believed him. Part of him expected her to doubt everything he said. But there was something different, something reassuring in her stillness, in how she listened without interruption.

Rose had told him, back then, to keep everything quiet. Their father was dead, and no one needed to know what had happened. So he did. He locked all the secrets up in his mind, sealing them away for years. But now, it felt like they were clawing their way out, one by one, dragging him back into the darkness.

Dr. Warrick took a slow breath, sensing the vulnerability in Jack's voice. "I don't think you're losing it, Jack," she said softly. "I think you're recognizing that you need help. Let me share a secret with you." She leaned in slightly, her eyes gentle but serious. "Everyone has moments of despair, of sadness. It's human nature. You, me, even Rose. We need these moments to make us stronger, more rounded. But what matters most is who is there for us when despair takes hold—who guides us, who helps us navigate the darkness."

Her voice caught slightly as she spoke, and an unbidden memory of her father and the suffering her family had endured surfaced. But she quickly refocused. This session wasn't about her; it was about Jack.

She pointed to a framed picture on her desk. "See that? My dog, Sig," she said, her voice softening. "When I feel lost or overwhelmed, Sig comforts me. He gives me a purpose, a reason to stay strong."

Jack's eyes shifted to the photo, and he spoke in a low, detached voice. "But you're going to lose your dog," he said.

Dr. Warrick's heart jolted. The statement felt too close to home, too unnervingly accurate. "How did you know that I might lose Sig?" she asked, trying to keep her voice steady, though a hint of paranoia crept in.

Jack turned to her, his gaze calm but distant. "We always lose our pets," he said. "They either run away or die. They don't live as long as we do." He turned his head to look at her fully, and she saw a flicker of something deeper, something rooted in painful experience.

"Did you have a dog, Jack?" she asked, gently probing.

Jack's expression darkened, and he looked away. "Yes. I loved that dog. His name was Dusky," he whispered. He paused, his voice thick with emotion. "They scared him away."

Dr. Warrick leaned forward slightly. "Who scared him away?" she pressed.

"The Miseries," he replied, his voice barely above a whisper. "Whenever they came, Dusky would growl and bite me. Then one day... he wasn't there anymore."

Dr. Warrick felt a chill run down her spine, but she knew she had to push deeper. Jack's childhood trauma seemed intricately tied to these so-called *Miseries*, and she had a strong suspicion that the heart of his issues lay with Rose. She needed to understand their connection. She sensed it went beyond sibling love, and she had to understand this connection if she was to help him heal.

"Let's start with Rose."

Jack shifted in his seat. "Rose has been there for me since the start. She's tough, you know? Hard, even. But she means well, always looking out for me. Doesn't trust many people, though."

"What about when you were growing up? Did you have fun with her? What was that like?" Dr. Warrick's tone was gentle, coaxing.

He hesitated. "Kind of. She took care of me after Mom... after she died." He paused, a flicker of unease crossing his face as he spoke. "I think I told you before, right? That she left when I was around six."

Dr. Warrick nodded gently. "Yes, you mentioned she left without saying goodbye. But you didn't say she had died."

"That's what Rose said," Jack replied, his voice softening, growing quieter, almost detached. "She told me last week that Mom had cancer, and she didn't want us to see her sick, so she left. Rose said she's probably dead now."

His gaze drifted away as he searched for fragments of memories that refused to fully surface. "I don't remember much about her. Just... that she was always sad."

Dr. Warrick remained silent, allowing Jack to sit with his thoughts, aware that the mention of his mother stirred something deep. There was a story there, buried beneath the sadness, something Jack seemed hesitant to uncover.

Dr. Warrick's pen hovered over the page though her mind was racing. Sad. The idea of a mother always being sad was a curious detail for a young boy to hold onto. She wondered if Jack had internalized that sadness, maybe even blamed himself for it. She had to dig deeper.

"Do you think her sadness had anything to do with you?" Dr. Warrick asked, watching his reaction carefully.

Jack shrugged; his expression guarded. "I don't know. Maybe. Maybe I was the reason she left. Maybe I made her sad."

The thought hit Dr. Warrick harder than she anticipated. She made a mental note: *Perhaps The Miseries are a manifestation of that guilt. Maybe he created them to externalize the sadness he believed he caused.*

"But," Jack continued, his voice faltering, "Rose always tried to protect me after Mom was gone. She was young herself, though. And Pops..."

His voice trailed off as if the words were too difficult to form.

"What about your father?" Dr. Warrick pressed, leaning in ever so slightly.

Jack's face hardened. "Pop wasn't kind. Not to me. Not to her either."

He paused momentarily as though wrestling with whether to share more. When he spoke again, his voice was bitter. "He used to beat me. Lock me in the cellar if I cried. Sometimes, worse things. He was always drinking. Always angry."

Dr. Warrick felt the weight of his words. The abuse Jack endured had shaped him. "And when you found him hanging... You were what, eight?"

Jack nodded. "Yeah. Eight." His voice sounded distant. "I don't remember feeling much. Maybe relief."

"Do you remember any good moments with him? Anything positive at all?" she asked, not expecting much.

Jack paused, staring at the floor. "Maybe the tree house," he muttered. "He built one for me when I was around six. Before everything went bad."

"And then it did get bad," Dr. Warrick echoed.

"Yeah. When Mom left, he got worse. Drank more, beat us more." Jack stopped himself as though some memories were still too painful to put into words.

But then, something shifted. His eyes flickered as if recalling something important. "Things changed when... when Rose met someone. I don't remember his name, but I remember his beard. Big, bushy. He had a tattoo on his arm. And a black car."

Dr. Warrick scribbled down the details. "This man, was he kind to you?"

Jack nodded slowly, his eyes softening. "He was. Took me on rides in his car. Made me laugh. Then one day, he was gone."

"What happened?"

"We were at the cabin one day," Jack began, his voice wavering slightly. "They had a big row—pretty serious. Rose slapped him, and he stormed out. She followed him, but when she came back... she was alone. I never saw him again." He paused, his gaze distant, as if replaying the memory in slow motion. "Rose was... sad for a long time after that."

His voice trailed off. It was as though Jack only now understood how much Bart's disappearance had impacted his sister and how deeply it had etched itself into her life.

Dr. Warrick absorbed this new piece of the puzzle, but the more she learned, the more questions arose. Who was this man, and why had he vanished? And what had happened to make Jack's mind conjure 'The Miseries' in the first place? Was it his father's abuse? His mother's abandonment? Or was there another, deeper trauma that had yet to surface?

As the session neared its end, Dr. Warrick leaned forward. "Jack, I think we're getting closer to understanding where these visions come from. But to get to the bottom of it, I'd like to run some tests. Blood work, to rule out anything physical that could be causing the hallucinations or blackouts."

Jack nodded, looking exhausted but resolute. "Yeah. Whatever it takes." He paused. "I don't want to end up like my father." The laugh that followed was hollow and unsettling. He then made a sudden, startling motion, miming a noose tightening around his neck and pulling him upward.

The gesture jolted Dr. Warrick. It was out of place and so unlike Jack that it made her uneasy. She had never seen him joke in such a dark way. Shaking off her surprise, she rationalized it as a coping mechanism—maybe a reaction to the intense session they'd just had.

Gathering her thoughts, she pressed the intercom on her desk and summoned a nurse. As the nurse prepared to take Jack's blood, Dr. Warrick leaned back, her mind still processing what he had said and the unsettling gesture he had made. The unease lingered, creeping into her consciousness. Something about his behavior felt deeply off as if a dark undercurrent had surfaced—a part of Jack she had never seen before. It was as though a different personality had emerged; one he might unconsciously bring forward to cope in certain circumstances.

She had never witnessed him act this way in all the time she had known him. Still, she tried to remain pragmatic, telling herself she would know more once the test results came back. Yet the worry stayed with her, gnawing quietly at the back of her mind.

The secrets of the Brooks family were tangled, the threads leading back to Rose, Jack's father, and a mother who had vanished under strange circumstances. There was something off about the official story. People with cancer don't usually leave their families to die alone. There was more to this.

"Jack, would you mind if I contacted Dr. Amen?" Dr. Warrick asked, gently. "He's been your family doctor since you and Rose were children. If he's willing to share your files, it could certainly help." She watched Jack closely, hoping he grasped the significance of her request.

Jack met her gaze, pausing momentarily before giving a slight nod. "Sure, if you think it could help."

"Excellent," she replied, making a note in her diary.

As Jack's blood was drawn, he sat quietly, lost in his thoughts. Dr. Warrick observed him closely, noticing the fatigue that had settled over him during the session. It had clearly taken a toll, but for the first time, there was a shift in Jack—he seemed willing, perhaps even ready, to confront his past. Dr. Warrick knew that this was the first step toward unraveling the dark mysteries that had haunted him for so long, and she hoped that by facing these demons, she could help him begin to build a better future.

After taking the blood sample, she briefly explained the next steps —what they would be looking for and how the results might help guide his treatment. A date was set for the next visit, and with any luck, she would have more answers by then. Together, they could begin to map out a plan.

Dr. Warrick wasn't one to rush toward medical interventions. For her, talking through emotions and untangling the threads of trauma and fear was always the first and most important course of action. But she also knew that if Jack's blood results revealed something physical, she couldn't rule out medication. It was a delicate balance, one that required care and patience. For now, though, the real work was just beginning, and Jack had taken the first crucial step.

FIFTY-SEVEN
THE CATZ CLUB

ROSE STOOD in front of the mirror, carefully applying a last stroke of lipstick. The reflection staring back at her seemed calm, almost radiant, as she adjusted the hem of her black dress. But inside, her mind was spinning. She could hear Jack in the next room, the dull hum of the TV barely cutting through the tension in the air.

She knew tonight was supposed to be about fun—heading out to The Catz Club, enjoying a night away from their mounting worries. But the visit Jack had made earlier that day to Dr. Warrick lingered in her mind like a dark cloud.

She spoke casually, trying not to sound too concerned, as she entered the living room. "How was the session today?" Her voice was light, but her heart was beating fast.

Jack looked up from his phone, the briefest flicker of discomfort crossing his face. "It was fine, you know... the usual stuff," he said quickly, his tone clipped. "Nothing major."

Rose forced a smile then, but she felt a knot forming in her stomach. Jack had never been the type to talk openly, especially not about something as delicate as his sessions with Dr. Warrick. But lately, she'd been worried that maybe he was saying too much—especially about the family. The fact that he had missed taking his medication only complicated the situation.

What if he slips? What if he tells the doctor something that should stay buried? The thought had been eating at her for weeks now.

She watched him now, sitting at the edge of the couch, tying his shoes with methodical precision. His movements were stiff, robotic even. He was going through the motions, but he wasn't really there. He'd been distant since the sessions had started—more so than usual.

"So, you... didn't talk about anything we had discussed?" Rose asked, her voice careful and measured. She didn't want to push too hard, but she needed to be sure, to hear it from him directly.

Jack kept his gaze fixed on the floor. "Nope," he replied, his tone flat. "Just talked about me going back to work, how I feel about it, and managing emotions. You know, all that stuff." It seemed to Rose as though he could tell she was probing for more, but he wasn't ready to reveal everything. Now was not the time.

Rose's stomach churned with unease. She forced a smile, pretending to accept his answer. "Okay," she said, nodding. "Good. You ready to head out?"

Jack finally looked up and gave a small, strained smile in return. "Yeah," he said.

The tension between them lingered; unspoken truths hanging heavy in the air. He stood and smiled, a smile that didn't quite reach his eyes. "Yeah. Let's go."

Rose tried to shake off the unease that had settled over her ever since they left the apartment. Jack was carrying something heavy on his shoulders, something he wasn't sharing. She could feel it. He hadn't been himself since that visit to Dr. Warrick earlier. But tonight wasn't about that—at least, she told herself it wasn't. Tonight was about unwinding, enjoying the music, and mending fences with Max.

They arrived at The Catz Club, its low lights and smooth rhythms washing over them as they entered. The band onstage were playing a slow, sultry tune, the kind of music that slipped into your bones and loosened everything that had been coiled too tight. Rose immediately spotted Max at a corner table, waiting for them with a wide grin, already nursing a drink.

Rose felt a pang of guilt as she approached. The last time they'd spoken, things had taken an ugly turn. She'd lashed out—not intentionally, but her emotions had overwhelmed her that night when Jack had gone missing. It wasn't fair—Max had always been a loyal friend to Jack, and accusing him of something unfounded was wrong. Tonight, she hoped, would be her way of making it right.

"Max," she said as she leaned down to hug him, the warmth of the gesture sincere. "I'm sorry about last time. I shouldn't have—"

Max cut her off with a shrug and a smile, his easygoing nature not letting the past weigh on him. "Don't worry about it, Rose—water under the bridge. Besides, we're here now, right? Let's enjoy the night."

Rose felt lighter after her apology to Max. The tension that had lingered between them for weeks was finally gone, and with that weight lifted, she could let herself relax. Jack and Max fell into an easy conversation, Jack animatedly discussing the model train Rose had gifted him for his birthday. His face lit up in a way Rose hadn't seen in a long time. For a brief moment, watching him, she let herself believe that things were normal again—like maybe the distance between them was just in her head.

But normalcy, she knew, was fleeting.

As Jack and Max became more absorbed in their conversation, Rose quietly excused herself, slipping away from the table. She moved through the crowd toward the bar, her heels clicking softly against the polished floor. The jazz band played on, the smooth rhythm blending with the murmur of conversations, but Rose barely registered the music. She had something else on her mind.

FIFTY-EIGHT
211

JACK, still chatting with Max, kept his voice light, but his attention wandered. With a subtle glance, he watched his sister from the corner of his eye. She had drifted to the edge of the bar, and his gaze followed her, curiosity sharpening his focus as he noticed her speaking to a man he didn't recognize.

Though he tried to maintain his conversation with Max, Jack couldn't help but feel a prickle of unease, his mind now split between the friendly banter and the unfamiliar figure engaging with his sister. The man was tall and slim, and there was something unsettling about him. The shadows of the dimly lit club seemed to cling to him in a way that made Jack's stomach tighten.

The man leaned in slightly, speaking to Rose. Jack couldn't make out the words, but there was something about their interaction—familiar, almost casual. It wasn't the professional or guarded demeanor Rose usually displayed around people Jack didn't know, and that unsettled him.

The man's face, partially obscured by the dim lighting, was sharp and angular. Then Jack saw it—the tattoo. A snake, curling from the man's neck up to his temple, its tail wrapping around his ear, its head poised just above his left eye. It slithered across his skin like it was alive, and the sight of it made Jack's chest tighten.

Rose glanced around, her eyes briefly sweeping over the room, but Jack made sure his gaze didn't linger too long on her. He didn't want her to know he was watching. His interest piqued when Rose pulled a brown envelope from her purse and handed it to the man. Jack tensed, his conversation with Max fading into the background. The man opened the envelope briefly, glanced at whatever was inside, and then slid it into his pocket with a satisfied smile followed by a brief nod. He took a final sip of his drink, set the glass down, and disappeared into the crowd without another word, vanishing as quickly as he had appeared.

Jack's mind raced. Who was that guy? What was in the envelope? And more importantly, why hadn't Rose mentioned any of this?

When Rose returned to the table, she smiled as if nothing unusual had happened. Jack felt his pulse quicken, but he kept his tone casual as he asked, "Who was that guy you were talking to?"

Rose's smile didn't falter, but there was a brief pause before she answered. "Oh, him? Just someone I know from work. He needed something from me, nothing important."

Her answer was smooth—*too* smooth. Jack sensed a lie lurking beneath her words, but before he could press her further, Scott appeared at the table. Jack reluctantly let the encounter go, but the feeling of suspicion lingered, simmering just below the surface.

"Hey, guys!" Scott greeted them with a grin, his presence easing the tension that had been slowly building between Jack and Rose. He slid into a seat next to Rose, his arm brushing against hers in a way that Jack had noticed happening more often lately. There was something unspoken between them—something Jack wasn't sure how to feel about yet.

Jack liked Scott. He seemed genuine—always upbeat, always positive. Jack enjoyed his company; it had a way of lifting his mood, and, if he were being honest, he thought Scott was good for Rose. The two had grown close, and Jack couldn't help but wonder if Scott was becoming more than just a friend to her. The thought made him smile, even if it stirred a sense of protectiveness in his chest.

As Scott launched into a story about something that had happened at work, the conversation seamlessly shifted, leaving behind the unsettling image of the man with the snake tattoo and the mysterious brown envelope. But Jack couldn't shake the moment from his mind. It lingered like a shadow, his thoughts constantly circling back to the strange exchange. Something wasn't right, and the growing certainty that Rose was hiding something gnawed at him.

The evening at The Catz Club was otherwise a perfect distraction. Smooth rhythms of live jazz filled the room, creating an atmosphere ripe for easy conversation and laughter. Jack tried to let himself unwind, letting the music wash over him, but his eyes kept drifting toward Rose and Scott. Their conversation seemed to have grown more intimate, their laughter a little too familiar, and Jack couldn't help but smirk.

"Get a room," he quipped jokingly, a playful grin spreading across his face. Rose shot him a mock glare, but the blush that crept onto her cheeks was unmistakable, while Scott just chuckled, shaking his head. The tension in Jack's chest loosened, replaced by genuine amusement at the sight of their growing closeness.

Sensing the shifting mood at the table, Jack and Max decided to give Rose and Scott some space. "Let's head out, give them some time alone," Jack suggested, rising from his seat.

Rose's smile wavered slightly. "Where are you going?" she asked, a hint of concern in her voice.

Jack gave her a reassuring smile. "It's getting late, and I'm back at work on Monday, remember? I need to catch up on as much rest as I can." He paused, his grin widening. "Besides, I thought I'd give you two some—you know—*together* time."

Rose managed a smile, though a hint of unease lingered behind her expression. But seeing Jack leave with Max by his side gave her some reassurance. She watched her brother and his friend head for the exit, then turned back to Scott, who had already gathered up their empty glasses.

"Time for a refill?" he asked, his eyes warm and inviting.

Rose's smile returned, more genuine this time. "Yeah," she said with a nod. Then a final glance at the exit; Jack and Max were gone.

THE MISERIES - THE HANGING TREE

AS THEY STEPPED out of the club, the cool night air hit them, sharp and crisp against the warmth of the evening. The original plan had been to move on to another bar, even though Jack had told Rose he was heading home. But as he stood outside, the pull of his earlier unease returned. Maybe the lie he told Rose about heading home would now be the better option.

"So, where to?" Max asked.

Jack shook his head, a tired smile playing on his lips. "You know what? I think I'm done for the night," he admitted. "Not really in the mood for more drinks," he added, his voice carrying a note of exhaustion.

Max raised an eyebrow but nodded, sensing that something was troubling Jack, something he wasn't quite ready to talk about.

"Same here," Max agreed. "I'll just grab a cab home." He raised his hand, and moments later, a taxi pulled up to the curb. As he opened the door, he turned back to Jack. "You coming?" he asked.

"Nah," Jack replied. "I think I'll take a walk first, clear my head a bit before heading home."

"Okay," Max said, climbing into the cab. "I'll see you Sunday. We can check out that new train of yours."

Jack smiled, more genuine this time. "See you Sunday," he replied.

He watched as the cab drove away, then took a deep breath of the cool night air. With the city quiet around him, he set off on foot, hoping the walk would help him sort out the thoughts swirling in his mind. As he wandered down the dimly lit street, the cool night air did little to calm the storm brewing in Jack's mind. His thoughts circled back to Rose—the envelope, the man with the snake tattoo, the secrets that seemed to cling to the night. Paranoia was settling over him. No matter how hard he tried, Jack couldn't shake the growing sense of dread, as if something dark was lurking just beneath the surface, waiting for the perfect moment to emerge.

As Jack sauntered down the sidewalk, his steps slowed, and the world around him started to warp. His vision blurred, and he felt the familiar signs of an attack creeping up on him. The voices began to swirl in his head, low at first, like whispers on the wind. But soon, they became a cacophony of torment—The Miseries, the demons that haunted him. They clawed at his mind once more, pulling him into a spiral he could barely control.

His breath quickened, and the sidewalk seemed to tilt beneath him. Jack stumbled into a nearby alley, doubling over as he was violently sick. He gasped for air, gripping the wall for support, but the shadows around him twisted, rising from the ground like dark figures. Shapes moved in the periphery of his vision, menacing and real. And then, from the shadows, a figure stepped forward, his face twisted with intent.

Before Jack could comprehend what was happening, his vision went black.

WHEN HE CAME TO, everything was a blur. The alley was bathed in harsh red-and-blue lights from police cars, their sirens wailing in the distance, surreal and disorienting. Jack stood unsteadily, his legs weak beneath him, and stared down at the unconscious man lying at his feet. In his hand was a gun, cold and heavy, its weight a terrifying reality he couldn't comprehend.

What had he done? His mind raced, but he had no memory of what had just happened or how the gun had ended up in his grasp. He stared at the weapon, his heart pounding in his chest, a sick feeling rising in his stomach. Panic and confusion clouded his thoughts as he tried to make sense of the scene unfolding around him, but all he felt was a deep, paralyzing fear.

DETECTIVES Harper and JJ arrived on the scene, responding to a call about a possible 211—a mugging in progress. As they stepped into the chaos of flashing red-and-blue lights, they immediately recognized Jack.

"Lower your weapons," JJ ordered the surrounding officers, his voice calm but firm. The tension in the air was palpable, and everyone complied cautiously, their eyes darting between Jack and the detectives.

Harper, meanwhile, quietly unclipped his holster and rested his hand on his gun. He watched JJ carefully, his thumb flicking off the safety just in case.

Both detectives began to approach Jack slowly, their movements measured and deliberate.

"Jack," JJ called out, his voice steady yet gentle, trying to gauge Jack's state of mind. Jack stood there, the gun still clutched in his hand, his eyes wide with confusion and fear.

"Jack, drop the weapon," JJ said, his voice calm but firm.

Jack's hands trembled, but he obeyed, letting the gun fall to the ground with a dull thud.

"I don't... I don't know what happened," Jack muttered, his voice hollow.

The man beneath Jack began to stir, groaning as he regained consciousness. He immediately started shouting, his voice loud and panicked. "He's crazy! He went all psycho on me!" he accused, pointing a shaky finger at Jack.

"It was self-defense," Jack murmured, though his voice sounded distant, almost unsure. The memories of the attack were fragmented, scattered pieces he couldn't quite put together. The voices that had roared in his head had faded, but the eerie echo of their presence left him feeling disconnected from reality.

Officers moved in swiftly, cuffing both Jack and the enraged man. An ambulance pulled up moments later, its lights flashing as paramedics rushed to attend to the injured man. A witness stepped forward, her voice clear and confident, confirming that the man had indeed attacked Jack first. The gun, as it turned out, belonged to the assailant.

But despite the evidence in Jack's favor, something about the way he had reacted—the way he had gone 'crazy'—cast a shadow over everything. His behavior had been erratic, and it left the officers unsettled.

Harper and JJ exchanged a grim look before arresting the suspected mugger. Yet they had no choice but to bring Jack in for questioning as well.

MEANWHILE, Rose and Scott had just left The Catz Club, savoring the calm after a night filled with music and conversation. They decided to take a leisurely stroll, the cool air refreshing and their laughter carrying softly down the street. But as they walked, their laughter faded, and their eyes fixed on a chaotic scene unfolding ahead.

Moments later, Rose recognized a familiar figure. "That's Jack!" she cried out, her heart racing as she quickened her pace, worry flooding her features.

Scott hurried alongside her, his expression growing serious as they drew closer, bracing themselves for whatever they were about to find.

Rose rushed toward the police tape; her eyes wild as she tried to push past the uniformed officers blocking her path. "Let me through! That's my brother!" she yelled, her anger rising.

The officers held her back, but JJ saw the commotion and gestured for them to let her through. Rose stormed over to JJ, her eyes immediately landing on Jack, who was being handcuffed and placed into the back of the police car.

"What the hell is going on?" Rose demanded, her voice trembling with fury as she confronted JJ.

"It seems Jack may have been attacked," JJ replied cautiously, his tone gentle but wary.

Before he could say more, Rose overheard the cursing and angry protests coming from the man being wheeled away on a stretcher. Something inside her snapped. Without a second thought, she lunged at the man, her fists flying in a blind rage.

"You did this! You hurt him!" she screamed, her emotions boiling over.

Officers scrambled to hold her back, their grips firm yet careful, as JJ stepped forward to intervene, his own voice raised in an attempt to calm her.

"Rose, stop!" he called out, concern and urgency mingling in his eyes. The chaos of the moment crackled around them, the rawness of Rose's fear and anger laid bare for everyone to see.

JJ pulled her back, his grip firm but gentle. "Rose, stop! Calm down. We're just taking Jack in for questioning. It's going to be okay."

Rose, breathless and trembling, glared at the mugger as he was wheeled away. Her fists clenched at her sides, but her anger quickly dissolved into anguish when she turned back to Jack. Watching him, handcuffed and being manhandled into the back of JJ's car, made her heart ache. "This is a mistake," she pleaded, her voice cracking. "Jack didn't do anything wrong."

Harper and JJ, their faces grim, drove past her with Jack secured in the back seat of the car. The sight of Jack, his eyes wide and filled with confusion, made Rose's chest tighten painfully.

"Jack, hold on! Don't say anything!" Rose called out, her voice desperate and breaking. "We'll be with you soon!"

The car sped off, sirens wailing and lights flashing, leaving Rose standing in the chaotic aftermath. Her heart pounded in her chest, a sense of helplessness threatening to overwhelm her.

FIFTY-NINE
BANGED UP

JJ AND HARPER arrived at the precinct and began the process of locking Jack into a cell. As the door clanged shut, Jack's voice trembled, the same desperate words spilling out like a broken record. "I don't know what happened," he repeated, his eyes wide and filled with confusion. "One minute, I was being mugged—attacked—and the next, I had the gun in my hand, and the guy was just... on the ground."

There was a raw, unfiltered disbelief in his tone that made JJ pause. Jack's voice was full of genuine fear, and he seemed rattled by the events. JJ felt a flicker of doubt. The man didn't seem to be lying; he looked more like someone who'd been caught in a nightmare he didn't understand. JJ believed him. Still, they needed to get to the bottom of what had happened that night, and this was also their chance to dig deeper into the bigger story.

As JJ and Harper walked away from the cell, a pensive silence settled between them. Harper was the first to speak.

"You know what this means, don't you?" His voice was quiet but tinged with urgency, each word deliberate, seeking assurance that JJ understood the weight of his question.

JJ nodded, his mind already racing through the possibilities. "Yes, I do. I'm already ahead of you," he replied. "But I need to act fast. We have about an hour at best—maybe two," he said, the urgency in his voice unmistakable. "The time it takes for Rose to get her attorney here," he added.

They both understood that every second mattered, and they needed to use the time wisely.

Harper crossed his arms, thinking quickly. "We could hold him overnight," he suggested. "There was a firearm involved, and that alone gives us some leeway. Might buy us extra time in the morning—time to ask more questions if Rose doesn't tell him to clam up."

JJ considered the idea and nodded slowly. "Good call," he said. "If we can use that to our advantage, we might get more out of Jack before his defenses go up. Let's hope we get something concrete."

With a plan forming between them, JJ and Harper knew they had to make every moment count if they were to get answers to the broader case that they were working on.

Harper headed for the front desk. He asked a uniformed officer to bring Jack to the interview room. Meanwhile, JJ made his way to the case room to gather information on the Brad Marshall case. He couldn't shake the feeling that Jack was more of an innocent bystander than anything else, not just in the mugging but maybe in the Brad Marshall case, too. Still, if questioning Jack could shed some light on Rose's involvement—or reveal more about her—it was worth it. This wasn't just about Jack and the incident that evening anymore; it was about getting answers to the questions regarding a more serious case.

Moments later, the door to the interview room creaked open. A uniformed officer stepped in, escorting Jack, his wrists bound in handcuffs. Jack's face was pale, the seriousness of the situation sinking in.

Harper leaned casually against the wall, his arms crossed, watching silently. JJ sat at the table, flipping through the file in front of him, a picture of calm focus.

JJ nodded toward the officer, his eyes landing on the cuffs. "You can take those off," he said.

The officer complied, uncuffing Jack. JJ offered a quiet apology. "Sorry about the cuffs, Jack. Procedure."

The officer turned and exited the room.

Jack sat down, rubbing his wrists, still looking a bit disoriented. JJ gave him a reassuring nod but knew there was little time for pleasantries. They had one, maybe two, hours before Jack's attorney would arrive, and once that happened, Jack would be advised to stay silent. JJ needed to work fast.

"Where's Rose?" Jack asked, his voice shaky.

"She's in the interview room," JJ replied. "Waiting for your attorney. Once he gets here, we can arrange for you to speak to her. That might take a couple of hours. But, Jack, if you want to tell us what happened now, we might be able to get this wrapped up quickly. Maybe even have you leave with them."

JJ leaned in, his voice gentle but firm. "How does that sound? You want to let us know what happened?"

He kept his eyes locked on Jack's, hoping the offer of a way out would be enough to get him to open up, even if just a little.

Jack had dealt with JJ and Harper before, and they weren't the type to intimidate or throw their weight around. They seemed like decent guys, and Jack appreciated that. He didn't feel the need for a lawyer—not yet, at least. After all, he knew he was innocent, even if the events of the night were a jumbled mess in his mind. He couldn't remember everything clearly, but he knew he hadn't done anything wrong.

Harper had now taken a seat at the table, leaning back casually, while JJ maintained a more focused posture. Jack, finally more at ease, leaned back in his chair, the situation starting to feel a little less oppressive.

"We know you didn't go after the mugger, Jack," JJ began, his voice calm but probing. "But we need to understand how things went down. You were standing over him, gun in hand, and the guy was unconscious. That's a problem for us unless we get some clarity. Walk us through what happened."

Jack rubbed the back of his neck, trying to piece together the foggy details of the evening. "I was just taking a walk for some fresh air before taking a cab home," he started slowly. "Next thing I know, this guy jumps me. I panicked, tried to push him off, and we struggled. Everything's blurry after that. When I came to, I had the gun in my hand, and he was on the ground."

JJ nodded, letting Jack speak without interruption. The story lined up with the witness account, but that wasn't what JJ was really here for. The mugging wasn't the issue—it was just a doorway into something bigger: Brad Marshall, Rose, and the tangled history that Jack seemed unwittingly tied to. JJ needed to slip those questions in without making Jack close up, and that would take finesse.

JJ leaned forward slightly, placing his elbows on the table and clasping his hands, his tone soft but curious. "I get it, Jack. Sometimes things happen fast, and your mind can't keep up. But I want to know if there was anything strange before that—anything unusual leading up to the mugging. Did you see anyone hanging around, maybe at the bar?"

The interview door creaked open, and a uniformed officer entered, balancing a tray of coffee. He carefully set three cups on the table along with a wooden spoon and a small bowl of sugar. There was a brief exchange of glances between the officer and JJ—silent, subtle, but clear. It was the kind of wordless communication every cop understood. JJ caught Harper's eye, and in the space of seconds, a decision was made.

Harper stood and walked over to the officer. They exchanged a few quiet words, barely a murmur in the air, and with a slight nod, the officer left the room, closing the door behind him. Harper returned to JJ's side and leaned in, speaking in a low tone so that Jack couldn't overhear.

"We've got about one hour," Harper whispered. "His lawyer's on the way."

JJ gave a quick nod. He'd expected as much. Rose wouldn't let Jack sit in a room with them for long, not without legal muscle. There was no time for small talk or easing into the conversation anymore. They were racing against the clock now.

JJ leaned back in his chair; his focus now razor-sharp as he fixed his gaze on Jack. Time was slipping away, and he needed more than vague recollections. "Anything else you can tell me?" JJ pressed; his tone steady but insistent.

Jack shifted in his seat, fidgeting with the edge of his shirt. He hesitated, and JJ could see the internal conflict playing out on his face. Jack was holding something back, and it wasn't hard to guess why. But before Jack could respond, the door to the interview room rattled slightly, a reminder that their time was running out.

"Well, that all seems clear, Jack. Looks like a simple case of self-defense," JJ said, his calm voice putting Jack at ease. The tension in Jack's body slowly melted away as he leaned back in his chair, visibly relieved. But JJ wasn't done. "Unfortunately, we still don't know what happened when you blacked out."

Jack nodded, his expression darkening. "Yeah, it's been happening a lot lately," he admitted, his voice dropping to a near whisper. "There's something wrong with me." He paused, running a hand through his hair. "I've had it for a long time, but the medication usually helps."

JJ's eyes narrowed slightly, listening intently.

"But since the incident at the school," Jack continued, his voice tightening, "you know, the Brad Marshall thing… since then, things have been getting worse." His gaze dropped to the floor, seemingly haunted by memories he couldn't shake.

JJ exchanged a glance with Harper, sensing that Jack was on the verge of revealing something important. The mention of Brad Marshall was a clue, a thread they needed to follow, and JJ knew he had to keep Jack talking.

"Sorry to hear that, Jack. Are you getting any help?" JJ asked, his voice sympathetic.

"Yeah, I've been seeing a therapist. The same one who looked after me while I was recovering from my coma," Jack replied.

JJ's ears perked up at the mention of Brad Marshall, but he kept his tone steady. "Who's your doctor? Maybe we can ask her to give a statement in your defense."

"Dr. Warrick," Jack answered quietly.

"Alright, we'll call her and let her know what happened tonight," JJ said, making a mental note. "Thank you, Jack."

"Now… can I go home?" Jack asked, his hope rising slightly.

JJ sighed and stood up. "Unfortunately, no. We still need to hold you while we finish our inquiries and get full statements from the witnesses and the guy who tried to mug you. But don't worry—we'll make sure you're comfortable in the meantime."

As JJ stood, he gathered the file from the table. In a subtle move, a handful of photos slipped from his hands and scattered onto the floor. One picture landed squarely in Jack's lap. Jack picked it up, curiosity in his eyes as he examined it more closely. It was a photograph of Lucas, the man with the snake tattoo.

"I've seen this guy," Jack said, his voice firmer now.

JJ, glancing at Harper, saw the flicker of satisfaction on his partner's face. "When, Jack?" JJ asked, playing it cool, though his heart raced a bit. This was the crack they needed.

"Tonight, at the Catz Club," Jack replied. "My head's still fuzzy, but I remember him. He was at the bar. The tattoo on his face—I recognized it."

"His name is Lucas." JJ informed him.

"Whatever his name is there is no mistaking that guy," Jack confirmed. He slid the photo back across the table to JJ.

"Do you recognize the name, Jack, or why he was there at the club?" JJ asked.

Jack shook his head.

"Do you remember who he was talking to?" JJ asked, his voice gentle but firm.

Jack hesitated, his body growing rigid. His eyes darted away, and his fingers fidgeted nervously. "Yeah, he was talking to…" He trailed off, the words lodged in his throat.

JJ held his breath, feeling the tension in the air. Jack was teetering on the edge of a major revelation.

"It was… I don't remember," Jack finally said, his voice unsteady.

Damn it, JJ thought, frustration simmering beneath the surface. He could see through Jack's hesitation—Jack knew the answer, but fear was holding him back. JJ understood what was happening. Jack was terrified, not just for himself but for his sister. If he revealed what he knew, Rose would be implicated, and that thought filled Jack with dread.

JJ could tell that Jack was struggling to balance his need to protect Rose with the weight of the truth. The fear in Jack's eyes wasn't just about the consequences for himself; it was about the danger and trouble his sister would face if the truth came out. JJ knew he had to tread carefully, or risk pushing Jack further into silence.

"No problem, Jack. I know it's been a rough night." JJ shifted gears, pulling out another image from the file—a picture of Bartholomew Harris, but without Rose in the frame. It was a family photo, faded around the edges.

"What about this guy?" JJ asked, tapping the image lightly. "Recognize him?"

Jack stared at the photo for a moment, then slowly nodded. "That's Bart. And that's his dad, Charlie, and his mom, Rosetta." He smiled faintly. "Rosetta made the best apple pie."

"Bart was Rose's boyfriend, wasn't he?" JJ asked, carefully piecing the puzzle together.

"Yeah," Jack confirmed. "He was a nice guy. We'd go for rides in his car all the time."

JJ placed another image in front of Jack, this time of a black Lincoln. "This car?" he asked.

Jack studied the photo, his expression darkening again. "That's the one."

The confirmation solidified JJ's suspicions, but he needed more. "When did Bart leave, Jack?"

Jack's face grew distant. "It was the day my father died," he said softly. The brief smile was gone, replaced by a shadow of memory.

"Sorry about that, Jack," JJ said gently, before pressing forward. "So, when did Bart go?"

Jack hesitated, gathering his thoughts. "We were all at the cabin. Bart and Rose had a fight, a pretty bad one. They went for a walk... but only Rose came back. We never saw him again."

JJ's mind whirled with the new information, but before he could fully process it, there was a sharp knock at the door. Before Harper could even get up, the door swung open, and in stormed Rose, with Jack's lawyer in tow. The interview was over.

JJ swiftly gathered the scattered images and tucked them back into the file, hiding any trace of what Jack had revealed.

"Come with me, Jack. We're going home," Rose demanded, her voice cool but firm.

"Unfortunately, that's not possible," JJ said, standing his ground. "He's still under arrest for the incident tonight. A gun was involved, and we need to take statements from everyone."

Rose glanced at her lawyer, who nodded in agreement with JJ. Frustrated but recognizing the reality of the situation, Rose let out a sigh. "Fine. Can we speak to him?" she asked.

"Of course," JJ replied, stepping aside but keeping close enough to monitor the interaction, his ears and eyes tuned to catch every detail. He didn't want to miss anything.

Rose approached Jack, her voice softer now. "Jack, are you alright?" she asked, concern etched across her face.

"I'm fine, Rose," Jack replied. But that was all he said.

JJ noticed the brief, guarded exchange, the way Jack's lips pressed into a thin line. It seemed Jack was deliberately holding back, as if there was something he didn't want Rose to know. Something he had shared with JJ in confidence, a secret he was intent on keeping from his sister.

JJ couldn't help but wonder what Jack was hiding and why he was so determined to keep Rose out of the equation.

They hugged, but before leaving with her attorney, Rose turned to JJ, her eyes blazing with a mix of desperation and defiance. "He's innocent," she insisted, her voice steady but fierce. Then came a promise, "And if anything happens to him, my attorney will be the least of your worries."

JJ raised an eyebrow, not entirely sure what she meant but understanding the underlying threat. He could have pressed the issue, called her out on it, but he let it slide. There were bigger things to focus on, and he had a more significant prize in his sights.

Jack and Rose hugged once more; a lingering embrace filled with everything they couldn't say aloud. With a final look at JJ, Rose left with her attorney. As they disappeared out of the door, a uniformed officer entered, re-cuffed Jack, and escorted him back to his cell.

JJ watched Jack being led away, with a pang of sympathy. But he quickly pushed it aside. He couldn't afford to let personal feelings get in the way of his investigation. There was still work to be done and more secrets to unravel before the case would yield its full truth. The interview with Jack had been incredibly revealing, but JJ needed time to process everything.

"That was close," Harper said, breaking JJ's train of thought. "Jack spilled a lot of beans there. What are you thinking?"

JJ sighed. "I'm thinking I need a coffee. You?"

Harper just nodded, and the two detectives headed out. Once they had their cups in hand, steaming and strong, they made their way to the evidence room. As JJ flicked on the light, the dim hum of the bulb filled the small, cluttered space. Harper leaned casually against the door, a smirk playing on his face.

"You pulled a blinder there, JJ. Bravo," Harper said, giving his partner a nod of approval.

JJ closed the door behind them and took a moment to gather his thoughts. "She may have shut down the interview, but I got enough," he said, moving over to the evidence board. He studied the threads he had gathered—threads that now pointed directly to Rose and the web of tangled secrets she was hiding.

Harper moved beside JJ, his coffee steaming as he took a slow sip. His usual playful demeanor had shifted to something more focused, the seasoned detective ready to work. "Alright," he said, his voice firm. "Let's break this down."

JJ's eyes scanned the board, his mind piecing together the puzzle. "So we have plenty of connections," he said, tapping on a series of photos and notes pinned to the board. "Jack's confession opened some doors, but it's Rose we need to watch closely. She's the key to this."

Harper nodded; his expression serious. "What have we got?"

"Well," JJ began, pinning up photos on the corkboard as he spoke. "Jack confirmed the key players. We now have a solid connection between Lucas and Rose. Jack was holding something back, sure, but it's obvious he's trying to protect her."

"Anything solid?" Harper asked, stepping closer to the board, his eyes narrowing in thought. "Something we can dig into?"

JJ nodded, pointing at a photo of Bartholomew Harris pinned to the evidence board. "Yeah. Remember what Jack said about Bart going missing? He was with Rose the morning he disappeared, and it was the same day as Jack's father's suicide."

Harper's brows furrowed in confusion. "I remember, but what's the connection?"

JJ grabbed a marker and circled Bart's photo. "Jack gave us a crucial timeline—Bart went missing on the day of the suicide. If we can confirm the exact date of his father's death, we'll have a clearer idea of when Bart disappeared. But here's the key: the last person to see Bart alive was Rose."

Harper scratched his chin, trying to piece it together. "Okay, but that was, what? Twenty years ago? What does that have to do with Lucas, Brad Marshall, and everything happening now?"

JJ leaned in, his voice lowering as if the walls had ears. "Think about it: no one ever really knew when Bart disappeared. They only knew he was never seen again. If we can pinpoint that exact day, we might be able to link it back to Rose. She may know something she's been hiding, and if we dig deep enough, we could crack not just the Bradley Marshall case but maybe even get a lead on the Mauler case. Two birds, one stone."

Harper's eyes widened slightly. "Now wouldn't *that* be something," he mused.

JJ's gaze hardened, the pieces beginning to fall into place. "My father always said there was something off about that case," he added. "Maybe now we'll finally figure out what it was—and why Rose has been keeping secrets all these years."

The two detectives exchanged a look, determination etched in their features. The past was coming back to haunt them, but it might also hold the key to solving the mysteries still gripping the present.

JJ shook his head as he looked at the board, tapping Rose's image. "There's one constant in all of this—Rose. She was there back then, and she's right at the center of everything now. I think there's more to her involvement in Bart's disappearance than even Jack realizes."

Harper leaned in, his eyes narrowing as he scanned the images. "So, she's our link. But we need something concrete."

JJ grabbed the photo of the black Lincoln; the same one Jack had confirmed belonged to Bart. "Jack mentioned something else," JJ said. "After Bart disappeared, Rose had the Lincoln. And now, that same car has been tailing us."

Harper's eyes widened slightly. "You think Rose is using it to keep tabs on us?"

JJ nodded. "It's possible. Or someone close to her is. Either way, that Lincoln is our connection between the past and the present."

The pieces were starting to fall into place, but the larger picture remained frustratingly blurry. There were too many unknowns, too many ghosts from the past still haunting the case. JJ knew he needed to pull a few more threads to see what would unravel.

Harper crossed his arms, his focus sharpening as he studied the board. "So, what's next?" he asked.

JJ took a step back, surveying the tangled connections they had laid out. "We dig into Rose's past, starting with Bart's disappearance," he said. "We pull the records on Jack's father's death, cross-reference them with the date Bart went missing. And we track down that Lincoln. Whoever's driving it knows more than we do, and we need to figure out what they're trying to hide."

Harper nodded, his expression turning serious. "Alright. Let's get to work."

JJ's gaze grew intense. "This is big, Harper. *Really* big," he said.

SIXTY
I'LL SHOW YOU MINE

BY 8 A.M. the following morning, the investigation into Jack's mugging had been completed, with all statements collected. The case had been deemed a straightforward act of self-defense, and Jack's release was scheduled for 10 a.m. Rose had been notified and was already on her way, expected to arrive around 9:30 a.m. JJ had one last opportunity to extract more information before Jack's release. He hoped that in a more relaxed, casual setting, Jack might open up, and having Dr. Warrick present could help him feel more at ease.

Before finalizing Jack's release, JJ made the call he had promised Jack. He explained the situation to Dr. Warrick, recounted the previous night's events in detail, and emphasized that Jack had specifically asked to see her. She agreed to come at once.

It wasn't long before Dr. Warrick arrived. The clock now read 8:25 a.m. She waited patiently in the reception area for her escort to take her to see Jack. Her wait was brief; JJ turned the corner, and she instantly recognized him from the hospital. She smiled remembering their encounter. JJ immediately recognized her as well, a blush creeping up his face.

"Officer Jackson?" she inquired, making the first move and holding out her hand, deliberately lowering his rank. She owed him one after their last encounter.

"Detective Jackson," JJ corrected with a smile. "But you can call me JJ. And you must be Dr. Warrick?" he asked. "Definitely not a nurse," he joked, a playful grin lighting up his face. "Dr. Warrick, I owe you an apology for the way I acted the last time we met. I was... well, less than professional," JJ began, his words tumbling out awkwardly in his haste to make things right.

Dr. Warrick waved off his apology with a gentle, dismissive gesture. "Don't worry about it," she replied, her voice warm and understanding. "Can you take me to Jack, please?"

JJ, relieved by her graciousness, nodded and gestured towards a door leading to the holding cells. As they walked, he filled her in on the details from the previous night, recounting the incident and Jack's troubling blackout. She listened intently, her concern evident, with her mind already working to piece together what it all might signify.

"I've been treating Jack for some time now, since his incident. The blackouts are a more recent development," Dr. Warrick shared as they neared Jack's cell. "I suspect there could be some underlying medical issues, but all the tests have come back negative so far. Physically, there's nothing wrong with him," she explained, then paused before adding, "but beyond that, I'm afraid I can't disclose any more due to doctor-patient confidentiality."

"I'll show you mine if you show me yours," JJ joked lightly, trying to ease the tension.

Dr. Warrick smiled, catching the tone. "Alright," she replied, playing along, "but I don't know how much I can actually show you at this stage. We've only had two sessions since his recovery, and I'm still waiting on files from the family doctor—especially regarding Jack's parents and Rose."

The doctor-patient confidentiality remark was mostly a formality; she knew that if the detective wanted her notes, he could get them through official channels. But from what she'd observed, JJ seemed to have Jack's best interests at heart, just like her.

WHEN THEY ARRIVED at Jack's holding cell, JJ informed him that he would be released soon and that his sister was on her way to pick him up. Jack seemed slightly embarrassed when he noticed Dr. Warrick standing beside JJ.

She gave JJ a knowing glance, and he immediately understood. "I'll be just down the corridor if you need me," he said, opening the cell door to let her in.

Dr. Warrick stepped inside, sitting down across from Jack as JJ locked the door behind them. She felt momentary unease as he locked the door behind them and left.

"Are you okay, Jack?" Dr. Warrick asked gently.

"I've got a slight headache, but I'm fine. I think the mugger got it worse." He smiled, though it didn't quite reach his eyes.

"Well, I have some good news," she began. "The tests came back, and there's nothing physically wrong with you."

"So I'm just going nuts, then?" Jack said with a half-hearted joke, though a hint of anxiety lingered in his tone.

Dr. Warrick smiled sympathetically. "I wouldn't put it like that. It just means we can focus on treatment and figuring out the root cause. We'll work together to find the best approach," she assured him in a calm, supportive voice.

She continued, "I've requested your family's medical records from Dr. Amen, and hopefully, there will be something helpful there. If not, we'll take things one step at a time and get to the bottom of this."

Before Dr. Warrick could finish, the heavy sound of a door swinging open interrupted their conversation, followed by the unmistakable clicking of determined footsteps echoing down the corridor. Moments later, Rose appeared, with JJ close behind. It was 9:30 a.m.

"Jack, are you okay?" Rose asked, her voice laced with concern, the emotional toll of the previous night still evident in her eyes.

"I'm fine. I just want to get home," Jack replied, his tone weary but steady. Rose's gaze shifted to Dr. Warrick, and a flicker of surprise and unease crossed her face. Sensing the tension, Jack quickly intervened.

"I asked her to come see me," he explained. "I blacked out again last night, and you know this isn't the first time. I told you I was going to get help. Dr. Warrick is helping me figure out what's going on."

Rose's demeanor softened, though a hint of reluctance remained. "Thank you, Doctor. Your help is appreciated," she said, her politeness edged with a subtle reserve.

"No problem. We both want Jack healthy and back on his feet—ready for action when he returns to work," Dr. Warrick replied, her tone professional yet warm.

Rose nodded. "Indeed, we do, Doctor. Let's go, Jack."

Jack glanced up at the clock. "It's not ten a.m. yet," he pointed out.

Rose turned to JJ, raising an eyebrow.

"I think we can make an exception and release you a bit early," JJ said with a smile, signaling to the uniformed officer at the end of the corridor.

The uniformed officer led Jack up the corridor, with JJ trailing behind, leaving Rose and Dr. Warrick standing alone for a brief moment. Rose stayed behind deliberately, as she had pressing questions that needed answers. Sensing the opportunity, Dr. Warrick remained as well, wanting to have a private word with Rose.

Once they were alone, Rose wasted no time. "So what's wrong with Jack? You need to tell me," she demanded, her voice firm and laced with urgency. The directness of Rose's question caught Dr. Warrick off guard, but she quickly composed herself, slipping into her professional demeanor.

"There's nothing wrong with Jack physically," Dr. Warrick replied, her voice steady and calm. "I ran blood tests, and they all came back clear. But that means we need to focus on his mental health. I've requested your family's medical history to get a better understanding of what might be happening."

Dr. Warrick didn't miss the way Rose's face tightened, though she could see Rose struggling to keep her emotions in check. It was a subtle change, but the flicker of fear didn't go unnoticed. Rose tried to mask it; her voice cool but probing. "Don't you need my permission to access our medical files?" she asked.

Dr. Warrick shook her head, her professionalism unwavering. "No, not in this case. If it could help diagnose Jack's condition, I have the right to access those records as his doctor. Dr. Amen is sending them over by courier today."

As Dr. Warrick watched, she could sense Rose's mind racing behind her composed exterior.

"Well, we all want what's best for Jack, don't we?" Rose said with a forced smile, her words sounding more like a defense than a reassurance. Without waiting for a response, she turned sharply and strode down the corridor, leaving Dr. Warrick alone.

Dr. Warrick watched her go, her own thoughts swirling. The way Rose had forced that smile, the tension that had seeped through despite her efforts to hide it—something felt off. Dr. Warrick couldn't shake the sense that Rose was holding back more than she was willing to admit.

She lingered in the hallway for a moment, trying to process the interaction. There was something unsettling about Rose's demeanor, something that went beyond concern for Jack's well-being. Unease crept into Dr. Warrick's mind, and she eventually decided to follow Rose up the corridor, her curiosity and worry pushing her forward.

By the time Dr. Warrick reached the front desk, Jack had already been processed, and she caught sight of Rose and Jack leaving the precinct together. JJ stood beside her, the two of them silently watching the pair exit. Dr. Warrick couldn't help but feel a growing sense of foreboding, a feeling that whatever secrets Rose was guarding were about to surface.

JJ noticed the thoughtful look on Dr. Warrick's face. "You okay, Doctor?" he asked, his voice breaking the quiet.

Dr. Warrick didn't respond immediately. She was sifting through her thoughts, trying to shape them in a professional manner. But after a brief hesitation, she let her true feelings slip. "That was... weird," she admitted, sounding genuinely puzzled.

"What was weird?" JJ asked, his curiosity instantly piqued.

Dr. Warrick turned to face him, a faint smile touching her lips. "You can call me Cara," she said, the formality softening between them.

JJ pressed again, sensing there was more to her unease. "What was weird?" he repeated, more insistently.

Cara met JJ's gaze, her expression shifting to something more serious. "I just had the strangest conversation with Rose. It wasn't so much what she said, but how she said it. It felt like she was hiding something."

JJ nodded thoughtfully; his face momentarily unreadable. Then, a slow, knowing smile spread across his lips. "Well, I guess it's time for me to show you mine," he said cryptically, his tone laced with intrigue.

Cara raised an eyebrow, intrigued but cautious. "What do you mean?" she asked, her voice careful, unsure of what to expect.

JJ turned and gestured for her to follow him down the hallway. "There's more to this than you know, Cara. Rose isn't the only one with secrets."

As they made their way to the case room, the tension in the air grew thicker. Just then, Harper arrived, slightly out of breath and clearly a bit late. "Nice of you to join us," JJ teased, the light humor barely disguising the gravity of the moment.

"Sorry, boss. It's our anniversary as you know, and she thinks I've forgotten," Harper said with a grin, holding up a swanky bag from *Rogers & Hollands Jewelers*. He chuckled. "I went to get her something nice."

Dr. Warrick glanced briefly at the bag, a flicker of amusement in her eyes. "Your wife is a lucky lady. It's been a while since someone bought me something like that," she said, her words warm but distant, her mind clearly elsewhere.

Harper, still puzzled by her presence, turned to her. "What brings you here, Doctor?"

Before she could reply, JJ jumped in with a grin. "I told her I'd show her mine if she showed me hers."

Harper furrowed his brow, confused. Before he could ask what JJ meant, they arrived at the case room.

JJ unlocked the door and gestured for them to step inside. The room was dimly lit, a small window allowing just enough light to cast long shadows across the walls. It had the eerie feel of a place where secrets had been whispered, theories debated.

As Dr. Warrick's eyes adjusted to the low light, Harper flicked on the switch, flooding the room with stark fluorescent brightness.

Immediately, her gaze was drawn to the corkboard at the center of the room. It was a sprawling mess of papers, photographs, notes, and red strings that crisscrossed between them like a web of conspiracy. But one image stood out—looming large, right in the middle of it all.

It was a magazine cutout of Rose.

Dr. Warrick's breath caught, her heart skipping a beat. "What... what is this?" she asked softly, her voice tinged with shock. She stepped closer to the board, her eyes darting from one photograph to the next. Familiar faces stared back at her—Jack, Rose, and others she didn't recognize. But then, one face jumped out at her: Brad Marshall.

It took a moment for her to place the name, but then it hit her like a punch to the gut. Brad Marshall—the boy from the news report. He had been the one who pushed Jack into the school cellar. The pieces were starting to connect. "Didn't he commit suicide?" she said. "I'm confused. What am I looking at here?" Dr. Warrick asked, her voice thick with apprehension.

JJ crossed his arms, his expression growing more serious as he watched her absorb the pictures in front of her. "First of all, we don't think Brad Marshall killed himself. We have evidence—circumstantial, but compelling—that suggests he was murdered."

Dr. Warrick glanced at him, half as a statement, half a question. "You think Rose has something to do with that?"

JJ shrugged slightly. "Maybe," he said, walking closer to the board. He stopped in front of a photo and tapped it with his finger. "This guy—his name is Charlie. We believe he witnessed Brad Marshall's murder," JJ continued.

"We accidentally shot him," Harper interjected, coughing awkwardly. "I accidentally shot him," he corrected, glancing nervously at the doctor, who threw him a sharp look. Harper shrugged helplessly. "It's a long story," he mumbled.

The doctor's attention shifted, and she pointed at a picture of a black Lincoln pinned on the board. "And the car?"

JJ sat back on the edge of the table, leaning forward slightly as he answered. "That car belongs to Rose's ex-boyfriend, Bartholomew Harris. He's... was Charlie's son."

The name struck a chord with Dr. Warrick. She furrowed her brow in thought as Harper moved closer to the corkboard. He tapped another photo, his voice cutting through the silence.

"This guy," Harper said, pointing at a familiar face. "This was Charlie's son, do you recognize him?"

The room fell silent as Dr. Warrick stared at the picture, piecing together memories. Finally, she spoke, her voice tinged with realization. "I know that name, and that face. That's…" the doctor paused.

JJ filled in the pause. "The missing teenager from the seventies. Allegedly—"

"The Mauler's last victim," the doctor interjected. "Never found."

"Exactly," JJ confirmed, his tone grim. "And that Lincoln, which is still registered to Bartholomew Harris and was apparently passed on to Rose when Harris disappeared, has been following us the last few days. We think it's the same car that was involved in Charlie's abduction."

Dr. Warrick's expression shifted as the full picture started coming together. JJ continued, his voice calm but urgent. "So, as you can see, we've been building this case for a while, connecting the dots. Rose is at the center of it all."

"And Jack too?" Dr. Warrick asked, her concern evident.

"Maybe," JJ replied. "You did mention something was wrong with him—he's been having these blackouts, and he has a motive. Marshall did throw Jack down a cellar, nearly killing him."

"Jack wouldn't hurt a fly," Dr. Warrick said defensively.

"Maybe not," JJ said. "But that's why we need your help."

Dr. Warrick stood there, silent, in disbelief, trying to process everything. The tangled connections, the names, the faces—it was all beginning to form a dark and twisted picture. Her mind raced, trying to reconcile the kind-hearted Jack she knew with the disturbing implications that JJ had set out in front of her.

Harper, stepped back, his gaze hardening. "We don't have all the answers yet, but what we do have points to, as JJ says, Rose."

Dr. Warrick gently sat in her chair, still processing, her mind racing. "So this is why she was so tense a moment ago," she murmured. Her heart pounded in her chest. "So you're saying Rose is involved in a murder and abduction."

JJ's face darkened. "We're not sure. But she is connected to everything that has happened, and whatever she's hiding is enough to make her nervous—really nervous. And if those medical files reveal anything that can help us then we can open an official murder trial."

She turned back to JJ, her voice barely above a whisper. "What do you need from me?"

JJ's eyes softened slightly. "I need those Brooks family medical records. All of them."

Dr. Warrick frowned. "You know there's doctor-patient confidentiality surrounding those records."

"I do," JJ said, not breaking eye contact. "But we don't have time to go through official channels. Charlie's missing, he's seriously ill, and we're not sure if he's even still alive. Every second counts."

Dr. Warrick had now fully absorbed the gravity of the situation. After a long pause, she nodded. "Okay. I'll help. I haven't received the records yet, but they should arrive this afternoon. We can go through them together."

JJ's shoulders relaxed, a flicker of relief crossing his face. "You're on. What time?"

"I'll call you," Dr. Warrick replied.

They exchanged contact information, and as Dr. Warrick began to leave, JJ spoke again, his voice softer now. "You can help crack this case, Cara."

She turned back, appreciating the familiarity in his tone. With a small smile, she nodded and left the room, the weight of her decision settling in.

As the door closed behind her, Harper turned to JJ with a smirk. "I think she likes you."

JJ shrugged, brushing off the comment. Now wasn't the time for distractions.

"So, what now, boss?" Harper asked, eager to move on.

"Breakfast," JJ replied, a hint of humor breaking the tension.

Harper's face lit up, excitement flashing in his eyes. So thrilled by the thought of doughnuts, he forgot the gift he had just bought for his wife. Moments later, they were headed to Mo's, the case had gained momentum, and they were both confident they had made further progress. Time to load up on coffee and carbs; it was going to be a long day.

SIXTY-ONE
CHIP OFF THE OLD BLOCK

AFTER A QUICK STOP at Mo's, it was time for another chat with Jack's alleged mugger. He had been released at the same time as Jack as there hadn't been enough evidence to hold him. He maintained his innocence, claiming he was nothing more than an innocent bystander. The detectives made their way across town to his apartment block. The building was run-down, seemingly untouched by the gentrification sweeping the city. It looked almost derelict.

As JJ and Harper walked down the corridor, a rat scurried across their path towards a torn-open bin bag. Another rat soon poked its head out of the bag, unfazed by the presence of the detectives as they passed by. Used syringes littered the filthy corridor floor, and the long, stained carpet, which stretched the length of the hallway, looked as though it hadn't been cleaned since the day it was laid.

Harper glanced back at the growing mischief of rats. "Do you think they've got a penthouse suite?" he quipped, raising an eyebrow at JJ.

Harper chuckled as they reached the door. "What number was it again?" JJ asked.

Harper glanced down at the back of his hand, where he had scrawled the number earlier, and as he unclipped his holster, he replied, "Nine."

Both men looked at the metallic number affixed to the door in front of them—it read '6.' Puzzled, they exchanged glances. Harper briefly stepped back to the previous door, which was numbered '8.' This had to be the right place.

Returning, he leaned forward and pushed at the crooked '6,' sliding it back into its correct position—it was, in fact, a '9.'

"Well," JJ said with a dry smile, "looks like we're in the right place after all."

As they stood outside the door of the mugger's apartment, the smell was beginning to gnaw at their senses and seep into their clothes; the quicker they got this done, the better. JJ glanced over Harper's shoulder and noticed more rats were beginning to arrive, so the quicker they took the statement, the quicker they could both get out of there and shower. Harper wasn't sure why they were there. They already had his original statement, but JJ's instincts told him there might be more to find out about last night.

JJ raised his fist and delivered a hard, sideways thump on the door, the kind that indicated authority—sharp and heavy, announcing that whoever was on the other side wasn't just knocking for a chat. It was a knock that carried weight, the kind that told you serious business was about to follow.

There was no answer. JJ, frowning, delivered several more blows—this time harder, with a sense of urgency. Still nothing. Both detectives, now on edge, instinctively removed their weapons from their holsters. They exchanged a glance, a silent agreement that something was off. JJ leaned in closer, straining to hear any sign of movement.

Then, faintly, they heard it—shuffling sounds from within, followed by a muffled struggle. Before they could react further, two gunshots rang out.

"Shit!" Harper swore, his body snapping into action. In a heartbeat, they flicked off the safeties on their weapons, instincts and training taking over in seamless unison. Harper charged the door, delivering a powerful kick, then followed up with a hard shoulder barge. The impact rattled through the frame, and with a final push, they forced the door open, the barrier giving way as they surged inside.

The frame holding the lock exploded inward, sending splintered wood flying in all directions as they charged into the apartment, guns raised, ready for whatever was on the other side.

The room was eerily still. A muted TV flickered in the corner, casting an unsettling glow across the dimly lit room. The only movement came from the curtains, billowing gently in the breeze that drifted through the wide-open window.

In the center of the floor, the mugger lay lifeless, his body twisted awkwardly, like a marionette whose strings had been violently severed. The gory remains of what was once his head were smeared across the faded carpet, the result of a point-blank gunshot. Blood and brain matter splattered the peeling wallpaper, marking the walls with a grotesque, crimson spray that was still meandering down the wall pooling at the bottom. It was an execution—brutal and cold.

JJ took in the details with a slow, deliberate scan of the room. The silence felt oppressive, broken only by the distant hum of the city outside. He didn't need to check for a pulse; the scene screamed of finality. The metallic scent of blood hung thick in the air, mingling with the stale odor of cigarettes and cheap beer and gunpowder.

"The window!" Harper barked, pointing towards it. Without hesitation, JJ bolted across the room, the sound of footsteps clattering down the fire escape spurring him into action. Harper lingered for a split second, quickly scanning the room for any clues or immediate threats before turning back towards the window. JJ was already halfway out, scaling the fire escape with purpose.

"I'll take the stairs!" Harper shouted after him, hoping to cut off the fleeing suspect from the front of the building.

As JJ's feet hit the metal grating of the fire escape, he caught a glimpse of movement below—a shadow darting around a corner. The fire escape clanged beneath him as he pursued, his heart pounding with adrenaline, but his breath steady and focused. JJ's peak physical fitness worked to his advantage; every step was fluid, every movement swift. The suspect, whoever they were, didn't stand a chance as JJ closed in with every step.

Harper, on the other hand, wasn't in the same shape as his partner. Years of police work, late nights, and the comforts of middle age had left him heavier and slower than he liked. "I'm too old for this shit," he muttered, pushing himself towards the stairwell. Despite his body protesting with every strained step, Harper knew time was critical. The suspect was armed, and every second counted, he was JJ's backup. This was one event being late for wasn't an option and he picked up a pace.

Harper hit the bottom of the stairs with a grunt, tumbling slightly as his feet met the ground. Gathering himself quickly, he burst through the building's front entrance, desperate to intercept JJ's chase.

Nothing.

He knew he hadn't beaten them to the bottom—he wasn't that fast anymore. Frantically, his eyes scanned the street. Then, he saw it—an alley beside the building yawned ahead. Instinctively, Harper sprinted towards it, though his muscles screamed in protest, every step heavier than the last. He had little left in the tank, but sheer determination pushed him forward; his partner needed him.

Just as he reached the mouth of the alley, a sleek black Lincoln screeched into view, tires shrieking as the driver floored the accelerator. There was no time for Harper to react.

The car slammed into him with bone-shattering force. The impact sent his body flying meters through the air in a blur of motion. The world spun violently around him, and then—thud—Harper's body and skull crashed against the pavement, the sickening sound of the collision resonating in his ears as the breath was ripped from his lungs.

Pain flooded his senses, every inch of his body throbbing with agony, and the world around him began to fade.

"HARPER!" JJ yelled as he arrived at the scene from the alley, his heart in his throat. He saw Harper crumpled on the pavement, barely moving. JJ rushed to his side, falling to his knees, panic tightening his chest.

"Help! Somebody get help!" JJ screamed, his voice cracking as he held his partner, feeling the warmth of blood seep through his fingers where Harper's head rested. Harper's breaths were shallow and labored, his chest rising and falling at an uneven rhythm.

People gathered quickly, forming a tight, suffocating circle around the wreckage of man and machine. The black Lincoln, now crumpled from its collision with a garbage truck, lay in ruins. Its driver slumped lifelessly over the wheel, was barely visible through the shattered windscreen. The wheel hubs, which had spun wildly, now wobbled to a gradual stop.

Shocked faces in the crowd were pale and wide-eyed, frozen in horrified silence as they watched Harper's life ebb away, blood pooling beneath him on the hard pavement. JJ knelt beside him; panic etched across his face. Desperation seized him as he looked around, his voice cracking with urgency. "Call an ambulance!" he shouted, his plea reverberating through the tense air. He frantically searched for his cell phone, not finding it and realizing he must have dropped it in the chase, again he screamed, "Someone please get an ambulance!"

In the distance, the rising wail of sirens cut through the chaos. A police car screeched to a halt, and uniformed officers sprang into action. They quickly moved to control the growing crowd, pushing the onlookers back from the scene. Another officer rushed to the Lincoln, handcuffing the driver, now conscious but dazed, dragging him out of the mangled vehicle.

Moments later, an unmarked car arrived, instantly recognizable to JJ—Frank and his partner. They leapt out, sprinting towards him and Harper, their faces filled with concern. The scene was rapidly escalating into a frenzy of flashing lights and uniformed officers.

Within minutes, an ambulance arrived, followed by more police units and finally a fire truck, its blaring horn echoing down the narrow streets. Medics rushed towards Harper, while more officers continued pushing the crowd back, creating a perimeter around the tragic scene.

JJ held onto Harper's hand, watching helplessly as his partner's breathing grew shallower with each passing second. The chaos swirled around them, but for JJ, time seemed to stand still.

The scene then became a blur of frantic movement. Officers took control of the chaos, securing the area, but JJ's world had shrunk to the bleeding, broken man in his arms. He cradled Harper's head, his own hands slick with blood as Harper's eyes fluttered open.

"Harper, stay with me, stay with me!" JJ pleaded, his voice thick with emotion. Harper's lips trembled, stained red with blood, coughing violently he tried to speak.

"Looks like..." Harper wheezed and coughed, his words barely a whisper. "Looks like I get my record played at Mo's after all." His face twisted into a weak, blood-streaked smile.

JJ's eyes filled with tears. "You son of a bitch, we're not playing any damn records. You're going to make it through this!" But Harper's body was growing colder, the light in his eyes dimming.

"Tell Maggie... tell Maggie I love her..." Harper coughed, blood spilling from his mouth. JJ squeezed his hand, his heart breaking as he watched his partner slip away.

"You can tell her yourself!" JJ begged, his voice shaking. Harper's breaths were fading now, each one more ragged than the last.

"And Chip..." Harper continued, the pain evident in every word. "Tell her... Tell Sophie."

JJ's breath caught in his throat. Chip had always been Harper's nickname for his daughter—a 'chip off the old block,' he'd always said. But Harper had never called her by her real name before. Tears streamed down JJ's face as he leaned in closer. "You tell her yourself, Harper. Don't you dare leave me."

But Harper's eyes had already begun to glaze over, his final breath rattling in his chest. His last words fell away, unfinished, as the life left him.

JJ held Harper's body tightly, his own chest heaving with sobs as the noise of the scene—the sirens, the shouting officers, the distant crowd—faded into a numb hum around him. Harper was gone.

JJ looked up, his eyes red and raw, his body shaking with grief. Around him, the world continued to spin in its chaotic, unforgiving rhythm. But for him, in that moment, everything had stopped. His partner, his friend, was dead, and nothing would ever be the same again.

As JJ held Harper's hand, the medics stepped in, their calm, practiced motions a stark contrast to the emotional storm brewing inside him. Reluctantly, he let go, backing away as they began working on his partner. But deep down, JJ already knew—it was too late. Harper was gone. The realization twisted his gut, reaching every breath from his lungs, leaving JJ feeling hollow.

His eyes, burning with unshed tears, darted around the scene, searching for something—anything—to make sense of the chaos. The crowd blurred in his periphery, but one figure stood out sharply. The driver of the Lincoln, the man who had stolen his partner's life, was being led away in handcuffs towards the back of a squad car.

JJ's heart pounded, the adrenaline surging back into his veins as the man turned slightly, and there it was—a snake tattoo, unmistakably marking him. Even through the blood and bruises, JJ recognized him instantly.

Lucas.

Rage, hot and blinding, surged through JJ. His breath quickened as he stood, slowly at first, but then moved with growing intensity. His feet seemed to carry him on their own, marching with singular purpose toward Lucas. His mind was clouded, focused on one thing—revenge.

But before he could reach his target, Frank intercepted him, moving swiftly. "JJ!" Frank shouted, his voice firm but pleading. "Don't do this, man!" Frank planted himself in front of JJ, bracing to hold him back. JJ pressed forward, his fists clenched and his muscles taut with fury.

JJ's rage fueled his strength, but it wasn't enough to overpower Frank. Frank held his ground, gripping JJ's shoulders and using every ounce of his strength to restrain him. Gradually, JJ began to feel the red mist dissipate, and his breathing slowed as a sliver of control returned.

In his heart, JJ knew Frank had done the right thing. He had seen that red mist descend on too many other cops, had watched them make terrible, life-ruining mistakes when no one was there to hold them back. But Frank had been there for him, had stopped him from crossing a line he could never uncross. JJ's fists slowly unclenched, and he met Frank's eyes, gratitude mixing with the fading anger.

"Thanks, Frank," JJ murmured, his voice shaky but sincere. He realized just how close he had come to making a terrible mistake, and he silently thanked Frank for being his anchor in that moment of blind rage. JJ's gaze shifted past Frank's shoulder, still locked onto Lucas as he was forced into the back of the squad car. The door slammed shut with a heavy thud, but JJ's eyes never wavered. He didn't blink, not even as the sirens began to wail, and the car slowly rolled away in front of him. Lucas's cold, unblinking stare pierced through the tinted windows as the vehicle passed by, his expression as lifeless as the body he'd left in his wake.

JJ stood motionless as the world around him buzzed with activity—officers shouting, radios crackling, lights flashing—but it all felt distant and muted to JJ. He was surrounded by chaos, yet utterly alone in his thoughts.

JJ snapped back to reality as the squad car disappeared into the rapidly encroaching night. His eyes drifted to the scene behind him, where Harper's lifeless body was being wheeled into the back of an ambulance, a bloodied sheet now draped over his face. JJ's heart sank, as the grim reality of the road ahead became painfully clear.

With a heavy sigh, he turned on his heel and headed toward his car. There was no time to waste—Lucas was pivotal in his case, and JJ needed to know how much he knew. Every second counted, and he couldn't let his grief slow him down—not yet.

JJ returned to the precinct just as Lucas was being led to a holding cell. "Patch him up," JJ muttered to the officers escorting Lucas. "I'll deal with him later." His mind was already elsewhere, lingering on Harper's family. His colleagues had tried contacting them, but no one had picked up. JJ knew what that meant—he had to go himself.

He made his way to the case room, needing a moment to gather himself. His eyes settled on the picture of Rose pinned to the evidence board. She was connected to this; JJ was sure of it. His anger simmered, but he had nothing concrete to bring her in on. He hoped his conversation with Lucas would change that.

His gaze shifted, landing on the small gift Harper had bought for Maggie earlier—before everything went wrong. JJ's chest tightened. It was up to him now. The burden of delivering the news to Harper's wife and daughter fell squarely on his shoulders. With a heavy heart, he picked up the bag and headed out, preparing to face one of the hardest moments of his life—informing them of Harper's death.

SIXTY-TWO
THE GIFT

JJ STOOD at the doorstep of Harper's home, clutching the small gift Harper had bought for Maggie. Today was their wedding anniversary. He opened the plush box to confirm its contents and instantly wished he hadn't. Inside, a bracelet glistened in the dim evening light—three delicate golden hearts linked together, each engraved with a name: *Margaret*, *Sophie*, and *Lou*. JJ knew Harper had been planning to give it to his wife as a token of his love for her and their daughter, a symbol of the family they'd built together.

Swallowing hard, JJ closed the box and slipped it back into the bag. His throat felt dry as he raised his hand to knock on the door. Today, of all days, he had to deliver the kind of news no one should ever have to share.

The door opened before he could even knock.

"Hi, Uncle JJ!" Sophie's bright, cheerful voice pierced the heavy silence. She stood before him, her face glowing with the joy only an eighteen-year-old could have on her birthday. "It's my birthday today, Uncle JJ! Did you forget? Of course, you didn't. Is that for me?" She grinned, her eyes flicking down to the gift bag in his hands, completely unaware of the storm cloud descending over their lives.

JJ froze. For a split second, everything inside him shattered. He had forgotten. Not only was this Lou's and Maggie's wedding anniversary, but it was Sophie's eighteenth birthday. In the chaos of the day, it had all slipped his mind. Now, instead of celebrating what should have been a joyful day for them all, he had to deliver the darkest news of their lives.

JJ smiled, but it was a fragile mask, barely concealing the devastating message lurking just beneath the surface. Sophie, or Chip, as Harper had called her, went on excitedly. "I passed my police academy tests! Can you believe it? I'm going to be a cop, just like Dad!"

Her hopeful words hit him hard, but he needed to hold on a little while longer. Harper's last moments flashed before JJ's eyes—the blood, the broken breath, the unfinished sentence. "Tell Chip…" Harper had never finished his final message for his daughter. Now, it was JJ's burden to create those last words and to somehow deliver them to Sophie, whose bright future was about to be shadowed by an unbearable loss.

JJ swallowed hard; his voice trapped in his throat. He let her continue, unable to ruin her joy just yet. She was so full of life, so like her father, he thought as sparks of emotion pierced his heart. He was so proud of what she had achieved, and he wished with all his heart that he could hold onto this moment for her. If only he could stop time, go back an hour, change everything. But he couldn't. Harper was gone, and a suffocating shroud of grief wrapped itself around JJ, tightening with every breath. It should never have happened this way. If only he hadn't pushed for more answers. If only they had been more careful.

His thoughts spiraled as he fought to keep his emotions in check, but Sophie's voice pulled him back to the present. "So is it?" she asked,

"Is it what?" JJ replied

"Is that for me?" She pointed to the bag in his hand. Her eyes gleamed with excitement, and JJ's heart sank even deeper.

He looked down at the gift—the bracelet that Harper had picked out so thoughtfully. It should have been part of a happy celebration, not a reminder of what had been lost. "No, it's for your mom," JJ replied, his voice rough with emotion. "Is she here?"

Sophie's face fell slightly, a hint of disappointment flashing across her features, but she brushed it off quickly, as she always did. "She's inside. I'll call her."

As Sophie turned to shout for her mother, JJ stood frozen at the threshold. His legs felt like lead, rooted to the spot. He could hear Maggie's voice before he saw her, and his heart ached at the thought of what was about to unfold. "Mom! Uncle JJ's here!"

Maggie appeared in the doorway, wiping her hands on a tea towel, her face lighting up as she caught sight of him. "Goodness me, Sophie, let the man in—" Her voice trailed off as she saw the look on JJ's face.

Those sparks of emotion he desperately tried to endure surged through his heart, he could hold on no more. The grief, the guilt—it was all there, plain as day. The tears that had been fighting to escape finally broke free, and JJ couldn't hold on any longer.

Maggie's smile faded, her breath catching in her throat. She didn't need words. The look on JJ's face, the tears, the expression told her everything she needed to know, the devastating news every cop's wife hoped would never reach them. She clutched her chest, collapsing into sobs, the realization hitting her like a wave of cold water.

Sophie stood there, frozen in shock, her bright birthday smile vanishing in an instant. "Mom? What's going on?" she whispered, her voice trembling as she looked between JJ and her mother.

JJ's voice cracked as he stepped forward, gently placing the gift bag in Maggie's shaking hands. Maggie needed to her the words, but she already knew. "I'm so sorry, Maggie… Harper—he's gone."

Maggie wailed, sinking to the floor in a mess of tears and agony. Sophie's world collapsed in that moment, the joy of her birthday turning into a nightmare she couldn't comprehend. "No… no… this can't be real," she whispered, her voice weak, as if saying it aloud would somehow reverse the truth.

JJ knelt beside them, helpless, guilt-ridden. He had lost his partner, his best friend, and his brother, and now he had brought the darkness to Harper's family. The weight was unbearable, but all he could do was hold them as they wept, their hearts breaking together.

Through her sobs, Sophie looked up at JJ, her tear-streaked face filled with desperate hope.

"Were you there? Did you see him? Were you with him? Did he say anything... before he...?" Her voice trailed off as if refusing to say the words might somehow make it less real, as though unspoken, it hadn't truly happened.

JJ's throat tightened. Harper had tried to say something—something for Sophie—but he had never finished. The words had died with him.

JJ hesitated, his heart thudding in his chest. He couldn't bear to let her down, not again. Placing a trembling hand on Sophie's shoulder, he felt his voice crack as he finally found the words. "He said... he was proud of you, Chip. More than you'll ever know."

Kneeling between them, JJ wrapped his arms around them both, pulling them close. Together, they wept, their shared grief heavy yet somehow binding them tighter in their sorrow, their cries filling the room. JJ's own tears finally fell, knowing that Harper's real last words had died with him, and now it was up to JJ to carry that unspoken burden forever.

SIXTY-THREE
TO HARPER

JJ STEPPED INTO THE PRECINCT, eyes red with the tears he had shed with Harper's wife and daughter, their sorrow was still fresh in his mind, but grief had to take a back seat for now; there would be time for grieving another day. He couldn't afford it. Not yet. Not until he had answers.

He stormed through the familiar corridors, the precinct buzz surrounding him like a dull hum. His mind, however, was elsewhere. Lucas was in custody—the man responsible for Harper's death, whether by accident or not, and JJ needed the truth. His mind raced with questions: Who hired Lucas to murder the mugger they were supposed to question? Where did he get the Lincoln? And, most importantly, where the hell was Charlie? JJ was running out of time, and so was Charlie, if he was even still alive.

As JJ approached the interrogation room, Frank caught up with him, his face etched with concern.

"Are you sure you're up for this?" Frank asked, his voice low, attempting to hide the doubt that flickered across his features. "You know Lucas killed Harper. You really shouldn't be the one in there, JJ."

JJ paused for a moment, knowing Frank was right. Protocol dictated he should steer clear of this interrogation, but protocol be damned. Harper was gone, and this was the only way JJ knew how to cope—by getting the truth. By making someone pay.

"I need answers, Frank. I'm not going to stand by and let someone else screw it up," JJ said, his voice hard, barely concealing the emotion threatening to break through. "As much as it cuts to say this, putting Lou's death aside for the moment, there's a bigger case at play here. And I believe Lucas holds the answers."

Frank nodded, though he seemed to be uneasy about the situation. "Alright. But I'm coming in with you. Someone has to keep you from doing something you'll regret."

JJ didn't respond. He didn't need to. They both knew that nothing was going to stop him from getting what he wanted—what he needed—from Lucas.

Inside the interrogation room, Lucas sat cuffed to the table, his eyes scanning the walls as though looking for an escape route. His smirk was gone, replaced with a hard, unreadable expression. He was a career criminal and cracking him wasn't going to be easy. JJ knew that. But he wasn't after easy. He was after answers. He was already one step ahead of Lucas.

"Let's get this over with," JJ muttered, striding into the room with Frank following closely behind. The door shut with a firm thud, the sound echoing through the stillness of the room. JJ took his seat across from Lucas and the court-appointed lawyer—whose disinterest was obvious, keen only to rush through the proceedings.

The lawyer, his tone clipped and devoid of any real engagement, spoke first. "My client has already confessed to the theft of the vehicle, and it appears we are dealing with what can be characterized as a straightforward accident. Given these circumstances, I suggest we expedite this process, allowing my client to be released without undue delay."

JJ remained silent, but his silence was deliberate, and it was clear Lucas had no intention of doing the same. Lucas leaned forward, his voice dripping with malice as he spoke, setting a far darker tone for the interview.

"How's your partner? I recognized him when his face smashed into the windscreen. Harper, wasn't it? That motherfucker bounced off the bonnet like a basketball hitting the rim of a hoop." A grin spread across Lucas's face, cold and unapologetic.

JJ's expression hardened, his gaze locking onto Lucas with an intensity that could bore through steel. The lawyer, realizing the gravity of his client's remarks, shifted uncomfortably in his seat. What he had assumed would be a routine, quick resolution had now taken a sharp turn, and it became clear this was going to be a long, difficult day.

JJ sat in silence, refusing to take the bait. Every fiber of his being strained to hold back the violent rage simmering beneath the surface—rage so intense that not even Frank would be able to stop him if it unleashed. But JJ was a professional. He took a deep breath, stealing a quick glance at Frank, who didn't say a word, but his eyes conveyed a clear message: *Don't let him get under your skin.*

Lucas's eyes flicked to Frank, then back to JJ. He leaned back slightly in his chair, his shackles rattling against the metal. "Look, I already told the other guy. I stole the car, and I'm sorry about your partner; he came out of nowhere. It was an accident."

JJ felt a surge of heat rising in his chest. The casual way Lucas spoke, as if Harper's life was just a footnote, sent a wave of anger through him. He leaned forward, his voice low and measured, but sharp with tension. "An accident?" He repeated, his words simmering. It took every ounce of control to keep his hands from trembling, to stop himself from lunging across the table and strangling the life out of Lucas. Instead, he clasped his hands tightly, forcing composure.

JJ leaned back in his chair; his tone deceptively casual as he glanced at the lawyer before turning his gaze back to Lucas. "And Jimmy? Why did you kill Jimmy? Why did you put two bullets in his skull?"

Lucas shifted in his chair, a flicker of unease crossing his face before a defiant look settled in. He turned to his lawyer, his voice hardening. "I didn't kill no one," he spat out, then faced JJ again. "I swear, man, I didn't kill no one—just Harper. And that was an accident."

JJ's fingers twitched, his patience wearing thin as the room seemed to close in, growing smaller, hotter. Frank, sensing the escalating tension, cleared his throat, but the air was thick with unsaid words.

"We'll deal with Harper later," JJ said, his voice strained but composed. He leaned in again, locking eyes with Lucas. "Were you sent to kill Jimmy because he mugged Jack?"

"What? No! I told you…" Lucas stammered, glancing nervously at his lawyer. "Are you gonna say something?"

But Lucas's slip hadn't gone unnoticed. He never asked *who* Jack was—never questioned the name. JJ clocked it immediately, his instincts buzzing. *Lucas knew Jack,* and that connection meant everything.

Lucas's eyes narrowed; his defiance clear. "You think I'm stupid? You're trying to pin something on me cos I killed your partner. I told you, man, it was an accident."

JJ let out a dry, humorless laugh, shaking his head. He remembered Jack mentioning Lucas on the night he was mugged, describing the man at the bar. It was time to test a hunch and make the connection. He reached into the file on the table and pulled out a magazine clipping, sliding it across—Rose's picture. He tapped the photo with his finger.

"What about her?" JJ demanded.

Lucas stared blankly into the distance; his expression unreadable.

"What about this woman? Have you met her before?" JJ repeated, his tone slow and deliberate, watching closely for any hint of recognition.

Lucas lowered his gaze, briefly glancing at the photo before looking up and shrugging. But JJ didn't miss the flicker of recognition in his eyes, as fleeting as it was.

"You know this woman, don't you?" JJ pressed, leaning in, his voice sharper now.

Lucas shook his head, his expression carefully composed, a mask of indifference. "Never seen her before."

JJ wasn't convinced. He saw the flinch, the subtle tightening of Lucas's jaw for just a second. "Don't lie to me. You were at the bar with her the other night—The Catz Club. She's behind this, isn't she? Her name is Rose. Did she hire you to kill Jimmy?"

"I don't know who you're talking about," Lucas said flatly, but JJ knew he was lying. Lucas might have been a seasoned criminal, but his reaction betrayed him. Rose was involved—JJ could feel it deep in his bones. But without solid evidence, he couldn't take her down. Not yet.

It was time to play his final ace. JJ pulled another image from the file, one that he knew would rattle Lucas to the core. He slid it across the table.

"One last question, Lucas," JJ said, his voice calm but dangerous. "Where's Charlie?"

He placed the photo of Lucas and Charlie leaving the hospital on the table. Lucas erupted with rage, violently yanking at the chains securing him to the chair. He shot to his feet, fury radiating from him.

JJ had him now.

Before Lucas could speak, his lawyer finally interjected, his tone sharp and defensive. "We're done here. Unless you have any further evidence connecting my client to the shooting, I expect you to release him."

JJ's expression didn't falter. "He's not going anywhere. We've got his gun, and it's being tested. Once we have the results, we'll know whether or not we're done."

Lucas's composure shattered completely. "Fuck you, motherfucker! I didn't kill no one! Just your fat fucking partner. Yeah, I enjoyed that. I almost missed him!" he screamed, kicking the table with such force that it rattled.

His lawyer, who had already closed his briefcase, stood and walked toward the door. What he had assumed was a straightforward case of grand theft auto had just become a tangled web of deceit.

JJ smiled to himself as Lucas was dragged out of the room, his fury barely contained while the officers manhandled him back to his cell. The outburst had been far more revealing than Lucas realized, and JJ knew they were getting closer to the truth. Lucas had cracked, and now it was just a matter of time.

JJ calmly placed the images back in the folder, his mind already racing ahead to the next step. He glanced over at Frank. "What do you think?" he asked.

Frank leaned back, crossing his arms with a satisfied nod. "I think Lucas is going away for a very long time. You nailed him."

JJ shook his head, his expression darkening. "I'm not after Lucas," he replied, standing up and heading towards the door.

Frank frowned, momentarily puzzled, before quickly following JJ out of the room.

As JJ walked down the hallway, his thoughts lingered on Lucas's reaction when he showed him the image of Rose. The flinch. That brief, telling, flicker of recognition in his eyes. She was involved—JJ could feel it deep in his gut. Now, he just had to prove it.

But for the moment, JJ knew he needed to let the grief in. It was clawing at him, relentless, waiting to break through the walls he'd meticulously built to keep it at bay. He was a professional; he had a job to do, he reminded himself. But even professionals weren't immune to the weight of loss. "Goddamn, I need a drink," he muttered to himself.

More than that, though, he needed to talk to his father. The captain was the only one who could ground him right now—the only person who truly understood where he was and what he was feeling. His father had lost a partner, too, back in the day. If anyone could understand the emptiness, the anger, and the grief gnawing at him, it was him.

JJ sighed deeply, feeling a glimmer of relief at the thought of speaking to his father. The conversation would offer the solace he so desperately needed, a steady anchor amidst the chaos swirling around him. It was late, but JJ was certain his father would still be awake, waiting with that quiet wisdom he always relied on. Tonight, he couldn't put it off any longer. He needed his father's counsel like never before—and he had to share the devastating news about Harper's death. Even as he thought of it, a pang of grief twisted in his chest, making the call feel both urgent and inevitable. He headed to visit him.

JJ SAT across from his father in the dimly lit room—his home, or at least it used to be. Now, it felt more like a mausoleum. The soft glow of the lampshade cast a warm light over his father's worn face. The cancer was taking its toll, and it pained JJ to see the once strong, commanding man fading before his eyes. His father's skin had taken on a pale hue, the lines in his face etched deeper with time and illness. Yet, despite the physical toll, the sharpness in his eyes remained. That fire, though dimmer, was still there.

JJ sipped his whiskey, the silence between them heavy yet oddly comforting. His father sat with the local paper in hand, quietly reading as if the world outside hadn't changed. It was clear he hadn't heard the news yet. JJ was faced with the painful duty of telling his father about Harper. He paused, his gaze drifting around the room, lingering on the cherished mementos that adorned the walls—each one a silent testament to happier, simpler times.

The space had become a shrine to bygone days—not just a testament to his father's long career as a cop, but to the life they had shared together. Medals and commendations hung in neat rows, each telling a story of service, of battles fought and victories hard-won, both on the streets and in the precinct. But the room also held pieces of JJ's own journey: his first swimming award, his high school shooting medal—snapshots of a life shaped by dedication and ambition.

It was more than just a room; it was a silent witness to their shared history, filled with achievements, milestones, and the moments that had defined them both.

On the table holding the lamp is a family portrait, capturing a time when things were simpler. All of them were there, Harper, his mother, even JJ's ex-wife—happier days, frozen in time. What JJ wouldn't give to be back in that moment, when life felt less complicated, as he now braced himself to deliver the news about Harper to his father.

JJ hoped he could add a few more memories to this room before the cancer claimed his father. Time was slipping through his fingers faster than he was ready to admit. He swallowed hard, trying to stay present, to hold on to this shared space of memories.

"Captain, I need to tell you something," JJ began, his voice low and steady, though his heart ached. "Harper's gone, Pop."

JJ's father, a man who had weathered countless storms during his time as captain at the precinct, set down the newspaper. He stared at his son, his expression momentarily blank, letting the sad news settle. Harper had been his first partner back when Harper made detective. They had been through thick and thin, facing dangers together that only forged a deeper bond over the years. Even after all this time, the connection between them had remained strong—unspoken but solid.

JJ's father finally spoke, his voice quieter than usual, "Harper... he was a good man. We've lost one of the best, haven't we?" The room, filled with the echoes of their pasts, felt heavier with the loss. He reached for his own glass of whiskey, raising it "To Harper."

JJ raised his own glass. "To Harper."

After a moment, JJ's father gave a heavy sigh, his eyes clouded with a sadness JJ rarely saw.

He took a sip of his whiskey. "Harper was my best friend," he said, his voice rough around the edges. "I'm so sorry, son. I know how much he meant to you, but he was more than just a colleague to me—he was like family. He was a great detective, one of the best—tough, instinctive, and always knew how to get the job done. This is a great loss to the force... and to you, JJ."

JJ nodded, grateful for his father's words. "We're having a family meeting tomorrow," JJ added, referring to the tradition upheld at the precinct when one of their own had fallen. "You should come."

His father met his gaze, understanding immediately. "Of course, I'll be there. We've lost too many good men, but Harper... Harper was special. I'll pay my respects, just like I have over the years. He deserves that and so much more."

They both lifted their glasses and in unison, they spoke, their voices low but firm, "To Harper."

The clink of the glasses echoed in the room, a small yet solemn gesture of respect for the man they had both admired and for the shared bond between father and son.

SIXTY-FOUR
HAPPENSTANCE

THE MORNING LIGHT filtered through Dr. Warrick's kitchen window as she poured coffee for herself and JJ, who had come by, as promised, to discuss the case, hoping the doctor could shed more light on the main suspects. The past few days had been harrowing, and before getting down to business, JJ knew he needed to tell her the news about Harper's death. JJ sat across from her, his expression grim, his hands tightly clasped around the mug in front of him.

"I don't know how to say this," JJ began, his voice low, "but Harper's dead. Lucas ran him over."

Dr. Warrick froze; the cup she was holding trembled in her hands. Her eyes widened in shock. "No..." she whispered, barely able to believe it. "Harper... Oh, JJ, I'm so sorry." Her voice broke as she realized how hard this must have hit him. Though she hadn't known Harper long, she had grown fond of him during their brief interactions.

JJ nodded, his expression distant, as though he were holding himself together by sheer force of will. "Yeah," he muttered, staring into his cup. "We've got Lucas locked up for now. He might get off on Harper's death, claiming it was an accident, but we're hoping to nail him for the murder of Jack's mugger. We're just waiting on forensics to match the ballistics from the gun we found on Lucas."

Dr. Warrick placed her cup down and sat in silence for a moment, letting the grief and the new information settle. "I know how much he meant to you, JJ. I can't imagine what you're going through."

After a moment of shared silence, JJ shifted in his seat. He needed to refocus, to push the grief aside for now. There was still the case to deal with.

"I'm more certain than ever that Rose is at the center of all this," he said, his tone hardening. "Everything keeps coming back to her. Lucas hasn't implicated her yet, but when I questioned him and mentioned Rose and Charlie, there was something in his response—something subtle, something I couldn't quite put my finger on. It felt like he was holding back, like he knew more than he was letting on." He paused, running a hand over his face, exhaustion and frustration creeping into his voice.

"I just hope he doesn't wind up dead like everyone else involved with this goddamn case." JJ's voice faltered for a moment as he mulled over the past week. "If only I'd accepted Brad's suicide verdict... a lot of people would still be alive, including Harper. It's all my fault."

Dr. Warrick looked at him, her eyes filled with concern as she watched him grapple with his doubts. JJ was beginning to question his resolve, and you didn't need to be a clinical psychologist to notice the self-blame written all over his face.

Dr. Warrick took a deep breath and sat up straighter. "Listen, JJ, you were right to question Brad's suicide verdict. Harper knew this, and he believed in you. If he were here now, he'd tell you to crack this case wide open. And I think I might have some information that's going to help you do just that."

JJ glanced up, a flicker of hope in his eyes.

"I've been going through the Brooks family's medical files," she continued, "and there's something you need to know."

JJ's attention sharpened. "What is it?"

"There were two files on Rose," Dr. Warrick began, choosing her words carefully. "One from the age of twenty-one onwards, and it's...

well, frankly, it's unremarkable. Nothing of significance. But then there's another file—a sealed one from before she turned twenty-one."

"Sealed?" JJ asked, his curiosity peaked. "Why was it sealed?"

Dr. Warrick hesitated, then continued. "It contains Rose's full medical history before the age of twenty-one, and she was diagnosed with schizophrenia at a young age. She's been on antipsychotic medications for years—risperidone, quetiapine, the works. But I don't think I was supposed to see this file. Dr. Amen, her primary physician, was away on a cruise, and I believe the receptionist mistakenly sent the whole Brooks family's medical records, including those I was never meant to access."

JJ's mind raced as he processed the revelation. It explained so much —the erratic behavior, the sudden mood shifts. "So, that's why her behavior was all over the place," he muttered. "I always knew there was something off, but I didn't know it was this."

"It would certainly explain some of her behavior, but schizophrenia doesn't usually lead to criminal acts," Cara explained. "People with schizophrenia can go on to live normal, even highly successful lives. Rose was on the best medication money could buy, which would keep any behavioral issues under control—as long as she took it. Besides, those with schizophrenia are far more likely to harm themselves than others. To commit murder requires a significant level of desperation and to cover it up demands manipulation—and under the right circumstances, we're all capable of that."

She paused, taking a breath as she gathered her thoughts. "I've read countless criminology books and papers, and there are many contributing factors that can lead someone to murder. Schizophrenia is very low on that list. What we need to look for are motives, circumstances, and hidden secrets—and Rose certainly seems to have plenty of those."

Cara's voice dropped as she picked up a file, her tone growing more serious. "I've been digging through her mother's medical records, and there's no evidence that she had more than one child. Which raises a very important question – who is Jack's mother? I assumed it was Rose, but if she was twelve when he was born, that would be... unlikely. Not impossible, but strange. And there's no mention of a birth in her medical file. That's the part that's worrying me," she admitted. "It's like Jack's birth never happened. His medical file and birth certificate lists his mother as Mary Brooks and his father as Ezra Brooks, but those could easily have been forged. And there's no medical file for him after the age of nine. It's as if he disappeared from the system."

"Or Rose could have taken him to another doctor," he suggested, his voice tense. "She might have secretly had Jack, keeping it hidden from everyone." He rubbed the back of his neck, frustration mounting. "This is the kind of secret people would kill to keep buried," JJ added. "Especially if you're a high-powered magazine editor with a reputation to protect. So, if we're accepting that Rose is his mother... then who's the father?"

Cara shook her head. "That's the million-dollar question. Rose's schizophrenia makes sense, though. And I've suspected for a while that Jack has it, too. Schizophrenia can be hereditary, and all the signs are there. But there's something more with Jack."

JJ looked at her, curiosity and concern mixing in his gaze. "What do you mean?"

Cara leaned forward, her voice calm but serious. "As you know, I've been treating Jack since the incident with Brad—when he threw him down the cellar. I've been noticing some troubling signs. I am working on a hypothesis that Jack might have dissociative identity disorder, or what was once known as multiple personality disorder. This could have been triggered by the trauma of being locked in the cellar."

JJ raised his eyebrows, his curiosity growing with each revelation.

"In one of our sessions," she continued, "he mentioned being locked in a cellar as a child. That kind of childhood trauma can leave deep psychological scars. Sometimes, when I speak to him, it feels like there's someone else behind his eyes—another part of him, separate. But I haven't been sure. Now that I have a working theory, I can conduct specific tests to confirm whether or not he's living with dissociative identity disorder."

JJ absorbed the information. This could explain a lot—Jack's unpredictable behavior, the secrets buried in the family's past. Jack's blackouts, his violent outbursts—the mugger can stand testimony to that—and his connection to Rose, possibly his real mother, all of it could be linked to or stem from this disorder.

Maybe Jack's violent tendencies are a result of these different identities. And Rose... She had always been protective of Jack, almost secretive when it came to him. If she was indeed his mother, the trauma that likely surrounded his birth and childhood could have fractured his sense of self. Everything seemed to be spiraling back to Rose and now Jack.

The possibility of dissociative identity disorder tied so many of the loose threads together. But it also raised more questions.

"So, if Jack has dissociative identity disorder, that would explain the shifts in his personality, his blackouts?" JJ asked, trying to make sense of it all.

Dr. Warrick nodded. "Exactly. It's possible that when Jack feels threatened or overwhelmed, another personality takes control. These identities could have formed as a way to protect him from trauma, especially from his childhood experiences. But until we run the tests, I can't say for certain."

JJ sat back, letting out a long breath. "This case keeps getting more twisted." He had been doing some digging of his own. "I've been looking into their mother's disappearance. Their father filed a missing person report, but she was never found. The notes say she vanished without a trace and didn't even take her purse. It's still an open case, though it's probably been forgotten over time."

"So she didn't leave him," Dr. Warrick said slowly, remembering the conversation she had with Jack. "She went missing."

JJ nodded. "That's right."

Dr. Warrick looked puzzled. "Jack told me his mother left because she had cancer, and that Rose told him that. But I've checked over the file. There's no evidence their mother ever had cancer."

JJ sat back in his chair at the revelation. "That's another lie, then. One more piece of the puzzle that doesn't fit." He rubbed his temples, the frustration building. "Rose has been feeding Jack false information for years. The question is, why? What's she hiding?"

JJ's mind raced, swirling with possibilities. *Was Rose protecting Jack from something darker—or was she covering up her own secrets?*

He shook his head in disbelief. "This family's buried in lies. And their father's suicide... there were inconsistencies there, too. The ligature marks around his neck didn't match a typical suicide and the case notes mentioned signs of a struggle in the room, but the investigation was closed, almost like no one wanted to dig deeper." He paused, his voice growing darker. "There was also an old report of domestic violence against their mother and the children. The cops at the time probably thought they were better off without him, and that's why they didn't investigate his death properly."

She frowned, her fingers tapping lightly on the table. "So their father's death may not have been a suicide at all. And if Rose was involved... what lengths would she go to in order to keep these secrets hidden?"

JJ nodded grimly. "That's what we need to figure out. There's more going on here than we realize." He clenched his fists. "It's not just about Jack anymore—it's about the entire Brooks family."

They both leaned back in their seats, grappling with the weight of the secrets they'd uncovered. Just as the silence deepened, JJ's eyes flicked toward the window. Something outside caught his attention. His posture stiffened.

Without a word, he stood abruptly and moved toward the door, his eyes scanning the area beyond the glass.

"What is it?" Cara asked, startled.

"I saw someone outside," JJ muttered, already heading out the door. He ran into the garden, scanning the area for any sign of the figure he'd glimpsed. But by the time he got there, they were gone.

When he returned, Cara was waiting by the door, a little rattled.

"Who was it?" she asked.

"I don't know," JJ replied, frustration lacing his words. "But we need to be careful. Someone's watching and may have heard everything we have just discussed."

Cara offered him a reassuring smile though her own nerves were frayed. She opened her hand, a small can of mace. "I'm not completely helpless, JJ. I'll be fine."

JJ sighed, though his concern was far from alleviated. "We've made a lot of progress today, Cara. But I need more time," he said. "I'll work on getting the warrants to arrest Rose, but it's going to take some doing."

Cara nodded, understanding the weight of the situation.

"I'd feel a lot better if someone was keeping an eye on you," JJ added. "I'll have a couple of squad cars patrol the area every half hour. If you see anything suspicious, call me immediately." He handed her his card.

Cara took the card, her fingers gripping it tightly. "In the meantime, I need to focus on Jack," she said. "I have a therapy session with him tomorrow, and I need to figure out his diagnosis and treatment plan. If my theory is correct, it could change everything."

JJ looked at her, his face still etched with concern. "Be careful," he warned. "If Jack contacts you, don't let on about what we've uncovered. If he gets suspicious, he might tip off Rose."

"Understood," she replied. "I'll act like everything's normal. But keep me in the loop if you find out anything new."

JJ nodded; his expression serious. "I will. Take care, Cara."

They exchanged a look, both aware of the precariousness of the situation and the danger that lay ahead.

With that, he turned and left to go to Mo's for Harper's eulogy. For the first time in days, JJ felt he was finally closing in on the truth. The tangled web of lies and secrets might soon unravel completely. The case could finally be solved. His thoughts drifted back to Harper—if only he were here to see it. Harper would have been proud, proud to know that his unwavering trust in JJ wasn't misplaced, and that justice was finally within reach.

SIXTY-FIVE
THE FAMILY PART 2

MO'S WAS PACKED. The usual hum of the coffee machines was absent tonight, replaced by the clink of glasses and the quiet buzz of conversation. Tonight wasn't about routine—tonight was about honoring a fallen hero. It was Harper's turn to be toasted. The precinct had gathered, all of them—brothers and sisters in blue—united in grief and camaraderie. They shared drinks, stories, and the heavy burden of loss. Though the occasion was somber, there was still laughter, the occasional joke, and even a song or two amid the low murmur of conversation and quiet reflection.

JJ sat at the end of the bar, a glass before him, untouched. His eyes were distant, his thoughts far away, yet his mind was fully present, absorbing the atmosphere. He could almost picture Harper here, grinning, leading a singalong as he always did at gatherings like this. *If only Harper were here...* JJ thought. *He loved a good singsong.*

The doorbell chimed as it opened, and the room quieted instantly. In walked Harper's wife, Maggie, and his daughter, Chip. For a moment, all eyes were on them. The precinct held its breath as JJ stood and crossed the room, gently gathering them both and seating them next to his father.

As they sat, the silence was suddenly broken by a spontaneous rapture of applause. The entire room stood, clapping for Maggie and Chip, a gesture of respect, admiration, and shared grief. Maggie, her eyes glistening with emotion, rose for a moment, nodding to acknowledge the gesture. She didn't speak, but the gratitude in her eyes said more than words ever could. The applause swelled, filling the space, a bittersweet tribute to the man they all loved and lost.

Frank stood up first, the weight of the room pressing down on him as he raised his glass. The low hum of conversation quieted, and all eyes turned towards him. He cleared his throat, but when he spoke, his voice still cracked with the strain of grief. "Harper and I… we went to school together, you know." He paused for a moment, collecting himself as he looked into the glass, the reflection of memories swirling back to him.

"He was older, a few years ahead of me, but even then… he knew how to handle himself. Harper was a bit of a legend at school." A faint smile tugged at Frank's lips as he spoke, his voice softening with the memory. "I looked up to him, like most of us did. He had this way about him, you know? Always stuck up for the little guy, even when it meant getting into trouble himself."

Frank glanced around the room, faces watching intently, knowing the truth behind his words. Harper had been larger than life, even as a boy.

"And yeah, sure," Frank continued, his voice growing more contemplative, "we had our differences later on when we became cops. You know, when you're partners, you clash sometimes. But if I'm being honest, I think it was because I was always jealous of him. The man was fearless."

He paused again, a bittersweet smile creeping across his face. "And then… he met Maggie." Frank turned to look at her, seated a few rows back, her face lined with quiet strength. "Maggie and Harper, childhood sweethearts. They were inseparable, like they were two pieces of the same puzzle. They stuck together through thick and thin."

Frank's gaze shifted to Chip, Harper's daughter, seated next to her mother. His eyes softened as he spoke, his words holding a different kind of weight now. "And then came Chip. What a day that was… he was over the moon. He never stopped talking about you, you know? You were the center of his world."

Chip managed a small, fragile smile, the kind that barely masks the deep ache of loss. Frank noticed, pausing to gather his thoughts before continuing, the room was so quiet it felt like the air itself was holding its breath.

"I remember he showed everyone this picture of you when you were a baby," Frank said, his smile widening at the memory. "When he showed it to me, all I could see was this chubby little ball of arms and legs. But Harper was so proud. You know," Frank added with a chuckle, "I'm the one who gave you your name. I said you were a chip off the old block, and from that moment on, 'Chip' stuck."

Frank's voice faltered, and for a brief moment, the man standing before them was no longer the seasoned cop. He was just a kid again, looking up to Harper with the same admiration and awe he had felt all those years ago. His eyes glistened with tears he could no longer hold back, and one slipped down his cheek. He quickly wiped it away with the back of his hand, trying to compose himself, but the room could feel the depth of his emotion.

"Damn," Frank said quietly, his voice thick with emotion. "He was one of the good ones. The kind you only meet once in a lifetime."

The room was still, everyone caught in the gravity of the moment, their own memories of Harper lingering in the air. Frank raised his glass, his voice steadier this time, though the emotion still lingered in his eyes.

"To Harper," he said, his voice carrying a mixture of pride, sadness, and respect.

As the words left his lips, the entire room followed, lifting their glasses in unison. "To Harper," they echoed. The simple gesture held a lifetime of love, admiration, and sorrow.

The clinking of glasses filled the room, a soft, collective tribute to the man they had all gathered to honor—a man who had touched so many lives and left a legacy far greater than he would ever know. As they drank, the stories and laughter would resume, but for now, in this solemn, shared silence, they remembered Harper, not just as a colleague or a friend, but as a hero who had left them far too soon.

JJ glanced at his father—'The Captain' to everyone else. He sat quietly in a corner, his once strong frame weakened by illness, but his eyes still sharp. Cancer had taken a toll, but nothing could diminish his presence. Tonight, though, he looked tired. JJ had noticed the way his father winced when he thought no one was looking, the way he shifted in his chair as if every movement sent a shock of pain through his body. But still, he was here, for Harper.

"Captain?" JJ prompted gently, and the old man stood, leaning slightly on his cane. His voice was soft but steady as he spoke.

"I remember Harper when he first came on the force—a rookie, eager as hell. He had something about him, though. Made detective in no time." He chuckled, his voice growing stronger as the memories surfaced. "Hell, I was his first partner. I saw him in action, and let me tell you, that boy was brave. Fit as a butcher's dog, too."

The Captain grinned as he continued, "Once saw him chase down a local hood. Big fella, an ex-linebacker for the Bears who had fallen on hard times. He stole a guy's watch and thought he could outrun Harper. He couldn't. Harper brought him down without breaking a sweat. Tough son of a bitch."

The Captain's smile softened as the room chuckled, but then his expression changed, a playful grin crossing his face. "But you know what brought him down in the end? Doughnuts. Yeah, Mo introduced him to the good stuff, and after that, we couldn't get him out of Mo's. Who would've thought, eh? Brought down by a doughnut."

The laughter rippled through the group, a bittersweet reprieve from the weight of the moment. The Captain raised his glass, his voice steady. "To Harper."

Maggie managed a faint smile, though tears threatened to spill, her grief barely contained. Sophie, however, remained stone-faced. There were no tears, no smile—just a look of unwavering determination. Her eyes burned with a quiet fury; a vow etched in her expression. She would become the type of cop her father had been, and she would see justice done.

"To Harper," the room echoed.

JJ stood next, all eyes turned to him and the room fell silent. He swallowed hard, forcing the words out through the lump in his throat.

"I owe my life to Harper. More times than I can count, he pulled me out of situations that should've ended me. Too many times to mention. And let's be real, I wouldn't be standing here right now if it weren't for him."

JJ's voice faltered slightly, but he took a breath, holding his emotions in check. "I could spend the whole night telling you stories about him, but I won't. What I will say is this: Harper wasn't just my partner. He wasn't just my friend. He was my brother. He was our brother. A damn fine cop, and we're never going to see the likes of him again."

For a moment, there was silence. A heavy, respectful silence as everyone raised their glasses and they all spoke in unison. "To Harper."

JJ moved over to the jukebox; his feet heavy but his purpose clear. He'd already paid the coin. He scrolled through the list, his finger lingering for a moment before selecting number twenty-one – Lou Harper. He knew this song meant something—Harper had always loved a laugh, but there was always a meaning behind the jokes. The music began, and as the first notes floated through the air, everyone paused, listening.

"Bum Bum Bum, Bum Bum Bum, Bum Bum Bum Bum Bum…"

The words followed, clear and unmistakable.

"Win or lose, sink or swim. One thing is certain, we'll never give in. Side by side, hand in hand. We all stand together."

The room fell silent, the disbelief palpable. For a beat, nobody moved. It was Frank who broke the tension first, chuckling softly. "'We All Stand Together' by Paul McCartney? Featuring the Frog Chorus? Harper, you son of a bitch, I love this tune!"

Everyone burst into laughter, the tension snapping in an instant. It was classic Harper—even in death, he found a way to give them one last laugh and message. They all joined in, singing along with the tune, their voices rising in unison. It was silly. It was unexpected. But it was Harper.

JJ stood by the jukebox, watching them all, the sound of laughter and music filling the room. He let himself smile, just for a moment, letting the grief slip away. For now, it was enough to remember Harper the way he would've wanted them to—together, laughing, standing side by side. The family.

JJ caught Joanna's eye, and she gestured for him to come over. JJ maneuvered through the room to where she was standing. On reaching her, he noticed her grim expression.

She cut right to the point. "Lucas's gun wasn't the one that killed Jimmy."

JJ's disappointment was fierce at the revelation. He had been banking on that gun as the critical piece of evidence to leverage against Rose. Without it, his case suddenly felt shaky, like it was losing momentum. But Joanna wasn't finished.

"However," she continued, her voice steady, "we found another gun under the seat of the Lincoln. We ran ballistics, and it's a match for the gun that killed Jimmy. We checked Lucas for gunshot residue, but... nothing. He wasn't our shooter."

JJ's heart sank further. His frustration was evident, he drew in a deep breath as he processed the unraveling lead. The breakthrough he had been hoping for was slipping through his fingers. Joanna, noticing his reaction, gave a faint, knowing smile and added, "Why the long face? The gun still matches, so we have the murder weapon, and do you want to know the best part? We ran the serial number, and guess who it belongs to... drum roll, please—Rose Brooks."

JJ froze, his mind racing. He fought to maintain his composure. "Any prints?" he asked, the question almost automatic.

Joanna shook her head. "No, unfortunately not. Whoever it was must have worn gloves."

A setback, but JJ knew he had something crucial—Rose was now tied to the murder weapon, even if indirectly. That alone was significant.

But Joanna wasn't done. She lowered her voice and glanced around as if ensuring no one else could hear. "There's more. One of the uniforms took a statement at the scene of the accident. After the car hit the truck, someone got out of the back of the Lincoln and ran."

JJ's pulse quickened. "Did they get a good look at who it was?" he asked, the words tumbling out faster than intended.

Joanna shook her head. "Nah, they were wearing a hood and disappeared down an alley."

JJ's eyes widened, his heart thudding in his chest. The pieces were beginning to fall into place. For the first time, he had concrete evidence linking Rose to Jimmy's murder, and now there was a potential eyewitness placing someone—likely Rose—at the scene of the accident.

This was the break he had been waiting for.

The walls were finally closing in on Rose. JJ had enough now to at least bring her in for questioning. As the puzzle pieces continued to align, he knew it was only a matter of time before everything unraveled for her.

SIXTY-SIX
CAT & MOUSE

IT WAS EARLY MORNING, and JJ, flanked by two uniformed officers, strode purposefully into the apartment block. The crackle of police radio chatter echoed through the foyer, drawing the attention of curious residents peeking from doorways. Today, JJ hoped, would be the day he finally got the answers he so desperately needed—answers that could close the case and secure justice for Brad Marshall, for Harper, and even for Jimmy Mercer—deadbeat or not, no one deserved to have their brains blown out over a mugging.

But more than anything, JJ prayed today would be the day they found Charlie—alive or dead. A fragile hope flickered inside him that Charlie might still be breathing, but deep down, JJ's instincts told him they were likely hunting for a body. Nearly a week had passed since Charlie vanished, and without treatment for the gunshot wound to his gut, the odds of survival were slim. Still, like Schrödinger's cat, Charlie hovered in that cruel space between life and death.

This case was riddled with dark secrets—secrets that needed to be dragged into the light if JJ was ever to get the answers he so desperately sought. And now, with his time running out, JJ hoped that if this was to be his final case before joining the FBI, he would at least uncover the truth.

Scott, the apartment concierge, greeted them with a defiant air, his disapproval practically radiating from him. JJ recognized Scott from the night Jack was attacked—he had been Rose's date that evening. JJ knew the moment he started heading towards her apartment, Rose would be informed of his presence. She would be ready.

Flashing his badge, JJ offered a brief, deliberately vague, explanation. Scott hesitated, visibly uneasy, but eventually stepped aside—he had little choice. Though JJ didn't secure a warrant for her arrest he had enough to bring her in for questioning. Besides, it felt best to keep things low-key. Scott's concern for Rose was clear as he hastily dialed his phone. Just as JJ deliberately stepped into the lift after the officers, he turned to see Scott, phone in hand.

"Bingo," JJ muttered, watching Scott make the call. "She knows we're on the way." He smiled as the lift doors closed.

They reached the apartment, and JJ knocked firmly. The door swung open almost instantly, and Rose stood there, waiting.

"Good morning, Detective," she said coolly, though she knew his name. Rose avoided using it, knowing this wasn't a time for pleasantries. Her eyes swept over the two uniformed officers, then briefly scanned beyond them as if searching for someone else.

"Where's your partner, Detective...?" She let her question hang, her pause deliberate.

"Harper," JJ filled in, his tone clipped, not offering further explanation. He wasn't ready to disclose Harper's death just yet—not here, not now. He intended to break that news in a controlled setting at the station when he brought her in for questioning.

Rose stepped aside, gesturing for them to enter. He wanted to keep things as informal as possible for now, so he maintained a casual yet informative demeanor. Once inside, he got straight to the point, not wasting any time.

"Jimmy was shot," he began, his voice calm but serious as he began to explain the situation surrounding the shooting of the man who had mugged Jack.

"Jimmy?" Rose did not recognize the name, though her voice remained steady. "I'm afraid I don't know who you're referring to."

"The man who attacked Jack," JJ clarified. "His name was Jimmy, Jimmy Mercer. Two days ago, he was shot and killed."

Rose kept her expression composed, though there was the slightest shift in her posture. JJ noted it but she remained unreadable.

"I see. And what does this have to do with me?" she asked, her tone still controlled, careful.

JJ took a breath, maintaining his calm demeanor. "The gun used in the shooting was found at the scene, and it's registered to you."

Rose blinked, her expression giving away little, save for a brief flicker of surprise. But JJ knew better than to read too much into facial reactions. They could be misleading.

"A witness also saw someone fleeing the scene," he continued, keeping his tone calm and matter of fact. He deliberately withheld the detail about the gunman crashing into Harper—he'd save that part of the story for later.

Rose's response was cool and composed, her voice steady. "Are you here to arrest me? Do I need my lawyer? And what time did this shooting happen?" She paused, then added nonchalantly, "My purse was stolen last week, and my gun was inside it. I meant to report it, but it slipped my mind."

How convenient, JJ mused inwardly, though his expression remained impassive. He kept his suspicion well hidden, his practiced poker face betraying nothing. This game was about patience, and he was determined to see it through without tipping his hand.

"Well, we can clear all of this up, down at the station," he replied, maintaining his neutral tone.

"So, you *are* arresting me?" she asked again, her tone sharper this time.

"We can, if you'd prefer it to be handled that way," JJ responded smoothly. He couldn't, not without a warrant, but she didn't know that. He knew it was only a matter of time before one was issued. "But since you've clarified that the gun was stolen, we just need to ask you a few questions—to clear up a few details."

Rose regarded him for a moment, then nodded. "I'll need to call my attorney. Give me a moment."

"Of course," JJ replied, his eyes never leaving her. He watched her closely, noting every subtle shift in her demeanor. As she turned to make the call, he asked casually, "Where's Jack?"

"He's out for a run," she answered, her voice smooth—perhaps a little too smooth. The lie slipped off her tongue effortlessly.

Rose knew Jack hadn't gone for a run; it was just a simple, convenient excuse that demanded no questions or explanations. In truth, she hadn't had a proper conversation with him in two days. Their interactions had dwindled to fleeting moments—like the brief glimpse she'd caught of him that morning.

Before JJ could probe any further, Rose slipped into a nearby room with her phone, her movements calm and deliberate. JJ's eyes narrowed slightly, his instincts on high alert. Something was definitely off.

She returned a few minutes later, her jacket and purse in hand, her expression still calm and collected. "Right, let's go," she said, almost as if she were in control of the situation.

JJ was surprised by how smoothly this was going; he had expected a more combative exchange. Instead, it felt as if Rose had been rehearsing this conversation. Was her calmness simply a coping mechanism, or was she genuinely confident that everything would be resolved in her favor?

As she prepared to leave, Rose turned to him with a smirk, holding her wrists out. "Are you going to cuff me?"

"That won't be necessary," JJ replied.

SIXTY-SEVEN
WHISPERS

MOMENTS LATER, they were outside the apartment block and as Rose was being guided into the back of JJ's car, Jack rounded the corner, catching a glimpse of his sister slipping into the vehicle. He froze, a sharp intake of breath betraying his shock. Instinctively, he stepped back into the shadows of a nearby alley, pressing himself against the cold, rough brick wall. His body tensed like a coiled spring, every muscle on edge.

He watched the car pull away, eyes narrowing as it disappeared down the street. His mind raced, calculating his next move.

The sharp pain in his shoulder flared, shooting down his arm like a searing blade. He clutched it reflexively, squeezing harder than he should—his fingers digging into his flesh, the pain rippling through him. But it wasn't just the physical agony twisting his features. Something far darker stirred inside him, something more than the pain. *Voices.* Familiar voices. They clawed their way to the surface, slipping through the cracks in his mind as they had for hours, days, maybe even years. Jack grimaced, feeling the battle within.

He knew he should have stepped out, maybe even intervened. Rose was his sister. But the voices—the ones that whispered in low, insidious tones, growing louder with each passing moment—ordered him to stay hidden. *Stay in the shadows, Jack.*

They told him not to act. Rose wasn't his problem anymore. She could handle herself. His task lay elsewhere now. There were things far more pressing, darker purposes pulling him forward. Jack hunched his shoulders, his hands sliding deep into his pockets, the muscles in his arms taut as the whispers shifted into a feral growl in his mind.

They're coming for you, Jack. You need to be ready. You need to be ahead of them.

The words pulsed through him, relentless and gnawing. And Jack understood. He knew exactly why JJ had come for Rose. He knew what would happen if he revealed himself now—it would ruin everything. He couldn't afford that. He needed more time—time to stay ahead of whatever was closing in on him.

The shadows seemed to throb around him, cold and unyielding, as if they welcomed him back into their fold. They wrapped around him, hiding him from view, shrouding him like a ghost retreating into the night. He slipped further into the darkness, the voices still whispering, still growing, guiding him toward his next task.

It wasn't long before Jack found himself standing outside the hospital, not knowing how he got there, as if he traveled in a hypnotic trance. His fingers twitched as the voices hammered in his skull. He needed to see Dr. Warrick, but The Miseries were louder than ever, each voice scrambling for control, tearing at his sanity. The demons he had warned her about—the ones she had tried to dismiss as figments—were very real to Jack. And now they wouldn't shut up. *They never shut up.*

"I told you... I told you they should've stayed locked away," he muttered, his eyes wild, as he paced in erratic circles, one hand gripping his head as if to hold the voices in. "But no, you wanted to fix things, didn't you? Wanted to clear them out. Now they're loose, and they won't leave me." His voice cracked into a snarl, the edges of his words splitting with the different tones of those inside him. "They won't stop. They want blood."

Jack dropped onto the bench facing Dr. Warrick's office, his pupils dilating, his eyes in a glassy stare as he watched her on the phone. His breath came in ragged, shallow bursts. *You like her, don't you, Jack? She hates you. She thinks you're a freak* a voice cackled from the depths of his mind, dripping with malice.

Who was she talking to? Another voice, harsher and more venomous, hissed and spat its suspicions. The chorus of hatred swelled, echoing inside his skull like a storm. *She's telling them everything. She's going to expose us. She's going to ruin everything, Jack.*

The whispers grew louder, mocking him with their laughter, cruel and taunting. Jack's jaw clenched, his fists tightening until his knuckles turned bone white. His head spun as the voices continued to swirl, twisting his thoughts, drowning out any hope of reason. His pulse quickened, the seething noise in his head becoming unbearable.

She'll destroy you, Jack. You have to stop her before it's too late.

The relentless whispers gnawed at him, pushing him closer to the edge, the darkness curling tighter around his mind.

"Shut up, shut up, SHUT UP!" His shout exploded out of him, startling passersby, their curious glances like knives cutting into his skin. He gritted his teeth, lowering his head. *Keep it together. Don't let them see. They'll know.*

She's a danger, Jack, one voice whispered, sly and convincing. *She'll tell them everything. She'll tell them about us. About what you did.*

Another voice, harsher, more insistent, cut in. *You need to silence her. Now.*

Jack's hand drifted to the cold steel of the knife hidden at his waist, fingers trembling as they curled around the handle. The touch was familiar, comforting in its menace. He pulled his jacket tighter to conceal it, his heart pounding in rhythm with the dark pulse in his mind. He needed Dr. Warrick. He needed her help. But the voices—*they*—were pushing him to something darker. Something he couldn't stop.

Do it, Jack, a voice hissed, louder now. *You know what you have to do. She's going to ruin everything. Kill her, before she kills us.*

"NO!" he screamed, his hand flying to his head, gripping his hair, pulling, trying to rip the voices out. People turned to look once again, wide-eyed, stepping back. But he didn't care. His mind was spiraling, each thought darker than the last. *Silence her, Jack,* another voice whispered, this one sweet, tempting. *We'll all be safe if you just silence her.*

He could feel his grip on reality slipping, the world tilting. His vision blurred as the dizziness washed over him, and he stumbled to his feet. He clutched his injured shoulder, feeling the pain shoot through his body—a pain that felt distant compared to the chaos in his mind. *Run, Jack. Before they take over. Before you hurt someone again.* Jack was back in control.

She's going to tell everyone about you, Jack, the voices sang in unison, mocking him, taunting him. *They'll all know.*

With a shaking breath, Jack turned and stumbled away from the hospital, each step heavier, each thought more fractured. The Miseries were winning. And soon, there would be no stopping them, he needed to get as far away as possible.

SIXTY-EIGHT
ONE MIND, MANY SOULS

DR. WARRICK WAS deep into reviewing the medical papers sent over by Dr. Amen's receptionist when something caught her eye. Amongst the neatly typed documents was a handwritten note on Jack's file that she had missed during her initial reading of the files. It simply read: *Referred - Dr. Chanler - Aurora.* The name struck a chord with her. She had heard it before but couldn't immediately place it. Then, it clicked—she remembered *Dr. Chanler.* Not someone she knew personally, but a figure she had come across in her professional circles, a fellow psychiatrist.

Suddenly, she began piecing it all together. Dr. Miriam Chanler wasn't just any psychiatrist; she was a highly respected clinical psychiatrist specializing in Dissociative identity disorder
. Dr. Warrick had once had the opportunity to speak with her at length at a psych conference. They had discussed complex cases and cutting-edge treatments—She was remarkable, someone Cara had admired instantly.

Feeling the tug of curiosity, Dr. Warrick crossed the room to a tall bookshelf. She ran her fingers across the spines of several books before finding the one she was looking for. Pulling it free, she read the title, *The Fractured Mind: One Mind, Many Souls.* The author, Dr. Miriam

Chanler. She opened the book and skimmed the foreword, which was titled 'Living with a Fractured Reality.'

"Perfect," she murmured to herself. What a stroke of luck. The very person who could help her piece together Jack's elusive medical history was not only a colleague, but someone she deeply respected.

Returning to her desk, Dr. Warrick flipped through her Rolodex, quickly locating Dr. Chanler's number. She dialed, and after a brief exchange with the receptionist, she was put through to the doctor. Before long, she found herself in an in-depth conversation. Cara explained that Jack was now her patient and that she needed as much information as possible to make an accurate diagnosis.

Dr. Chanler remembered Cara immediately and was more than happy to assist. She spoke at length about Jack, Rose, and even Bart, revealing that she hadn't treated Jack for nearly fifteen years.

When Dr. Chanler mentioned Bart, Dr. Warrick felt a sudden surge of tension in her chest. *This was the breakthrough she needed.* She listened intently, ensuring she didn't miss a single detail. As their conversation drew to a close, Miriam promised to fax over everything she had on the Brooks family. Cara thanked her, mentioning that she hoped to see her at the next conference. With that, she placed the phone back on its receiver, a sense of satisfaction settling over her.

Leaning back in her chair, she exhaled deeply and glanced out the window. The bright light filtered into her eyes, momentarily distracting her. She picked up Dr. Chanler's book and opened it where she had previously placed note stickers. Although it had been a while since she last read the book, the markers helped refresh her memory. The chapter heading read, 'Dissociative Identity Disorder (formerly known as Multiple Personality Disorder).' She had always been intrigued by the condition and believed she had found a possible explanation for Jack's symptoms. As she read further, the book discussed trauma as a primary cause, particularly stemming from family dysfunction. It suggested that DID was not linked to a chemical imbalance or genetic mutation, though biological factors could increase susceptibility, especially if a close relative, such as a mother or father, had experienced the disorder.

The increasing brightness from the sunlight was becoming bothersome, prompting her to stand and adjust the blinds. Before doing so, she glanced outside once more. It was a beautiful day, and for a brief moment, she caught a glimpse of someone disappearing around the corner at the end of the street. Their gait was familiar, though she couldn't quite identify whose it was. Before she could dwell on it further, the sharp sound of the fax machine interrupted her thoughts—Dr. Chanler had kept her word.

She stood and walked over to the machine, watching document after document slowly emerge. She glanced at the papers as they came through, one by one. Everything was there: Jack's past treatment and the history she had been searching for. Detective Jackson needed these missing pieces, and she needed to tell him what she had found out. Picking up her phone, she dialed.

The doctor let the phone ring, but it was clear the detective wasn't available as the voicemail kicked in. He needed to know she had called and hear what she had to say. When the voicemail beeped, she sighed and began to leave a message, hoping he would listen soon.

"Hi JJ, it's Dr. Warrick... Cara here. I've just got off the phone with Dr. Chanler—long story, but she was Jack's former psychiatrist. She had some very interesting things to say about the Brooks family. She faxed over everything. Call me when you get this. Oh, and I know who Jack's father is—it's..." *Beep.* The voicemail cut off abruptly.

SIXTY-NINE
JACKY BOY

JACK HAD RETURNED to the hospital, but something about him had shifted. His walk was different—deliberate, with an unsettling confidence. The smile that flickered across his face wasn't quite right, more of a smirk, like a teenager up to no good. Was this Jack at all? There was a slyness in his movements, a predatory awareness in his eyes.

At the hospital entrance, an emergency caused a distraction—paramedics rushing in, staff scrambling to assist. It was the perfect cover. The security guard turned his back just as Jack slipped inside unnoticed. He made his way down the sterile corridors, moving with purpose. Then, suddenly, he paused. His face twisted in pain, and his hand shot up to clutch his injured shoulder. His expression contorted, a grimace of fear and agony distorting his features.

"Where you goin', Jacky boy?" he muttered under his breath, his voice low and menacing. It was Jack's voice, but something about it was wrong—off, as if someone else was speaking through him.

Jack straightened up, releasing his grip on his shoulder. His face smoothed into something almost blank, emotionless. He turned back towards Dr. Warrick's office, his posture again transforming into that unnerving swagger. "That's my boy. 'Goosey goosey gander, where shall I wander?'" he whispered, the rhyme slipping from his lips with a sickening playfulness. His movements were fluid, almost jaunty as if he were enjoying the game.

As Jack passed by nurses and hospital staff, they greeted him with warm smiles. "Hello, Jack," they said. They knew him well—he had been here many times before.

Jack smiled back, his responses effortlessly charming, as though they were old friends. Yet, beneath that exterior, he was silently screaming, *stop me*. Trapped within the confines of his mind, his desperate cry went unheard. None of the staff suspected something sinister was hidden behind those friendly eyes. No one realized that a darker, malevolent force was moving undetected among them.

Jack was there, somewhere, but locked inside his mind, desperately clawing at the walls of his consciousness, trying to break free, to stop what was coming. The voices were louder now, drowning out his thoughts. *You can't stop me, Jacky boy.* They were in control.

Finally, he arrived at Dr. Warrick's office. Jack leaned in close to the door, his ear pressed against the wood, listening. A smirk curled at the corner of his lips.

Outside the door, Jack had been listening intently to every word, his ear pressed against the cool wood. A slow, menacing smile spread across his face. Leaning back, he whispered darkly to himself, "Oh, that won't do... that won't do at all."

INSIDE, Dr. Warrick cursed under her breath. "Damn it, I hate voicemail," she muttered in frustration. Just as the words left her lips, a soft knock echoed from the door. Without thinking, she called out, "Enter."

As she began to walk back to her desk, the door creaked open—slowly, deliberately. She turned to face the door, expecting the receptionist, but instead, there stood Jack. He said nothing, his movements unnervingly controlled as he pushed the door closed with a soft *click*. Cara's heart skipped. She hadn't expected him.

A little flustered, she stammered, "Jack, did you—did you have an appointment?" Her eyes darted to the diary on her desk, hoping she had simply forgotten something. Still, Jack remained silent. He didn't move; he just stood there, grinning, the smile stretching from ear to ear, a full, soulless toothy grin, cold and empty. The longer he stood there, the more oppressive the room felt, and the more suffocating the silence became.

Then it hit her—her heart seemed to stop, her stomach twisted in on itself, and a sharp, panicked breath tore through her lungs. Dr. Chanler's words flooded her mind, the warning about Jack's treatment. A sudden wave of realization coursed through her veins, icy and paralyzing. Fear gripped her, more intense than anything she had ever felt before. This wasn't Jack... at least, not the Jack she knew.

Without a word, Jack slowly parted his jacket. Cara's breath hitched as his hand slid inside, revealing a knife. The blade caught the light, glinting with a cold, lethal sharpness. He moved with eerie calm, no rush, no sudden gestures—just deliberate, chilling control. His other hand rose to his lips, his eyes locking onto hers, dark and malevolent.

"Shhhhh," he whispered, his finger pressed to his lips, a sickening smile fixed on his face.

SEVENTY
THE INTERVIEW

WHEN THEY FINALLY ARRIVED AT the station, Rose was greeted by her attorney, who was waiting at the entrance. She cast a glance at JJ, silently requesting a moment of privacy. JJ nodded, stepping back as Rose had a quick conversation with her lawyer. Moments later, she introduced him.

"This is my attorney, Mr McCarthy."

JJ extended his hand. "We've met briefly."

"Indeed," McCarthy replied, his tone curt as he shook JJ's hand. "Shall we get on with this?"

JJ offered a friendly smile and gestured for them to proceed. As they made their way to the interview room, McCarthy was the first to speak.

"My client wishes it to be noted, on record, that she has come in voluntarily to assist with your investigation."

"Of course," JJ responded, his composure steady, revealing nothing. He was saving his thoughts and questions for the interview. First, he needed to ensure the mouse was well and truly cornered. He opened the door, and they all entered.

JJ had chosen a more comfortable setting for the interview with Rose;

an interrogation room's cold, sterile atmosphere just wouldn't do. He needed her to be relaxed and at ease. The chairs were cushioned, the lighting soft, and the room warm and inviting—a soft glow filtered through the vertical blinds, casting gentle stripes of light across the space.

"Please, take a seat." He gestured toward the two chairs positioned in front of a low coffee table. JJ's mobile suddenly burst into life as they sat down, vibrating and ringing in his pocket. He frowned—this was not the time for interruptions. Without hesitation, he retrieved the phone, pressed *end*, silencing the call, and returned it to his pocket. The room returned to its calm stillness.

JJ pressed *record* on the tape machine. After stating the time and date, the interview began. Rose's attorney methodically opened his briefcase, retrieved a notepad, and sat ready to take notes.

"So, Rose, thank you for coming in," JJ began, calm yet deliberate. "We just have a few questions for you."

JJ started by asking about her movements on the afternoon Jimmy Mercer was shot. Rose provided a confident, well-rehearsed alibi. JJ made a mental note to follow up later but wasn't buying it.

"So, you say your purse was stolen," JJ continued, leaning forward slightly, his eyes fixed on hers. "So the gun found at the murder scene was in your stolen purse?"

Rose held his gaze, her tone casual. "That's right."

"Do you always carry a gun, Rose?"

"It depends on where I'm going and what time of day," Rose replied, her demeanor calm and composed, giving nothing away. "I was at a bar last week—not one of my usual spots, but somewhere a little more... edgy. That's where it was stolen."

JJ's eyes narrowed slightly. "Calhoun's? The Alamo?" he probed.

Rose shook her head, her expression neutral. "No, I can't say I've been to those places."

JJ tried again, leaning in just a fraction. "The Cattle Drive?" He looked her directly in the eye, waiting to see if she would lie or tell the truth. He needed Rose to make a choice.

Rose hesitated, only for a moment, before responding. "No, I haven't been to the Cattle Drive in months," she said, a touch too casually. "I think it was Fraser's, yes—that was the bar. A bit rough and ready, but they have live music, and I love a live band."

JJ pressed, his tone insistent. "So, not the Cattle Drive?"

Rose held his gaze. "No, as I said, not for a long while."

JJ mentally noted her words. *Her first lie.* He knew for a fact that she had been at the Cattle Drive the night Charlie disappeared. He couldn't yet confirm if she was in the black Lincoln that night, but her connection to the car stretched back twenty years. To link her definitively to the Lincoln, he needed Lucas to confess that he had gotten the car from her. But so far Lucas was keeping silent. JJ studied her carefully. Her story was too smooth, too convenient, but there was no way he could disprove her claim. He reached into the file before him and slid a photo of Lucas across the table. Rose glanced down at it; her expression guarded.

"Do you know this man?" JJ asked. What decision would she make this time?

She could have lied. She could have denied ever seeing him. But she knew there were witnesses at The Catz Club who'd seen her with Lucas at the bar the night of the mugging. So, playing it cautiously, she nodded.

"Yes, I've seen him before," she said, her tone measured. She wondered if JJ knew about the envelope and waited for him to ask. He didn't. Sticking to the purse story was her only story for now. "Did he steal my purse?"

"Maybe," JJ replied. He knew he couldn't tie Lucas directly to the murder weapon or the theft of Rose's purse containing the gun. The gun had been found in the car Lucas crashed, but no gunpowder residue linked him to the shooting. JJ pressed on.

Her attorney leaned forward; his tone curt. "Is this going anywhere, Detective? My client has provided her alibi, and she's told you her gun was stolen. If you have any real evidence, let's hear it. Otherwise, I think we're done here."

JJ's time was running out. He needed something—anything—to link Rose to Jimmy Mercer's murder. If he could nail her for that, he could likely tie her to Brad's death, and maybe even the abduction of Charlie.

"We are nearly done I've just got a few more questions," JJ said, his tone darkening.

He pulled out another photo—this one of the black Lincoln IV. Not the shiny, pristine version they had seen in earlier images, but the wreck that had killed Harper. He placed it on the table in front of Rose, watching her closely.

"I think you've seen this car before, haven't you?"

Rose's face remained neutral, but a flicker of recognition in her eyes betrayed her. JJ knew she had ridden in that car countless times with Jack and her missing, presumed dead, boyfriend Bart. She picked up the image for a more detailed look, giving her time to gather her thoughts.

She looked at the photo. The seconds ticked by as she carefully crafted a lie. She did recognize the car, but she also knew that, again, JJ could not link it to her.

"No," she finally said, her voice steady. "I've never seen that car before. Looks like it's been in a bad accident."

Lie number two, JJ thought.

"It has," JJ replied coldly. "The driver, Lucas, ran over my partner—Harper, remember him? Harper is dead now. Perhaps it was an accident, perhaps it wasn't. That's for the courts to decide. But one thing's certain—if Lucas is found guilty, he might just take others down with him."

Rose shifted in her chair, her composure cracking for a moment before she regained control.

"I'm truly sorry about Harper," she said softly, her voice measured, but JJ noticed a slight hesitation. "He seemed like a decent man."

JJ wasn't about to let her off that easily. He knew she was lying about the car, the gun, and knowing Lucas, but his time was slipping away, and he had one final card to play.

Reaching into his file, JJ pulled out the last photo—a picture he knew would rattle her. It showed Rose, Bart, Charlie, and Rosetta. Parked in the background was the black Lincoln IV. A small child could be seen peeking out from the back seat. JJ placed the photo in front of Rose and tapped his finger lightly on the image of the girl.

"Is that you, Rose?"

Rose froze. The calm mask she had worn throughout the interview cracked. The tension in the room spiked. JJ could see fear creeping into her eyes, though she was trying desperately to hide it. Slowly, she turned to her attorney, her silence louder than any words.

"This interview is over," her attorney declared, standing abruptly. "The next time you call in my client, you'd better have more than this... nonsense. She has an alibi for Mercer's murder, and her gun was stolen. You've got nothing."

He snapped his notepad shut, placed it in his briefcase, and gestured for Rose to follow. She stood, her eyes never leaving JJ. The brief moment of humanity she had shown when Harper's death was mentioned was gone, replaced by a cold, calculating stare. She turned and headed for the door, her attorney at her side.

But JJ knew he had unsettled her. He had loosened something beneath the surface, though he was still no closer to tying Rose to anything concrete just yet. Nevertheless, he sensed he was on the verge of a breakthrough.

As she reached the door, JJ called after her. A faint smile spread across his face as he made a promise. "See you soon, Rose."

JJ felt satisfied with how the interview had gone. There hadn't been a definitive 'gotcha' moment, but he had managed to unsettle Rose. He just needed that one crucial piece of evidence or a single confession, and he would have her. Even if not for Brad's murder or Charlie's abduction, there was still a chance he could connect her to Jimmy Mercer's murder.

Just then, he remembered the missed call from earlier. He pressed the voicemail retrieval button and listened closely. After hearing the doctor's message, he snapped the phone shut and headed out. The new information confirmed that the Brooks family was hiding a dark secret. With this, JJ knew he had leverage. It might just be the key to uncovering the whole truth behind the events of the past few weeks.

SEVENTY-ONE
TAKEN

AS JJ LEFT THE PRECINCT, he called Cara back, but her voicemail cut in. "I'm sorry, I can't take your call right now, so leave a message, and I'll get back to you." The beep followed.

"Hey, Cara, it's JJ. I got your message. I'm heading to your office now. I hope you're there. If not, meet me there if you get this message." He hung up. He didn't know it, but it was a message she would never hear. Her phone lay abandoned on the floor of her empty office, a silent witness to something JJ had yet to uncover.

The drive across town felt like pure torment. Traffic crawled at a snail's pace, but JJ's mind was racing. Cara's phone message had been frustratingly vague. *Who is Jack's father?* he wondered. He needed answers, and it felt like they were the key to cracking the case. Dr. Warrick was the only person who could provide them, but the traffic seemed determined to keep him from getting to her. As his frustration mounted, a garbage truck lumbered before him, blocking his path. That was the final straw; he activated the siren. The piercing wail sliced through the thick congestion, but it did little to calm the knot tightening in his stomach. An uneasy feeling gnawed at him, a sense that something was wrong.

When he finally reached the hospital, JJ didn't bother parking properly; he leaped out of the car and strode purposefully towards the entrance. The security guard barely glanced up, giving him a cursory nod and waving him through—he knew who JJ was.

Reaching the front desk, JJ wasted no time. "I need to see Dr. Warrick," he demanded, his tone sharp and urgent. "Can you call her and let her know I'm here?"

The receptionist dialed quickly but frowned as the phone rang endlessly. "She's not picking up," she said, glancing at a passing nurse. "Is Dr. Warrick on her rounds?"

The nurse shook her head. "No, she left about forty minutes ago with Jack."

"Jack Brooks?" JJ's heart slammed in his chest.

"That's right," the nurse confirmed, oblivious to the storm brewing inside JJ.

"Take me to her office." His tone left no room for debate. The nurse hesitated momentarily until JJ flashed his badge. "This way, Detective."

The moment he entered Dr. Warrick's office, the chill hit him. Her phone was on the floor; the screen cracked—a bad sign. JJ's pulse quickened as he scanned the room, eyes landing on a file on the desk: 'The Brooks Family.' He flipped it open. Empty.

Where the hell was she? His mind raced. Why had she left with Jack? The knot in his gut twisted tighter. Had Jack fooled them all? JJ had been focused on Rose, but what if Jack had been pulling the strings all along? Every fiber of his being screamed at him to move faster. He had to get to Rose. She was the only one who could make sense of this mess.

The drive to Rose's apartment felt endless despite the sirens blaring. When he arrived, he barely acknowledged Scott, the concierge, as he tore through the lobby, moments later he arrived at Rose's apartment closely followed by Scott. He hammered on Rose's door, each knock echoing like a gunshot in the empty hallway.

Nothing.

"Open it," JJ ordered, eyes burning into Scott as he fumbled with the keys.

"I—uh—"

"OPEN IT!" JJ barked, drawing his gun. He wasn't taking any chances.

Scott's hands trembled as he fumbled with the lock, and JJ's grip on his gun tightened in response. The moment the door clicked open, JJ didn't wait—he shoved it wide and charged inside before Scott could even pull the keys free, leaving them jangling in the lock. As he moved swiftly into the living room, his heart sank at the sight before him. Rose was crumpled on the floor, her body shaking with sobs, an empty pill bottle lying abandoned on the coffee table. In her hands, she clutched an old photograph, the image blurred by her tears: it showed her, Bart, and a young Jack smiling in a moment that now seemed a lifetime away. Her sobs filled the room, each one heavier, more broken than the last, but it was her words that truly sent a chill down JJ's spine.

"I'm sorry," she whimpered, her voice barely more than a whisper. "I'm so, so sorry. It's all my fault."

JJ's mind spiraled, grappling with the implications. What had he missed? What crucial detail had slipped through his fingers? He holstered his gun and crouched beside her, gripping her shoulders firmly, trying to steady her and himself.

"Rose, where's Jack?" he asked, his voice low but urgent, almost pleading.

"I don't know," she managed to choke out, her words barely audible through her sobs.

JJ's eyes flicked to the empty pill bottle. He picked it up and waved it in front of her, his frustration and fear bubbling over.

"And these—what are these? It's empty. Have you taken them? Talk to me, Rose."

She shook her head, her eyes unfocused, as if she were trying to make sense of her thoughts. "I haven't taken anything. It was empty when I found them," she said softly. "They're my sleeping pills... I think Jack took them."

JJ's heart skipped a beat. "Why would Jack take your pills, Rose?" he demanded, a mix of disbelief and urgency in his tone.

She shrugged, her expression vacant, but then her gaze sharpened, meeting JJ's eyes. "He's taken the kitchen knife, too," she said, her voice trembling with a new layer of fear.

"What?" JJ asked, his mind scrambling to keep up. "Why would he take a knife?"

"I went to prepare dinner, but the chef's knife was missing," she explained.

JJ's patience was wearing thin, his mind reeling, as he pieced together Rose's disjointed words. Then, a chilling realization dawned on him, and his pulse quickened. He looked at Rose.

"Rose, listen to me," his tone was sharper now, laced with urgency. "I think Jack has abducted Dr. Warrick. You need to tell me everything."

Her tear-stained eyes met his, wide with panic. The raw fear in her gaze was unmistakable like something had snapped inside her.

"No," she muttered, shaking her head. "Jack wouldn't... he couldn't. He got better. He's not capable of hurting anyone—"

But even as she said it, her voice faltered. She knew the truth, and so did JJ.

Rose's sobs turned to gasps as reality began to sink in. "He... he took my gun; it wasn't stolen," she confessed, barely above a whisper. "I tried to protect him, but I couldn't. He's out of control. Please... don't hurt him."

"What gun? The one that killed Mercer?" he asked, his mind connecting dots faster than he could rationally comprehend.

Rose just nodded, her body shaking with grief. The strong, calculating woman JJ thought he knew was replaced by a broken shell.

"I asked Lucas to keep an eye on him," she continued, her voice trembling. "I needed to protect Jack... he's all I have left." She paused. "He is just like his father."

The puzzle pieces were falling into place, but the picture they revealed was far darker than JJ had anticipated.

"What are you saying, Rose?" JJ pressed. "Who is Jack's father, and what does that have to do with all of this?"

Rose hesitated, and then the words burst out of her, raw and ugly. "Bart Harris is his father! And I'm Jack's mother. I was so young; we had to keep it a secret."

The revelation hit JJ like a freight train. His breath caught in his throat as he stared at her, disbelief and shock warring for dominance. Scott, standing in the doorway, looked equally stunned.

Noticing Scott's wide-eyed disbelief at her revelation, Rose's expression twisted, and she snarled, "What the hell are you looking at?" The venom in her voice was unmistakable. The terrified, broken woman from moments ago had vanished, replaced by a woman he didn't recognize, her eyes sharp and wild. "Get out!" she spat, her tone threatening and vicious.

Scott didn't need to be told twice. He bolted, shoving past the onlookers gathered outside, their faces a mix of curiosity and concern. As he disappeared into the crowd, the uneasy murmur of whispers followed him, but no one dared to linger too close to the doorway.

JJ stood, headed to the door, and closed it, shutting out the prying eyes. When he returned, an uneasy calm was beginning to return. "I need you to stay here, Rose," JJ commanded, his voice firm. "If Jack contacts you, call me. Don't do anything on your own."

But before Rose could respond, her phone rang, raising the tension once again. The shrill sound froze them both in place, and the room fell eerily silent. Rose's eyes widened as she frantically searched for her bag, her hands trembling. JJ held his breath, every second stretching unbearably long.

The ringing seemed to echo more loudly with each passing moment until, finally, Rose's shaking fingers found her phone. She glanced at the screen, her face draining of color.

"It's Jack," she proclaimed, then flipped the cell and answered.

"HEY, sis, are you okay? I saw them take you. Are you alright?" Jack's voice crackled through the line; his words frantic, unsteady. He had pulled over at a gas station. His eyes darted around, holding his shoulder as the pain throbbed relentlessly.

JJ RAISED his hands in a calming gesture, silently urging Rose to stay composed. She had to get information—she had to find out where Jack was. Dr. Warrick's life depended on it.

"Oh, Jack... that was just the detective. He needed to talk to me about the night you got mugged, to take a statement, that's all." Rose's voice wavered, her lie barely holding together.

JJ's gaze fixed on her, urging her to keep going.

SHE'S LYING TO YOU, *Jack*, a sinister voice hissed in Jack's mind, cutting through his thoughts, slicing away his sanity. He glanced over at the doctor's car he had stolen, but Dr. Warrick was nowhere to be seen. The voices were louder now, demanding, insistent. *Hang the bitch, Jack. Let's end it and get out of here.* Jack pressed the phone tighter against his head, his face contorting with the strain of keeping control. He glanced towards the trunk of the car.

"Leave me alone!" he growled, banging the receiver against his brow. "Get out of my head!" His knuckles whitened as he gripped the phone, shaking.

"JACK, WHO'S THERE WITH YOU?" Rose's voice trembled as she overheard him arguing with himself.

JJ leaned closer, whispering urgently. "Where is he?"

Rose put the conversation on speaker. "Come home, Jack," Rose pleaded, trying to keep her voice steady. "We can figure this out. We'll talk. Please, just come home. Don't hurt anyone... don't hurt Dr. Warrick."

JJ's first instinct was to snatch the phone from Rose—this was a hostage situation, and his training had drilled into him how to handle moments like these. But he held back, his eyes scanning the scene with a practiced, calculated calm. He knew that sometimes the calming presence of a familiar voice could be more effective than anything he could say. Right now, Rose's voice might be their only hope, the lifeline they desperately needed if they were to save Cara.

"I can't." Jack's voice cracked, desperation seeping through. "They won't let me. They're going to hurt her."

"Jack, you need to come home," Rose urged her tone soft but filled with dread. "I know you have Dr. Warrick. Please don't hurt her. We can fix this, but you have to bring her back."

YOU HEAR THAT, *Jack? I told you she was lying. That detective is right there with her.* The voice twisted, venomous. *She knows you killed Brad. She likes the detective, Jack. They're going to lock you up and throw away the key, Jack. End this.*

JJ LISTENED INTENTLY over the speaker, hearing Jack's struggle, his voice fractured and desperate, arguing with itself. Each tone and hiss overlapped in a chaotic, frenzied mess, with different voices commanding Jack to act. JJ could sense that Jack was teetering on the brink of complete madness. Yet he clung to the hope that the real Jack, the part of him that cared deeply for Cara, was still in there somewhere. He had to believe Jack wouldn't hurt her, but they needed to hold on until they could reach him. And to do that, they had to figure out where Jack was—and where he was headed.

JACK WAS BATTLING demons of his own, internal beasts snarling for dominance and dragging him closer to the abyss. His grip on reality was slipping fast. His hands shook violently, and cold sweat dripped down his brow. The voices roared louder, and the urge to silence them, to give in, gnawed at his very sanity. The struggle was becoming unbearable, and the edge of madness loomed dangerously close.

Jack's demeanor shifted in an instant. He straightened up, the pain in his shoulder seemingly forgotten, as a sinister smirk spread across his face. Then, his voice broke through the silence, but it was no longer his own. It was cruel, mocking, and dripping with malice—a twisted, warped version of Jack's usual tone. Jack was gone—only his voice remained, commandeered by the demons now ruling his mind.

"Hey, bitch, you heard him. He's not coming home," it taunted, each word sharp and brutal. The voice grew louder, more vicious, screaming down the phone, "We're all heading back to the old place to have some fun with the doctor."

This wasn't just a slip but a deliberate threat, a taunt crafted to instill fear. And though Jack's body stood there, it was clear he was no longer in control. The demons had seized him entirely, and they were reveling in their dominance, their cruelty echoing in every twisted word.

It wasn't Jack anymore. He was gone—or worse, buried deep within his mind, trapped as The Miseries, the demons that had tormented him for so long, took complete control. Their twisted laughter echoed endlessly, filling every corner of his thoughts, suffocating him with their cruel glee.

Yet, even in the suffocating darkness, Jack fought. Somewhere within the chaos, a small, stubborn part of him still clung on to his mind, desperately clawing for control, struggling against the tide of voices that sought to drown him. He managed to force out a few words; the effort was monumental, as if clawing his way to the surface —the old place. The words echoed in his mind, lingering like a faint beacon in the gloom. He had let it slip, made those words escape his lips. Had he just revealed where they were going?

Had Rose heard the clue, a secret message hidden amongst the snarls, the vile threats of the madness that had gripped her brother? It was the only hope left to save the doctor.

A mocking laugh bubbled up from Jack's throat, his lips curling into a sneer. "Cute, Jack," he muttered to himself, his voice dripping with scorn. "Now you've gone and told them where we're going. Never mind, though... they won't get there in time. Let's go have some fun with your doctor."

The demons spoke through him, their words twisted and mocking, relishing every moment of their control, dragging Jack deeper into the abyss. Yet, somewhere beneath their suffocating grip, a glimmer of Jack's defiance still flickered, desperate to break free, fighting against the darkness that sought to consume him entirely.

Jack's hand trembled as he let the phone slip from his grasp, the receiver dangling precariously, swaying back and forth. From the other end, a crackled voice pleaded, desperate and fearful, the words barely audible through the static. For a moment, Jack's eyes flicked down to the receiver, his gaze unfocused; then, with a cold, detached motion, he reached out and pressed the hook switch, cutting off the call mid-sentence.

"JACK, JACK..." Rose's voice trembled as the phone went silent, the eerie hum of the disconnected call lingering. She stared at the dark screen, frozen in dread. JJ's piercing gaze bore into her, the tension was so thick, it was suffocating.

JJ leaned in, his voice sharp and barely controlled. "Damn it, I should have spoken to him," he muttered to himself, frustration etched across his face. "I'm trained for this kind of thing. Now we don't even know where he's headed." His words came fast and urgent, the pressure of the situation pushing him to the edge. He paused for a split second, then barked, "Rose?!"

His voice cut through the tension, demanding an answer, a direction—anything that could lead them to Jack before it was too late.

Rose flinched at the sudden rise in JJ's voice, snapping out of her paralysis. Her gaze flickered to the phone in her hand, her breath shaky, uneven. "The old house..." she stammered. "He's going back to the old house in Alexander. We never sold it. It's where I left Charlie."

JJ's heart lurched. "What do you mean, where you left Charlie?" His eyes narrowed as he began making connections. "You took Charlie. It was you driving the Lincoln the night Lucas abducted him?"

Rose didn't respond, but the truth hung between them like a dark cloud. She simply nodded.

"Is he alive?" he demanded, his voice nearly breaking.

Rose hesitated; a confession heavy on her tongue. But the truth didn't matter anymore—only getting Jack back and saving the doctor. She met JJ's eyes and nodded again, her voice barely a whisper. "Yes, Charlie is alive."

JJ exhaled sharply, a flicker of relief crossing his face. There was no time to process the chaos of Jack's fragmented conversation—every second, every minute was precious now. "Let's go," he commanded, his voice steely and resolute. "You're taking me to Jack, and you'd better pray Charlie is alive and that we get there in time to save the doctor."

Deep down, Rose knew the cruel reality—only one of those things might be possible.

SEVENTY-TWO
DEAD WOMEN WALKING

JACK ENTERED the store just off I-72, the kind that sold everything from snacks to hunting supplies. But Jack—or rather, the twisted part of him now fully in control—only wanted one thing. When he emerged, that thing was in his hands: a thick length of rope, the heavy-duty kind, strong enough to tow a truck.

His fingers moved with precision as he walked, expertly crafting the rope into a noose. This wasn't the first time this had been done. Whoever was pulling the strings inside Jack's fractured mind had hung someone before, and they were ready to do it again.

As Jack passed by the trunk of the car, he thumped it twice, each knock reverberating through the stillness of the empty parking lot. After the second thump, a muffled noise responded from inside, a desperate sound stifled by layers of confinement. Jack's eyes flicked around, scanning for any signs of life, but there were no witnesses, no prying eyes. Satisfied, he popped the trunk open, and the sight inside made his twisted smile widen.

Dr. Warrick lay bound and gagged, her eyes wide with terror, her breathing rapid and shallow. She struggled against her restraints, but the effort was futile. Jack held up the noose, letting it sway in front of her, dangling like a grim promise. The gag swallowed her muffled screams, her body twisting frantically as if sheer willpower could somehow free her. Jack's smile deepened—a cold, soulless grin—and he pressed a finger to his lips.

"Shh," he whispered, the sound almost tender yet laced with menace. His eyes were dead and unfeeling. He casually tossed the noose into the trunk, letting it land near her feet, a silent reminder of what awaited her if she dared resist.

"Thirsty?" he asked, his voice mockingly polite. Dr. Warrick hesitated, then nodded, understanding that her only chance, however slim, was to cooperate. Jack's smile stretched wider, pleased by her compliance. He retrieved a water bottle from his jacket, but the cap had already loosened. Cara hadn't noticed, but the water inside was tainted; Jack had laced it with sleeping pills, ensuring her resistance would soon fade. He twisted off the lid, still holding her gaze, and brought a finger to his lips once more. "Shh."

Then, he slowly opened his jacket, letting the handle of the knife glint in the dim light, a chilling reminder of the consequence of any sound she might make. The message was clear, and Dr. Warrick, eyes locked on the blade, remained silent. Jack removed her gag, and she reluctantly took a sip from the bottle, the liquid sliding down her throat, as she fought the urge to scream. The gag was back in place before she could even think of protesting, her momentary freedom snatched away as quickly as it had been granted.

Jack tossed the half-empty bottle into the trunk, letting it roll beside her, then glanced around the parking lot again, ensuring they were still alone. When he was satisfied, he slammed the trunk shut with a violent, final thud, the noise echoing through the empty lot. The sound was like a closing door, sealing her fate as the darkness enveloped the car, leaving only silence behind. With a skip in his step, Jack moved toward the driver's seat, a chilling satisfaction settling over him. "Today we're gonna have a hanging," he promised to no one in particular, his voice gleeful, detached from any semblance of humanity.

He started the car and sped away, the road stretching ahead like a dark promise of what was to come.

SEVENTY-THREE
I-72

WITHIN MOMENTS, JJ and Rose were speeding down the highway, sirens screaming as JJ weaved through traffic on I-72. He wasn't done with Rose—not by a long shot.

"So if you took Charlie," JJ pressed, eyes fixed on the road, "you knew he saw something that night. He saw you kill Brad." The pieces were all aligning now, faster than he could process them. "You killed Brad because of what he did to Jack, didn't you?"

"I didn't kill Brad," Rose's voice was firmer now, the lies peeled away, exposing raw truth. "But I know who did."

JJ's mind raced, his suspicions swirling. "Then who? The evidence never supported the idea that Brad committed suicide."

Rose inhaled deeply; her breath shaky as she struggled to maintain her composure. The truth poured out like poison. "Jack... Jack killed Brad. He's not well, JJ. He hasn't been well since..." Her voice wavered, cracking under the weight of painful memories. "Since he saw my father hanging at the old place—the one we're heading to now. Something snapped in him that day. After that, he was never the same."

JJ listened as she continued. "You see, Bart wasn't well," Rose explained, her voice distant, as if she were trapped in a memory, reliving an old nightmare.

"What's Bart Harris got to do with all this?" JJ's voice was sharp, confused. The connection eluded him, and he needed answers.

"He did bad things, but it wasn't him—it was the voices," Rose continued, her words thick with a history that JJ was only beginning to glimpse. His mind raced, trying to piece together what she was saying. None of it made sense—what could events from twenty years ago possibly have to do with the crisis they were facing now?

"Hold on a minute, Rose. Why are you telling me this?" he asked, glancing at her, his tone demanding clarity.

"Jack... Jack is Bart's son. He must have inherited that sickness. But it wasn't just Bart's illness," she said, pausing as if struggling to weigh whether to reveal more. "He also inherited my issues."

JJ's jaw tightened, but he remained silent, letting her words sink in. There would be time to dig deeper later and unravel the tangled mess of lies, secrets, and generational scars that plagued this twisted family. But for now, he needed to listen. They were speeding toward a volatile situation, and every piece of information, no matter how fragmented, was critical.

"You see Bart—" Rose began, but her voice faltered, her eyes drifting toward the window. Whatever she was about to say, it was clear it was something she struggled to confront.

"Bart, what?" JJ pressed, his voice firm but not unkind, trying to coax the truth from her.

"It doesn't matter," Rose said quietly, her voice tight, as though holding back a flood of emotions. "What matters is I tried to get Jack's help. For years, it worked. He was stable as long as he took his medication. But when he stopped..." She trailed off, the weight of her unfinished sentence hanging in the air, heavy and foreboding. The consequences were now painfully clear to both of them.

JJ's mind raced, trying to absorb everything Rose had confessed. His thoughts darted, a chaotic blur like the landscape speeding past outside the car windows. Rose was hiding something about Bart—something dark that still cast a long, unsettling shadow over this situation. But there wasn't time to pry it out of her. Whatever dark secret

Bart had taken to his grave, whatever questions needed to be asked, they would have to wait.

Right now, Jack was the immediate threat, the danger they were hurtling toward, and if they didn't act fast, whatever happened next would be far worse than the darkness Rose had hinted at.

The urgency in the air was suffocating, the tension mounting with every mile. Each second felt like it was ticking toward something inevitable, something terrible. The old house, the one Rose had mentioned—where it all began—loomed closer with each passing minute, pulling them toward its secrets and the horrors unfolding within its walls.

"We need to stop him," JJ muttered under his breath, more to himself than to Rose. His mind raced through grim scenarios, knowing they were headed into a confrontation with a man who had already crossed the line. Jack had spiraled into a darkness that might be impossible to pull him back from.

As the miles blurred into one another, JJ's thoughts fixed on Dr. Warrick. Her life hung by a thread. They had to reach her before it was too late—before Jack, or the voices controlling him, did something irreversible.

Danger loomed ahead, and JJ knew they were heading straight into it. But there was no other option. They had to get there before Jack's madness claimed another victim.

SEVENTY-FOUR
THE OLD HOUSE

JACK PULLED into the driveway of the old house, the car's tires crunching over the gravel of the overgrown, unkempt road. The house loomed ahead, isolated and desolate, standing alone on its patch of land like a forgotten relic. The nearest neighbor was half a mile away—far enough for no one to hear or see anything.

Time had not been kind to the place. The house was in a state of decay, its windows boarded up, the paint peeling and flaking, clinging stubbornly to the weathered wood. An old, rusty swing hung from a solitary frame in the front yard, swaying slowly in the breeze, its chains creaking with a haunting, rhythmic groan. Near the swing lay an upturned red tricycle, tangled in the overgrown grass, a forgotten relic of a childhood long past—*Jack's* childhood. The sight of it, faded and rusting, seemed to mock the innocence it once represented. The fence surrounding the house was broken and rotting, with sections missing entirely, as if the place had stopped caring about keeping the world out—or perhaps, about containing what lay within.

The air was thick with silence, broken only by the soft rustle of the wind and the creak of the swing. It was as if the house was holding its breath, waiting for something inevitable. Jack stepped out of the car, his eyes scanning the scene, his expression cold and detached yet tinged with a hint of nostalgia. He had been away for so long, but standing there, it still felt like home. The house had been a silent witness to so many secrets and pain; now, it would bear witness to another horror.

Jack stood in front of the house, his lips curling into a smile, arms wide, as if welcoming an old friend. The gesture was unnerving, almost reverent, like a dark parody of an embrace. As if in response, the house seemed to stir. The front door, which had been shut tight, slowly creaked open despite the absence of any breeze. It was as if the house recognized him, beckoning him inside, ready to engulf him in its shadows once more.

Jack's smile widened, and he stepped forward, the threshold yawning open before him, inviting, dark, and full of secrets. He was home.

He stepped inside, the air thick with a musty, stale scent, as if the house had been holding its breath for years, waiting for this very moment. The creaking floorboards groaned beneath his weight, but to Jack, the sound was comforting, familiar, like the murmurs of an old friend. For a brief moment, he forgot about the captive in the trunk—Dr. Warrick wasn't going anywhere. The sleeping pills had done their job, and she was fast asleep, slumped inside the dark confines of the trunk, oblivious to the horrors awaiting her. She would stay that way long enough for him to do what he needed to do, or rather, what The Miseries had planned for her.

Jack knew what they wanted. The dark whispers in his mind grew louder as he crossed the threshold, seeping into his thoughts, taunting him, guiding him. But he could do nothing to resist; The Miseries had taken control, twisting his actions to suit their cruel intentions. He was merely a vessel now, a puppet dancing to their discordant tune, his own will buried beneath the cacophony of voices that echoed relentlessly in his head.

The hallway stretched out before him, dimly lit by slivers of the late afternoon sun sneaking through the cracks in the boarded-up windows. The old wallpaper was peeling, revealing patches of crumbling plaster underneath, and the air was heavy with the scent of dampness and decay. Every step he took seemed to stir the house awake, its creaks and groans welcoming him back as if acknowledging the return of its prodigal son.

Jack's smile faltered, his lips twitching as his mind drifted to the past, to memories that flickered like shadows—fragments of a life, not all of them fond. Dark memories crept to the surface, unbidden and unwelcome, and for a moment, the dread on his face betrayed a sliver of control. Somewhere, deep beneath the twisted voices, a part of Jack still existed, still clung to his thoughts, but it was a feeble resistance, slipping further away with each breath.

He recalled the darkest memories of his past, the ones he had tried so hard to bury: his father's harsh words, the sting of his fists, and the unrelenting cycle of abuse that had marked his childhood. And then, the day he found his father hanging, swaying lifelessly from the ceiling, the old rope cutting into his neck. Jack could still see it, could still feel the cold shock that had spread through him as he stared up at the body, his father's face twisted in a grim, final expression of torment. Those memories leaked out, spilling into the present, drawing him back to that moment like a dark tide. He gripped his shoulder; Jack was back in control, for how long he couldn't know. He wanted to run, but the house pressed down on him, restraining him.

His eyes shifted to the open living room door, and he found himself standing on the threshold, staring inside. The room was frozen in time, as it had been left it all those years ago. An upturned chair sprawled in the center of the room, the same chair his father had stood on to end his life. The sight of it sent a shiver through him. He quickly averted his gaze, turning instead toward the darkened kitchen, where the door to the cellar beckoned.

The cellar. Jack's heart pounded as he stared at the darkened doorway, his pulse quickening, nausea churning in his gut. That place held secrets—sickening, twisted secrets that no child should have ever known. Memories flickered at the edges of his mind, threatening to drag him under. He remembered the cold stone walls, slick with dampness, the suffocating air that seemed to grow thicker with every breath, and the feeling of being trapped, like there was no escape, no way out.

"Stop that crying, boy," his father's voice echoed, clear and sharp as if the man was standing right behind him. Jack's body tensed, the sound chilling him to his core. "If you don't stop crying, The Miseries'll git ya." Those words, once used to terrify him into silence, still had the power to freeze him in place. Jack's body shook as the past and present blurred together, and the voice rang in his ears. He could almost hear the footsteps, the slow, deliberate creak of the cellar door opening, and what would follow next—the darkness, the pain, and the feeling of being utterly alone.

His father had thrown him down there, time and again, forcing him to endure things he could never speak of—things that had scarred him far deeper than any visible wound. The cellar had been a place of punishment, a place of fear, but worse than that; it had been a place where the seeds of darkness were sown deep within him, twisting his childhood into something unrecognizable. It was down there, in that cold, suffocating pit, that The Miseries had first taken root, whispering to him, feeding off his terror and pain, growing stronger with each night he spent trapped in the dark.

Now, all these years later, those memories still haunted him, festering like an infection in his mind.

But the more he thought of those dark, sickening memories, the stronger the voices—The Miseries—became. They fed off his pain, drawing power from his anguish, twisting his thoughts until they no longer felt like his own. The demons inside him thrived on his suffering, and in this house, where every shadow seemed to echo with the past, their grip on him grew tighter, their whispers louder.

This place had been waiting for him. It had never truly let him go. It was as though the house itself was alive, breathing in the darkness that Jack carried, feeding off it, drawing him back to the very place that had broken him. The evil lurking within these walls needed him, but it was no longer satisfied with Jack alone. It wanted more.

The thought of Dr. Warrick, still unconscious in the trunk outside, flickered through Jack's mind, and his lips curled into a twisted, hollow smile. He let go of his shoulder, wincing slightly from the lingering pain. It didn't matter now; he was no longer in control. The Miseries had seized him, stronger than ever, imprisoning him once more within his mind, leaving him nothing more than a spectator.

Thank you, Jack, for the doctor, the voices whispered, their tone mocking as if savoring their victory. *It's time we introduced her to the family, but we haven't got long. That bitch of a sister will be here soon with the detective to spoil our fun.* The words dripped with malice, and they sent a shiver through what was left of Jack's consciousness. He could do nothing but watch, powerless, as his body responded to the commands, moving without his will.

He turned on his heels, his movements precise and deliberate, and headed back into the fading light. The sun was beginning to dip behind the house, casting long, creeping shadows across the yard as the day slipped away. The night was approaching fast, and Jack knew he needed to act before darkness fully enveloped the place. He approached the back of the car, but something immediately caught his attention—the trunk was slightly ajar. A flicker of panic spread across his face, and he quickly yanked it open.

The trunk was empty, except for the noose and the half-empty water bottle. His eyes darted to the damp patch where Dr. Warrick's head had lain. It was then he realized that she hadn't swallowed the drugged water. "Fuck," he cursed under his breath, the panic quickly turning to rage. "How the fuck did she get out of—"

He didn't have time to finish the thought. Before he could react, a sharp pain exploded in his right side; Dr. Warrick had slammed a screwdriver into him, the metal sinking deep into his flesh.

SHE HAD USED the screwdriver to escape, hid behind the car, and waited for her chance to strike. But as she stood there, expecting to see him recoil in agony, she saw something far more chilling—Jack's demeanor didn't change. Sure, his body felt the pain; the wound was real, but whichever demon was controlling him didn't. The Miseries had him, and they felt nothing.

Jack turned slowly, expressionless, his eyes dark and empty. The screwdriver protruded from his side, blood beginning to seep through his shirt, staining the fabric a dark red. He reached around, grasped the handle, and, with a slow, deliberate motion, pulled it out, examining it briefly before letting it drop to the ground. "Now, that was uncalled for, Cara," he said, his tone calm and almost mocking, as if scolding a child. "You don't want to hurt Jack now, do you?"

Dr. Warrick stumbled back, her heart pounding, every instinct screaming at her to run. But there was nowhere to go, and she needed to find something—anything—to defend herself. Her eyes darted around, landing on an old, rusted shovel leaning against the side of the house. Jack slowly walked towards her. She lunged for the shovel, gripping the handle tightly, and swung with all her might. The metal whistled through the air, aimed straight at Jack's head, but he leaned back, the motion smooth, almost casual as if it was all a game to him.

The patch of blood on his shirt was growing, spreading across his abdomen, but it didn't seem to faze him. Dr. Warrick swung again, aiming lower, but Jack was ready. His hand shot out, grabbing the handle mid-swing, stopping the shovel dead in its tracks. She barely had time to process what had happened before he brought his other hand around in a quick, brutal hook, the punch landing squarely on her jaw.

The force of the blow snapped her head to the side, and the world spun around her. Pain exploded across her face, and before she could even think to react, she was falling. The ground rushed up to meet her, and she collapsed, the shovel slipping from her grasp as her vision blurred.

JACK STOOD OVER HER, watching as her body crumpled to the ground, unconscious; the fight knocked out of her in an instant.

He stood there for a moment, breathing heavily, his eyes glazed over as if waiting for something. Then, his twisted smile slowly returned, and he let out a low, dark chuckle. "There we go," he murmured, almost to himself. "Much better."

He glanced down at the blood soaking through his shirt, the pain still rippling through his body, but it was nothing compared to the voices in his head urging him on and guiding his every move.

He bent down, his hands slick with his blood, and scooped up the limp body of Dr. Warrick and, like a rag doll, slung her over his shoulder. The Miseries were stronger now, feeding off the violence and the fear. They didn't care about the wound, didn't care about the damage. They only cared about control, and as long as they had Jack, they would continue to push him forward, deeper into the dark path they had carved out for him.

Jack turned back to the house, carrying Dr. Warrick's unconscious form in his arms, her head lolling against his shoulder. He moved with a grim, steady purpose, but then he stopped abruptly as if something had tugged at the back of his mind. For a moment, he stood there, still and silent, his head tilting slightly like someone trying to remember a forgotten task. Then it came to him.

He turned back toward the car, his eyes narrowing as he glanced at the open trunk. There, coiled and waiting, was the noose. He looked into the trunk and let out a quiet, almost satisfied sigh. "Mustn't forget the noose," he murmured to himself, the words dripping with dark amusement.

SEVENTY-FIVE
A SIMPLE MATTER OF TRUST

JJ AND ROSE were making good progress, the car speeding down the highway as the sun dipped lower, casting a reddish hue across the horizon. They were running out of light and time, but at least they were getting closer. That was until they reached exit 76 off I-72, heading into Alexander, and saw the flashing lights ahead. The ramp was blocked, and a row of orange cones diverted traffic. JJ's frustration boiled over as he slowed to a stop and slammed his hand against the steering wheel.

"Damn it! Must be an accident up ahead," he muttered, his jaw clenched. The delay was the last thing they needed, every minute wasted feeling like another chance slipping away. His mind raced, trying to figure out another route, but then another thought hit him, colder and more alarming—he hadn't called for backup. In his rush to get to Jack, he'd let his emotions cloud his judgment, and now they were heading into a dangerous situation without any support.

"Stupid," he cursed, reaching for his car radio. A moment later, he hastily requested backup and gave as many details as possible about the incident. Rose had provided the address. The radio crackled as the dispatcher acknowledged the call, promising to send units as quickly as possible. JJ let out a slow breath. He knew backup was on the way, but he couldn't wait; the quicker he got there, the better chance Cara had of getting out of this alive.

JJ glanced at Rose, a sudden realization dawning on him. She was implicated in this mess—Charlie's abduction, Jack's unhinged state—and now she was leading him straight to Jack. But Jack was her son, and if things got out of hand, if she had to choose, JJ wasn't sure whose side she'd be on. He couldn't afford to take any risks, not now. She had to be restrained.

He sighed, feeling the weight of the decision pressing down on him. "Rose, get out of the car," he said, trying to keep his voice steady.

She looked at him, confused. "What? Why?"

"Just... step out for a moment," JJ said, opening his door. He waited as she reluctantly followed, with a wary curiosity on her face. "I need to make sure you're not going to interfere when we get there," he said, pulling a pair of handcuffs from his belt.

Rose's eyes widened, and she took a step back. "What are you doing? JJ, I'm trying to help you."

"And I appreciate that," JJ said, his tone firm. "But you're also Jack's mother. I don't know how this will go down, and I can't risk you complicating things. This is for your safety and mine."

She hesitated, glancing down the empty stretch of highway as if considering running, but then she looked back at him, and something in his expression made her stop. With a resigned nod, she held out her hands, allowing him to cuff her. The metal clicked around her wrists, and JJ guided her back into the car, securing her in the back seat.

Rose's face was a mixture of frustration and sadness. "I just want to help my son," she said quietly, her voice barely above a whisper.

"I know," JJ replied, softer now but still resolute. "But right now, I have to be sure you won't get in the way. When we get there, I need you to let me handle this. Do you understand?"

She nodded, her eyes downcast, and JJ shut the door, locking her inside. As he returned behind the wheel, he took a deep breath, trying to steady himself. The road ahead was still blocked, but they would find another way. They had to. They were running out of time to stop whatever was happening at that old house, and JJ couldn't shake the feeling that the night would end badly.

SEVENTY-SIX
BASTARD

JACK HAD NOW SET the scene. The noose was rigged, and Dr. Warrick, slowly coming to after the brutal punch Jack had delivered, was beginning to stir. Her face was bruised, a dark purple swelling under her eye, and a trickle of blood ran from the corner of her mouth. Her vision was hazy, the world tilting slightly as she blinked, trying to make sense of her surroundings. Panic set in as she realized where she was—at the top of the stairs, seated on a rickety old chair, her hands tied tightly behind her back. The rough, scratchy rope of the noose was looped around her neck, connected to the attic balustrade above. One swift kick, and she'd be hanging.

Jack sat on a step a few feet below her, his posture slouched, his eyes dark and distant. He watched her as she began to cry soft, desperate sobs that echoed in the stillness of the house. The sound seemed to snap something in him, and for a moment, Jack's blank, detached expression softened.

"Please, don't do this, Jack," she whispered, her voice choked with fear. "I know you don't want to."

Jack's eyes flicked up, locking onto hers. For a moment, it seemed like he was trying to grasp her words, to reach out from whatever dark place he was trapped in. But then his lips curled into a cold, lifeless smile. "Jack's not here," he said, his voice unnervingly calm. "Well, he is, in here," he mocked, "but he's up here and not coming out." He tapped the side of his head.

Trapped inside his mind, Jack could see everything. He could see Dr. Warrick, the terror in her eyes tearing at him. He wanted to help her, to stop this, but he was weak, drained from the blood loss that was slowly sapping his strength. The Miseries—the dark, cruel voices that had haunted him for so long—were pushing him, urging him to kick the chair out from under her, to end it. But Jack fought back, using every ounce of strength he had left to resist. If he could just hold out a little longer, if the blood continued to drain from him, he'd pass out, and she'd be saved. It was a grim, desperate plan, but it was all he had.

He looked down, his gaze drifting to the papers he had taken from Dr. Warrick's office, strewn across the floor beside him. A thin sliver of light filtered through an upstairs window, illuminating the words on the page. As he read, the lines blurred and shifted, and a cold realization began to creep over him. His whole life—everything he thought he knew—was a lie, and it was all here for him to see.

The first lie cut deep. He found out who his real father was—Bartholomew Harris. The name stared back at him from the paper, taunting him, mocking everything he thought he knew. *Look here, Jacky boy, guess who your daddy is—well, was. Bartholomew Harris*, the voice sneered. *You were not only a weak, sad little boy but a bastard.*

Jack's head snapped up, and he began to mutter to himself, trying to drown out the voices, to hold back the urge to hurt Dr. Warrick. "Bart was a good man," he whispered hoarsely. "He looked after me. He was my friend."

But then another voice, deeper, colder, and all too familiar, echoed through his mind. *He wasn't a good man, Jack. He was bad. Very bad. Just like you.* Jack's breath hitched, and his chest tightened as he recognized it—his father's voice, creeping back from the grave to haunt him.

He began to cough, blood bubbling up and spilling over his lips. He was getting weaker, his vision swimming, but he forced himself to speak. "You were bad… you hurt me," he rasped, his voice cracking with raw emotion. "I'm glad you weren't my father. I was happy you died. You made Momma leave."

The voice only laughed a low, dark chuckle that reverberated inside his skull. *Your mother didn't leave, Jack. She's always been with you. She never left you.*

Jack's eyes widened, confusion and fear flashing across his face. "What does that mean?" he shouted, his voice a strangled cry. "What are you talking about?" But before he could press further, before he could make sense of the twisted riddles the voices were feeding him, the sound of a car engine pierced the silence outside. Tires crunching over gravel, coming to a stop.

Jack's head snapped up, his heart hammering hard, almost audible. Someone was here. He strained to listen, trying to discern if it was one car or two; if it was help or danger. The voices in his head quieted, waiting as if curious to see what would happen next.

The sliver of control Jack had been clinging onto began to slip. If this were the police, if this were someone coming to stop him, The Miseries would fight back. He could feel their dark presence rising, ready to lash out, to protect themselves at any cost. Jack hoped it was Rose, and she had heard him when he mentioned the old place and understood his clue.

Jack glanced back at Dr. Warrick, her eyes wide and fearful, her breaths coming in short, ragged gasps. He had to hold on a little longer to stop The Miseries from making that final, fatal move. But time was running out, and Jack's strength was waning.

Jack got up and peered out the window, squinting as the sunlight pierced his eyes. He raised his hand to cast a shadow for him to see, and he spotted Rose sitting in the car's back seat. Then, the driver's door opened, and Detective Jackson stepped out, scanning the area. JJ was here, along with Rose—two people he hoped would stop the nightmare he was trapped in. For a fleeting moment, salvation seemed possible, but it was quickly crushed by The Miseries' dark whispers, urging him to give up control.

Jack's hand instinctively reached for the knife at his belt, and he shouted through the open window, his voice harsh and desperate. "Any further, and the doctor is dead!"

THE THREAT ECHOED through the quiet yard, freezing JJ in place. JJ ducked behind the car door, uncertain if Jack had a gun but aware of the knife. He glanced into the backseat, where Rose was waving her cuffed hands frantically, signaling for him to release her. JJ hesitated, knowing she might help Jack, but the look of determination on her face pushed him to make a choice.

JJ opened the rear door, leaning in to unlock her cuffs. "Listen," he said, his voice low and urgent. "I don't know what's happening in that house, but you must keep him occupied. Talk to him, distract him. I'll sneak around the back. Don't let me down, Rose. You could end this peacefully."

Rose nodded, a mix of fear and resolve in her eyes; she stepped out of the car. She began walking toward the house, her hands now free, and called out to Jack. "Let me in, Jack! We can sort this out. Let the doctor go."

Jack's eyes flared with anger. "Fuck you! She belongs here with us," he spat back, the words twisted by The Miseries' influence.

"You don't want to hurt her, Jack," Rose said, her voice steady but pleading.

INSIDE, Jack turned back to face the doctor, tied to the chair with the noose tight around her neck. He could feel the dark urge rising, pushing him to kick the chair out from under her, but he fought back, his mind splitting under the strain. He needed a distraction, something to focus on, and he seized on the question that had haunted him. "What did you mean, my mother has always been with me?" he asked, speaking to The Miseries.

Come on, Jacky boy, surely you've always known, the voices teased, their tones laced with mockery. Jack glanced down at the papers on the floor, trying to piece together the fragments of his shattered reality.

THE MISERIES - THE HANGING TREE

MEANWHILE, JJ had taken advantage of Jack's distraction. He slipped around the back of the house, climbing onto the roof and inching through an upstairs window, quietly making his way into the bedroom. He could hear Rose's voice drifting up from below; she was now in the house looking up at him from below the stairs, trying to keep Jack engaged. "Jack, we need to talk," she called out, her tone soft but firm. "Jack, I'm your sister; you must listen to me. Those voices in your head aren't real."

Jack's head snapped up, his eyes locking onto hers. *She's lying, Jack, see, she can't help it.* The Miseries are still in control. "You're not his sister," he spat, his voice breaking. "Tell him the truth, Mommy," the voice mocked.

"Yes, Jack I am your mother," Rose said, her voice gentle but urgent. "We can talk about this, but we must let the doctor go."

Kill the doctor, Jack. Kill them all. Kill your mother, the voices hissed, louder now, almost deafening. Jack was fighting, struggling to hold onto the last shreds of his sanity. "I don't want to kill anyone," he whimpered, his eyes welling with tears. "I'm sorry, Rose."

"I know, Jack," Rose said, stepping closer. "Put down the knife."

Jack's gaze drifted to the blood-stained blade, his hand trembling. He was losing the battle, his strength ebbing as The Miseries tightened their grip. He heard a faint creak behind him, and before he could react, JJ lunged forward.

The two men grappled, the knife flashing between them. Jack's hand thrust forward, the blade sinking into JJ's shoulder. JJ gasped, his vision blurring from the pain, but he didn't let go. They struggled, their movements frantic and desperate, but Jack, fueled by The Miseries, had the upper hand. With a final surge of strength, he threw JJ down the stairs, the detective's body hitting the floor with a sickening thud, leaving him unconscious.

You see, Jack, you can't trust her, the voices taunted, triumphant. *She wants you dead, just like everyone else.*

Jack stood there, panting, the room spinning around him. He staggered back toward the doctor, his vision darkening, the world narrowing to the thin, taut line of the noose. The Miseries had won, and he no longer had the strength to stop them.

Dr. Warrick's eyes were wide with terror, but she could see something else in Jack's face—a deep, unbearable pain, the agony of a man torn apart by forces he couldn't control. "Please, Jack," she whispered. "Don't do this."

He lifted his leg, ready to kick the chair out from under her, his heart screaming against the action even as his body betrayed him. But before he could, a gunshot rang out, the sharp crack echoing through the house. The force spun Jack sideways, knocking him away from the doctor.

He staggered, barely able to keep his footing, as another shot echoed through the room, then another, each one driving him back with a jolt. His movements grew more frantic, jerky, and unsteady. Dark patches of blood blossomed across his chest, seeping through his shirt. Jack slowly turned, his eyes wide with shock and a raw sense of betrayal, to see Rose standing there, her hands shaking, the gun still raised. Every shot had struck true. Thin wisps of smoke curled from the barrel, the sharp, acrid scent of gunpowder hanging heavy in the air.

Now, Jacky boy, do it, The Miseries whispered. *See who wants you dead.* But they were wrong. Jack's gaze softened as he looked at the doctor and then back at Rose, the chaos inside him quiet for the first time in what felt like an eternity. His beautiful sister, his mother, with tears streaming down her cheeks, had her finger on the trigger.

One more shot rang out, and Jack crumpled to his knees dropping the knife, the strength draining from his limbs. He looked at the doctor and softly spoke, "I'm so sorry." He coughed, blood erupting from his mouth. He slumped forward, tumbling down the stairs, finally coming to rest at the bottom.

Rose ran to him, cradling his head in her lap, her sobs echoing through the hollow, empty house. "I'm sorry, Jack. So sorry," she whispered, her voice breaking.

Jack's eyes fluttered open, his breath ragged and shallow. He reached up, his hand weakly cupping her cheek, a gentle, almost childlike smile tugging at his lips. "That's okay, Mom," he murmured, his voice barely audible. A moment later, his hand slipped from her face, and his body went limp. It was over.

Rose's scream filled the house, a raw, anguished cry that seemed to echo for miles. She had killed her son, the boy she had failed to protect, and now, nothing could ever undo that.

JJ stirred, groaning as he regained consciousness, his eyes widening as he saw Rose cradling Jack's lifeless body. He forced himself to his feet, his shoulder throbbing, and rushed up the stairs to free Dr. Warrick, his hands shaking as he untied the rope.

SIRENS BLARED IN THE DISTANCE, growing louder as police cars pulled up outside, their blue lights flashing, cutting through the dim evening light. An overhead chopper circled, its searchlight scanning the grounds, illuminating the house that now stood silent and still. Within the hour, the scene was swarming with officers. Rose was arrested and led away in handcuffs, her face blank, her eyes vacant with grief. JJ and Dr. Warrick were taken to ambulances, the chaos of the scene unfolding around them as Jack's body was carried out, covered and anonymous.

The house, once filled with screams and whispers, was now silent. The wind picked up, rustling the overgrown grass and sending the old swing creaking back and forth. In the garden, a gust swirled, lifting a cloud of dust, nudging the red tricycle until it righted itself, its wheels turning slowly. It rolled across the yard, stopping at the front step as if it had been summoned home. The door, which had been left ajar, swung open, and the gust rushed inside, slamming it shut behind it with a loud, echoing thud.

The wind swept through the darkened halls, whispering down the corridors, slipping up the stairs and into each room, pausing where the blood had pooled on the floor. It lingered momentarily, then continued into the kitchen, reaching the cellar door. With a soft creak, the door opened, and the gust rushed down, disappearing into the blackness below. The door slowly creaked shut, leaving the house still once more, as if it had swallowed something whole, settling back into silence, waiting for the next secret it would be asked to keep.

SEVENTY-SEVEN
DARKNESS RISING

THE SOFT FLICKER of the TV cast fleeting shadows across the room. The room wasn't cold or sterile like the usual hospital spaces. Instead, it carried a quiet warmth, a lived-in feel, as though time itself had slowed within these walls. Pale blue curtains framed the single window, filtering what remained of the fading afternoon light. A modest lamp on the side table offered a comforting, dim glow that barely reached the far corners of the room.

At the center of the room lay George, the long-forgotten occupant. For over twenty years, his life had remained suspended in stillness, his body trapped in an endless, dreamless sleep. His chest rose and fell in slow, measured breaths, while the heart monitor beside him, silent and coated in dust, had long been redundant. Saint Joseph's, a donation-funded Catholic care facility, was resourceful but relied on expensive equipment only for those deemed salvageable. George, however, was a fixture, a remnant of a time when hope was brighter.

Sister Margarita sat beside his bed, her black habit flowing around her like a shroud. Her hands moved delicately as she turned the pages of the well-worn book in her lap, its pages yellowed with age, soft from years of handling. She read to George almost daily, her voice a gentle murmur in the silence, as though her words alone might pierce the veil of his deep sleep. The stories were familiar, re-read in the hope that someday, they might stir something in him.

The room, usually so still, so peaceful, suddenly changed. Low but persistent, the quiet hum of the television broke through Sister Margarita's concentration. She glanced up from her book, her gaze lingering on the screen. The news flickered across the dim room, its images sharp, but the sound too soft to discern. She hesitated momentarily, torn between her reading and the tug of curiosity pulling her toward the broadcast. Her eyes flicked back to George, unmoving as always, before the lure of the television drew her away.

Placing the book gently on the small bedside table, she rose, her habit whispering against the chair as she moved. Each step was careful and deliberate, as though any sudden movement might disturb the stillness that had settled like a veil over the room for years.

The television was old, without a remote, so Sister Margarita had to pull a chair close to stand on. The legs of the chair scraped softly against the floor, and despite knowing George wouldn't wake from his unbroken slumber, she instinctively lifted it, trying not to disturb him. The absurdity of her caution wasn't lost on her, but she did it anyway —out of habit, out of respect.

She turned the knob, and the voice of the newsreader filled the room, clear and urgent, slicing through the quiet like a knife.

"Here at this old, dilapidated house is where the events unfold, Ray," the reporter began. "It seems this whole case involving the Brooks family—Ezra and Mary Brooks, and their two children, Rose and Jack—may stretch back twenty years. Ezra and Mary Brooks are no longer with us. However, Rose and Jack are implicated in an incident that transpired here two days ago."

Sister Margarita, still perched near the television, leaned back and sat on the bed's wooden frame, her brow furrowing as the report continued. The gravity of the presenter's voice caused her pulse to quicken. The light outside had almost disappeared, leaving the room cloaked in shadows, with the only light from the flickering TV.

"Jack died at the scene, shot by his supposed sister, but there is speculation that she may not be Jack's sister after all, but his mother…" The reporter paused for feedback.

"What else can you tell us John?" the studio reporter asked

"Well it seems Jack is implicated in the abduction and attempted murder of local psychiatrist Dr. Cara Warrick and possibly the murder of Brad Marshall, a local boy originally thought to have hanged himself. However, Detective Jackson's investigation revealed otherwise, unraveling a mystery that spans twenty years."

Sister Margarita crossed herself as the deaths were mentioned, her fingers trembling slightly. As the reporter spoke, she couldn't shake the feeling that something was shifting in the room—something unsettling.

"Rose Brooks," the reporter went on, "is now in custody, but her involvement in these crimes is still being investigated. A source tells us that she may have played a role in the abduction of a local man, Charlie Harris, who, if viewers remember, was the father of the missing teen Bartholomew Harris. Charlie Harris was also found dead earlier today at the scene, and his body is being autopsied."

Sister Margarita made the sign of the cross once more as the body count rose higher, unaware of the scene unfolding behind her. For the first time in twenty years, George stirred. At first, it was a subtle movement—his eyelids fluttered as though the name Rose had awakened something deep within him. But at the mention of Charlie Harris's name, his eyes snapped open, wide and alert, instantly bringing him into the present.

Sister Margarita had no idea what was transpiring behind her, too engrossed in the report, but George was awake. He blinked, squinting against the dim light, his gaze flickering around the room as if he was trying to place himself. Slowly, he raised his hands, staring at them in disbelief as he flexed his fingers into fists and released them—they looked old. His eyes fell upon the back of Sister Margarita's head, still oblivious to the incredible transformation taking place behind her.

"Tell us more about Charlie Harris, John," the studio anchor continued. "How was he connected to these events?"

"Well, Ray," the reporter replied, "Charlie Harris was abducted from the local hospital, where he was recovering from a gunshot wound. His abduction led to his death, as he was denied necessary medical care."

As the voice droned on, George sat up in bed, his movements deliberate. He flexed his arms, staring at his hands—familiar, yet strangely older. His gaze shifted to the mirror across the room. At first, he didn't recognize the face staring back, his mind clouded with fog. Then his eyes caught the tattoo, and everything clicked. He scratched his chin, expecting a scruffy beard, but found his face clean-shaven. Though he knew who he was, the reflection told a different story, leaving him struggling to make sense of it all.

George's gaze shifted to the TV, watching over Sister Margarita's shoulder as the story continued to unfold. His face remained expressionless, but there was something cold and calculating in his eyes—something that had been dormant for two decades. He wasn't just waking up; something far darker had returned with him.

As Sister Margarita crossed herself once more and whispered a prayer, George slid the covers silently away from him and crawled to kneel behind the sister. She didn't sense him, not yet, too engrossed in the flickering images on the screen.

THE NEWS REPORT was wrapping up when she glanced at the mirror before her, her prayer unfinished. That's when she saw him—George, fully awake, kneeling on the bed behind her, eyes locked on her reflection. Her breath caught in her throat; her body paralyzed by shock.

Before Sister Margarita could turn, George's arm snaked around her neck, his grip tightening like a vice. Panic surged through her as her hands flew to his arm, her fingers clawing desperately, but his strength was unrelenting. She tried to scream, her mouth opening in a silent, futile gasp, but no sound came. Her wide eyes locked onto the mirror in front of her, forced to witness her own reflection as her final moments slipped away.

Her gaze dropped to George's arm, catching sight of the tattoo—an intricate dagger entwined with a death's head skull, dark and menacing. The horror of it flickered through her fading consciousness, but it was already too late. The edges of the world began to blur, the mirror growing dim as the life drained slowly from her body. She looked up, desperate, into the cold, empty eyes of a demon wearing George's face. If that wasn't enough, the grin that twisted his lips—a cold, soulless smile—was the last thing she saw before everything went black.

AS SISTER MARGARITA'S body went limp, George held her for a moment longer, staring into the mirror at the lifeless figure slumped against him. Her struggle over. Without a flicker of emotion, he released her, letting her crumple to the floor like a discarded rag doll.

He stared at her for a moment, tilting his head sideways, unmoving, watching the still figure before him. The room, once warm with a quiet routine and filled with the soft sound of prayer, had shifted into something cold and sinister.

With deliberate, almost mechanical precision, George rose from the bed, his body casting a long, creeping shadow across the dimly lit room. Slowly, he turned toward the television, standing motionless in front of the screen as the flickering light danced over his face, casting shadows on his now expressionless features.

George's lifeless eyes remained fixed on the screen, his face a mask of indifference, as though the horrors being recounted meant nothing to him. Yet, in truth, they meant everything; it was as if they were reawakening echoes of a distant past within his mind.

"That's it from me, Ray," the reporter concluded. "Stay tuned, as I'm sure this story has more to reveal."

THE BEGINNING

Printed in Great Britain
by Amazon